TOUCH OF A STRANGER
20TH ANNIVERSARY EDITION

A Wicked Tale of Suspense,

Mystery and Chills,

by

ROBERT E. GELINAS

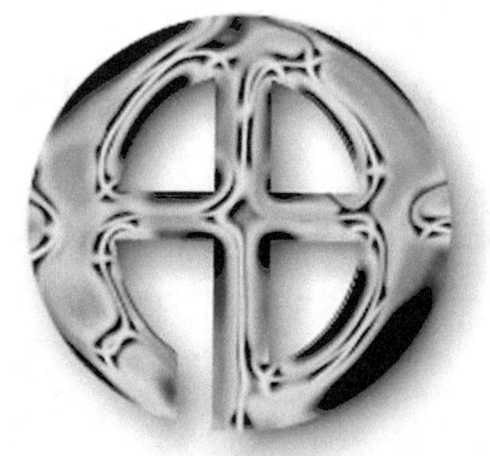

ARCHEBOOKS PUBLISHING

TOUCH OF A STRANGER
20TH ANNIVERSARY SPECIAL EDITION

By

ROBERT E. GELINAS

Original Copyright © 1994 by Robert E. Gelinas
20th Anniversary Edition © 2013 by Robert E. Gelinas

ISBN-10: 1-59507-252-7
ISBN-13: 978-159507-252-8

ArcheBooks Publishing Incorporated
www.archebooks.com

20th Anniversary Special Edition: 2013

DEDICATION

(Original from 1994)

This book is in honor of Mrs. Virginia Schelper, Senior English Honors Teacher, Oliver Wendell Holmes High School, San Antonio, TX—my creative writing teacher—who is probably the last person in the world who would believe I'd end up a novelist.

To Susan (and her little Anna Grace) for just being my friend, and being there in the dark times.

But most of all, to Patsy Ann Yarbro, my mom, who taught me to dream big, to always have fun, to imagine, to face fear—and who instilled in me the fundamental belief that one can accomplish most anything if you just bother to give it a try.

(Updated for 2013)
For Joanna, and our ability to "just keep swimming."

PROLOGUE

BISHOP TAKES PAWN: CHERYLL DUPRIS

Friday
June 7, 2013

"With a complete stranger?" Her eyes flashed with no apology, "Yeah, I'd do it."

All eyes turned to her in open-mouthed disbelief.

Sitting in the crossfire of three chilled glares, Cheryll Dupris absently glanced across the packed and undulating Friday night dance floor. The air was charged with youthful spirits. No one said a word. She returned the icy stares of the Spanish Inquisition boring into her with a curt grin of defiance, adding a coquettish addendum of qualification, "Well... *you* know, I mean, if it was the *right* guy."

He stood across the room—silently waiting and watching.
Perfect. Soon, and very soon.

The three other young women gathered about the tiny, round cocktail table continued to hold a clenched breath of appall, measuring their companion's brazen countenance, then simultaneously burst into dark, raucous laughter. As was the case on many a Friday night, the festive foursome was strategically situated in their usual spot along the crowded periphery of the pandemonium that comprised the dance floor of the Caribbean Club. The Caribbean Club was one of Dallas, Texas' most popular and chic, crowded to the brim, neo-hipster meat-markets. Each of these four attractive, young working girls was arrayed in her most alluring, form-fitting, low-cut, high-thigh hem line party dress—choice cuts on full display.

The pounding, thumping, driving music suddenly swelled in intensity as a new song started. Sweating, smiling bodies separated and fanned out to the periphery. New partners were selected. The urban mating rituals proceeded without interruption.

It was barely 11:00 P.M.

The odyssey of sight and sound was just getting cranked up. Nested in the black tangle of iron battens and steel rafters overhead hung the robotic panorama of "Spielbergesque" LED lights. Their pulsating brilliance was pierced by a dazzling web of green lasers, bathing the crowd below in a rainbow of fluid colors and electric hues. The dense throng of beautiful bodies on the dance floor gyrated and squirmed in a turbulent electric sea of jubilation. Similarly, the alcohol flowed as deep as the river of bullshit from the mouths of all the pretty boys hoping to get laid.

All the pretty girls would make that final determination.

Cheryll Dupris, a paralegal assistant at Kinsley, Holt and Turner, a small law firm in Richardson, just smirked, offering neither repentance nor defense for her brazen candor. With her eyes lightly closed she stole another long sip of her sixth frozen Margarita, leaving a few large grains of salt on the corner of her mouth and a speck on her chin. Her eyes came open again, glassy and bright, the pupils swollen like a pair of summer cow ticks. The corners of her smile curled into a devilish crook, announcing she was teetering on the threshold of having a little too much fun—as if there was such a thing.

It didn't escape his notice.
So... succulent. Available. Unsuspecting?

Cheryll's three vivacious friends: Taylor Price, the brooding executive secretary; Morgan Galen, the devil-may-care dental hygienist; and Clancy Harvey, the effervescent and volatile travel agent; were all just as well-lubricated and glassy-eyed as Cheryll was, if not more so. Clancy still had a small speck of white on her upper lip that she missed on her last trip to the bathroom. Her pupils were pinpoints of energy. All four were hovering precariously over the precipice of the danger point: that fuzzy, impertinent zone where judgment, moderation, and inhibition takes a back seat to the more... shall we say... *primitive* desires. It was no wonder the incessant banter of their conversation continued to escalate in bravado and sorority-flavored daring with each passing moment—and swallow.

"Ohhhh!" Morgan, moaned with exaggerated emphasis, shimmying her shoulders with mischievous glee, "The *right* guy. So what makes a total stranger *right* for you?"

6

"A great big bulge in his pants," snickered Clancy, a dark-eyed red-head. She listed over against Morgan's shoulder, then righted herself with a sputtering wheeze, wiping her nose with the back of her hand. The little white speck was gone.

Morgan tittered, bringing her index finger up under the bridge of nose, her bright green glassy eyes scrunching tight. Her shoulder length, over-moussed and styled blond curls brushed forward over her flushed cheeks. "You mean, if it's a big bulge in his back pocket."

Taylor's frail smile disappeared. She was the philosopher and part-time den mother of the group. Her dark eyes narrowed like a serpent over a fresh laid Robin's egg as she leaned forward, repeating her earlier question at Cheryll, point-blank. "You could really do it? You'd do it with a complete and total stranger?"

Cheryll rolled her eyes, "Like you haven't?"

Morgan and Clancy both leaned closer, exchanging a fleeting conspiratorial glance.

Clancy set her glass down, peering at Cheryll beneath a drawn brow. "You already have, haven't you?"

Cheryll just smiled and downed the rest of her glass. "Perhaps once. Maybe twice."

Morgan dropped her chin in mock appall, "Miss Dupris, you *slut*."

Cheryll flipped her shoulder-length mousy brown hair over her right shoulder with a huff—the way most of the blondes in the place did every few minutes to attract attention. "So why is it if a man seduces you, he's a friggen hero among his horny buds. But for a woman, if *you* do it, or let it happen, then you're a slut?"

Taylor nodded, leaning back in her chair, her devilish eyes flashing, "She's right. It's not fair." Her eyes were coal black and scolding, as black as her short velvet dress and inverness hair. She addressed Morgan and Clancy in Cheryll's defense, "As if you two little tramps hadn't let a scrumptious suitor sample your womanly delicacies for as little as a steak and lobster dinner."

Morgan frowned, pointing a defensive finger back at Taylor, "It was Steak Diane, prepared table-side, and it was a *second* date."

The table burst into riotous laughter again.

Taylor propped her elbows on the edge of the table and laced her long, narrow fingers together, cradling her delicate chin. Her inch long nails were polished a deep, passionate violet. "But our dear sister said she *does* have her standards where strangers are concerned. True?" A sharp sliver of a smile reappeared, creeping across her thin lips as she turned her attention back to Cheryll, melodramatically asserting, "*However...* we're still eagerly waiting to hear what virtuous qualities merit precious access to her treasured... *intimacies*."

Morgan and Clancy renewed their girlish giggles.

"Excuse me," came an intruding male voice. Another unsolicited submission.

All four women looked up at a long blond-haired, but otherwise well-groomed young man attired in business casual: a teal button-down shirt, khaki Dockers, and brown Italian slip-ons. He held onto a long-necked bottle of Corona beer with a twisted sliver of lime crammed down the clear neck. The tell-tale whiteness of his knuckles around the bottle neck foretold of a pair of anxious knees invisibly trembling beneath his Dockers. He smiled down at them, doing his very best to look at ease.

All four women took and deep breath and eyed him from head to toe as if he were a questionably operational, but potentially functional item at a garage sale. These interruptions were numerous, occurring every five or ten minutes—all part of the game. If the suitor-to-be was acceptable-looking enough, he might get a dance. If he was also charming *and* gracious he might also get a phone number—that is, if he was *very* lucky, *very* charming and *very* gracious. However, the vast majority got a polite smile and quick dismissal.

The young man smiled at Morgan, making eye contact, "Would you like to dance?"

Morgan looked him over once more from head to toe, prolonging the poor fellow's ego-agony in a well-practiced and painfully deliberate pregnant pause of judicial consideration. After all, it was a woman's sacred right. The fate of this poor fellow's fragile male self-esteem hung in the balance. The decision was made.

She wrinkled her nose, "I don't think so. But thanks anyway."

Without missing a beat, the young man just shrugged and turned to Clancy. "So how about you, honey?"

Clancy laughed, "No, sorry, Sport. It was a possibility, but you blew it when you went for the blond first."

Cheryll covered her mouth with her fist, suppressing a giggle that rumbled in her chest and throat of its own accord.

The young man was about to say something else, but wisely caught himself, recognizing he was vastly outnumbered by four slightly drunk and bluntly outspoken women. *Warning, warning, danger, Will Robinson.* All that awaited was further rejection and potential embarrassment. *Retreat.* He disappeared as quickly as he came. The music and the teeming crowd swallowed him like an outgoing tide.

All eyes instantly returned to Cheryll.

Another pair of calculating eyes continued to watch with wry amusement. He chuckled softly to himself.

Cheryll threw her head back and lifted her upturned palms, rebuffing their accusing glares yet again. *"What?"*

Taylor challenged, "So tell. Who's your handsome stranger? Your mister right for one night? What's he like?"

Cheryll didn't flinch. "Weeeeeell..." She thought for but a moment, wanting her rendition to be good, before smiling with a look of almost fond recollection. "Of course he's good looking, sweet and charming."

"Yeah— yeah— no shit— of course—" the other three chimed in, nodding, and prompting her on to get to the good stuff.

Cheryll leaned forward ever so slightly, drawing her titillated companions in as well, relishing in her fantasy description. *"And...* he's *very* romantic and passionate, with a sizzling bedroom technique that lasts till dawn."

More giggles. It was getting better.

"And naturally he's successful. A man of awesome means. Not old money. Self-made. But not just *rich*. Oh, no." She took a quick breath, putting her hands out before her, fingers sprayed wide, "No, he's a man who has time to *enjoy* his success." Her hands found her hips, elbows pointing out on either side, then moving forward toward the edge of the table as she spoke, "And sharing it with me goes without saying. He's a generous man who likes first class things—like *me*, and never settles for anything second best."

Morgan bristled with excitement, "Ooo, I like that."

Cheryll continued, "He' s got a captivating sense of humor, but not a silly ass always trying to make a joke out of everything. Just a carefree way of looking at everything with a smile and a twinkle in his soul-enslaving eyes."

Clancy sniffed, then cooed, "So where do we get one of these?"

Taylor waved an admonishing hand at Clancy, her dark eyes reprimanding, then challenged Cheryll, "But how do you know all that from a complete stranger? That all sounds like virtues discovered over time, like, in... a *long*-term relationship."

"Oh, no," Cheryll contradicted. "He wouldn't have to say it. And it wouldn't take long to notice. You wouldn't even have to completely see it." She paused for effect, "But it would be as obvious as his good looks. You'd just know. You could *feel* it in the first instant. It would wash over you like a tall wave at the beach."

9

Clancy pretended to swoon, "And make you just as wet!"

Morgan jabbed Clancy with an elbow of rebuke, then said to the group, "Yeah, well, of course, who wouldn't do it with a guy like that? But unfortunately, both guys in the world who fit that description are unavailable. One's dead, the other's married."

Their cackling laughter filled the air once more rivaling the volume of the thundering music.

Cheryll tossed her head back, "Oh, I think there might be a few more floating around. You just have to keep a careful eye out..." All the talk and fanciful imagining triggered a sudden taste for the hunt. She took a deep breath and abruptly rose to her feet, causing the glasses on the table to clink into one another. "...and not sit around in a gaggle of other geese. So, I guess I'll say good night, ladies." She rolled her eyes, "So wait and watch if you want to see how it's done. I don't think I'll be needing a ride home."

Soon. Very soon.

Clancy and Morgan pretended to be offended when Cheryll sauntered away from the table to the end of the long bar lining the entire length of one wall of the club. Taylor just watched her go with that thin, all-knowing smile of hers. Like most Friday nights, Clancy and Morgan, who were roommates, would chip in a couple of twenties for their part of the tab and go home. Neither had a steady boyfriend at the moment, and wouldn't dream of finding a man in a nightclub. Hanging out and laughing with the girls, dancing and drinking to silly excess was fun; but for those two, romance came in an entirely different package, properly scrubbed and washed and planned in an imitation leather bound appointment book.

On the other hand, Cheryll Dupris would routinely stake out a place at the end of the bar and appear to ignore everyone until someone of her liking happened along. She was always waiting for her fantasy prince to show up, but routinely settled for a lesser nobleman on many occasions. Taylor's own methodology was much more direct and effective. She would target someone of her own choosing and pursue him, like a sleek black jungle cat in the brush spying a Gazelle grazing on the small flora. She delighted in the teasing thrill of the chase—and the taste of the prize.

Neither method took much time. In fact, no sooner had Cheryll gone off to bait her trap, taking her seat at the bar, when Taylor spotted an older man in a smartly tailored suit talking to another man who appeared to be a business colleague or possibly a client. He would do nicely. He was probably married with a family. Not that it mattered. It never did: rarely to her, and never to the guy. As soon as Morgan and Clancy made their imminent departure, he would be in for a most pleasant surprise.

It was time.

Thirty feet away, Cheryll sat quietly at the bar, staring at the reflection of the crowd in the long mirror behind the neat rows of bottles of distilled spirits. She saw Taylor wink at her, a salutation of "happy hunting," which made her smile. They never discussed the actual details of their exploits, but each had an unspoken respect for the others' abilities. A few minutes later she noticed Morgan and Clancy were gone. Taylor was staring across the dance floor at two suits with that dark "look" in her eye, like a vampire alone in a neo-natal ward. Cheryll chuckled to herself. It never took Taylor long. Meanwhile, over the course of the next ten minutes, Cheryll turned down four more offers to dance and two free drinks.

Now.

It was the sound of his voice which first caught her attention.
"Vodka martini, please. On the rocks."
It was a cultured voice, smooth and elegant, not urgent, but filled with a tangible sense of power and quiet authority.
Out of the corner of her eye, Cheryll saw the nearest bartender immediately stop what he was doing and hasten to the task. She turned to her right and caught her breath, her eyes going wide. There stood one of the most incredibly handsome men she had ever laid eyes upon—not just one of the numerous "pretty boy" suits or plastic hipsters littering the bar—oh, no. Something much more. It was a rare occasion indeed when Cheryll Dupris was so struck by a man's mere appearance. But there was more standing there within arm's reach than good looks. Here was a man surrounded by an utterly enigmatic and alluring aura, riveting her complete attention.
He appeared to be in his early- to mid-thirties perhaps, with impeccably groomed brown curls, beautiful deep blue eyes, and chiseled aquiline features. He wore a stunningly formal, dark blue, double-breasted suit which screamed "Armani" and dollar signs in the thousands. Yet it fit him like a comfortable, casual garment you might see him wear everyday as he politely bought and sold small countries over tea at his polo club; or while he notified the Queen and senior officials of Her Majesty's Secret Service

that the nuclear bomb had been disarmed and they could all comfortably return to the cricket match. She noticed his crisp white Italian silk shirt was highlighted by a stunning dark blood-red silk tie. She'd never seen one quite that exact shade before. The peppery, inviting, and sexy fragrance of cologne wafted past her nose.

"Let me guess. Shaken, not stirred?" Inwardly she prayed he was amused.

He turned to her, those dark blue eyes finding hers, piercing deep with uncanny ease; his devilish smile making her head feel lighter and her legs feel weak.

"Naturally."

Her heart was racing. In that one word, he had graciously and kindly acknowledged her, not with condescension, but with a gentleman's elegant charm and polite affection for a lady of high birth. However, by the same token, all of his manner flatly announced that he wasn't a man who was ever required to storm the gates of a woman's heart. He would be eagerly invited, if not begged to come in. When he politely turned away to face the bartender, she felt a strange sinking feeling. Cheryll was an attractive brunette, with a decent figure she worked on very hard at her gym four times a week; but at that moment, in this handsome stranger's presence, she felt woefully inadequate, if not invisible.

When the bartender set the handsome gentleman's drink down, he lifted it to his lips and drained a third of it away with those beautiful eyes closed. He returned the glass back down on the bar, blinked twice, and turned directly to face her, his words momentarily startling her, "You obviously have a taste for James Bond films. Mystery, intrigue, action and adventure? Yes?" His smile warmed her. "But tell me. Are you merely a spectator, or are you an adventurer yourself?"

Cheryll didn't quite know how to respond, but was more than a little pleased to receive his attention again. Her mind tumbled forward and fell back. She returned his smile, hoping he didn't see her blushing. The alcohol did most of the talking, resorting to familiar ground in a moment of confusion. A salutation.

"My name's Cheryll." She held out her hand. "Cheryll Dupris."

He took only her fingers and raised them effortlessly to his lips, those warm endearing eyes of his never leaving hers. For any other man, the gesture would have appeared contrived and foolishly melodramatic. That was not the case. For him, it was natural and effortless, the gentle pressure of his lips sending wicked electric chills rippling up and down her spine. In that instant she wanted to feel them elsewhere—several places quickly came to mind. Her heart was racing again. She knew she was blushing now and felt the desperate need to pee.

He released her fingers. "It's my pleasure to make your acquaintance, Cheryll Dupris. But you didn't answer my question."

That crazy little voice inside Cheryll's head was laughing, telling her that if this guy was even the least bit interested in her, he didn't have to play games. If he wanted her, he just had to say when, and she'd be there. Thus, in a strange twisted frame of her own logic she realized he *had* to be merely playing with her, charmingly flirting—a harmless game. Wasn't it? Getting her hopes up would be a foolish mistake. Her heart began to sink in the gray fumes of disappointment, then buoyed for a moment, considering even the enjoyment of the game amusing for the time being. Who knows? Maybe he would drink too much and—

She cocked her head, sliding her jaw to the side, trying to sound confident and perhaps even a little bit alluring, answering his question, "Oh... I've had my share of adventure."

His smile broadened with genuine amusement. He leaned closer, a hair's breadth away, his intoxicating fragrance enveloping her like a morning mist, making her noticeably tremble. His eyes burned brighter with forbidden cunning.

"No you haven't. But you've wanted to."

She laughed, leaning back defensively. "What makes you say that?"

He didn't answer. His eyes did. They looked right through her, probing beneath the festive make-up and the party costume, the big hair and the false bravado. The trembling had spread down to her legs. At that exact moment she wanted to either fall helplessly into his arms, or run away in tears. The tension of the moment only increased when he reached into his pocket and pulled out a folded deck of cash bound with a bright gold and diamond studded money clip. He peeled a hundred dollar bill off the top and tossed it on the bar at the bartender with a wink that told the bartender to keep the change.

Cheryll knit her eyebrows in confusion.

He held out his hand, "Come with me."

"What?" She looked around to see if anyone was looking at her. Taylor, Morgan and Clancy were long gone. She was off the trapeze, flipping end-over-end, flying without a net.

"Please." The word fell from his lips with protracted patience. He wasn't begging, just asking—adding a touch of polite etiquette, which was rapidly dissolving the confusion.

"Where?" she almost whispered.

"To adventure." He wouldn't ask again. His eyes made that perfectly clear.

Three minutes later, and without another word, Cheryll Dupris was sitting in his car. Car? That word was so unworthy. It was a hand-crafted automobile. Cheryll had seen many Porsches, but never one like his. It was a gorgeous, custom-made, midnight black, Carrera Cabriolet. The top was down and the night was warm, but Cheryll folded her arms tightly across her chest to stave a tingling chill of excitement. Just the smell of the rich tan leather hugging her skin was intoxicating.

He removed his jacket and laid it in the small back seat, more of a deep shelf really, barely large enough for a set of golf clubs. When he spun the key in the ignition the smooth roar of the powerful German engine seemed to be an extension of the man himself. The Porsche's bug-eyed lights came on, peering into the darkness. His left foot found the clutch as his right hand pushed the leather clad stick into first gear. The automobile flew away into the night, bound for adventure.

•

An executive suite at the Rue de Royale Hotel was something Cheryll Dupris had only seen in magazine articles or in luxury real estate brochures. The lavish twenty-first floor room was enormous, elegantly appointed like a furnished penthouse apartment in Paris, with a breathtaking view of the Dallas city skyline from the balcony. The sea of lights at night was a mesmerizing landscape of glittering fascination.

He bade her quietly enjoy the luminescent splendor while he turned on the sound system. It filled the air with the quiet romantic strains of a stringed symphony orchestra. He busied himself fetching a chilled bottle of champagne from the fully stocked wet-bar. She knew the last thing she needed was more alcohol, but she didn't refuse. Sipping the glistening bubbles from the tall crystal flute just seemed to usher her deeper and deeper into the heart of the exquisite unfolding adventure.

The moment arrived.

He spoke not a word as he approached, quietly taking the glass from her trembling fingers and setting it gently down aside his own atop a small iron table on the balcony. A cool breeze from the night, permeated with the scent of an approaching rain, whispered gently across her flushed cheeks. A strand of hair flowed across her nose. His finger came up and tenderly brushed it away, folding it behind the curve of her ear, letting his palm graze her cheek as he withdrew his hand.

Another touch.

Again, the chills tingled the length of her as her mind deliciously washed away into fluid fantasy, as it had repeatedly done on the short ride from the club, wondering exactly what it would feel like to be touched by him, held by him—and more.

And fantasy became reality.

Her breath stilled as she felt his strong and powerful hands masterfully rise to her upper arms—gently holding her at a distance, those bright blue eyes of his staring into hers for a mesmerizing eternity. She wanted to fall into his arms right then. But no. He held her just inches away. Her legs turned to quivering gelatin. An enchanting rhapsody struck up from the electronic orchestra playing inside. The moment was perfect.

What was he waiting for?

Yet, those eyes measured and studied every inch of her, returning to her face and stopping at the gateway of her eyes, probing deeper and deeper, cutting through any and all chains of potential resistance or inhibition. It was completely unnecessary. Yet her heart hurried all the more. It was becoming increasingly more difficult to breathe, and her head was beginning to feel faint—it was no longer just the alcohol. How long would he just stand there, drawing what remained of her strength away with but a glance?

Her question was answered in the next instant.

At last...

His lips descended upon her like a thief, taking what he wanted with a polite violence, deliciously exacting more and more with the passing of each moment. She willingly fell forward as he crushed her body tightly into his own, embracing her into the vice grip of his long, athletic arms. She desired to give him whatsoever he wished, and accept whatever gratifying graces came in return. She relished the scintillating sensation of his hands quickly and meticulously undressing her, never taking his lips from hers, expertly completing his task in mere seconds. The pace of bodily motion accelerated, arms and legs intertwining, hands touching and exploring, mouths feasting and consuming.

Her head swam again when he lifted her into his arms, gallantly twirling her around once in the night air, making the lights of the city below blur around her in fluid contagion. She could hardly suppress a giggle of swelling anticipation when he carried her back inside the suite, straightway through a wide set of tall double doors into the luxurious bedroom. He placed her gently down upon the king-sized bed, stripped off his suit, never pausing an instant in the ever increasing ravishing of the helpless and vulnerable—*but most willing*—fair maiden in his arms.

Cheryll Dupris was in ecstasy.

Making love had never been like this with a boyfriend, stranger, or acquaintance alike. Just as she had imagined, he magically knew precisely where to touch, to kiss, to caress, to pet, to stroke, to taste, to please. He was so delectably patient and persistent—sensing, as if by instinct, exactly where to run the tender tip of his tongue, the smooth tips of his talented fingers, the sweet moist graze of his lips—arousing her and pleasing her in ways she didn't know was physically possible.

After bringing her to the heights of her pleasure again and again for well over an hour, she was approaching delirium.

And then he abruptly stopped.

She looked into his eyes, confused.

He declared, "Beware, my love. This is where the adventure really begins."

His words touched her, shook her, making the small hairs on the back of her neck rise to attention, then faded. Could it be true? Yes, adventure. She wanted adventure. *More* and *more* adventure. If only her body could endure any more.

"Hang on tight," she heard him say.

Her heart was bathed in a surge of glee when he suddenly rolled them both over in one strong motion, taking his place beneath her. She eagerly sprang up straddling him. Her excitement was instantly renewed with a rush of energy, as she was now free to feed her voracious bodily appetites to gluttonous excess.

Cheryll winced a few moments later when she felt his hands roughly grip her upper arms and forcibly arrest her movement. Her eyes came open, again in puzzled confusion at the unwelcome interruption.

"Are you *sure* you're an adventurer?" His eyes challenged and taunted, threatening to deprive or enrapture, depending on her answer.

She vigorously nodded. "Yes. Don't stop."

Cheryll was barely aware of his right hand lifting his beautiful blood-red silk tie from the pillow to his right. It was still tied, just loosened enough to remove his head.

"Here," he commanded, "then put this on."

She giggled, obediently threading her head through the loop and pulling the smaller of the two ends, cinching it around her neck. "How's it look?"

"Beautiful," he grinned, his eyes glinting with a haunting quality, the pupils constricting, harder and colder, "Absolutely beautiful. Now don't stop until you explode." With that he snapped his hips up beneath her, prodding her into an adrenaline charged sprint to the finish line.

Oh, Good God, yes... oh yes, oh yes....

Cheryll didn't have to be told twice. Her head flopped back, a moan of desperate delight easing past her pursed lips. Her fingers kneaded into his rock-hard abdomen. The sweet tingling within had returned, like the initial plummet of a roller coaster. She seethed each shallow breath through clenched teeth. A devastating tidal wave was building, growing, expanding, amassing just off shore, nearing its crest. It was only seconds away.

Oh, yes, yes, yes. Here it comes!

The tidal wave had just begun to crash, towering across the sky, eclipsing the sun, and toppling—everything in its path was about to be utterly consumed in the next instant. Her mouth fell open, sucking in a huge, desperate breath—

The searing pressure hit her throat halfway into the second breath.

However, in that exact moment Cheryll Dupris was completely oblivious to her mysterious lover's strong hands grabbing the knot of the tie in one hand and the small tail in the other, then yanking it taut with murderous intensity. Her windpipe was completely constricted. Her face flushed blood red, her heart pounding, her temples about to burst. But the ferocious orgasmic wave crashed down upon her regardless, thundering down with an unimaginable power and intensity. A shrill screech knifed painfully into her ears.

The frantic sensation of drowning flashed briefly across her mind, and in some macabre way—it was welcome. Her body convulsed and constricted in potent fits and jerks. A deep primal instinct knew in the next second the sheer weight of the sensual tide would surely crush her into oblivion.

Phantom fireworks exploded behind her closed eyelids in darting patterns and tangled webs of lightning. Her hands weakly shot forward, reaching for an invisible mooring to life that was no longer there. Her long slender fingers sprayed wide in the air, shuddering with rigid strain. Yet she was far too spent and weary to fight for what remained of her life, only to slowly sink into the boiling blood-red darkness which beckoned. Her last conscious thought was one of resignation to complete ecstasy.

Cheryll Dupris' lifeless corpse fell forward into her lover's waiting arms. He just lay there for several minutes, sweetly enjoying the moment, his body still joined to hers. He tenderly held her close, lightly stroking her silken light brown hair, gently kissing her forehead—chuckling softly to himself.

It had begun.

PART I

FACTS ARE STUBBORN LITTLE THINGS

Detection is, or ought to be, an exact
science, and should be treated in the same
cold and unemotional manner.

Sir Arthur Conan Doyle
The Sign of the Four, 1889

CHAPTER 1

OPENING MOVES: THE RUE DE ROYALE

Saturday
June 8, 2013

The crime scene photographer's camera flashed two more times. He turned to Ralph Weatherstrom, the chief detective assigned to the murder of Cheryll Dupris, nodding once, indicating he was done.

"Did you get the close-ups of the bruises around the throat?" Ralph asked, as several other technicians combed the room, picking up tiny samples, dusting for prints, making notes, and scurrying about like ants on a freshly dropped crust of a chicken-salad sandwich.

Dallas Homicide Detective Ralph Weatherstrom was fifty-three years old and less than two years away from full retirement. His wife Mari was happy about that. For her it wasn't soon enough. Ralph was happy about it too on some days. This was one of those days.

Ralph Weatherstrom stood six foot tall, with Marine-styled short hair, buzzed high and tight. He took a great deal of teasing about his "poster boy for Duncan Doughnuts" figure; but he knew he could still move when he had to. He had a notorious temper, which had cost him several promotions along the way. But Ralph Weatherstrom had a good heart and was extremely persistent and bull-dog thorough in his work, boasting a very distinguished and colorful arrest record.

The photographer nodded again, answering Ralph's question. "Sure did. Anything else?"

"No," Ralph shook his head. "Take off, and get me prints as soon as you can. I want to see 'em all right away."

Ralph looked down at the bed in the Rue de Royale hotel suite again, shaking his head in wonder, feeling the usual numbness of professional detachment envelope him. It was welcome. After three decades, it never stopped: the endless inhumanities and depravities of the species. The girl lying before him was pretty, probably about the same age as his daughter, Carla, who lived in Wisconsin with a husband and three kids. The lifeless, pale-blue nude body lay in the center of the wide bed with her hands folded neatly across her midsection. Her head lay in quiet repose on the satin cased pillows. Thankfully, her eyes were closed. At first glance she looked like she was merely asleep. A paradoxical look of contentment seemed to frame her face. A single long-stemmed red rose was carefully tucked in her right palm, the fresh petals of the rose bud lying the in the gentle valley between her breasts.

A very petite young woman dressed in a pair of very faded and ripped jeans with no knees, an oversized Dallas Cowboys jersey, a dirty pair of tennis shoes, and her waist length brown hair pulled back into a loose pony tail came up to Ralph. She was chewing a piece of Juicy-Fruit gum, tapping out numbers on the calculator app of her phone and scrawling a few more notes in a small seven-ring notebook with a broken pencil stub.

She smiled up at him with big cheerful brown eyes, "Hi. You're Detective Ralph Weatherstrom, right? This your party?"

Ralph scowled, running his thick tongue between his upper lip and teeth, "Yeah. Who are you? And how'd you get in here?"

She fished her badge and ID out of her front pocket and held it up, grinning. The Juicy-Fruit smacked, "Pembrooke. Megan Pembrooke. I'm heading up your lab team."

Ralph nodded with a note of amused, yet apprehensive recollection. "Oh, yeah. The new *forensic specialist*." He made no attempt to hide his skepticism, as though the title was an offensive absurdity. "I heard about you. A *gen-u-ine* college grad-ja-tated criminologist. Zat right?"

She said nothing. Her lips tightening into a fine line of self-control.

"Seems here-abouts, they also tell me you're *supposed* to be real clever-like." He frowned, lifting his thick eyebrows high, announcing like a school principal reciting the gum policy, "I don't like people who are... *too* clever. Understand?"

Megan stopped munching her gum and opened her notebook, looking down at the top page. "I just try to be observant, sir. Wanna hear what I've got?"

Charlie McManus stepped up next to Ralph. Charlie, a tall man in his late forties but in good enough shape to pass for mid-thirties, was Ralph's partner; and had been for the last seven years. He looked Megan up and down from toe to head. "Who's this, Ralphy?"

Ralph turned to Charlie, "Hey, Charlie. Uh...this is... uh...*shit*... uh... Pam Brooks. The new lab girl."

Megan cleared her throat, "It's Pembrooke. Megan... Pembrooke..." Her voice trailed off and she tossed a futile hand in the air when she saw neither man was listening to her, just mumbling among themselves. "...Megan. Meg. Elvira, mistress of the night. Queen of Sheba. Shamu, the killer whale. Whatever..."

Ralph turned back to her, "Okay, so what do you got for us, Pam?"

"Meg," she tried to keep her smile in place. "It's... Meg."

Charlie looked at Ralph in confusion. "What's 'MEG'?" He looked back at Megan, "I'm sorry, honey, what does that stand for? Is that like one a them damn acronym things?"

She folded her arms and puckered her lips, "It stands for me. My name. It's Megan. Meg. Not Pam."

"I thought you said her name was Pam," Charlie chastised.

Ralph looked more confused, "I thought that's what she said." He shrugged, lifting his hands as if to indicate the issue was beyond his powers. "It's okay. Give her some slack. She's new."

Megan mumbled under her breath, "Oh, this is going to be fun. I get Dumb and Dumber." She spoke up, "So do you want to hear what I've found, or not?"

They both turned to her and smiled.

Ralph nodded, "Go ahead, darlin'."

Megan scrunched her face into a brief thank-you, then flipped a few pages back in her notes, reciting facts quickly, professionally, without emotion, gesturing toward the bed with her pencil stub, "Okay, you can see the obvious, the strangulation sex thing. Victim on display. Must have got pretty kinky before he snuffed her. Semen stains everywhere. So we have plenty of DNA to work with." She cleared her throat. "Okay. Your killer was Caucasian, approximately six-one, one-hundred eighty seven pounds, with brown curly hair. I put time of death at between three-thirty and four-forty-five. You'll have to wait for the lividity tests and a thorough blood matrix from the Medical Examiner for a little more accurate window."

Ralph's eyes went wide. "The desk clerk said it was just a guy of medium height and build with dark sunglasses. You got yourself another witness?"

Megan blinked once. "No."

"Then how the hell do you know all that height and weight shit about the killer?" Charlie leaned in closer. "Who told you all that?"

Megan put her hands on her hips, always weary of explaining the obvious to simpletons. "The carpet told me."

Both detectives looked at her in silence for several seconds, then at each other and laughed out loud. They weren't laughing at the message but the messenger.

Ralph did his best to repress a smile behind a his plump fingers. "How long have you been a police officer, Miss... *Megan?*"

The twenty-four year-old's stomach was starting to knot. "Fourteen months... *sir.*"

Ralph threw his head back with fatherly aplomb. "Well, that's about how long I have to go to retirement. I been a detective for nearly thirty years, darlin'. Doing this kinda thing long before you was even born. I've put away hundreds, if not thousands, of murderers, rapist, thieves, and various an'sundry scum of every sort for *long* periods of time. And I never did it by listening to no carpet."

Megan's tender pink lips bowed into a patient smile. She curled her finger and scrunched her nose at both of them, indicating they should follow. Explanations would obviously have no effect on the ego impaired. Demonstration time.

She led them over to the entrance of the bathroom, where a fine layer of light blue powder, actually pool-cue chalk from a cube in her bag, was brushed on the rug. It revealed two imprints of a heel spaced vertically from each other as if in stride.

Ralph and Charlie peered closer, eyebrows lifted high.

Megan knelt down and pointed to the imprints, pulling a thin steel tape measure out of her pants pocket. "I marked these before the crew came in and matted the rest of the carpet down. Distance of the casual pace was thirty-seven and three quarter inches." She re-measured, showing the detectives her mark on the tape. "Multiply that by a vertical male heel-to-toe walking stride factor of 1.93 and you get approximately seventy-three inches in vertical height. Checking the tensile fibrosity and depth of penetration of the carpet nap, I put the man at slightly over average weight; therefore, at approximately one-hundred eighty-seven for that height category. Give or take a pound to a pound and a half."

Dead silence reigned for almost ten full seconds.

"Bullshit," Charlie spat out a mocking laugh, shaking his head.

Ralph didn't know *what* to think. He never was very good in math. He just kept looking down at the highlighted heel prints with his bottom lip protruding in deep thought.

Megan huffed. "Okay, I'll prove it. How tall are you Detective Weatherstrom?"

"Six foot on the nose," he muttered.

"Stand up," Megan instructed, "and take a step for me."

He did. Megan marked his heel prints in the rug, then looked up to Charlie. "And you, Detective? How tall are you?"

"Just under six-two."

"Give me a step, please," she asked politely.

Charlie reluctantly complied. Both of the detectives eyes went wide when they observed Ralph's stride measurement was a little smaller than the powder-blue one originally marked on the floor; and Charlie's was just a wee bit longer, almost the same length.

She cocked her head, pointing to Ralph, "Let's see here. You're six foot, and he's almost six two, and my measurement of the killer's stride is in between the two of you, so I'd say approximately six-one was a pretty safe guess. Wouldn't you?"

Charlie was smug. "Big fucking deal. How do you *know* it was the *killer?*"

"Because we're in a hotel, *sir.* A nice one with expensive carpet. Pretty basic. The rooms are vacuumed between each guest's use, raising the nap to a very revealing vertical. A first class hotel room is the worst place in the world for a murder. For the killer, that is. Great for us. The woman on the bed isn't six-one. This heel belongs to someone else."

"And the time of death?" Ralph asked, still skeptical of the young woman's talents, but overwhelmed with curiosity. "How do you know about that?"

Megan stood up. "From hotel records and the rose. As you know, our John Doe killer and attractive date discreetly checked in just after midnight, paying with cash. Like you said, the night clerk doesn't remember them other than the five one-hundred dollar bills he threw down in exchange for a quick key. The rose was obviously a post-mortem decoration, confirmed by one of the thorns breaking the skin and drawing no blood.

All three police officers looked back to the bed.

Megan continued her explanation, "On the way in I noticed the rose probably came from one of the bouquet arrangements placed at the end of each hallway. The stem cuttings match exactly, and there's an empty vase at the south end of the hall on this floor—that *isn't* supposed to be empty. No telling what he did with the other eleven roses. Who knows? Maybe took 'em home as a souvenir. But it all fits. I checked with the management downstairs and they tell me they're put out fresh every night between three and four, so we know they weren't even available prior to that time."

Ralph and Charlie looked at each other, obviously impressed, but both unwilling to say so.

Megan glanced at her watch. "It's just after ten now, and from the fact that rigor is just now starting to set in, I'd say she's been that way for at least five or six hours. Pretty basic, really."

"Yeah, right. I still think it's a load of bullshit. I'll go talk to this clerk myself." Charlie pinched a cynical tight-lipped smirk, shook his head and strode away.

"Don't mind him. He's just crotchety in his old age," Ralph called after Charlie as he gave Megan a slight smile.

Charlie flipped Ralph the finger.

Ralph waited until Charlie was out of earshot then leaned over toward Megan, mumbling quietly, "Not bad, Pembrooke. Not bad. I assume then that you found a brown curly hair or two and Caucasian skin samples on the victim?"

She returned his smile, suddenly feeling more at ease with Charlie gone. "Yeah. Pretty basic."

Megan was tempted to hurl a snide comment after Detective McManus, but thought better of it. Asking why Charlie felt the need to keep his wedding ring in his left front pants pocket while at work, in all likelihood, would just make Detective Ralph Weatherstrom think she was being too clever.

CHAPTER 2

THE STAGGER INN

Saturday
June 8, 2013

The Stagger Inn was discreetly tucked at the end of a neighborhood retail strip center in Plano, an upscale North Dallas suburb. The quaint little pub was about three blocks (easy walking or staggering distance) from Megan's four-story apartment complex, the Stratford Arms Apartments. The almost invisible little tavern shared a parking lot with a grocery store, a cafeteria, a small laundromat, an off-brand music store, Jesse's Military Collectibles, a pawn shop, and a Seven-Eleven convenience store on the corner. It was as close an approximation to an authentic Irish pub as the owners and proprietor's, Hal and Sally O'Brien, could fabricate. They had lined all the interior walls and covered the front plate glass windows with dark stained wood panels, and installed heavy beams across the black spray-painted acoustical tiles on the ceiling. From the inside it created the proper cavernous effect.

The actual bar itself was a gorgeous antique, brought in from New England. It was originally part of a Boston pub down on Beacon Street, just off the Commons. The front bar was almost ten yards long and over 100 years old, made of ornately carved dark mahogany, with a gleaming brass foot rail and polished rounded elbow rail. The back bar featured a long beveled-glass mirror etched with an ornate boarder of grapes and bold Baroque strokes. Flanking its sides were intricately carved niches bearing bottled spirits of every shape and size. A dozen round tables with ill-matching chairs were scattered between the bar and the small stage on the far wall, which hosted an occasional local music group on weekends—that is, whenever Hal and Sally could afford it, which was rare.

Four lethargic ceiling fans wound around in excruciatingly slow, hypnotic futility, never disturbing the fine layer of gray haze drifting up from the smoking patrons. It smelled like any other bar: spilled whiskey, beer, smoke, and unwashed humans. There was no juke box, but Hal had a small Sony stereo with four shelf-speakers tacked up along the walls to fill the place with a background of Irish ballads and an occasional Polka from a hand full of old CDs he bought at the Wall-Mart down the street. The Collin County fire marshal said seventy-eight people could physically occupy the pub at any one time, but there were rarely more than thirty people present, even on Saturday night. Then again, there were rarely less than a dozen in attendance, from opening to close. Ten of those were the core regulars who considered the charmingly dark and quaint watering hole the center of their own small, social universe.

Megan Pembrooke had fallen in love with The Stagger Inn two years ago, just after she graduated from Stanford with a Bachelor of Science degree in criminology, minoring in both chemistry and mechanical engineering. California didn't really suit her, so she decided to move back east. She made it as far as Dallas, subsequently enrolling in the Dallas Police Academy to become a cop—always telling herself with a smile it was only because she didn't exactly have the necessary equipment to be a topless dancer. A pity though, she mused with a giggle. Lap-dancing sure as hell paid better than being a cop.

Being a cop took up practically all of Meg's waking hours. But off duty she was one of those ten regulars that could be found down at The Stagger Inn on a fairly consistent basis. The Inn suited her well. The people there knew her and accepted her like family. And she needed that. She had no real family of her own, orphaned when she was five-years-old and raised by a cruelly strict Presbyterian aunt and uncle in Pennsylvania.

The happiest day of her life was the day she left Allentown for California to finally start her life—and get away from *him*. Out of sheer courtesy (habit?), she still exchanged Christmas cards with her aunt and uncle, but never saw them. She never wanted to see them again. The wincing memories of his unwelcome and inappropriate touches—the leering looks in his eyes—

—*come here, Meg, honey. Just give me a hug. I'm not going to hurt you. Just don't you tell. Don't you tell. Don't you tell*—

—it all returned in the form of an occasional nightmare when she was under a lot of stress. For the most part it was forgotten. At least that's what she told herself—again and again and again. Yet, deep down she knew there was more, little taunting whispers of demons she didn't let herself think about or remember.

Just the wind...

Yes, thankfully, they were far, far away.

Megan liked Dallas: the endless Metroplex of urban civilization, stretching out as far as the eye can see; the land of the world's longest traffic lights; and in her view, the Mecca of nouveau-riche vanity and wanton materialism, where no self-respecting woman would walk out her front door to check the mail without full make-up and her hair styled.

But on the upside it was a growing, thriving city, which in many ways still behaved in bewildering, emotional fits and starts like a small town. At least that's the impression Megan got of the city council. But all in all, it had everything one could want, a low cost/high standard of living, clean streets, reasonably good and available jobs; and endless amusements, from amusement parks to the Dallas Cowboys. So for now, to Megan, it was home, hearth, and career. Career came first. There didn't seem to be much time for amusements, other than swinging a few cold brews with her colorful circle of friends down at The Stagger Inn.

Now, as a second year police officer, but still considered a rookie, Megan was attached to the Third Dallas Metro Division as a chief investigative forensic technician. Megan busied herself by day as the wizard of forensic science. Her uncanny gift for noticing the minutia, combined with her dizzying IQ of 169, processed and assimilated facts and figures, deducing the truth faster and more accurately than anyone had ever seen. It was something spectacular to behold. Hal O'Brien constantly reminded her that in a previous century she'd have been burned as a witch. But it wasn't that bad. Megan richly enjoyed her job as a technician, and made no secret about her desire to be a full-fledged gold-shield bearing detective one day.

Third Dallas Metro was assigned to primarily investigate North Dallas: from DFW Airport west of Dallas, east past all the sleazy dives and strip clubs on Harry Hines Blvd. and Northwest Highway, up through residential Farmers Branch, through North Dallas past the glitzy Galleria Mall, across Addison, Richardson, and Plano, through the high dollar homes of Bent Tree and Willow Bend, all the way to middle-class Garland on the east side of town. It was a lot of territory, and kept Megan very busy. That was all right. She liked her work. In any case, each evening after work, usually between seven and eight, after she had time to grab a sandwich and a shower, she'd saddle up her favorite stool at the bar, order a Samuel Adams lager, and trade bizarre anecdotes of the day with the other blithe spirits which haunted the dark, private, comforting shadows of The Stagger Inn.

"Hey, Meg," called Shannon Bolinski, cheerfully bringing a reluctant new face Megan didn't recognize in tow.

Shannon's bubble gum popped almost as loud as her words. She was a bleached blond, who wore far too much make-up for a non-prostitute, and went to great lengths to make everyone else's business her business. She'd never been seen in a dress, opting always for painted-on skinny jeans or ass-high cut-offs, and T-shirts or tank-tops stretched to the limit over her bountiful bosom. Unfortunately, years of bra-less liberation had migrated her pendulous endowment south almost equidistant from her collar bone and her hips.

Shannon grinned, bobbing her penciled in eye-brows, "This here's Kyle. Ain't he cute? I told him about you. He's an unbeliever. Go ahead, Meg. Do him."

Megan set her mug of Boston lager down, wiped her mouth with the back of her hand, and looked at the young man Shannon had by the arm. He appeared to be in his mid-twenties, needing a shave and a haircut, with the same fashion sense as Shannon: worn-out jeans, dusty working man's cowboy boots, a sweat-damp tank-top, sporting an incredulous grin. He said nothing, just kept smiling.

Megan wrinkled her nose, "Sorry. I'm really not in the mood, Shannon. Long day. Maybe later."

"Oh, go on, Meg," Hal prompted from behind the bar, mixing a Jack Daniels and Coke for Jesse Phillips two stools away to Megan's left. Jesse owned the gun shop a few doors down, Jesse's Military Collectibles. The thought of how much liquor Jesse consumed on a daily basis, and then went to work in a room full of lethal firearms and ammunition always gave Megan a nervous chill.

"Yeah, come on, Meg," Shannon pleaded, bouncing down once with her legs pressed together, her bosom flopping like an empty pair of tube socks with a tennis ball in each toe. "Just once more."

The young man huffed, speaking to Shannon out of the side of his mouth, but keeping his eyes on Megan. "Ah, you're a lying sack of shit, honey. This gal ain't got no magical *powers*."

Megan felt a quiver of irritation run up her spine. She didn't like the smug arrogance on this "Kyle" face. Her eyes narrowed on his, speaking slowly and deliberately, "So I bet you felt pretty stupid crouched there on the side of the highway after you finally figured out it was just clog in your fuel filter and not the carburetor."

His eyes widened, his chin dropping slightly.

She grinned. "You should have known to check that first. They're not that complicated on a Harley. But then, your mind was probably too busy figuring out what to do when her husband finds out. It was a close call, wasn't it? You're getting careless. You'll probably get caught red handed next time. You might think she's a real pretty red-head, but you gotta ask yourself if she's worth it."

Kyle's face went completely pale. He swallowed with visible difficulty. His eyes went to Shannon's. "How does she know all that? She don't know me! Did'jou tell'er all that?"

Shannon's eyes darkened, "*What* red-head?"

Kyle looked back at Megan. "You're a witch. You know that? You're a fucking *witch*." He turned and bolted from the bar. Shannon just watched him go, folding her arms over the top of her breasts in a huff.

Hal and all the others burst into a cloud of laughter.

Pete Brumley, sitting on the stool on the opposite side of Megan piped up, "Okay, I saw the marks on the top of his left boot from the gears of his bike, so I knew he was a biker. And the grease under his nails says he's probably a mechanic, but you lost me on all the rest."

Megan turned around and faced Pete. Pete Brumley was a rosy-cheeked, Captain-Jean-Luc-Picard-bald, cigar-smoking, heavy set, fifty-year-old retired trucker who spent the majority of his time profitably hustling newcomers at the dart board on the back wall.

She gave him her cheery grin, "It's pretty basic, Pete."

Hal leaned closer, as did Shannon, always eager to hear the meticulous magic of Megan's hawk eyes and cunning mind. Even Jesse set his drink down and cocked one of his ears.

Megan counted the points on her fingers, "Okay, you saw the marks on the boot. Pretty basic. Very obvious, he drives a bike, and yes, he's a mechanic. Older scars on his fingers and knuckles said that more than the grease. As to the kind of bike—his upper chest was sunburned and peeling. From the size of his chin, he'd have to be leaning back on a chopped Harley as opposed to the forward lean of a Japanese-styled bike. The first knuckle on his right hand was just scabbed over, the cut obviously from today. A trace of light oil in the same direction from the cut came from an oil-pan, not axle grease. I could smell the gas on his shirt, and a few of the drops had already started to bleach out the dye. That, combined with the dust on the front of his pant legs, and I knew—"

"Okay, okay, fuck that shit," Bobby O'Fallon, a tow-headed bag boy from the grocery store, urgently interrupted from a nearby table. "Tell us about this red-head."

Shannon leaned closer, "Yeah. What's this about a red-head?"

Megan frowned in acquiescence, "All right, forget basic mechanics. The red-head." She took a deep breath, "First, he had another long, fresh scratch and an indentation on the inside of his right forearm. Both left multiple traces and a fine penetration. The head of the indentation was very distinct, and oddly squared. I'd say it was from a piece a jewelry, perhaps a diamond ring, marquis or pear cut, pressed tight at close quarters. The marks came in a moment of haste." She paused with a mischievous grin, polling the eyes of her eager pupils. "Plus... he had a long red hair hanging down from his fly, and he missed a belt-loop on the left side trying to get his pants back on in a hurry."

Everyone burst into laughter again.

Megan nodded at Pete, "Pretty basic." She leaned over to Shannon, who still appeared miffed, whispering in her ear. "Shannon, if he comes back, stay away from him. He also keeps a very large knife in his right boot."

Shannon's eyes grew wide, "Thanks, Meg."

The two women exchanged a brief hug, then Megan watched Shannon totter over to where Clyde Mallory sat on the far wall nursing a Miller Lite. Clyde was the locksmith by trade, who suffered from chronic Bass-fisherman Syndrome (BS). BS is a disease common in rural areas where the sufferers become thoroughly obsessed with plucking unsuspecting aquatic life out its natural habitat to the exclusion of all other human activity—with the exception of talking about it every waking hour they're not doing it (also known as BS). Shannon climbed in his lap, removed his Red Man chewing tobacco ball cap, put it on her head, and smothered his face in her generous bosom for a second. He laughed and proceeded to tell her about his new radio activated lure he received from a mail order house in Alaska. Megan swallowed the last bit of her beer with smile and set the empty mug back on the bar.

"One more?" Hal asked, already fishing an ice cold bottle of Sam Adams out of the cooler. He knew Megan always had at least two on a normal day, three on a bad day, and at least ten when something was really bothering her.

"Thanks," Megan nodded, watching him pour the amber brew in a fresh chilled mug. She felt a soft hand rub across her back. The scent of Chanel announced Carol had arrived.

"Hey, sweetie," Carol cooed next to Meg's ear. "Come over for a second. We need to talk."

Megan turned around and gave Carol a brief hug of welcome, feeling Carol's lips peck her cheek. Carol was very physically affectionate to everyone in which she came within an arm's length; as was Carol's roommate and lover, Linda, just sitting down two tables away, hanging her purse on the back of the chair and waving cheerfully. They were a very attractive pair of brunettes, who also lived in Meg's apartment complex, on the same floor in fact. All the men at the bar always murmured about what a waste it was, two such beautiful young women, and not the least bit interested in men. Although, Jim Tucker and Stanley Myers readily admitted they'd be content just to sit and watch some time.

For Megan, they were both very sweet and kind friends, who had been there for her through more than one crisis: when her little Yorkie, Schnapps, got run over by the garbage truck on Valentine's Day; when her place was robbed last spring and she wasn't insured; and when the senior detectives at the department wouldn't listen to her on the Highland Park rapist case last year resulting in two more twelve-year-old girls being savagely raped and dismembered. It wouldn't have happened if they had listened. On each occasion, Carol and Linda had graciously provided strong shoulders and warm hugs for her tears, a couch to sleep on when she didn't want to be alone, and provisions when she had none. Megan didn't really think about her friends' sexuality as an issue of concern. If she had, it might have disturbed her all the more.

In her own right, Megan Pembrooke was very attractive, but never really dated. She was attracted to men, in general, she thought. She just never had much of an opportunity to ever be that close to one. Her ruthless powers of observation and deduction, as well as the awesome scope of her intellect were stumbling blocks few men ever made it past. It was all but impossible to lie to her, which most men couldn't begin to handle. Somehow she not only instantly knew a lie, but from her explicit observations, could tell exactly what the liar *had* been up to.

So despite all Megan Pembrooke had to give—with the exception of her colleagues at work and her colorful little family at The Stagger Inn— she lived a quiet, reclusive life of solitude. She would never openly admit she was lonely, not really even to herself. But that empty little ache deep down in her heart continually longed for someone to share the most minute secrets of her heart, for someone to draw close to, for someone to instill a sense of trust and security. Oh, the distant echo of that hollow little ache was never very far away.

Just the wind…

Well, it wasn't as if she had no suitors. Technically, Bruno lived with Megan. He loved to cuddle and loved her dearly, but officially he didn't count. He was more like family. She laughed at the thought of Bruno's cute legs and dark eyes.

With a half-laugh she'd readily admit there was always Dominic, the nerdy young man with the thick black framed glasses who lived in the apartment across the hall from her. Unfortunately, he had never quite captured her serious interest, nor were his prospects very high on improving that status. They were "just friends," per her insistence. Dominic wasn't repulsive or obnoxious, nor was he anything to write home about; just painfully average. On the positive side, Megan had to give him high marks for effort—unceasing effort.

Dominic Callaghan was a fastidious self-employed software engineer who worked from home, munching on cheese popcorn, Cheetos, and pizza rolls, playing his old classic Beatle albums without end. Every day when she came home, he'd *coincidentally* pop out of his door to say hello, and flirt in his bashful, inept way. He had invited her to dinner at his place twice. She'd politely declined once and reluctantly accepted once. He was actually a pretty good cook and wished she'd accepted the first time.

"What's the matter?" Megan asked Carol as she picked up her beer and headed over to the small wooden table. Linda rose and gave Megan a hug and a brief kiss of her own. Megan took a seat, the look in Carol's eye giving her cause to worry.

Carol sat down with a frown, "We need your help."

Megan nodded, "Sure. Anything." She meant that. Something in her gut told her she already knew. "What is it?"

Linda leaned close, gently setting her hand on Megan's forearm, speaking softly, "Meg, we've started to get the calls again."

Megan's face darkened, "Is it Troy?"

Carol swallowed with difficulty and returned a curt nod, bringing her shoulders in close and taking a deep breath, "It could be. We think so, despite all we've done. We don't know how he found us this time."

"What makes you think it's him again?" Megan asked.

Linda looked embarrassed. She glanced around the bar once, careful to make sure she attracted no undue attention. She opened her purse and pulled out her phone with earphones and handed it to Megan. "Listen to this voicemail."

Megan put the earphones on and pressed the play button on the screen. She heard a raspy voice say, "*...answer the damn phone, bitches! I know you're home. Hello? Hello? Fuck you two! Answer, dammit! Or are you too busy playing grip-and-slide on that double-ended dildo of yours? You like that don't you? (a laugh) But why are you settlin' for a fuckin' piece of plastic when you can have the real thing? What you both really need is a real man, who can more than do you both, with nine inches of—*"

Megan switched the tape player off. It was him. "When did the calls start?"

"Yesterday," Carol replied, reaching over and taking Linda's hand for comfort.

Megan's mind was whirling while her stomach was sinking. No one should have to go through what these two poor women had already been through. Carol and Linda had been forced to move three times in the past two years, fleeing from an obsessed psychotic stalker named Troy Bigham. It had all begun quite innocently with a series of flirting phone calls and letters. Then flowers and small gifts started showing up at their door. When they didn't respond to his advances, they began to receive threatening messages, and then gifts of broken glass and sometimes animal excrement. In the beginning they had tried to shrug it off, hoping he would just get bored and leave them alone. When they found the little German Shepherd puppy butchered and hanging from their apartment door handle by a piece of piano wire, they called the police.

Unfortunately, despite the bloody mess on their doorstep, with no proof who had done it, the police professed complete impotence to do anything about it. The authorities went so far as to tell them that until their tormentor actually *hurt* one of them, the police couldn't really get involved. They were outraged, but were summarily dismissed by the guardians of the peace nonetheless.

They tried legal restraining orders. It didn't stop the calls or the revolting packages from arriving. They changed apartments. They bought deadbolt locks, window bars, and even a fifteen-hundred dollar security system, automatically connected to the 911 emergency service—battery backed up of course. It was quiet for a little while, almost a week, then the calls started up again. The only thing the girls could surmise was that he knew where one or the both of them worked, and followed them home. With enough effort and persistence, anyone can get a phone number or an address, even if it's unlisted. Mr. Troy Bigham was a most persistent individual.

Last year they thought they could finally have him arrested when Carol found all the tires slashed on her car and a profane message scrawled into the paint of her hood; but again the police professed no proof specifically linking Mr. Bigham to the crime. In fact, none of their precautions stopped the break-in when their second apartment was devastated; nor the shots fired through their window on a separate occasion—which precipitated their most recent move into The Stratford Arms, where Megan now lived. Just looking into the two pairs of frightened eyes made Megan's heart heavy. Of all people in the world, Megan had a special sensitivity to being in a situation of persecution and unwanted invasion of privacy.

She knew that menacing beast first hand.

Linda's chin was trembling, "Meg, it *has* to stop. Somehow. I has to stop!"

Megan forced a smile, flexing her arms out in front of her for a second, fingers laced, palms pressed out, popping her knuckles. "It will." A ripple of nervous energy was tingling up her spine as the ideas formed. "Soon. Very soon."

"What can we do?" Carol was almost pleading.

"First, I want you two to pack some things and come and stay with me for a week or so. All right?" Megan looked from face to face to let them both know it was more of an order, not a question.

Linda nodded, "You don't mind?"

Megan's smile came out as she flipped her long brown hair back over her left shoulder. "Not at all. You're right, this has to stop."

"But how? What good does coming to stay with you do? He'll just find us there too." Carol's voice still cracked with a trace of anxious emotion. "We don't want you to get hurt."

Megan leaned forward, "Carol. This... *thing*... that's stalking you is nothing but a diseased animal. It doesn't understand reason like a human being. It doesn't comprehend compassion or civility. It's just a brute beast, like a hyena or a jackal. It sees you two as nothing but two plump gazelles on the fringe of the herd just waiting to be devoured. He thinks you're weak and vulnerable, incapable of defending yourself."

Both girls looked warily at each other, then back to Megan.

Carol sniffed once, holding her composure intact, "Then what can we do?"

Megan paused for a second, then took a deep breath. "There's only one way I know of to deal with ferocious beasts, and that's to trap them, and then show them your claws."

"And then what?" Linda was almost afraid to ask.

Megan locked her eyes on Linda's, unflinching, instinctively knowing what had to be done. "And then you do whatever you have to do. It's pretty basic."

"Yeah right. And pretty scary," Linda mumbled under her breath.

CHAPTER 3

DOMINIC

Saturday
June 8, 2013

"Hi, Meg!" came the cheerful voice from across the hall.

Megan Pembrooke had no sooner stabbed her door key into the thick deadbolt lock on her front door when her regular evening greeting halted her progress.

She turned around, "Hi, Dominic."

Dominic pulled his door open and stood in the doorway, asking with curious cheer, "So how was your day?"

Megan opened her door, calling over her shoulder as she went inside, knowing he'd follow, "Pretty ugly. I got assigned to work a new murder case, so there's a lot of tedium to sort out."

"The woman killed at the Rue de Royale?" he asked, his smile betraying a little morbid curiosity.

Megan stopped for a second in the doorway of the small, but comfortable one-bedroom apartment, her eyes taking in a quick survey of her private domain. She liked having her own place, unlike sharing an efficiency apartment with three other college girls in California. It was certainly a lot quieter.

Her little one bedroom unit was attractive, only about four years old, with a vaulted ceiling and a five-blade ceiling fan in the single-living area. A tiny brass-trimmed fireplace, barely big enough to hold a single starter log, accented the corner just inside the door to the left. A black metal mesh screen draped across its opening. It was primarily there just for looks, but she did get the urge to fire it up once or twice in the winter time. A warm, cozy mood would arise for a fire, but sitting in front of it by herself, huddled in an old quilt never failed to bring on a gray case of the melancholies.

A sliding glass patio door led to a small balcony overlooking the inner courtyard of the complex. The door was graced by a new set of off-white vertical blinds which took up the bulk of the far left wall. She bought the blinds herself, thinking the heavy drapes which came standard in each unit were hideous. She left the blinds angled open most of the time so she could see her potted plants out on the balcony, and let sunlight in on the ones lining the top of a low bookshelf positioned along the stationary glass pane of the patio door. Another set of shelves, leftovers from a previous tenant, hung on angle brackets just inside the door on the bare wall to the left.

Her nineteen-inch color television, DVD player, and stereo sat in a light oak armoire on the far wall. She loved her stereo, with bookshelf-sized speakers that sounded like professional recording studio monitors. Consumer Reports had given them the thumbs up, and that was her cue. She had almost three hundred CD's in every genre, from Mozart to Metallica. But that was just for atmosphere. Her favorite amusement was her TV, or more precisely, her satellite service. Megan got everything. She spend over two-hundred dollars a month just to watch TV. But for her it was well worth it.

She was an avid movie buff. Her personal goal was to try and see every movie ever committed to film, recording the ones she wanted to see again and again. She used a yellow highlighter to mark in Leonard Maltin's review digest every new film she saw. The book was well worn, and very yellow. When friends noted her obsession, she'd routinely remark that the visual arts served to refine her powers of observation.

The entertainment center was just to the left of the phone booth-sized hallway which acted as the intersection of three doors: her bedroom door, facing the front door; the bathroom door was to its immediate right; and the central Air Conditioner/Furnace half-door above an intake register to the left. Megan's bedroom was little more than a twelve by twelve foot drywall cube, whose most attractive feature was the queen sized sleigh bed she bought at an antique store in downtown Plano.

Similarly, the bathroom was functional, but featured an oversized Roman-styled oval tub which was perfect for stretching out in long, hot, stress-relieving bubble baths. Its perimeter was lined with a dozen or more half-used bottles of shampoo, conditioners, honey body lotions, her pink disposable razor, a container of clove scented bath beads, a few remnant slivers of bath soap, an indestructible glycerin bar for her face, a coarse loofah pad, an abrasive foot brush, and several other indispensable needful things she hadn't touched in six months.

On the right wall of the main living area was a munchkin-sized breakfast nook, separated from a efficiency kitchenette by a waist high breakfast bar. Megan didn't have a dining table, just two barstools at the breakfast bar. However, she usually ate standing in the kitchen, or sitting cross-legged at the coffee table watching TV. She let out a thankful-to-be-home sigh and dumped her bulging white canvass book bag atop the breakfast bar. Her head was still a little tipsy from the three Sam Adams she had down at The Stagger Inn.

"Yeah, that's right. The girl killed at the Rue de Royale," she answered Dominic's question, feeling a little puzzled. "How'd you know about it?"

He remained by her door.

She peered over and looked inside the ten-gallon aquarium on the end of the breakfast bar and tapped the glass slightly, "Hey, Bruno, you hungry, baby?"

A ten inch in diameter (from foreleg tip to hind-leg tip) Mexican Indigo Tarantula, sitting in quiet repose on a piece of driftwood, lifted his two long forelegs in mute response. Megan spun open the perforated lid of a large mayonnaise jar with several live field crickets bouncing around inside, then lifted the thin metal lid on the aquarium and dumped three of the wriggling insects inside. The plump, juicy brown bugs leapt to freedom, eager to be out of the jar—*little did they know*. While Bruno's unsuspecting dinner flitted about the glass walls, exploring their new domain, Megan carefully reached in the tank and rubbed the back of Bruno's black fuzzy thorax lightly with her finger tip. He was most pleased.

"There's my baby doll," she cooed with maternal affection.

Dominic felt his stomach sink seeing Megan's dainty little hand so perilously close to something so loathsome. His eyes widened with a rush of alarm at the sight of Megan leaning down close to the opening of the tank and then making a sudden long, high-pitched squeaking chortle with her tongue pressed tightly behind her teeth. It had an uncanny resemblance to the song of crickets in the field. The three insects in the tank even stopped hopping about to listen. Bruno reared his forelegs high and bared his fangs. He had heard it too. It was the dinner bell.

Dominic shrank back from her doorway, always politely waiting to be invited in, but secretly terrified of the gargantuan spider she so affectionately cherished. He inwardly prayed she left him securely in the tank for the time being. On several occasions he had nearly screamed in terror watching her let the hellish creature lethargically wander at will over her arms and shoulders. Nor could he believe she actually allowed the hairy eight-legged beasty to nestle down on top of her head or curl up on her shoulder snuggling against the side of her neck while she watched television. It wasn't natural. It was patently unnerving, to say the least.

He stammered slightly, still in awe, abruptly recalling her question about his knowledge of the new case, "It... uh... was on the news."

"Really? Already?"

Megan glanced at the oversized Mickey Mouse clock on the wall in her small kitchen as she replaced Bruno's lid. Mickey's fat yellow gloves announced it was approximately eight-fifteen. Her hand found the TV's remote and the thirty-seven inch flat screen came to life, filling the apartment with its familiar background noise. A talking head was busy reciting the latest news. Megan looked back at Dominic, noting the tell-tale trace of orange powder on his right forefinger and thumb. More cheese popcorn than usual. He had a busy day. The two small, purple, grape Kool-Aid marks on both corners of his mouth made her smile. That was Dominic, a thirty-something year-old kid.

"Yeah," Dominic nodded, fidgeting around in the doorway. "Channel eight had a special report."

Megan just stared at him for several seconds standing the doorway, then gently admonished him in a patient, motherly way in her no-hurry Pennsylvania/California accent-less voice, "Dominic, why don't you close the door and come on inside for a minute? The air conditioner's on and you're letting the heat in."

A toothsome smile erupted from his lips. The tall, lithe young man dashed over and pulled his own front door closed, making a hasty return, carefully closing Megan's door behind him. Megan thought of Dominic like a stray puppy she made the mistake of feeding. He was always scurrying around her feet, eager to be petted and told he was a good boy—but if she wasn't careful to watch him closely, he might piddle on the rug. Although, she had to admit in his own way, he was kind of cute.

Dominic was just over six foot tall, somewhat athletically built, with bright blue eyes and brown hair which always sported a tussled cow-lick in the back that reminded Megan of Alfalfa from The Little Rascals. He wore heavy Clark Kent styled black-framed spectacles, blue jeans, high-top Reeboks, and a lemon yellow short-sleeve button-up shirt worn open like a jacket over a purple tank-top. It was his usual office attire. He was a character, but for Megan, his extreme intelligence compensated for an annoying clumsiness and irritating shyness.

He stood just inside the door, resting against it with his arms folded loosely across his chest. "Was it, like, *really* gross?"

She moved into the kitchen and pulled open the freezer to determine which exotic frozen dinner selection would be tonight's sumptuous microwave fare. Megan could cook, and was rather good at it; she just never felt inclined to do so unless the mood really hit. That happened about four times a year. Nuclear food was so much more efficient. No messy dishes to wash; just toss the tray in the trash and pitch the fork in the dishwasher.

She shook her head, "No. It was just a strangulation. Looked to me like a typical A.S. episode. That is, it might have been an accident; but I don't think so. The killer decided to get cute."

Dominic frowned, "What's A.S.?"

Megan opened the microwave door, responding clinically, "Asphyxiation Sex. Pretty kinky stuff. During intercourse, just prior to orgasm, one partner cuts off the oxygen and blood flow to the brain with a throat ligature of some kind, then releases it for a blood rush during the orgasm. It's alleged to prolong and intensify the erotic sensation. Pretty dangerous though. I wouldn't recommend it."

Dominic's eyes went to the toes of his perfectly clean tennis shoes, his cheeks reddening slightly. "I wouldn't know about things like that."

Megan giggled, peeling open the box of Salisbury Steak. "Well, don't worry, neither would I. I think it's sick."

He looked back up, "So what was so *cute* about it, as you say?"

She made the appropriate slits in the plastic membrane and uncovered the imitation peach cobbler, per the instructions, then tossed the tray in the oven and set the timer with five expert beeps. "Well, if it was just an accident, he might have called 911, or just fled. But he took the time to position the body and decorate it and everything, just for us to find. I believe it was definitely intentional."

"Wow," he mused. "Who was she?"

"No one special that we know of. The detectives are still checking her out. Not my department," Megan replied with a noticeable trace of longing in her voice. It was difficult to say those words. Someday it *would* be her department. She really wanted to be a full-fledged homicide detective. It's what she had trained for. It was in her blood. Just sifting the clues for the detectives was enjoyable, and she was very good at it; but she knew in her heart she was capable of doing so much more. But who knew how long that would take? Many of the police officers who applied for detective duty waited as long as ten years or more for the chance—if it *ever* came. That was too long. She knew she had to find a way.

It was as if he read her mind, "You know, I bet you'd get your chance, Meg, if you caught a killer like this."

She stopped cold in her tracks, her hands perched on her hips, chin angled slightly off center, her eyes downcast. "Yeah. But unfortunately I don't get the chance."

"Why not?" he asked, stuffing his hands into his pockets.

"I told you," she replied. "Not my job."

He brightened, "What if you *make* it your job?"

She shook her head as she walked back into her small living room and noticed the red light blinking on her answering machine. "No. I could get in a lot of trouble. I don't want to screw up my chances by being labeled a meddler." She tossed a hand of exasperation in the air, "Or worse, go to jail for obstruction of justice."

"What if you were just being helpful?" he challenged. Dominic grimaced slightly as he noticed Bruno leap upon one of the crickets. The huge spider's long, sharp mandibles were already piercing into its savory prey. The other two crickets, suddenly alert to their impending peril, were jumping as fast and hard as they could, making little pinging sounds as they made blunt contact with the thin metal lid. Dominic made a conscious effort to look Megan in the eye, keeping his arms tightly folded across his chest. "You know, I mean, helping like in following up on your own on some of your observations and reporting your findings to the higher-ups?"

That made her smile with intrigue. "I don't know. Maybe."

The mental gears were already shifting and the cerebral RPM's revving. Was that really possible? Could she get away with it? *Would* she get in trouble? What could she do? Would it even be *worth* it? The numbing memory of the Highland Park rapist flashed across her mind. She shook her head to dislodge the thought as she absently reached down and hit the message machine.

Maybe...

Ralph Weatherstrom's voice beeped in, "Meg. This is Detective Weatherstrom. Sorry to bother you at home. Look, it's just after seven this evening. I just wanted to tell you that I liked your work this morning. You done good. Very impressive. Charlie's still bitching, but that's just Charlie. Don't pay him no mind. Anyway, I though you just might like a quick update."

Megan's eyes flashed to Dominic. He seemed just as pleased and interested in the information.

Ralph's voice continued, "That girl today was identified as one Miss Cheryll Dupris of Arlington. Don't worry, she's no one you'd know, just a Jane Doe Citizen. Good news is, we found a friend of hers named Morgan Galen who was supposedly with her earlier last night. They were at the Caribbean Club on lower Greenville with a couple of other gals. And get this, we questioned a bartender there who remembers Cheryll Dupris leaving with a well-dressed man about six-one, a hundred and eighty-five pounds. Thought you'd get a kick out of knowing that."

Dominic's eyes glanced over to Bruno's aquarium as he was slowly stalking six-legged victim number two. He quickly looked away.

Ralph's voice chuckled on the tape then continued. "That's about all we know. We still got no idea if the guy was a friend or a pick-up. So, anyway, if you come up with any more nuggets, let me know. You got my number." Another beep terminated the message.

Another message came on. It was Carol, "Meg? Linda and I will be over at your place about ten. Hope you get this message and are home when we get there. We're not bringing that much and don't want to be in the way. Thanks so much again. See 'ya." A final two-tone beep announced there were no more messages.

Dominic offered hopefully, "Gee, sounds to me like they really *want* you to help."

She nodded, "I think so too." The excitement was building in her voice, "So why don't you go home and get dressed up."

Dominic's eyebrows rose quizzically. "Why?"

"We're going to the Caribbean Club," she announced.

"*We?*" his smile was about to break his face.

•

Just before racing out the door Megan had thought to hit the cancel button on her microwave oven, abandoning her Swanson dinner. She left her apartment door unlocked with a hastily scrawled note taped to it for Carol and Linda. She advised them she "had a date" with Dominic, sarcastically adding "ha-ha" in parenthesis. The note also invited them to just make themselves at home and she'd return soon. She added a P.S. indicating they shouldn't wait up and were more than welcome to take advantage of her queen-sized bed. She would just crash on her sofa.

With that she was gone.

Megan had to send Dominic back inside his apartment to change twice before she accepted him as presentable in public. On his third appearance, wearing a very handsome gray suit and dark tie, she thought he actually looked pretty good, older in fact. However, it took much more coercion to get him to abandon the Reeboks. He had wet his hair to slick it down securely in place. The black-framed glasses made the Clark Kent persona almost perfect. Megan tried not to laugh.

She had quickly slipped into a bright green, low-cut cocktail dress she hadn't worn in years. Fortunately, it still fit and seemed appropriate to the occasion. At least Dominic was impressed, though his endless litany of complements quickly grew tiresome. In less than half an hour Megan had fixed her hair, touched up what little make-up she wore, and she and her conscripted escort were heading south down Central Expressway toward the popular lower Greenville Avenue night spot. They were both giggling and babbling along with excitement—but each for a totally different reason.

The Caribbean Club was more of a zoo on Saturday night than it was on Fridays. Megan and Dominic valet parked Megan's little blue Honda Accord and went into the jammed-packed club pretending to be a couple. Although, in Dominic's mind it was no illusion. Megan insisted on paying the ten dollar cover charge for both of them, especially since she dragged Dominic out on such short notice, but he wouldn't hear of it. Once inside, there were no tables available, nor barely even standing room at the bar. Megan wondered how people could call this writhing pandemonium a good time. The live band, Emerald City, thundered from a wide stage across the back wall. Dancers moved and bopped as best they could in the virtually nonexistent SRO space on the dance floor. Megan aggressively elbowed her way through the sea of humanity up to the bar with Dominic in tow.

A smiling bartender acknowledged her, yelling above the ear shattering decibels, "What can I get you, Miss?"

Megan stepped up on the foot-rung of an occupied barstool next to her and hoisted her small frame up, leaning over the bar, bringing her face within inches of the bartender. She pawed through her purse and showed him her police badge, still having to yell to be heard. "I need to speak with the bartender on duty last night who identified the girl who was killed. Is he working tonight?"

The bartender's smile faded and he gave her a curt nod. "Yeah. That'd be Mike. Hang on." He disappeared for several minutes, then returned with the young man who had waited upon Cheryll Dupris and her handsome date the previous evening.

Dominic politely stood back hidden in the throng and let Megan work, content to watch all the excitement on the dance floor.

The bartender, Mike, nodded politely at Megan. "Hi. What can I do for you?"

"Is there somewhere we can talk?" she bellowed, also showing him her badge.

Mike nodded, and pointed toward a door down at the end of the bar. Megan gave Dominic strict instructions to stay put and order them a beer, a Sam Adams for herself. She was most grateful to be shown into a manager's office where the deafening rumble of the music and the crowd was thankfully muffled to a dull roar with the door closed. At least she could now hear herself think.

Mike noted with a smile, "You don't look like a police officer."

She didn't know quite how to take that. "I'm plain-clothes. You know, undercover."

"Oh," his expression sobered. "So what do you want to know? I told the guys earlier everything I saw."

"I just have a few more questions for you." She sat down on a small vinyl sofa. "It'll only take a minute. Please, sit down. There are just a few things Detective Weatherstrom and Detective McManus wanted me to follow up on."

Mike obediently sat down on the sofa as well. "Okay."

Her mind was already pulling out its probes and high-powered lenses. "The man that was with Ms. Dupris. How exactly was he dressed?"

Mike pursed his lips, "Sharp. Real nice suit and tie. He looked like big money. Doctor, lawyer maybe. Tipped big. Can't really tell you much more than that. It was almost as busy last night as it is tonight."

Megan nodded, making mental notes. "All right. Fair enough. But tell me this, did you happen to notice if he touched the woman at any time or in any way, a peck on the cheek, shake hands, a hug, anything?"

"No. Not really." Mike casually crossed his legs. "She just took his arm when they left. That's all. She'd been sitting there for a few minutes before he showed up. He wasn't there long."

Megan nodded, "I see. And did you overhear any of their conversation?"

"No, ma'am," he replied. "The other detectives already asked me that."

"I know," she added, as though it were true, "but what *I* want to know is if you were able to tell anything about their conversation from their behavior. Were they laughing, joking? Having a good time, acting like old friends?"

He shook his head, "No. But you gotta realize, like I said, I was like really busy. I mean, all I can really remember was that she looked a little nervous and he sure didn't. That's all."

Megan smiled. That's what she had wanted to hear. "Thanks, Mike. You told me what I needed to know." She rose.

"That's it?" he asked.

She nodded, "That's it. Told you. Quick and painless."

Megan returned to Dominic and shared a beer with him, then agreed to one more. He begged her to dance, but she declined, not feeling very confident of her dancing skills nor having any desire whatsoever to be trampled to death in the bouncing throng. Nevertheless, they stayed at the nightclub for almost two hours, making minute observations about the establishment and its colorful assortment of patrons, until finally Megan flatly announced it was time to go. Dominic wasn't very happy to be leaving so soon, but Megan insisted that she learned everything she needed to know for the time being. She resolved to next find a woman named Morgan Galen first thing tomorrow morning, and pick up the trail from there.

•

When they arrived back at their apartment building, Megan turned Dominic's quiet little pout back into an ear-to-ear grin with a warm peck on the cheek and a brief, but warm, hug of thanks.

"Thanks for coming with me tonight," she told him, the beer and the long hours bringing her eye-lids down to half-staff. "That was real sweet of you."

"Anytime," he grinned, then looked very serious. "Oh, by the way. Bishop to Knight five."

Megan grinned. "Bad move. Queen takes pawn, check. Mate in four if you're not careful."

Dominic frowned. "We'll see." With that, he disappeared inside his door.

Megan knew he'd be up half the night feeding moves into one of his chess programs to try and come up with a defense. There was one move he could make that might save him, but she doubted even his computer would deduce it. She enjoyed playing the game with him. They used no board. It was a mental game, where all the pieces and their positions were committed to memory. They were each allowed one move per day. They had played over a dozen games in the past few months. Dominic had yet to post a win, even though Megan knew he cheated and used his computer.

She awkwardly jiggled her key in the lock of her own door. Despite the overwhelming sense of physical fatigue, Megan could still feel the wave of excitement washing over her. No matter how tired her body felt, she didn't know if she was going to be able to sleep that night. Dominic was right. There was nothing preventing her from "following-up" on observations and physical evidence to help the investigation. In fact, her thoroughness might even be commended. Who knows where it might lead? And if she got lucky, she might find out much more than just how it was done—but *who*.

Closing the door behind her and relocking it, Megan switched on the living room overhead light under the five-blade ceiling fan, then walked over to the breakfast bar and tossed her keys down with a sliding metallic jingle. She threw a weary glance at the clock in the kitchen. Mickey said it was almost midnight. Bruno was fast asleep, curled up in a little ball next to the driftwood log. She had the sudden desire to hold him, to feel something warm and affectionate against her neck, but didn't want to wake him up. The three brown field crickets were noticeably gone.

Megan let out a wide, arm-stretching yawn. She kicked off her shoes, unzipped her dress and trudged slowly into her bedroom. She stopped in the doorway, reaching for the light switch, then froze with a slight gasp. In the light spilling in from the living room she could see Carol and Linda fast asleep in her bed, snuggled tightly together.

The bedclothes were pulled down around their hips. Both women apparently slept nude. Linda's head was resting gently on Carol's left shoulder. Carol's arms held Linda close, like a baby, her cheek cuddled against the top of Linda's head. Linda's left arm draped across Carol's middrift, her fingers absently cupping Carol's right breast. Neither stirred to Megan's intrusion or presence. Megan just stood there for several moments, strangely frozen to the spot; watching the couple sleep, somewhat awestruck, virtually hypnotized by the graceful rise and fall of their ribs in slow, even rhythm.

They looked so peaceful and secure in each other's arms. The sight of the gentle swells of their bare breasts initially sent a warm bolt of voyeuristic embarrassment through Megan, but something held her gaze fast. She couldn't look away. Furthermore, as she continued to stare, she realized that the sensual image before her didn't appear to emote an inherent sexual connotation at all. Yes, it was an intensely intimate image; but in a quiet, tender, almost maternal way. Her hot-cheeked embarrassment quickly dissolved into an almost childlike curiosity and sense of wonder, like watching a deer give birth in the wild. For a brief, fleeting second she genuinely wondered what it might feel like just to be held close like that while she peacefully slumbered—by *anyone*. Sadly, it was an experience she couldn't remember.

Just the wind...

Megan felt another hot wave of embarrassment wash over her when she realized she was just standing there, rudely staring. She retreated as quietly as possible, discreetly closing the bedroom door behind her, ensuring the girls' privacy.

Alone again in the living room, the disturbing sense of embarrassment quickly cooled into an empty feeling of solitude. Megan silently plodded into the bathroom to wash her face, pee, and brush her teeth. Her own weary reflection looked so detached and forlorn, her eyes bloodshot and dark. Staring back in the wide mirror was a lonely face. Another heavy sigh eased past her lips.

You're pathetic, Pembrooke. You know that?

It was true, though she hid it well by the light of day. She didn't really know why. It didn't seem like a question that had a precise answer. It was just something that was. Therefore, as usual, in mute resignation, she opted to avoid confrontation with the seemingly unchangeable and unfathomable. She retrieved an extra blanket and pillow from the small linen closet in the bathroom, returned to the living room, and made herself comfortable on the couch.

As she slowly drifted into the twilight of sleep, cuddling one of the sofa's little square throw pillows tightly against her tender bosom, Megan Pembrooke's mind was still whirling with a disjointed montage of facts and figures, heights and weights, distances and pressures, stranglers and victims, stalkers and friends, careers and mentors, interviews and witnesses, embracing arms and kisses, and the nagging dilemma over whether she should castle if he figured out his bishop could be sacrificed for her queen, or whether just to move the queen.

CHAPTER 4

THE COMMISSIONER

Monday
June 7, 2013

"Sit down, Ralph," Police Commissioner DeWayne T. Bragg ordered, not looking up from his desk.

Commissioner Bragg was an intimidatingly tall man, even seated behind a desk. His hair was almost completely silver; his face hard and haggard, bitten and callous, like a trail boss of a century ago. A faint pink and purple web of broken capillaries streaked across his long, sallow cheeks. His reputation as a tyrannical autocrat over the department was well-deserved. Even the most veteran, battle-hardened members of the police force reverently trembled in his presence, and usually had great reason for concern if unexpectedly summoned to his office.

Such was the case with Ralph Weatherstrom.

All the way down the chain of command from Chief Moranzano, to Captain Trevino, down to Lieutenant Prescott—they all wanted to know why Commissioner Bragg wanted to see Detective Ralph Weatherstrom in his office the first thing Monday morning. What had he done? What did he know? He was repeatedly threatened and browbeat to keep his information brief and in concert with the department's party line: everything's fine, we're all doing a good job.

They were more afraid than he was.

Detective Weatherstrom carefully closed the tall glass door behind him and obediently took a seat in one of the two chairs in front of the commissioner's desk, glancing apprehensively at his watch. It was 8:05 A.M. "You asked to see me, sir?"

Bragg nodded, picking up his finely etched Castello pipe and tamping down the black Cavendish tobacco as he spoke. "They tell me you're supposed to be on top of this new strangler case. There any truth to that vicious rumor, Detective?"

"Yes, sir," Ralph affirmed.

The commissioner took several moments of agonizing silence to light his pipe and blow the darkly aromatic blend high above his head toward the hex panel of florescent lights in a slowly spiraling gray cloud. He leveled a hard gaze at Ralph, his hazel eyes cold and accusing. "Then tell me exactly, and I mean *exactly*, what you have so far."

Ralph swallowed, "Have you had a chance to read through the case report, sir?"

Bragg grunted, his pipe clicking against his teeth, "Do I *look* like a fucking rookie to you, Weatherstrom? Huh? Do I look like some piece of shit, just fell off the turnip truck?"

"Naw'sir," Ralph meekly replied in one and a half syllables.

"*Of course* I've seen the damn reports, son," Bragg leaned forward, his teeth yellowed and bared, "But reports don't tell me shit. I want to hear it from you. What have you got? And I want to hear it all."

Ralph squared his shoulders, knowing it would do no good to lie or hide the ugly truth. He gave it to him straight. "In a nutshell: Nothing, sir. And we don't really have anything substantial to go on yet. And it doesn't look too promising either. We got us a high-dollar suit picking up a trollop at a lower Greenville body shop, taking her to the Rue de Royale, pokin' her brains out, chokin' her to death, then leaving her neat-n-purdy for us to find. No significant prints. Plenty of DNA splashed around, but that doesn't mean shit until we have someone to match it to. No distinguishing description of the killer by anyone. Not squat."

Bragg nodded, leaning back in his chair, a thin crack of a smile emerging from his stony mask. "Thank you, Detective. I *appreciate* your candor..." He huffed, "...as opposed to the bullshit I'm being fed. Metro is telling me they're hot on the trail, following up leads, expecting a break, the usual wagon load of shit they think I want to hear."

Ralph felt better. "We do have more we gotta check into, sir. But just between you and me, my gut tells me this was just a random thing. No connection to find, just a fucked-up one-nighter. Hell, as far as we know it could have even been accidental, and maybe made to look intentional by some poor bastard with a twisted imagination sitting at home scared to death. No way to know at this point. Then again, the poor woman's blood-alcohol level was pretty high. Either way, I'd say in all likelihood we're not going to find any prior association between the killer and victim."

The commissioner took another long cloudy puff, his hazel eyes receding to a sullen gray stare down the end of his sharp nose, "Which means if it *was* random, and it *wasn't* accidental, then it's more likely to happen again."

"Yes, sir. Possibly," Ralph nodded, then hesitantly asked, "But... if... uh... if you don't mind my asking, sir... what's *your* interest in this? It's a fairly routine investigation. Nothing special. The girl wasn't some society rich bitch. Nobody else really seems to give a shit. It barely got covered in the news. And I don't see any bad exposure for the department—"

"Until it happens again," Bragg said softly, taking one more deep drag on his pipe, eyes closed.

"You really think it will?" Ralph was serious.

Bragg's eyes came open, revealing a weariness, or perhaps a wariness, that wasn't there a moment earlier. "Don't you?"

CHAPTER 5

FRIENDS IN LOW PLACES

Wednesday
June 9, 2013

"Hey there, girlie-girl, you look like your itsy-bitsy spider just died."
Pete Brumley leaned over on his stool, moving his soggy, half-smoked cigar from one corner of his mouth to the other and back again. His brow
knit with concern, "What's wrong?"

Megan just sat there on her stool with her elbows on the bar in a mo-
rose puddle, cupping her face in her palms. Her beautiful hair was no
longer in a ponytail, but hanging loose across her shoulders and down her
back like a full-length brown veil.

She shrugged with an apathetic roll of her big brown eyes, "Nothing."

"Obviously." Pete put a fatherly hand lightly on her shoulder, waiting
for Hal O'Brien to move further down the bar out of earshot to assist another customer. "You aren't a very good liar either. You know that?"

Megan picked up her mug and took another long sip of her beer, leaving a swath of thick white foam on her upper lip. She looked at the
reflection in the mirror of the happy patrons seated behind her at The
Stagger Inn.

She sighed, "I'm just a little disappointed. That's all."

"At what?" He ran a thick hand over his bald head, garnished with a
few age spots and freckles. His cherub cheeks pinched up to his eyes with
empathetic interest, making the large reddish-brown mole in the middle
of his right eyebrow stand out more prominently.

"It's stupid." She tossed her head back, sticking out her bottom lip
and blowing a few straggling hairs out of her eyes. "I just interviewed a
girl today in the murder investigation I was telling you about yesterday,

hoping it would turn up something significant, but it didn't."

"So why the long face?" He retrieved his own mug of Fosters and sucked down a long gulp, wiping the corner of his mouth with the back of his free hand.

She didn't answer for a minute. "I don't know. It wasn't actually an *official* interview. I was just hoping I'd find a connection to someone or something. Something I could use."

Oh.

Pete smiled as understanding filled his eyes. He remembered sitting through many an evening listening to Megan tell him how bad she wanted to be a detective. In his opinion, she'd certainly be a good one—that is, if she didn't let her burning ambition turn into foolishness. Ambition was a good motivator; but unless tempered with wisdom, could be a patently dangerous dragon. Throughout his life Pete Brumley had seen too many cases of that on the open road. He often wondered how many of his fellow truckers died or were permanently disabled, having pushed on down the road a little farther, collapsing from exhaustion behind the wheel, having refused to give up any precious time to rest, just to make a few dollars more. In the Brumley Almanac it said that the secret to life was pacing.

He patted her arm, "Don't worry, Meg'lin." Meg'lin was Pete's contraction of Megan and Darlin', always meant affectionately. "Your time will come. Just give it a chance. All things happen in their time."

Megan glanced over into his glassy expression, measuring the growing redness in his cheeks: a barometer if Pete's level of inebriation. His concern for her was always comforting, and it never failed to touch her. Megan had known Pete for less than two years, but in so many ways she had adopted him as the surrogate father she really wanted, and needed. It was an unspoken relationship, but seen and understood by everyone at The Stagger Inn who knew them. The old walrus was a treasure.

"I know. Thanks, Pete." With that, she leaned over and gave him a brief hug, which he appeared to enjoy immensely.

However, Pete could tell his sagely platitude had minimal effect on her mood. On many occasions, he enjoyed sparring wits with her on the subject of crime and punishment. He was a big mystery novel fan, with shelves and shelves and boxes and boxes of them all over his house. He dearly loved Raymond Chandler the best, but the old dime store gum-shoe pulps were consistently his favorites. Consequently, he loved to sort out logic with Megan. His mind wasn't as sharp or quick as hers, but his natural common sense was indefensible. Unfortunately, at the moment, something dark and quiet, deep in those big brown puppy-dog eyes of hers told him that she didn't just want to hash out facts and figures. She obviously still had something painful festering inside her that needed to be squeezed out.

He asked off-hand, "So tell me what happened? Was this girl you interviewed uncooperative?"

Megan shook her head, "No, not at all. She was only too happy to talk to me. Although, she was still pretty shaken up from the tragedy. The funeral was this morning. Maybe it was bad timing. I don't know. I went to it myself, just to see who showed up. It was depressing. I hate funerals. There was hardly anyone there. A few friends and co-workers. She had no family in the city. A couple of relatives came in from out of town. That's all."

"So what did the girl say?" Pete prompted.

"She just confirmed what little we already knew," Megan droned in a quiet monotone. "She and the murdered girl and two other friends had gone out for drinks and dancing. Apparently it's a regular social ritual for them on Friday nights. The girl I talked to, this Morgan and her roommate, left the club first, sometime between eleven-thirty and midnight. At the time they left, the murdered girl had gone off to sit by herself at the bar."

"Why?" he asked innocently. "Was she angry at the rest of the group?"

"No," Megan smiled, glad to hear Pete's mind already moving into analysis mode. Perhaps he could shed a little light on something she wasn't seeing. "Apparently, she was looking for a little romance and found it from Mr. Wrong. Mr. *Very* Wrong."

Pete took a deep breath, "Then that's that."

She shrugged, "Yeah, that's that. I just didn't want the trail to end there."

"Perhaps it doesn't," he arched his wiry gray brows, thinking that perhaps a little stimulation of the wits was what she needed after all.

Her eyes found his, questioning—demanding, "What do you mean?"

He took his cigar out of his mouth, gesturing with it like a pointer to an invisible map a few inches in front of them, plotting little invisible points as he made them verbally. "I mean, it sounds like to me you went to talk to this girl today under a false assumption—that is, that the killer was known to the murdered girl and you could somehow make the connection. This, I take it, you figured out was the part that wasn't true."

"Right," she lamented.

"Well, *there's* your mistake." He poked his cigar at her, "You know better than to look at any puzzle with assumptions. Look only at your facts. Let them tell you what's true. Hell, you're supposed to be a scientist by trade. You know you don't start with a hypothesis and then find facts to prove it. You look at the facts and form a hypothesis from them." He chuckled, "Come on, Meg'lin. Think about it. From what you learned about the murdered girl today, just from what you've told me, I think tells you *much* more about the killer himself than you knew before. Not necessarily who he is, but certainly *what* he is."

"How so?" she asked, genuinely intrigued. Megan liked Pete's straightforward logic. Her heart was starting to shrug off some of its lethargy.

His eyes darkened, pensive, concentrating. "Well, let's consider only the issue of motive. Nothing else. *Why* did he do it? Money? No. Not applicable. What then? A man picks up a young woman at a night club. A deliberate act. Yet, they're complete strangers, so there's no prior hate or malice. Thus, no direct motive. From what you said yesterday, she's a simple working woman of modest means just out for a good time. On the other hand, he's a man of substantial means, throwing a lot of money around, and getting an expensive suite at one of the nicest hotels in town. The poor girl must have been very impressed. Don't you think perhaps he wanted her to be impressed? I do. And I would also think a girl being treated to a first class time, a very *romantic* time, with champagne and flowers and all, would be very, very... *vulnerable.*"

Megan's mind meshed into his gears, pointing at him for emphasis, "Yes. Which he would have known, for it was his intention all along to do more than seduce."

Pete nodded, "Which means—"

She was already ahead of him, her words accelerating as she spoke, "That is was a completely premeditated act. But since she was a stranger, a random victim, then motive is by definition pathological."

He nodded, "*Psycho*-pathological."

Her eyes went wide, "That's right."

He pursed his lips, soberly adding, "And since you've found no other bodies in similar fashion—*yet*—I think you can safely assume that this is just a *first* kill."

Her head nodded slowly in anguished realization, reciting almost verbatim her text book delineation of the degenerative psychopathic homicidal personality type. "That's right. Only now he knows what it feels like to kill. His experience is now more than just a twisted fantasy or a dark obsession. He didn't know that before. He does now. Any inhibition he might have felt in killing is now gone." She huffed, "Why, I bet the flower decoration was his way of telling us how much he really enjoyed it."

"And his lack of any remorse," Pete added.

Megan shuddered. "You're right. The trail *has* just begun."

•

Megan's mind was still whirling when she arrived home. She was so distracted in thought she dropped her keys trying to unlock the door.

A familiar voice came from a few feet away, "Hi, Meg."

Megan scooped up her keys and turned to see Dominic's smiling face. "Hi, Dominic."

"How was your day?" He stepped out in the hall, cautiously closing his door behind him.

"Fine."

She really didn't feel like talking to him at length. She just wanted to get inside, slip out of her clothes, and take a long, hot, soothing, steamy bubble bath with a few of her clove aroma-therapy bath beads thrown in for good measure. Pete Brumley had inspired her anew and she had to get alone and think. She felt they had merely scratched the surface in their brainstorm session, and clearly there was a lot more to be assimilated and considered. Yes, it had to be a bath. Some of her best logic and deductions came while lying in almost scalding water up to her chin in her big Roman tub, playing with the water spout with her big toe.

It was hard to mask the impatience in her voice, "But if you'll excuse me, I've got a lot to do this evening."

The subtle dismissal wasn't wasted on Dominic. His expression sank into a mask of futile disappointment like the kid who arrived at the candy store five minutes after it closed with his allowance in hand. "Oh. Okay, I guess I'll see 'ya around." He put his hand back on his door, then shot back with a grin, "Oh. Bishop takes pawn."

Megan frowned. *Damn.* He figured out the move. But it didn't matter, he was dead in six moves anyway. She opened her door, "Clever. All right. Queen to knight three."

Megan made an about face over his exaggerated chuckling and went inside, closing her door behind her. Just inside she stopped short. Carol sat on the couch holding an ice pack on the left side of Linda's face. Linda was softly crying.

Megan moved toward them, "What happened?"

Carol's face was twisted with concern. "*He* did it."

"Who?" Megan implored.

"You know," Carol fired back. "Linda just went over to our apartment to get some things and he was there. He was waiting *inside* the damn apartment!"

Linda sobbed, "I..I..I started screaming. He just walked over and back-handed me, daring me to prove anything. He threatened to be back. Then he just ran off."

"Oh, my God." Megan knelt before the two women, putting a hand of reassurance on Linda's knee.

Linda whimpered, "We have to get out of here, Meg. We should just move out of the city."

"No," Megan announced flatly. "This is your home."

"No it's not," Carol lamented. "It's more like a prison. We can't come and go without looking over our shoulders, wondering what he's going to do next."

Megan stood up with her hands on her hips. "Did he say what he wants this time?"

Carol huffed, pulling her arm around Linda's shoulders, "He wants to make our lives a living hell. That's what he wants. He wants to control us. He gets off on it."

"He just wants to *fuck* us," Linda lashed out with vulgar venom, fresh hot tears streaming down her cheeks. Carol pulled her close and hugged her tight.

Just the wind...

Megan ground her teeth together, steeling herself, "Shhh. Stop it. Does he know where you are now?"

Linda shook her head, "I don't know. I don't think so. God, I hope not."

"Don't go back to your apartment. Under any circumstances." Megan turned around and wandered back to the breakfast bar, still deep in thought, her fingers tapping along the edge of the counter like she was playing and invisible piano.

What should I do? What CAN I do?

She lifted the lid on the aquarium and pulled Bruno out, gingerly setting him on her left forearm and gently stroking him with her right hand. He appeared to like it, scampering up to her elbow and scrunching into a black hairy ball in the crook of her arm.

Her eyes turned back to the two frightened women sitting on her couch. What other choice was there? She whispered matter-of-factly, "I'll take care of it. I promise."

"What are you going to do?" Carol asked, almost afraid to hear the answer.

Megan cuddled Bruno up to her cheek, kissing his plump abdomen, and feeling his fuzzy forelegs stroke her cheek. A haunting, tight-lipped smile emerged, her eyes distant and pensive.

"You don't want to know."

CHAPTER 6

PAWN TAKES PAWN: SANDY DEPAGLIA

Friday
June 14, 2013

"Vodka martini, please. On the rocks."

Sandy Depaglia had noticed the handsome gentlemen long before he walked up to the bar next to her and gave the bartender his order. Even the sound of his voice was attractive, so politely smooth and cultured, like a distinguished statesman or part of some charming aristocracy. He was probably an investment banker, a high-powered corporate lawyer, or a commodities trader. As an insurance underwriter at one of the local Dallas investment banks, Sandy knew the type on sight: carefree, with the world tucked securely in his hip pocket. She didn't hold out any real hope he would take any notice of her.

Sitting patiently at the bar of the Zanzibar Club for over an hour, she had hoped someone nice might come along—someone like this guy. She was starting to get a slight headache. Another glass of white wine would take care of that. She picked up her pack of cigarettes on the bar and a book of matches from a stack next to a bowl of bar nuts and lit up. The almost instantaneous rush of nicotine helped her relax. She wanted to appear relaxed—and available. Her eyes stayed fixed on the gorgeous catch standing next to her.

Yooo hooo...

Like most Friday nights, Sandy would nurse a couple of glasses of Chardonnay, and with a little luck meet a nice guy for drinks a little dancing, and if he was really nice, maybe more. Sandy desperately hated to be alone, especially on a Friday night. She hadn't been in a relationship in over three years and longed to find one—a *good* one this time. Half of her knew she'd never find "Mr. Right" hanging around in the neon-plastic nightclub scene; but at the time, the other half of her didn't really know where else to look, and figured it was worth a shot. She believed in luck, and was just waiting for her luck to change.

Over the past hour a few cute guys had ventured over and asked her to dance; and she had accepted one or two offers with coy interest. But no one had really impressed her beyond idle chit-chat and cheesy come-on lines. What few really hot-looking guys there were in the Zanzibar Club that particular Friday night busied themselves vying for the meager attention of two air-head-looking blondes sitting together at a tall table near the dance floor. She glanced back at them again.

Just look at that...

The bubbly pair were dressed up in ass-high, low-cut, slutty, skin-tight party dresses, four-inch spiked "come-do-me" heels, big hair, lots of make-up, the works. Sandy thought they looked like complete whores, sitting there seductively sucking the straws of oversized umbrella drinks and giggling hysterically. They were obviously having too much fun—more fun than Sandy was having at any rate. And she was even *more* incensed at how much attention they garnered—which only seemed to increase as the evening wore on. She wondered how long it would take for the delicious prize standing next to her to notice them and be gone. He'd surely succeed with one or both of them where others had failed. Why kid herself? With her luck, he was probably married, or gay, or both.

Hi, handsome. I'm alive and as charming as anyone else in here.

Sandy genuinely believed she was attractive enough for even the most discriminating man: five-seven, a trim one-hundred and twelve pounds, with a decent figure, an ample cleavage, and a pleasant face, highlighted by beautiful bright green eyes. She didn't put on too much make-up and wore a comfortable, yet tastefully attractive knee-length ruby red dress. Her auburn hair was curled nicely, styled just that afternoon. She looked hot. While she didn't consider herself a major head-turner, men noticed her—and she dearly liked being noticed.

Would HE notice?

He finished a healthy sip of his drink and softly returned it to the square napkin the bartender placed under it. The abrupt intrusion of his sultry voice instantly masked every other noise in the place.

"It's difficult to find exactly what you want. Isn't it?"

Sandy turned toward the voice, *his* voice, not exactly sure who he was speaking to; but seeing no other within earshot, said, "I'm sorry. Did you say something to me?"

He turned to her, his movements smooth, lithe and cat-like, idly adjusting the lapel of his slate-gray double-breasted jacket, nodding with a polite smile, "You haven't found what you're looking for. Have you?"

It was those deep blue eyes which captivated her and impeded her breathing for an instant. They seemed to look down inside her, piercing deep, beyond the friendly facade she propped up with a cheerful smile. Her tone was almost defensive, "What are you talking about?"

He didn't answer for a moment, just reached for his glass and took another quiet sip. His smile was positively mesmerizing. He leaned over next to her ear, his lips barely making contact with the edge of her carefully styled hair. His words sent an icy chill up her spine.

"I'm talking about an adventure. That *is* why you came. It *is* what you're looking for. Yes?"

•

Sandy had never been so overwhelmed in all her life, instantly smitten to the very core. To say she had been literally swept off her feet was an obscene understatement. His flawless seduction was utterly beguiling and soul-enslaving. It was as though he stepped out of a dream come true, dripping with intoxicating charm and bewitching enchantments. In less than an hour since she had first laid eyes on her handsome stranger, they were together in an Imperial Suite at the Regency Park Plaza Hotel, locked in fervent embrace in the oversized bed.

Sandy lay securely buried beneath him, their bodies shrouded in the finest silk linens. Her legs and arms encircled him like an octopus on a spiny lobster, cradling his sinewy body tight. Every languid thrust of his hips driving the firm heat deeper and deeper within her was like nothing she had ever experienced—but had often dreamed of.

Oh, yes...

This was so unlike her; but from the second she laid eyes on him there had been no decision involved, so sense of choice or deviation. It all happened so effortlessly and devoid of reservation. Never in all her life had she so wantonly given herself to a man, with such unabashed, absolute, and total sensual abandon. But never had such a man come to take her—and take her he did.

It was insane.

It was incredible.

He barely spoke a word. He didn't need to, his eyes, his lips, his hands, even the intoxicating scent of his cologne—all of it told her exactly what she wanted to hear and see, what she had so longed to experience. He made her feel the way she has so longed to feel. She couldn't help herself. She wanted to be plundered and consumed by such a voracious beast. It was like sliding off a cliff and plummeting farther and farther into sensual oblivion. From the moment he first touched her, kissed her, caressed her, undressed her, tasted her, entered her, filled her, massaged her, delighted her, devoured her—she had to have more.

She had to have it all.

It was sometime after her third orgasm, well into the second hour of their passion, that he prompted her to roll over and get on top, straddling his lap. She was thrilled to do so. Sitting up face to face, he coaxed her hips into a leisurely ride toward erotic peak number four. She could feel the heat easily growing within her again.

Oh, yes, yes, yes, yes...

It was like a forbidden erotic narcotic with instant addiction—the more she consumed, the more she wanted. She knew she was almost to her climax again when she felt his forearms tense and his hands roughly grab her hips and forcibly stopped her.

"What's wrong?" she whispered through a dry throat. She thought if he was about to finish, he was more than welcome. "It's okay, don't stop. Enjoy it."

He just held her gaze, silently measuring. His eyes searched her face the way he had done at the Zanzibar Club, contradicting her assumption, "Oh, no. We're far from over. It's time for an altogether new adventure. I want to do something different. I want you to experience something even more incredible than any delight you've tasted thus far."

Was that possible?

Her eyes grew eager, "Will I like it?"

He started to laugh, "You'll just die."

Her smile came out, "That's hard to imagine. You're incredible." She started rocking her hips slowly forward and back again. "I can't imagine anything getting better."

"You'll have to trust me." He reached over to the pillow where his shirt and tie lay in a rumpled pile, picking up the tie. He held the loop up, moving it toward her head.

Sandy leaned back, feeling a twinge of apprehension, "No, I don't need that. I mean it. You're more than enough all by yourself. Let's just keep doing what we're doing. Okay?"

His voice was firm, but still laced with his unique blend of irresistible witchcraft, "Oh, you'll like it. I promise you, it will be the ultimate adventure."

Her hands caught his wrists, "Please, no. I don't want it. I'm not into anything kinky or being tied up. Okay? Come on, let's just go with what we've got. All right?"

His eyes chastised, then softened. "It's nothing kinky. I just want to see you wear it. It arouses me. Thus far, I've been most entertained. But you've only begun to see what happens when I'm fully aroused. You really should see what happens next."

Just wear it?

Breathless, Sandy's grin reemerged, her head still spinning, "Okay. Sorry. I misunderstood." She took the tie and put it around her neck, cinching the not up secure. The ends of the blood-red silk hung down in her tantalizing cleavage. Her shoulders tossed back and forth in a brief, teasing display. "So how's it look?"

"Beautiful," he grinned, coaxing her hips into motion again. "So very, *very* beautiful. Go *faster*. And it's very, *very* arousing. It makes me want to explode inside you. Would you like that?"

Her hips accelerated as she nodded. Their gaze fused together.

Sandy's vision was starting to blur. Her lungs were on fire. Her knees and thighs began to scream and burn in searing pain. But it couldn't stop. No, she had to feel it. She was about to explode. He was about to detonate. The heat between her legs intensified. This time she didn't know if she was going to survive it. The tingling at the base of her spine had already begun.

NO! Not yet...

She had to hang on until he joined her in the torrid conflagration of sensations about to ignite. Just a few more seconds.

"Yes," he panted, "I have to have you now!" He sucked in a hard breath, flexing the muscles in his legs. "I can't hold back any more!"

Yes! NOW!

Sandy knew in the next instant she would feel the pounding pulses deep inside her and the thought was more than sufficient to tear any semblance of self-control from her grasp. Her body instantly constricted in sweet throbs and throbs of wicked ecstasy, devastating her entire being anew. She never noticed his hands grabbing the tie and yanking hard until she felt the iron pressure hit her throat.

She gagged.

Her eyes flew open, her hands flying up and pulling at the smooth cloth cutting into her skin. She couldn't see. Bright flashing strobes of white light and disjointed purple and pink exploded before her. Her temples thundered. Her lungs screamed in agony for release. The demons of fear and panic swooped in and began to encircle her head, tormenting and taunting, reaching out with poisoned talons.

SMACK!

By sheer reflex her right hand had swung hard with all the power she could muster, defensively and accurately, sharply coming into contact with smooth stinging flesh.

The tension on the tie immediately went lax.

Her left hand clawed at the deadly noose about her neck, now finding it pliant, and pulling it out a life-saving inch from her bruised skin. Her lungs surged, sucking in breath after breath. Her vision began to clear. In the fog before her she thought she saw the image of the man beneath her falling back on the bed and grabbing at his discarded trousers.

The haunting waves of panic had begun to recede—that is, until she saw the blurred image of the man's torso rising quickly, and felt strong hands slam into her shoulders and drive her down on her back, bending her legs back an excruciating angle. She cried out in pain. Tears streamed down her cheeks. The image above her came into warped focus. It was the face of her lover hovering inches above her own; but the expression was now one of cold, murderous fury.

"Mistake, pretty girl," he whispered with acid venom.

Horrified, she tried to strike out again, but froze when he brandished a lock-back hunting knife before her face.

Oh, God, no....

"Ah, ah, ah," he chastised, bringing the point less than an inch from her right pupil. "Unnecessary movement could be quite painful and costly. Understand?"

Sandy's heart was about to pound out of her throat. Fresh rivulets of tears cascaded down her face, bounced along amid sobs of fear and pain. The panic was returning.

He began to smile. "It would have been so good, if you had just sat back and enjoyed the adventure."

"Please don't hurt me," she whimpered, scarcely able to get the words past the searing burn in her throat. "Please? I'll do anything you say."

He chuckled, still thrusting, "Why would I do that? I don't want to hurt you. We just wanted to have a little fun. That's all. A little adventure. That's what you wanted, wasn't it? Adventure?"

She began to cry harder, then forcibly stifled her sobs when she felt the tip of the knife blade prick her underneath her chin.

"Shhh," he hushed, still gliding slowly in and out of her body. "Just a little more and then it'll all be over. We're almost finished."

Finished?

Sandy wondered if that was true. Would he just let he go and not hurt her? Was this all just a cruel joke? Did he get off on frightening women? It would figure. When everything seemed so perfect, there just had to be something desperately wrong. It was just her luck. All trace of the exquisite passion was gone, replaced with a the single desperate desire to break free and get away—far, far away.

Would there be the chance?

A cold shiver wracked through her from one end to the other. She silently prayed he would just finish his business, let her go, and then disappear. But for the time being, she just lay there in frozen terror, holding her lips tightly between her teeth, letting him do what he desired. Minutes later, when the invading presence withdrew completely from her, her heart jumped.

Oh, thank God. It was almost over.

She groaned out loud as she straightened one cramped leg.

"Turn over," he commanded.

The cloud of panic and fear came thundering back. It wasn't over.

"No, please, no," her tears returned.

He grabbed her hips and positioned her on her knees and plunged back inside her from the rear, holding the knife in his left hand against her ribs, and the neck-tie in his right, like reigns on a horse, or a dog on a short leash. His hips surged again into maniacal motion. Sandy was praying again amid her tears.

Oh, God, please, please, PLEASE...

The surging sensation behind her was soon of no consequence, as Sandy's fingers came up to claw at the increasing pressure of the tie. The terrifying emotional exhaustion, the draining fear, and physical devastation prevented her from doing anything about it, save vainly picking and scratching at her own throat. The pink and purple lights had returned. Her face was almost completely purple, her eyes swollen and glazed.

Oh, please, just let it be over...

Soon not even a thimble-full of air made it in and out of her mouth. A long, thin strand of saliva dripped from her chin to the bedspread. The ringing in her ears obscured all other sound. Her tortured diaphragm went into involuntary spasms, tearing and surging—the last vestige of her frame with the will to fight. The terrible burning from her waist to her neck had returned, intensifying with the passing of every tortured second. But after almost a full minute, even those sensations slowly began to numb—until the blackness came.

...please...

And the silence.

When the tall man's molars finally ground together, with his entire body drenched in sweat, his eyes clenched tight, the muscles in his legs and abdomen straining taut with his release—Sandy Depaglia had been dead for almost five minutes.

CHAPTER 7

THE REGENCY PARK PLAZA HOTEL

Saturday
June 12, 2013

"Wonderful. Just Wonderful."

Ralph Weatherstrom stood in the doorway of the Imperial Suite of the Regency Park Plaza Hotel with his hands stuffed in his pants pockets, looking at the flurry of activity inside. A piece of yellow crime scene tape spanned the doorway about chest high. Ralph ducked under the tape and stood just inside the doorway in his white short-sleeved shirt and an ugly blue and red striped tie. He left his suit jacket in the car, prompted by the high-ninety degree temperature. It normally didn't get quite that hot in Dallas till later in June or early July. Sweat stains stood out along the edge of his brown leather shoulder-holster bearing his snub-nosed 357. As usual, the forensic technicians combed the crime scene for every shred of evidence they could find.

He knew this day would come, though he hoped if it did, it would be more than just a week away. A dark, unsettled feeling early that morning got him out of bed just before dawn, long before he planned to get up. His wife Mari was still sound asleep with her mouth hanging open, leaving a little brown spot of saliva on her pillow. This was one Saturday he would have enjoyed sleeping in. He had aimlessly walked around his house for hours, bored and restless, with a deep sense of foreboding. There was no sense of surprise when the call came from Charlie McManus just before noon. It had happened again. He knew it. As usual, his instincts had been right. They were rarely fooled.

He looked across the spacious suite to the bed. The scene wasn't exactly identical to the last one, but the similarities were most evident. This time, as was the last, the body was lying in peaceful repose with the head on the pillow, the legs stretched out straight, palms tastefully folded over her lap. And also like the last time, the animal that did this put roses in her right hand, the red bulbs resting attractively between her breasts. Only this time there were two of them instead of one. But unlike the last murder there were several lesions and abrasions of various sizes on the woman's arms, legs, and torso, like she had been beaten as well as cut. Megan Pembrooke was seated on the bed next to the body carefully looking over the surface of the skin with a small hand lens and making notes in her notebook.

Charlie McManus came out of the bathroom and smiled at Ralph, "Nice of you to drop by."

Ralph shrugged, "Yeah. Had nothin' better to do today. Is it the same guy?" He already knew the answer before he asked. The routine babble helped settle the acid churning in his stomach.

Charlie nodded, "Looks that way. According to the desk clerk. Good looking dude. About six-foot tall. Nice suit. Brown hair, blue eyes. Paid cash. Quick and easy. No questions."

A sinking feeling washed over Ralph. "No other witnesses. Right?"

"Naturally," Charlie affirmed, turning around and walking with Ralph over to the bed.

Ralph tapped Megan on the shoulder, causing her to jump, "Hey?"

Megan spun around in alarm, her long hair billowing around and settling against her back. She smiled, with her free hand pressed against her upper chest when she saw who it was. "Oh, you startled me."

"Sorry," he grinned, looking over at the dead woman's face. "Your team turn anything up?"

Megan arched her brows, "A few new wrinkles."

Charlie was still very skeptical of the talents of Ms. Megan Pembrooke and took no pains to disguise that fact in his tone. "Yeah, like what?"

Megan stood up and put her small lens in her canvass book bag on the floor. "Well, to begin with, your Handsome Strangler, or Mr. Friday Night , or whatever you want to call him now, is left-handed."

Charlie scowled, "Come again?"

Megan reached over and lifted the dead woman's chin slightly. Just under her jawline, slightly to the left, was a small cut and a drop of dried blood. "See here? This particular puncture wound, as well as the others here and there along her arms and legs, they were made with the tip of a knife blade. So it wasn't just fun and games gone awry this time. And I can tell from the angle of penetration on this wound, he was in front of her, holding the knife in his left hand."

"That doesn't make any sense." Ralph shook his head back and forth. "If he'd wined her and dined her and brought her up here to this suite for some hanky-panky, what would he need a knife for?"

Charlie huffed, "Maybe she didn't want to put out for him?"

Megan gestured to the body again, "Not hardly. They definitely had a good time in this bed. Look at the semen stains all over the sheets." She shook her head back and forth, "But for some reason this one *did* put up a fight—right at the end. See the scratches at her throat. She didn't like what was happening to her at all." She frowned, "Although, it's weird. Look. The ligature marks around her neck have multiple impressions. He started, stopped, then finished the job on a second try."

"So was it a rape?" Ralph asked.

She stepped closer and lowered her voice. "No. They definitely had intercourse. Lots of it." She awkwardly cleared her throat. "But... uh..." She paused. looking back at the body.

Ralph prompted, "But what?"

"Well, you'll have to get corroboration from the ME's office, but I... uh... took a close look at her... you know." She absently gestured toward the body's pubic region. Megan felt her cheeks start to redden and willed it to stop. This was silly. She cleared her throat and spoke professionally, "And from the condition of the external tissues, my suspicion is that a portion of the intercourse was... uh... post-mortem."

Both Ralph and Charlie looked at each other with a distasteful grimace.

Ralph whispered back, "Really? You sure?"

"Not a hundred percent," she candidly admitted, dropping her eyes to her feet, feeling unusually uncomfortable again.

Actually, it had been strangely awkward for her to pry the corpse's stiff legs apart and examine the bruised vaginal opening. Even the dried semen on her skin and bed sheets bothered her in an uncanny way. Rationally, the unsettled feeling made no sense to her. She had done pathological investigations for years on both murder and rape victims and she never had anything but a one-hundred percent clinical perspective on it. Yet seeing this poor girl just sitting there, propped up with the flowers in her hand had given her a hollow chill. Even in death, she was still very pretty, the look on her face almost peaceful, like the last one. Consequently, her gynecological examination had been extremely brief and cursory.

She looked away, "And, I'd also say that with the single exception of the small puncture under the victim's chin, the other cuts and bruises were also post-mortem. There's no significant blood drainage on any of them. I'll have the coroner's office verify it in the lab. They'll do some more detailed tests."

Charlie looked a little pale. "Anything else?"

Megan grinned, relieved to press on to a different subject. "Well, he wears Aramis cologne."

"What?" Charlie rolled his eyes.

The petite brunette pointed to the bed. "It's still on the pillow and sheets. Smell it if you want. A friend of mine wears it. It's easy to recognize, kind of peppery and sexy."

Charlie chuckled, "I'll remember that." He turned to Ralph, "What do you bet we find she's another Friday night pick-up?"

"I'm sure of it," Megan added.

"Why?" Ralph asked.

She reached over to the nightstand and retrieved a small matchbook in a cellophane bag, handing it to Ralph, "I found this under the bed, near her discarded purse and clothes."

The matchbook read: Club Zanzibar.

Ralph handed it to Charlie. "Great. Let's get over there and check it out. Maybe we'll get lucky this time and find someone who saw something or knows something."

"Right." Charlie agreed as they turned and started to leave.

"Gentlemen?" Megan called after them politely. The conversation with Pete Brumley came to mind. She had to share what she thought and see if her unofficial follow-up help was going to be accepted or rejected. "Before you go. There's one more thing."

They stopped by the door, looking at her expectantly.

"Just a circumstantial observation. It obviously isn't an isolated incident anymore," she added, pointing to the roses. "By his flamboyant signature, we've apparently got a serial killer on our hands, who has now escalated his attack scenario."

Ralph took a step back toward her, "What do you mean?"

"I mean he's demonstrating signs of rapid desensitization. Last week it appears he learned how to kill in a moment of passion, a twisted fantasy perhaps, but only a strangulation." Her voice was cool and even, giving both veteran detectives an uncanny chill. "Only seven days later he's now using a knife." She pointed at the body on the bed. "But this girl wasn't *killed* with a knife. So he's learned to add fear to intensify the thrill. In all likelihood, unless he also decides to accelerate his schedule, there's a good chance we'll get to see his next twisted fantasy by next Friday. And you can bet it'll be worse. Probably *a lot* worse."

Ralph just shook his head back and forth with a dark sense of foreboding in his gut. He knew she was right. He gave her a nod of thanks, turned with Detective McManus, and then left. Neither detective said another word.

Megan just stood there, watching them leave, inwardly wondering what they were thinking at that moment. She thought by the look in Weatherstrom's eye, he believed her. McManus had an arrogant scowl which said he'd believe it when he saw it happen first hand. She could tell Charlie didn't like her. He was like so many simpletons whose egos wouldn't allow them to accept anything insightful from someone younger, less-experienced, or a woman.

Asshole.

•

As they rode the elevator down, Charlie asked, "You believe any of that shit she said?"

Ralph shrugged, "Does it make any difference?"

Charlie pursed his lips, "No, probably not. But answer the question anyway."

Ralph's voice became grave. "I believe the part about having a serial-psycho on our hands. We know it's not revenge. It's not a bad drug deal. It's not a cheating wife or girlfriend. That eliminates better than ninety percent of our homicide motives. Right? So what's left? Sick-o. Hell, Charlie, we've seen it before."

"Yeah," Charlie agreed. "You're right. But not quite like this. There's an arrogance to it. Like he's fuckin' showing off. You know? And though I'll never admit it, just between you and me, despite all the psycho-babble, I think the girl's probably right. And odds are, he ain't done either."

"No. He's not done. I'm scared shitless he's just getting started." Ralph shook his head, feeling a dark cloud of apprehension looming over him. Pembrooke *was* right. It was sure to get worse before it got better. He sighed, "Well, hopefully we can keep it all very quiet and avoid all this getting blown out of proportion. I know I'm going to get another call from Commissioner Bragg. He's watching all of this personally."

"Super," Charlie sighed. "That's all we need."

"So don't talk to anyone," Ralph admonished, "Nobody inside or outside the department, no lawyers, *nobody*—and especially *no* fuckin' reporters."

The elevator stopped on the ground floor announced by the single chime of its electronic bell.

Charlie touched his arm, "Right. This has to be kept very low key."

Ralph nodded, then stopped short as the elevator doors parted and he witnessed a hungry mob of press teams, armed with cameras, lights, and microphones flooding into the lobby of the hotel.

His eyes turned back to Charlie, "Wonderful, just wonderful."

CHAPTER 8

HOPES AND FEARS

Tuesday
June 18, 2013

Megan's dart landed dead center of the triple-twenty section of the dart board. Pete Brumley groaned, reluctantly reaching into his pocket and pulling out his thick money roll. Shannon Bolinski squealed and clapped her hands together. Clyde Mallory laughed out loud and pulled Shannon down on his lap, hugging her close. Megan victoriously sauntered over and pulled her three darts out of the board, chalked her score of sixty down to a perfect zero, and strolled triumphantly back to Pete holding out her upturned left palm..

He handed her a crisp ten dollar bill. "Double or nothing?"

Megan threw an arm around his shoulder and squeezed him. "No, but I'll buy you a beer."

Megan and Pete saddled their usual stools in the middle of the bar. Megan laid the ten dollar bill down and slid it toward Hal, "A Sammy Adams for me and a Fosters for my friend, Hal."

Hal O'Brien slid over, "Can do." He winked at Megan, then cast a disparaging sideways glance at Pete, "So how'd you let her beat you so bad, Pete? I heard you're supposed to be pretty good at a toss."

Pete frowned. He didn't like to be teased. "She's just lucky."

Hal popped the tops on the two bottles of beer and slid them down the bar, reaching into the cooler to fetch two frosted mugs. "Well, if luck means you win, then if I had to choose, I think I'd rather be lucky than good."

"*Amen*," sounded Jesse Phillips with good Baptist fervor as he lifted the last swallow of his bourbon and coke in a slight toast to Hal's back-porch wisdom. Jesse's drooping basset hound eyes were already well glazed from a happy-hour binge he started mid-afternoon.

Pete pulled a fresh Dutch Masters panatela out of his wrinkled shirt pocket and nipped off the end with his front teeth, spitting the bitter little plug on the floor. "I'm surprised you could concentrate so well on the game, thinking about your case and all. I guess they're keeping you pretty busy, right? I saw the news reports. Sounds like the circus is in town."

Megan poured her bottle into the empty mug, expertly holding it at an angle to keep the foam to a minimum the way Hal taught her. She leaned over, bumping against her friend's shoulder with a friendly nudge. "The circus? Yeah, that about hits it right on the head, with lions and tigers and bear, oh my."

Pete chuckled.

She took a sip, "And with all the other clowns from the local as well as national press thrown in, it makes it that much harder to get anything done. The department has been trying to keep it pretty low key, but the attention's already getting out of hand. It's crazy. If we find another body, there's likely to be a panic."

"You really think so?" He raised his eyebrows as he flipped the top on his brushed stainless-steel Zippo lighter and fired up his cigar.

Megan nodded slowly, "We'll see. But you were right about one thing. We definitely got a real sick puppy out there. And I got this nasty feeling it's far from over."

"You think you got any real chances of catching him?" Pete was studying her face.

Megan's eyes narrowed, "Who knows? It's weird. There are clear variances from a typical serial case. He's very smart and very efficient in committing the crimes. He knows exactly what he's doing. But apparently he has absolutely no fear of being caught, as though he knows ahead of time exactly what we'll be looking for."

"Like a professional criminal?" Pete mused.

"Perhaps." She turned to him, "Or a cop. He leaves no fingerprints, which leads me to believe he may have a prior record of some kind he doesn't want us to know about. He avoids security camera's. But I think he's made one small mistake." She paused, collecting her thoughts for a second, then continued, "He's left us plenty of semen samples for DNA matching, should he *ever* be caught—which you know is even *better* than fingerprints. Hell, we've even got witnesses in the clubs, as well as the hotels, who could easily pick him out of a lineup, should he ever stand in one."

Pete blew a rank cloud to his right and licked his chubby lips, "Then you're right. He apparently has no fear or intention of being caught. Even if it means going out in a blaze of glory."

Megan smiled at Hal when he put her change on the bar in front of her. She left it there. "Yeah. And if he keeps on going the way he's going. He just might be right."

It was Pete's turn to lean into her shoulder, returning his pretty young friend's encouraging nudge. "Then you got no choice. If you can't corner your quarry on your own time," he took an exaggerated breath, "then you'll just have to find a way to trap him in his native habitat. Catch him in the act. That's how most of the big carnivores are caught. Set up a blind, then get the right bait. Something you know ahead of time he likes to feed on."

Megan looked him in the eye. "That's right." She was about to say something else when the sound of the door opening and urgent footsteps growing louder, diverted her attention.

Carol was running inside Linda close on her heels. "Meg, *there* you are." Their faces were white, their eyes filled with fear.

Just the wind...

Megan's heart jumped up into her throat. "What is it? What's happened?"

Linda rushed up with them, "He's in the parking lot."

"What?" Megan started to get off the stool. "Here?"

Carol blurted out, "He followed us from the apartment. He tried to run his car into ours, bumping our back bumper. We could have gone off the road. He was just laughing and cussing. Dammit, Meg, he could have *killed* us."

Megan bit her lip. "I have my badge and gun in the car. Do you want me to arrest him?"

"Lord, NO!" Carol lamented. "That's not enough. You know they'll just let him go and he'll be back. Meg, he's going to *kill* us!" She looked so helpless and afraid.

A smoldering rage bubbled up in the back of Megan's throat looking into the horror filled eyes before her. Her mind shuffled and reshuffled the facts and options. Carol was right. If she just busted him, he'd call a lawyer; and then a bail-bondsman would have him back on the street in less than four hours. And then what would happen? The truth was too evident. It would just continue, and get worse—until it was stopped.

She made up her mind. A pretty basic choice.

"All right. It stops right now. Tonight. Stay here. Stay right here with Pete." She turned back to Pete. "Pete, you just got some company for a little while. Don't let them out of your sight. I have to go take care of something."

Pete chuckled, "No problem. They're safe as a baby in its mother's arms."

Linda and Carol both moved to the other side of Pete, safely away from the door.

"What are you going to do?" Carol asked.

"Just what I said. I'm going to put a stop to this. Once and for all." Megan started to leave, then shot back. "What kind of car is he in?"

Linda gulped, "A blue Corvette with a white top."

"Fine," she replied. "Look, I want you to stay here until you see he's gone. Then wait another hour and then go straight back to the apartment. Lock the door. Let *no one* in. Is that clear?"

Both girls nodded vigorously, still visibly trembling.

Pete's hand caught Megan's arm. "Meg'lin, what *are* you going to do?"

Her eyes were hard and determined, though she tried to make her voice sound light, almost joking, "Don't worry. I'll be all right. I just have to go explain to an infantile bully on the play yard how to behave around a lady."

"And?" He hadn't let go.

"And..." her eyes flashed with an icy confidence, her voice even and in complete control, "...then I do whatever's necessary to make sure he understands."

He let go of her arm. "Be careful. And you know if you need any help...."

She headed toward the door, calling back, "I know. Thanks, Pete. But I won't need any help."

Linda and Carol were crying softly, huddled against each other on Pete's plump shoulders. He hushed them with quiet words of assurance as Megan walked out of The Stagger Inn.

Outside, Megan saw the blue and white Corvette the instant she walked out the door, but ignored it, hastily climbing into her inconspicuous little blue Honda Accord and leaving the parking lot. She made one quick lap around the block and pulled up alongside the Seven-Eleven on the corner, careful to stay in the Corvette's blind spot. She couldn't see the man's face in the driver's seat, just the back of his head. She still hadn't worked out all the details of what she was going to do, but the ideas were forming quickly as she watched and plotted. The more she thought about it, the more convinced she was she had to do it. There was no choice.

Mr. Troy Bigham was in for a shock.

She watched him just sit there, waiting in his car for the better part of an hour, patiently sipping a tall-boy, just staring at the door of The Stagger Inn. Finally, he started his engine, turned on his headlights and pulled out of the lot. Megan discretely followed him for miles, all the way to an attractive middle-class neighborhood in Richardson with older homes and lined with mature trees. She carefully noted which driveway he pulled into, pausing on the roadside just long enough to see him walk to the mailbox and check the mail before heading to the front door. She smiled, writing the address down in her notebook. It was his house. She'd be back very shortly after picking up a few necessary items for the task ahead.

•

Dominic Callaghan was thrilled that Megan asked for his help that night. He had never seen her so determined, so focused. It sent a chill through him. Her instructions had been extremely explicit and he knew exactly what to do. It would be easy. He had all the necessary equipment and supplies. It wouldn't take more than an hour. He promised he'd have it finished before she came home. It was a pleasure. He'd have done anything for Megan—literally. Megan could have asked him to commando-crawl naked over disease-tainted broken glass to retrieve a live hand-grenade and he would have done it without question.

After Dominic finished his task, he sat alone in his own small apartment in front of the wide color computer monitor on his desk. Megan Pembrooke was all he could think about. She was all he could *ever* think about. It was a quiet torture. He intentionally kept his stereo turned down low during the day, especially between seven and seven-fifteen in the morning, and between eight and eight-thirty in the evening. That's usually when she came and went. He tried to never miss an opportunity to pop out and see her. It was awkward sometimes, and he knew she must find it a nuisance, but a chance was a chance.

He was intelligent enough to know that as things stood, he really didn't have much of a *real* chance with her; but that didn't stop him from hoping. He wanted her to see him as he really was, without pretension, without the airs. He could deceive her and play games like he had done with others; but he didn't want to. That was too unsatisfying. He had the money to impress, more money than he could spend in a lifetime. So many women were so impressed by money. But no. Megan wouldn't be impressed with money, even if she found out how many millions of dollars he had made over the last five years with his private software business. That's why he liked her. That down-to-earth quality was what was most attractive about her.

Dominic had known for quite some time that in order to win Megan

Pembrooke's heart it would take something much more personal, much closer to her own desires and ambitions. That's why he put so much thought into the project. The project would impress her. It had to. He had worked so hard already. It was coming along so well.

Yes. She'd love it.

Furthermore, Megan Pembrooke would never know, nor would he ever reveal, that the last three hit action-adventure video games Dominic had written all starred a caricature of her as the beautiful princess who had been captured by evil villains and was perpetually in sore need of rescuing. His damsels-in-distress all had a waist length fall of gorgeous brown hair. The hero character of the games was always patterned after himself, naturally, but with an almost super-human James Bond persona. It was his favorite fantasy. When all the forces of evil had been outwitted and vanquished, he'd pluck her from the brink of doom and disaster, take her into his arms, and then usher her into his animated pixel and sprite processed version of happily ever after.

Dominic hit his keyboard and executed the animation sequence he was debugging. The image of his handsome hero taking his pretty princess in his arms and warmly kissing her repeated itself. Small angelic cherubs flew around their heads. The headless carcass of the great dragon lay at the hero's feet. The princess was safe. A pang of apprehension swept across Dominic's brow.

Was his princess really safe at that hour?

At that exact moment, she had just arrived at her destination.

CHAPTER 9

CREATURES GREAT AND SMALL

Tuesday
June 18, 2013

Troy Bigham was more irritated than surprised when his doorbell rang at ten-thirty that night. He staggered to the door with eight beers in his system and peered out through the peephole, surprised to see a small, attractive, brown-eyed brunette with a canvass book bag on her shoulder standing on his front porch. He assumed she was selling something.

"Yeah? What do you want?" he asked, opening the door a crack, keeping the safety chain on.

Coward.

She smiled, "Hi. Look, I'm *so* sorry to bother you so late, but I'm…" she looked back over her shoulder at her car with the hood standing up and feigned a stifled sob of helplessness, "…having car trouble and I need to call someone to give me a tow. Could I please use your phone?" She gave him her best damsel-in-distress look. "Please? I'd really appreciate it."

Oh? That's different.

Troy Bigham gave her a wide grin, lecherously glancing up and down her body, wondering just how much she would appreciate his gracious assistance. The scenario reminded him of a sexploit article he had just read in Hustler magazine. This could be fun. "Sure, honey. Come on in and make yourself at home. Take a load off."

Megan gave him a brief, demure curtsey of thanks and walked past him into the small foyer of the small ranch-styled dwelling, her hand deftly slipping inside the book bag and closing on a small rubber handle. Troy reclosed the door and locked it, already fantasizing about what kind of amusing games he could conjure up with his unexpected playmate. When he casually turned around to face her, with the same silly grin of expectation plastered on his face, he never knew what hit him. All he felt was a sharp prick sting his chest, heard a loud crackling pop, and saw a bright blue light as a freight-train slammed into him head-on, rendering him unconscious in the next instant.

Megan smiled with satisfaction, walking over to the man's limp body lying in a heap and pulled the TASER darts out of his chest, winding the wire back up and returning the device to her book-bag.

"Phase one complete." She hummed the *Mission Impossible* theme song to herself, then huffed with reluctance as she gently set her book bag on the floor, careful of its fragile contents. Standing back up with her hands on her hips she frowned, studying her quarry.

"Now to get you moved."

•

Troy Bigham's next conscious sensation was the acrid burning stench of ammonia as Megan waved the broken plastic capsule under his nose, reviving him with an abrupt start. He had no idea how long he had been unconscious, but his entire body ached with a universal soreness like he had been badly beaten. Troy hadn't felt that bad since he used to ride bulls in the stockyards in Fort Worth. He moaned softly as he tried to sit up, but a sharp pain bit into his wrists and ankles, holding him in check.

"Don't even move a little bit," he heard an unfamiliar female voice nearby say. "Or you'll bleed to death in less than ten minutes."

His eyes came open slowly, weary and blurred. He saw a petite woman with long brown hair and big brown eyes sitting calmly on a chair a few feet away. A quick recollection flashed though his mind. Yes, he remembered. It was the same woman who had come into his house shortly before everything went black. What had she done to him? He wondered what had happened and where he was. Still shrouded in a confused daze he glanced around, noting he was in his bedroom, lying on his own brass bed. He looked up at his wrists and gasped.

Megan grinned, "It's a very fine and specialized piano wire. Razor wire. *Very* special. Point oh-oh-nine gauge. As thin as an E-Sting on an electric guitar, but much stronger. It's routinely used for garrotes. It goes through a windpipe and carotid arteries like a hot knife through butter, with less than ten pounds of pressure. Amazing how something so frail can be so strong. Isn't it?" It felt good to say that. A warm rush coursed up her spine, intensifying her voice. "You struggle against it, your skin slices long before the wire breaks. In fact, you could cut yourself down to the bone before *that* wire breaks. Understand?"

What!!!

No one dared treat Troy Bigham like this. Especially not some sawed-off fucking cunt! There was a shit-load of hell to pay—right now! His eyes filled with black venom and his head started to clear, fueled by an explosive rage.

He bellowed, "*Fuck you*, bitch! Let me up from here or I'll beat your ass black and blue! You hear me?!"

Megan just continued to sit there and smile.

He started to writhe back and forth, then stopped when he felt a foreign sensation on his stomach.

Megan chuckled, "Like I said... I wouldn't make any... sudden movements—*at all*—if I were you." Her eyes glanced midway down his body to just below his waistline.

Troy looked down his chest and froze. Up to that point he didn't realize he was completely nude, but at that moment the indignity was completely irrelevant. His lungs gripped tight.

Oh, FUCK!

If Troy Bigham could have squeezed any air out of his paralyzed lungs he would have shrieked like a five-year-old with a finger caught in a car door, but he couldn't. He was paralyzed with fear, trembling at the sight of the largest spider he had ever seen in his life moving slowly up from his navel toward his face. With every languid step, its two long black forelegs reached out, deliberately and precisely, followed by the fluid contagion of the other six. He felt the warm splash of his own urine arcing down on his knees. It didn't matter. He knew he was about to die.

His body began to quake in uncontrollable fear as he watched the hellish beast scale over the gentle rim of his rib cage and pause briefly on his sternum. He could see the multiple rows of shiny black eyes. The ghastly inch-and-a-half long black fangs of the horrific arachnid flexed apart and moving in and out, audibly clicking together. Step by step, it crept closer and closer to his face. The helpless image of the half-man/half-insect caught in the spider's web in the final scene of "The Fly," screaming in terror in its tinny little voice flashed to mind.

Help me! Help me!

"It's a Mexican Indigo Tarantula," Megan advised matter-of-factly. "Not only is the bite extremely, and I mean *extremely* painful, as you could well imagine—kind of like being stabbed with a pair of scissors or a barbecue fork—but the venom is highly toxic. Almost always fatal. A rarity among Tarantulas. Actually, the Mexican Indigo is very rare species from the Central American jungles of extreme southern tip of Mexico. And in case you missed the episode on the Discovery Channel, you might want to know that death comes very, *very* slowly over about forty-eight hours, amid bone-wrenching convulsions, frothing at the mouth, spontaneous lesions all over the skin, loss of control of all bodily functions, and excruciating agony. I think you get the picture." She shrugged, "And unfortunately, there's no known antidote—other than perhaps a bullet in the head."

"Please take it away," he whispered, trying not to panic. "Come on. Don't fool around. For God sake, lady, please."

She shook her head, "Sorry. Can't do that, stud. He's hungry right now. *Very* hungry. Not a good idea to touch a Mexican Indigo when he's hungry. He might mistake my hand for a rat or a rabbit."

He could barely speak, "W-w-w-what d-d-do you want?"

Megan reached into her canvass bag again and rose. She walked over next to him snipping a huge pair of pinking shears twice before his face, then reached down and with latex-gloved hands lifted his fear-shriveled penis straight up. It was still dribbling.

Her words were callous and cold, but deliberately amused, "What I *want...* is for you to know how *helpless* and *vulnerable* you are. I just wanted you to know what it feels like." She opened the scissors, bringing the crotch of the blades up against the base of his flaccid organ. "And I particularly want you to know how easily I can get to you and hurt you—*anytime* I want. And I will. And I'll enjoy it." She looked down at the wrinkled nub of flesh in her hand, "I don't think you'll be needing this anymore—"

"No!" He seethed through clenched teeth, then whimpered, hot tears filling his eyes. "Please, lady, don't. Please? I'm so sorry for what I said. Honest to God, I am. I'll do anything you say. I swear. Anything."

Bruno was almost to his collar bone.

Megan lifted the scissors up and down, scraping his tender flesh, "I know you will. It doesn't feel too good to be in your position. *Does* it? So pitiful. Tell me, Troy-honey. How does it feel to know you're about to die, and it's going hurt more than you could possibly imagine?"

"*Please*," he strained through chattering teeth. "*Please* don't kill me. I'll do anything for you. I swear to God. Anything."

Bruno stood on the man's throat and put a single foreleg on his chin.

Troy's eyes clamped shut, bracing himself for the piercing pain he expected to sustain in his jugular in the next instant.

And nothing happened.

Megan took a deep breath, removed the scissors, and stood up pursing her lips. "Humm. Now that I think about it, perhaps there is something you can do for me. You see, Troy-baby, the main reason I'm here is because you've offended two of my nearest and dearest friends. I think you know who they are. Two beautiful young girls? In a car just today? And it wasn't the first time. Was it? You've been a very naughty boy for quite a while. And you know, by offending them, you've deeply offended me." She leaned close to his face, "I don't take offense lightly. And as you can see, it isn't wise to offend me. Understand?"

Troy kept his eyes closed to the horror around him, "I'm sorry, ma'am. It was all a joke. You gotta believe me. I never meant nothing. I won't ever go around them ever again. I-I-I s-s-swear to God."

"I don't believe you." Megan bit into the inside of her lip as she looked at Bruno, trying very hard not to laugh.

Bruno was curling up on Troy's Adam's apple, snuggling under his chin, getting comfortable and preparing to go to sleep, the way he did when they sat together on the couch and watched TV. While Bruno *looked* quite menacing, in truth, he was about as dangerous as a hamster; but Troy Bigham obviously didn't know that. Nor was he poisonous, though his bite did hurt a bit if you pissed him off, which was pretty hard to do. He was very affectionate and loved to cuddle even more than getting a snack from his jar of crickets. He looked very comfy at the moment.

Troy barely whispered, "Please lady. You're right. I was dead wrong. If I ever come near 'em again, you *can* kill me. But I don't want to die. Not like this. Please? I'll stay away. I swear. I *don't* want to die. I'll leave them alone. Just give me a chance."

Megan leaned over and picked Bruno up, who appeared to have been quite at home where he was, and returned him to the large Hellman's mayonnaise jar. Bruno tapped on the glass with his forelegs to register his displeasure. Megan put the jar back in her book bag and returned to her chair. She didn't really realize it until that moment, but the rushing sense of power and control she felt was actually quite arousing. In a strange way, this was starting to be a lot of fun.

She kept her voice terse and short. "Very well. You get *one* chance, Mr. Bigham. But understand one thing very clearly." She leaned down next to his ear, speaking softly. "I'm going to be watching you. Day and night. And waiting. You won't see me, but you'll know I'm there. Day *and* night. If you even *think* about it. One phone call. One package. One letter. *Any* contact of any kind and I'll know it before you do. And I'll get you. Day or night. You'll never see it coming. You'll never know how or when.

But it'll happen. And I'll enjoy doing it."

His eyes reluctantly came open, moist with fresh tears. "Thank you, ma'am. I promise, you don't have to worry."

Megan could tell by the look in his eyes she already had reason to worry. He wasn't that good of an actor. He was just scared and would say anything to save his miserable hide.

"We'll see." She stood up and started to leave.

"Hey," he called after her. "Don't leave yet. A-a-a aren't you going to cut me loose?"

She stopped at his door, adjusting the book bag on her shoulder. "No. I've had enough fun with you for one day. But tell you what. In an hour or two I'll call you a cab and leave a note on the door that you're back here waiting in the bedroom. You can explain your situation any way you want." She smiled. "Assuming, of course, whoever shows up speaks English and gives a shit. Have a nice day, Mr. Bigham."

Their eyes locked for almost ten agonizing seconds. She could tell it took everything within him to bridle his tongue, sensing his present danger had momentarily passed and that he'd get another day to fight. The gentle flutter in her stomach told her she'd see him again all too soon.

And then it would end.

•

Megan stopped at Dominic's apartment door and knocked twice.

He pulled the door open and smiled when he saw her. "Hi!"

"Is it all fixed?" she asked.

"Yeah," he nodded. "Come on, I'll show you."

They walked across the hall back to Megan's apartment. Carol and Linda were sitting on the sofa, cuddled protectively together, engrossed in the television. A tabloid talk show host was interviewing a man who hired prostitutes to sleep with his wife while he watched and took pictures for a scrapbook. The wife was secretly a lesbian and working as a topless dancer, unknown to the husband until the show. The hubby seemed upset about his wife's behavior and considered it deviant. The host held his microphone under the many chins of an obese woman from the audience who was shaking her finger and giving the man on stage a piece of her mind.

Carol noticed Megan and Dominic come in. She asked with deep apprehension, "Hey. Is everything okay?"

Megan's expression was cool. "Fine." She turned her attention back to Dominic who was still standing by the door. "Show me."

"That's it." He pointed to a small table lamp he had placed on top of

Megan's entertainment center. The shade was removed and a dark red bulb replaced the white one. "I've wired it into the security system in their apartment. Any door or window penetrated or motion detector set off, and you get continuous flashes."

"Great." She reached over and hugged him. "Thanks, Dominic. I owe you."

"My pleasure," he said softly.

"Look," she gestured to the door, "I need to talk to the girls in private. If you'll excuse us."

"Oh, no problem," he bowed slightly and made a hasty exit, thinking he'd save his chess move until tomorrow.

Linda huddled next to Carol, pressing the mute button on the television remote. "Meg, what happened?"

After the door was closed, Megan came over and sat next to them on the end of the couch, considering how much she really wanted them to know. "I got the message across. That's all you need to know."

The two girls exchanged a nervous look.

Carol asked the obvious, "Well, is it over? Is he going to leave us alone?"

Megan glanced back at the red light. "It's almost over. His kind don't listen well to things that are in his best interest. His particular subspecies has a basic need to be in control, and they get very agitated when they're not. But don't worry. He'll leave you alone very soon. I promise." Her gaze went back to the two pairs of frightened eyes, like startled deer caught in a pair of headlights. This wasn't easy. "Listen, when that red light begins to flash, if I'm not here, I want you to call me, no matter what time day or night. You have my pager number. Use it. The instant it goes off, I want to know. Understand?"

They both nodded.

Deep down Megan knew Pete was exactly right. Large carnivores had to be trapped in the wild. Troy Bigham would be no different. She knew ahead of time the evening's episode would only serve to provoke the animal and draw it out. But it had to be done. She hoped when the time came she had enough courage to take care of the next step.

CHAPTER 10

CONFLICTS OF INTEREST

Thursday
June 17, 2013

Ralph felt just as uncomfortable sitting in front of Commissioner Bragg's desk this time as he did the last time, and every occasion prior to that over the last ten days. Nor did he appreciate the grilling he received from Captain Trevino the instant he left Bragg's company. The press had gone completely ballistic after the second murder with up-to-the-minute wall-to-wall "crisis journalism." Thus, the Commissioner insisted on frequent progress updates directly from Ralph, who headed up the investigation team. It always made for a much longer day. Ralph continued to silently fidget while Commissioner Bragg lit his pipe and rummaged through a thick sheaf of computer generated notes and memos on his desk.

A framed eight-by-ten family portrait sitting behind Bragg on his credenza caught Ralph's attention. It depicted the commissioner and his rosy-cheeked carrot-topped wife, Daphne, standing on either side of their son. Ralph had met Daphne Bragg once at a formal department dinner about a year ago. She was the commissioner's second wife of about five years. The woman looked half Bragg's age, hardly much older than the young man in the picture. The son was in formal graduation cap and gown holding a ribbon-bound diploma. The gold Harvard University Ve-Ri-Tas emblem was emblazoned on the lower right corner of the picture. Ralph squelched a smile noting how much better looking the son was than the father. Bragg must be very proud, Ralph thought. His eyes strayed up the wall to the Commissioner's vast array of certificates, diplomas and sundry accolades. They told a distinguished story of the powerful man sitting behind the wide mahogany desk.

Commissioner Bragg was a Harvard Law School alumni himself; a Magna Cum Laude graduate of Vanderbilt; a City Councilman for six years; twice voted "Man of the Year" by the Dallas Law Enforcement Association; there was a Distinguished Service Award received many years back as Chief Council for General Dynamics in Fort Worth; and he even had a certificate of appreciation from the Dallas Country Club, one of the most distinguished "old money" (and BIG money) institutions of its kind in the state of Texas. The image of that much personal achievement, power and wealth was very impressive—and *very* intimidating.

"So what have you got for me today, Weatherstrom?" the Commissioner gruffly broke the silence, sucking a deep puff from his pipe. "And don't tell me jack-diddly. You're better than that."

Ralph's eyes attentively flew back to Commissioner Bragg, as he anxiously cleared his throat, "Well, sir, we definitely believe it's a random serial problem. And since we got no clear motives, we've had to rely pretty heavy on guidance from Dr. Jamison, our staff shrink. He's pretty good. I like him. The good news is that with Jamison's input and some good work by forensics, even in these first two murders, we've got some fairly identifiable patterns. He apparently likes what he's doing, and for the most part, likes doing it the same way."

Bragg leaned back in his leather-backed judge's chair, the leather squeaking beneath his weight. He nodded pensively, blowing a perfect ring up toward the florescent lights, "Such as?"

Ralph opened the folder on his lap, pulled his black framed reading spectacles out of his shirt pocket and put them on. The first sheet was an investigation summary. "It's all here in the file, sir. You should have a hard copy. ...uh ...here we go." He found the place on the page he wanted. "He apparently likes Friday nights. He likes upscale bars to pick up his victims, usually just before midnight. But he's smart and we suspect smart enough not to go to the same one twice." He lifted a page. "Eyewitnesses at the hotels and bars could only give us general descriptions, nothing useful, but we learned a lot about him. We've been able to determine he's six-one, a hundred an eighty-seven pounds, brown hair, left-handed, and even wears Aramis cologne."

Bragg leaned forward again, furrowing his hard crag of a brow, "Jamison helped you find all that?"

Ralph smiled, "No, sir. Forensics. Specifically, Officer Pembrooke, Megan Pembrooke." He gave a half-laugh. "Actually, it's kinda scary watching her work. She's new, but she's very good."

Bragg's thin lips came out thoughtfully, "Pembrooke, eh?" He picked up his pen from the desktop and made a note, then looked back to Ralph,

"So what does your team plan to do?"

Ralph closed the folder, "If the pattern holds true, he's likely to strike again tomorrow night. There are way too many bars to cover in the city, so we're putting surveillance teams at all of the major high-dollar hotels. Plus, I've asked Captain Trevino to expedite a special emergency ordinance for the next thirty days. Normally, all the hotels renting rooms for cash are required to at least register guests with a valid ID, but we both know for enough money that don't happen. *Even* at the best places in town. The new ordinance would hold the hotel criminally liable if another murder occurs on the premises and holds the on-duty desk clerk and management responsible as criminal accomplices."

"I like that," Bragg nodded with approval. "It ought to solicit a little cooperation. I'll see what I can do to help it along. I'll call the mayor's office myself. The city council is meeting this afternoon. I think I can make sure it's in effect before noon tomorrow."

That made Ralph feel good. "Thank you, sir. But to be honest, it's just a little incentive. All we're really looking for is a phone call. We know that even if the killer gets carded, he's likely to have false identification. So, as a verbal addendum to the order, we're making it *very* clear to local hotel management staff, that any Friday night couples checking into the hotel without a reservation for cash need to be reported immediately. We know some folks'll be pissed-off and inconvenienced, and perhaps a few extra-marital dalliances will get curtailed, but right now it's the best we have to work with."

"All right." Bragg set his pipe down. "I like it. But keep it quiet. Very, very quiet. If word of this gets out, you've potentially got two problems. One, our strangler hears and runs. Two, the civil libertarians hear and make all our lives a living hell. Either way we're all fucked."

Ralph chuckled, "I know what you mean. It was hard enough keeping a lot of the details out of the papers and off the tube. It seems like legions of reporters are on a feeding frenzy with hourly updates on most of the local channels. Hell, I've already turned down three interviews with CNN, Fox News, and MSNBC." He took a deep breath, lowering his voice. "And just in case you haven't heard, we've had to keep the connection to the nightclubs very hush-hush. The restaurant association insisted on it. They're threatening a court injunction if we don't. They say it's just a *coincidence* the killer made his pick-ups in their establishments. If the media splashes the potential of a homicidal stalker in the bars on Friday night, they're terrified what the effect on business would be. They think all the single women would stay home, along with the men, and all the profits."

"Quite understandable," Bragg noted with harsh sarcasm, "Even if it gets more women killed. Bastards. But it doesn't help us."

"Yeah," Ralph shrugged, "And all it leaves us with is the notion of going public with some naive, general-sounding warning for single women not to accept any invitations to go to nice hotels with strange men. It'd be a waste of breath. I imagine even our killer would probably find it pretty damn funny."

"Undoubtedly..." Bragg's eyes weren't on Ralph anymore, just staring pensively down at his desktop. A hollow moment of silence past, then Bragg looked up, taking in a deep breath. "Yes, well.... I *do* think your approach is sound, Ralph. Go to it. Work the hotels. Just keep playing it close to the vest and do what you can. Like I said, I'll do what I can and see you get all the support you need, manpower-wise, and with this ordinance thing. If Chief Moranzano gives you any shit, I want to know. *Immediately.* Understand?"

Before Ralph could answer, the phone rang on the Commissioner's desk. He glanced down at it. "...if there's nothing further, then thank you, Weatherstrom. That'll be all."

Ralph rose with a respectful nod and headed for the tall glass door as Bragg stabbed the hand's-free button on his desk set with a long, boney forefinger. Bragg's secretary's voice chimed in, "Commissioner, your son is on line two."

Bragg smiled, his fatherly pride visibly blossoming into a broad smile as he eagerly poked another button and lifted the receiver to his ear, "Richard! How's my boy? ... Great! How about lunch?"

Ralph grinned as he quietly closed the door and paced off down the hall. Bragg wasn't such a bad guy, he mused, despite what everyone else thought. Admittedly, he was a bit rough on the outside, but appeared to be a caring, concerned, decent sort deep down. Ralph could tell. Perhaps Megan Pembrooke had a gift when it came to observation and physical detail; but Ralph Weatherstrom knew people. He had to know people to survive for almost thirty years working the streets.

It didn't take long for him to get a solid impression of someone. He could size up most people with a mere handshake or a deep look into their eyes. It never failed. That's why he knew he could trust everything Megan Pembrooke told him—and everything she was about to tell him when he met her and Charlie later in the day for lunch.

•

He pointed the infra-red auto-security remote hanging from his keychain at the elegant black Porsche. It squawked twice, indicating the vehicle was secure. The gravel crunched softly under the gentle pad of polished Italian leather as he moved quickly toward the door. Garth Brooks' classic "I got Friends in Low Places" greeted him in concert with a cool rush of chilled air as the front door swung back. It took only a moment for his eyes to adjust to the darkness as he stepped out of the bright Texas sun into the small, dark, hole-in-the-wall bar in Irving, just off Northwest Highway, near the site of the old Texas Stadium. There were less than three bar-flies in the establishment at eleven-thirty in the morning.

Perfect.

Ferndale was waiting for him in the last booth, cloaked in the shadows, as agreed. The tall man took a seat opposite Ferndale in the booth, suppressing a wry smile.

Samuel Ferndale did his best to look so straight and respectable, dressing conservative, keeping his hair trimmed neat and clean; but all he had to do was open his mouth and everyone knew what a flaming queen he was. But despite being a voracious homosexual, the wiry little man possessed other qualities of great value: he was extremely gullible, a loner, and most importantly, very discreet. Discretion was absolutely essential to the completion of the project. Samuel hadn't been hard to find—*much* easier than Ferndale's current lover. That took months of research. All the record searches, profiling, computer look-ups, clandestine third-party interviews, narrowing the choices and candidates, even "augmenting" a few public computer databases and social networks. But it had all been worth it. Everything was proceeding precisely according to plan.

"Well, hi," Ferndale greeted him with a cheerful wave. "Thought maybe you weren't coming."

"Excuse me, Samuel. I'm rather in a rush today. Do you have it?" the tall man asked, his cultured voice rich and smooth. He carefully set his Louis Vuitton sunglasses on the table between them.

Ferndale nodded vigorously, "Of course, silly!" He reached next to him, opened a neon green gym bag, and pulled out a thermos, placing it in the center of the table between them.

The tall man pulled it toward him. "Very good. Then I gather your *dates* have been enjoyable as well as profitable?"

Ferndale almost blushed, "I should say. *Every* Friday night. He's absolutely marvelous! But you know, I think I'd be head-over-heels after this one, even if you weren't paying me. He tells me I'm his number one customer."

"Excellent. And no one has seen you together?" he asked, pulling out his gold and diamond studded money clip, peeling off ten one-hundred dollar bills and tossing them on the table.

Ferndale shook his head as he swept the bills up, "No, sir. I call him at the club where he works, just as you instructed, and then he slips over to my place for the entire night. He thinks I'm a real high-roller."

"And he doesn't ever ask you about the samples?" he probed.

Again another garish denial, accentuated with his palms bent over his wrists, fingers wide, like his nails were drying, "Oh, *no*. After we're *finished*, you know. I just tell him to give me the rubber and dispose of it with mine. It's *remarkably* easy. I go in the bathroom, dispose of mine and save his for you. They're all safely in the thermos and in the freezer less than an hour after he's gone in the morning. Just like you wanted."

"Excellent." The man picked up his sunglasses. "And do you already have your date scheduled with him for this Friday?"

"Of course," Ferndale shot him a coy smile. "Wouldn't miss it. I hope you need plenty more samples for your research, Doctor, because I absolutely adore my work." Samuel found his quip wickedly amusing.

The tall man just smiled as he rose, taking the thermos with him, again suppressing the urge to laugh, keeping his tone even and serious, "I think I'll be needing a great deal more, Samuel. As I told you before, this subject has the exact genetic profile I require for *my* work. But you have to remain completely discreet. Our secrecy is absolutely essential to the success of the project."

"Not a problem," Ferndale rolled his eyes. "He'll *never* know."

As the tall man started the engine of his black Porsche, he began to laugh. It suddenly occurred to him what he told Ferndale was half true. With the bullshit of the genetics experiment aside, Samuel Ferndale's lover's genetic profile was indeed the key to the ultimate success of the entire project.

•

All three Dallas police officers sat around a small table at a Chinese restaurant on LBJ Freeway, just off the Abrams Rd. exit, wolfing down a late lunch. It was almost two o'clock in the afternoon. Megan was quietly eating her lunch while Charlie continued to berate Ralph on the current state of affairs.

"It's bullshit, Ralph," Charlie stuffed another bite of pork fried rice in his mouth, a few grains toppling over his lip and trickling down his tie. "Pure bullshit."

"You got a better idea?" Ralph fired back.

"Yeah!" Charlie huffed, "I say we dig harder for more real material witnesses. *Someone* saw something. They *had* to. You know it. Come on, a car, a license plate. *Something*."

88

"You're not going to catch him with a license plate," Megan offered flatly. "He's too smart for that. It's a waste of time."

Charlie turned to her, wiping his curly brown hair back with the fingers of his left hand, his deep blue eyes angry, "Like *you* know how to catch a serial killer? Give me a fucking break. How many serial killers, or killers of any kind, have you apprehended in your day, Missy?"

Megan just ignored Charlie's curt patronization, focusing her comments on Ralph, "*Your* plan is on the right track, Ralph. You've definitely got to catch him in the act. There's no other way. It's the *only* way. He may be crazy, but he's not stupid. He won't leave us enough evidence to find him otherwise. You can be sure of that."

Charlie was incensed, his cheeks flushing. "How do you *know* that? I don't care *how* lucky this guy has been so far. Everyone makes mistakes. And believe me, this guy will too."

Megan looked Charlie dead in the eye, "That may be true...Detective. But whoever we're looking for is pretty ballsy. Like I said, he's obviously *not* stupid. He *knows* he can easily pick up willing victims in a public place with virtually complete anonymity. He also knows he can easily get a hotel room, a private place to commit his crimes, in a *public* building, also with complete anonymity. And he's also smart enough to know that what *little* physical evidence he leaves behind for us is *only* relevant if he's *caught*. Which means you *have* to catch him in the act, because he doesn't think *you're smart enough* to catch him!"

Charlie raised his hand like a fire and brimstone preacher and was about to fire off his next acid rebuttal when Ralph cut him off with a forearm across Charlie's chest, "*Which is why...* " He pulled his arm back, "Which is *why*, we've solicited the help of all the major hotels. Everybody simmer down. With a little luck we *will* catch him in the act."

"Assuming he decides to do things the same way again," Charlie said.

"Right," Megan agreed, "assuming he's a creature of habit."

"So, Miss know-it-all, what if he decides to do something a little bit different this time?" Charlie's terse condescension hung in the air like the stench of burnt beans.

"Then we deal with it when it happens, and learn what we can from it," Megan replied matter-of-factly, holding her temper in check. It wasn't easy; but she surprised herself with cold resolve. A familiar pang twisted across her mid-section. She hadn't been called a know-it-all since she was in junior high school. She hated that epithet with a passion. It sounded so derogatory, yet always came from the mouth of a know-nothing.

"S'right," Ralph affirmed with a stiff nod. "We just deal with it. So come on, guys, let's stop this bickering. This isn't helping."

"No, Ralphy. It's *bull*-shit," Charlie shook his head back and forth. "You're putting too damn much stock in Miss Shirley-lock Holmes' theories here, when we *should* be busy digging up more on what's *happened*, not betting on what *might* happen."

Icy glares fired back and forth between Megan and Charlie.

After an awkward pregnant pause, Ralph put his fork down, weary of the needless confrontation between colleagues. He knew he needed to get Charlie alone and let him cool off. He was just frustrated. Hell, they were all frustrated. Pissing and moaning certainly wasn't getting them anywhere. To make matters worse, Charlie wasn't the least bit fond of women on the force, let alone competent women who appeared to be making more progress on a case than himself.

Ralph wiped his mouth with a paper napkin, "Come on, Charlie. Time to go. Maybe you're right. Let's go do some more digging."

Megan caught Ralph's wink to her. It made her feel better. She said nothing further as the two older officers rose from the table and departed. Charlie didn't even look at her as he went. The tension in the air noticeably cleared the instant they were gone. Another ten minutes went by as Megan just sat at the table amid the undulating din of lunchtime conversation around her, sipping her iced tea, lost in quiet thought.

Yes, Ralph was doing the right thing to stake out the big hotels around town, but in her heart she felt it would do little to trap the killer—unless they got incredibly lucky. She wasn't going to hold her breath. Even Ralph's emergency ordinance idea would probably do little more than precipitate litigation with hotels after they found more bodies. Would some minimum wage desk clerk *really* make that call with five one-hundred dollar bills in his hand? And if so, would it even be in time? And what if Charlie was right and he decided to change tactics and just go somewhere else?

The odds were decidedly against whatever poor unsuspecting girl was unfortunate enough to say yes to the wrong handsome stranger tomorrow night. Meg's eyes widened with a burst of inspiration.

That was it!

They just needed a *suspecting* girl—someone prepared for him. But how? Where? There were so many popular high-dollar nightclubs from Addison through North Dallas to lower Greenville to the West End. He could be at any of them. Which one? Would he stick to working his way through the lower Greenville Avenue area? Was he indeed a territorial beast, like a great white shark or a pack of wolves, which fed in one place as long as the food supply was plenteous?

A strange thought prompted Megan to reach down next to her chair and pulled a MAPSCO out of her canvass book bag, flipping open to the grid-scaled page of the lower Greenville Avenue area. The page she looked at from the minutely detailed book of maps of the Dallas Metroplex streets covered an area just south of Highland Park to Woodall-Rodgers Freeway.

Megan knew first-hand the area was thick with world-class restaurants, nightclubs, hotels, and popular local attractions. She lifted a red felt-tip pen out of her bag and marked the approximate location of the Caribbean Club with the number one and drew a small circle around it. She put a number two at the intersection where the Rue de Royale hotel stood a few blocks away. She annotated the Zanzibar Club with the numeral three. The Regency Park Plaza Hotel became site number four. All four locations were within six blocks of one another, almost equidistantly spaced. The image she had just created before her eyes riveted her attention and made the small hairs on the back of her neck stand tall. The numbers formed a small crescent—in order.

Coincidence?

No. It was a pattern—an obvious pattern. A little too obvious for her liking, which meant it was meant to be seen.

Why?

She looked just beyond the end of site number four, following the gradual arc of the crescent approximately equidistant from the other sites to a popular intersection she knew had three hot night spots. One was called Jinx, another club was nearby was called Sensations, and another one about a block away was called the Purple something, she couldn't quite remember the exact name. Purple Panda? No. Purple Pogo? No. That wasn't it, but something like that.

But which one?

Was he indeed working a circuit, moving down the street each Friday night in search of his next prize? Her face suddenly felt hot and it was becoming a lot more difficult to breathe. Her pulse accelerated. Who was she kidding? What was she thinking? The harsh voice of Charlie McManus echoed in her ears:

Like YOU know how to catch a serial killer? Give me a fucking break. How many serial killers, or killer of any kind, have YOU apprehended in your day, Missy?

Nevertheless, she couldn't take her eyes off the page. Her heart was still pounding. It didn't matter what Charlie McManus thought. It didn't matter what he would say. Only one question remained: Would "he" be at one of those three clubs tomorrow night?

One thing was certain: Megan Pembrooke would be.

CHAPTER 11

SENSATIONS

Friday
June 18, 2013

"*Oh*, watch out!" Linda exclaimed in alarm.

Megan instantly snapped out of her pensive trance and slammed on her brakes, screeching to an abrupt stop. Her little blue Honda narrowly stopped short of rear-ending a sleek black Porsche rag-top stopped at the traffic light in front of them. They were on Greenville Avenue, only a block from the Sensations nightclub. That's where they were headed. Megan figured they had a 33.33% chance of guessing right. She was still hashing over the decision in the back of her mind, lost in thought, when Linda cried out. She still had the option of heading over to Jinx or the Purple Pagoda. Carol and Linda had volunteered to split up and cover the other two clubs, but Megan patently forbid it. Troy Bigham was still out there somewhere. The girls were gracious enough to come along for moral support. Megan had no intention of putting them in any more danger— not from Troy, *or* the other carnivore she was hunting.

"I'm sorry," Megan apologized, her heart pounding in her temples. She waved an apology to the driver in front of her. He looked in his rear-view mirror and raised a single hand of acknowledgment.

"It's okay," Carol assured her. "Just take it easy. Nobody's hurt." While they all took a few deep breaths Carol frowned, "This is really kinda nuts, you know. How come you have to do this all by yourself?"

"I told you," Megan insisted as she carefully pulled her little blue Accord up in front of the nightclub entrance, "I couldn't tell any of the detectives about this just yet. They'd just laugh at me. Besides, if I'm wrong they'll never believe another word I say." She was dressed in her green cocktail dress once again. Her make-up had been nicely improved with Carol and Linda's help. Her long waist-length brown hair was elegantly twisted together in an elaborate French braid down the center of her back.

Linda sat in the front seat and Carol rode in the back, both dressed to kill in wickedly attractive party dresses and spiked heels. Linda's dress was whisper-thin gold lamé, low-cut and tantalizing. Carol's dress was strapless white Spandex which clung to her like Saran Wrap. As the small car came to a stop at the valet parking station, two uniformed attendants opened the doors. Megan stepped out into the steamy night air and accepted the square yellow ticket. The festive clamor of celebration was only a few feet away.

The hunt was on.

As the three young women huddled together at the door, Linda asked, "Meg, you know we'd do anything for you, but this is kind of scary. I think I'm having second thoughts."

Megan tried to sound assuring, fishing in her wallet for enough cash to pay the ten dollar cover charge for all three of them. "Look, there's nothing to worry about. We're just looking. *Looking.* That's all. *Nothing* can happen here in public. If you see *anyone* you think might be suspicious, we call in the cavalry. That's all. Trust me." She paused, searching their eyes. "Hey, I need you guys on this one. I really do. Please stay. Okay?"

Carol nudged Linda, "It's okay, Lin. She's right. Nothing's going to happen in here. Besides, we haven't been dancing in a long time. It'll be fun."

Linda shrugged, "All right. But just in case, I have my pistol in my purse. It's loaded."

Megan's eyes went wide, "Oh, shit, Linda. You don't have a CHL. That's illegal."

"So arrest me, Officer," Linda smiled.

Megan's .40 caliber Beretta PX4 Storm and an extra magazine was in her purse as well, but she was authorized to carry it, even when off-duty. She just rolled her eyes, "You guys are impossible. You know that?"

Linda shook her head, "No, just cautious."

Inside Sensations, the three women leaned against one of four bars, nervously chatting amongst themselves for almost an hour until they saw a table open up and pounced on it. From there they established a command and control center for Megan's impromptu surveillance operation.

Carol shimmied her shoulders with a nervous, almost giddy giggle, "This *is* kind of exciting. You know?"

"Make it fun," Megan suggested, then dryly added, "And just try to forget we're after a psychopath strangler who has already killed two innocent young girls, and in all likelihood will be here tonight looking for number three."

Both Meg's companions' eyes enlarged by a factor of two.

"I'm just teasing," Megan huffed.

Carol and Linda both looked at each other and said in unison, "No she isn't.

They all laughed together.

Carol pointed at Megan's purse on the table. "Let me smell the card again."

Megan opened her black leather purse she packed for the evening, careful not to let her pistol be seen, and pulled out the square cardboard perfume tester she picked up at Dillard's, saturated with Aramis cologne. She handed it to Carol.

Carol held it to her nose, sniffing lightly, "Okay. This is what we're looking for.. er... *smelling* for. Got it."

Linda took it from her and took a fresh sniff, nodding with recollection. "Yeah, couldn't miss that one."

Offers to dance with all three young ladies came in at almost a regular five minute interval. Megan politely turned down her would-be suitors, still not very confident about her dancing ability. On the other hand, Carol and Linda occasionally gave a hopeful smiling face a yes, then promptly shuffled out on the packed dance floor to gyrate around for a song or two, returning happily covered in sweat and in search of a fresh, cold beverage. Megan noted that her two friends seemed quite talented dancers and attracted a lot of attention, from both men and women. There was no rational reason why that fact bothered her slightly. She wasn't jealous. Well...not really. It had to be something else.

Megan looked at her watch. It was just after eleven. It didn't seem like they had been there that long. A disturbing question flashed across her mind: Was he already here?

It was time to find out.

She leaned toward Carol and Linda, "I'm going to stroll around and have a look at the shadows. Watch my purse. Be right back."

Carol and Linda lifted a cheerful toast to her as she got up with wine her glass in hand and started a slow patrol of the entire club, looking for well-dressed men approximately six-one, a hundred and eighty-seven pounds. If she spotted any man even vaguely resembling that description, she would squeeze up near them and nonchalantly sniff. One or two guys noticed her and tried to strike up conversation, but she'd profess to be on her way to the ladies room and move on into the throng. She was actually a little disappointed when she made it back to the table without seeing anyone even remotely close. It blatantly showed in her downcast expression and her heavy plop back into her seat.

"Well?" Carol asked. "Nothing?"

"Not even a nibble," Megan replied. "He's not here yet, or maybe not coming."

"Do you want to go over to one of the other two clubs?" Linda offered enthusiastically.

Megan thought about it. It was still early. Something in her gut told her that this guy didn't come to stay long. He didn't have to. He'd be in and out very quickly to minimize recognition. She shook her head, "No, we'll give it a little longer."

Her last thought suddenly propelled her eyes back toward the entrance. *Yes.* That was it. He wasn't there yet. If he was coming, he'd show up just in time for the pick-up and then leave.

Carol saw the alarm in Megan's eyes, "Did you see something?"

Megan half-turned her face, but kept her eyes on the door, "No. Not yet. I'm just watching the door. I don't think he's here yet."

Carol and Linda looked at each other again in confusion, both of them more than a little bit tipsy from the numerous rounds of frozen Margaritas, served in glasses bigger than a baby's head. Halfway through the next round both of their mouths dropped open when the DJ announced a golden-oldie interlude. The thundering music abruptly transitioned from a hip-hop number to the crisp acoustic guitar introduction of Bad Company's "Feel Like Makin' Love."

Carol and Linda exclaimed together, "Our song!"

Megan was oblivious to her two friends leaving the table together hand-in-hand, careful to keep her eyes vigilant on the entrance of the club. She meticulously scanned the face and general build of every patron coming in. A few moments later she heard a few whistles and cat calls which distracted her enough to suddenly realize she was sitting alone. Her eyes looked about for Carol and Linda. Turning completely around, she was chagrined to find them on the dance floor—dancing together.

Dancing?

Megan's jaw dropped slightly in awe. On the heavy backbeats in the refrain of the song Carol and Linda's bodies were locked together at the hip, writhing forward and back, snapping sharply in unison like a buggy whip, giving the phrase "dirty dancing" an whole new connotation. Other dancers on the floor gave them room and applauded. When the song dropped back into the ballad-styled verse, both girls' bodies moved in an effortless, fluid rhythm, like a well-rehearsed ballet performance, or a pair of champion ice dancers.

It was amazing.

Linda would spread her arms wide and lean back into a gentle back-dive, supported by Carol's arms; then arch her back forward returning erect. As she did so, Carol's lower lip would trace a fine line from Linda's waist through her cleavage to her chin, eliciting more raucous applause from the crowd. Carol and Linda never noticed the adulation, lost in the enchantment of "their song" and the inebriated euphoria of the moment.

On the next high-energy chorus, Carol stood behind Linda with her hands on Linda's narrow waist. Linda's hands reached back and clung to Carol's hips. Linda's head slowly tilted back, resting on Carol's right shoulder. Cheek to cheek, their hips pressed together, rocking seductively back and forth, left and right, in perfect time with the music, their bodies sinking lower and lower with every wide sway, bending slowly at the knees, all the way to the floor.

When they reached the lowest point, on the instrumental verse, they rose in unison, Carol's hands coursing up Linda's torso, lifting and massaging her sumptuous breasts. Simultaneously, Linda's hands slid from Carol's knees along her inner thighs, gathering the stretched hem of Carol's Spandex dress up between her legs as her own body flowed into a parade-rest stance. Her hands then rotated out in wide arcs over Carol's rock-hard hips and buttocks, pulling Carol's thin white dress completely up to her waist, revealing her thong-cut white lace panties from Victoria's Secret. More riotous applause and cheers echoed above the music.

Megan couldn't believe it. It was like nothing she'd ever seen. A nervous tug yanked across her mid-section and a cold chill rippled up her spine. She was both confused and fascinated like everyone else in the club—and couldn't look away.

It was repulsive. It was beautiful. It was outrageous. It was incredible. It ought to be stopped.

What did it feel like?

When the music stopped, the two girls received a riotous standing ovation for their unwitting performance. It was only then that Carol and Linda realized how much attention they had attracted. They made a hasty retreat back to the shadows of their table. Megan was still sitting there, mutely staring at them in a mild state of shock.

Carol blushed slightly as she took her seat, "Sorry. We...uh...got a little carried away."

"I should say," Megan scolded politely.

Linda just sat there looking like the cat who ate the canary—the one who enjoyed the crunch of the tiny bones.

All three of them burst into laughter again, breaking the tension of the moment. However, Megan still felt uncomfortable and would never admit to anyone, not really even to herself, how what she just saw made her feel. It was quite unsettling to put it mildly.

Suddenly feeling the need to make a trip to the ladies room, Megan politely excused herself, and pressed her way through the festive throng once again. When she returned to the table, Megan was a little annoyed to see two strange men sitting there at her table, obviously flirting and joking with Carol and Linda. She had to ask to have her seat back. It was reluctantly surrendered. It took almost twenty minutes for the two guys to come to the conclusion that the girls weren't interested in them and make their exit. Megan was further annoyed when she looked at her watch and saw that it was just after midnight.

Linda grabbed Carol's arm, "You were right. This *is* a lot of fun. I'd almost forgotten what it like to just get out, get crazy, and let our hair down. This is great! Thanks, Meg."

"No, thank you, for coming along with me," Megan muttered.

Carol grinned and nodded in agreement, then looked at Megan to see if she was also having a good time. She could tell by the look on Megan's face something was wrong. Her smile faded, "What is it?"

Megan let out a long sigh, sobering all three faces at the table. "It's too late. Sorry. I guessed wrong. This wasn't the place."

Linda felt bad for Megan. "It's too late?"

Yes.

For someone, Megan thought. Somewhere else.

CHAPTER 12

KNIGHT TAKES PAWN: MANDY HOLDEN-WORTH

Friday
June 21, 2013

"You have quite a beautiful place," the tall man complimented, loosening his blood-red silk tie and unbuttoning his perfectly starched collar. He slipped out of his navy blue double-breasted jacket and laid it gently on the padded arm of Mandy Holden-Worth's overstuffed sofa.

He told her the truth. The spacious twelfth-story unit at the Centennial Towers, a Highland Park high-rise condo, was absolutely gorgeous. It was almost as nice as the one he sold in Boston a few years ago. Ms. Holden-Worth's charming abode had tall ceilings and was decorated in stunning contemporary furniture and abstract art pieces.

A fountain graced the entryway, burbling and trickling down into a recessed basin in the Italian marble tiled floor. The outside wall was comprised entirely of three wide panes of glass, floor to ceiling. Thus, the view from the terrace overlooking the skyline of downtown Dallas was gorgeous. The tall green-trimmed "Jolly Green Giant" building stood out from the rest of the tall glass monoliths. The glowing lollypop ball of Reunion Tower stood just beyond it. White and red car lights drew long ribbons of motion down the twisting multi-lane expressways below. He looked at his watch.

It was exactly midnight.

Mandy mirrored his inviting smile, "I was just so glad to get away from all that smoke and breathe. The Purple Pagoda's a lot of fun. I hadn't been there in quite a while. Have you been there before?"

"No." Again, the truth.

There hadn't been a need to go there prior to that evening. He didn't even like to drive in the area, especially on a Friday night. It was too crowded and busy. In fact, someone almost rear-ended him that very evening. That would have been most unfortunate. But all his purposes had been served, and the primary objective achieved.

The attractive red-head before him—Mandy Holden-Worth she announced more than once, as if he was supposed to impressed by the name—had been a third choice; but an acceptable choice, once he learned exactly where she lived. Location was very important. She was a little older than the other two, perhaps in her mid- to late-forties, and from the posh trappings, obviously had quite a bit of money. Undoubtedly, the police would vainly attempt to read something into that, then frustrate themselves trying to comprehend the significance; and in the end conclude it to be a further permutation of his madness. But in reality, the deviation was of no real consequence. Other factors were much more critical.

The irony made him chuckle quietly to himself.

No. There would be no hotel suite tonight; although convenience was still most important, and geography an equally vital element of the game as well. Sadly, the pack of hounds were appallingly slow to catch the scent; and naturally, that only made the game, oh, so dreary. Sooner or later they'd have to at least provide a bit more challenge to the affair—just before he confounded them anew. There was one hunter up to the challenge. He knew she would be. But even she hadn't risen fully to the occasion as of yet. Pity. He chuckled again as a ripple of energy tingled up his spine. It was all too easy, and delightful fun.

Mandy Holden-Worth reached behind her, slowly and seductively unzipping her short blue satin dress, doing her best to appear alluring, letting it slowly slip from her shoulders and fall to the floor in a shimmering pool around her feet. Her eyes stayed fixed on his, breathlessly awaiting his reaction. She wore neither bra nor panties, only a black lace garter accented with two tiny red satin bows encircling her waist and tethered to a pair of full-length black fishnet hose sheathing her long legs. Her svelte figure was exquisite and she knew it: her breasts firm and supple, her waist trim, her hips rounded with not a trace of cellulite, her skin creamy smooth and tanned. She worked very hard on her appearance in addition to paying a small fortune for the surgical refinements which improved the parts she couldn't help with her religious regimen of diet and exercise.

Mandy couldn't believe her good fortune that evening to meet such a charming and devastatingly good-looking catch to satisfy some of her more libidinal appetites. This one was an exceptional find. She didn't go out prowling for romantic entertainment very often, but when the mood hit her, it became a craving she could not suppress. Not that she ever tried to bridle her succulent urges. Oh no, not Mandy Holden-Worth. She loved to explore them, deeply and exotically. Tonight would be no different, and portended to be an exceptional undertaking.

Like her handsome companion. Mandy had her own unique criteria for erotic adventure. First and foremost, it could never be with someone she knew. Oh, no, no, no. That wouldn't do. It had to be with a complete and total stranger—no expectations, no preconceptions, no questions, no strings, no inhibitions, and no remorse. From that vantage she could play every role her vivid and lurid imagination could conjure: from sinner to saint, whore to maiden.

Pure adventure.

She slowly ran her tongue lightly around her plump collagen-injected lips giving them a fresh sheen as she stepped forward, her sultry voice reduced to a smoldering whisper, "So, handsome, where's my *adventure* you promised?"

He couldn't help but laugh out loud now, a deep percolating laugh, shining out through his piercing blue eyes. He slipped his blood-red necktie over his head and dangled it from is forefinger with forbidden invitation in his voice, "Right here, my dear. Right here."

•

In his own expert opinion, this Mandy Holden-Worth was as gifted a sexual athlete as he had ever encountered in his life, phenomenally so. It was a genuine challenge to keep up with her, not to mention the hope of ushering her to into any convenient state of vulnerable fatigue in a short period of time. She was wantonly aggressive and unquenchably hungry for endless passion. He sincerely appreciated that quality in her, and thoroughly enjoyed it. Funnily enough, it seemed to make it all that much more sporting in the end.

To his amusement, she was also one of those delightful women who preferred to meticulously and exotically choreograph each erotic event, making frequent and minute adjustments to heighten her own sensual pleasure. That was wonderfully acceptable, and quite entertaining to observe, not to mention pleasurable to accommodate.

She was good at it.

With both of their bodies bathed in rich, glistening perspiration, lungs heaving like marathon runners, eyes glazed, still joined as one, she sat across his lap. She was most impressed he had been able to persevere so long, his masculine prowess not diminishing a trace in quality nor quantity from the first minute. The dark haunting look in his eyes only kindled the fiery hunger within her, and set her hips ablaze in fresh motion. What forbidden delicacy would be next? He answered the question by handing her his blood-red neck tie.

It was time.

She quivered with excitement, already anticipating an experience she had only heard about. It went over her head and cinched tight in the next instant.

"Oh, yes, do it," she begged, instructing him as though he were the novice. "But not yet. Right before I come. Make it real tight. Count to five and when you let it go, I want to explode."

He was laughing again.

It wasn't his initial intention, desiring to be more expedient than in his last outing; but for a reason unknown even to himself, perhaps out of mere curiosity, he *did* release the tension on the tie when she crested the wave of her next climax. He really wanted to see what she would do. As promised, red-faced and trembling, she indeed exploded like a geyser in a fit of thrashing, spastic movement, her voice reverberating in wall-shaking moans and groans, drowning in cataclysmic gyrations. Surprisingly, to his amazement and delight, in the aftermath of the sensual storm, at long last, she finally fell into his arms, winded and immobile.

NOW, it's time.

It was at that point he realized how physically sore he had grown himself. His arms, legs, and lower back mightily ached as though he'd just chopped two chords of fresh felled oak. His loins were actually getting raw. But none of that mattered any longer. Curiosity had been satisfied. Amusement had passed. The novelty of her sexual acrobatics had waned. It was indeed time for an altogether "new" thrill. Even the tie wouldn't be sufficient.

Still lying on his back, he pushed her up into a sitting position, coaxing her hips back into motion, "One more time."

She pulled at the knot of the tie, "No, lover. Not that again. I don't think I could survive it. Let's try something else. Something quiet and easy for a while. Give me a chance to get a second wind."

His smile was back, but no longer warm, instead icy cold and hard. He grabbed her hands. "I *said*, one more time."

She slapped his hands, her eyes stern, dominant, and hotly defiant, "And *I said*—no. Eat me if you want to. *I'm* going to lay down. My legs hurt. If you've got so much damn energy *you* do all the work."

He never broke their gaze. "As you wish."

The movement was massive and sudden. He rolled her onto her back pinning her body beneath him, careful to stay firmly inside her. The rush of what he was about to do threatened to imminently send him into his own pulsating climax. He forced himself to focus and relax.

Not yet.

Mandy was giggling, "Oooh, there we go. I like that." She barely heard the small metallic "click."

Her eyes flew open in bulging alarm when the burning sear swept across her throat, instinctively aware something was horribly, horribly wrong. It happened so quickly, her mind barely registered it. Her eyes watered, distorting the images floating above her face. Hovering above her, he was still smiling down as though nothing were wrong.

Was anything wrong?

She could still feel him inside her. But the tingling sensation of pleasure was instantly gone. The gentle hush of the breath from his nostrils produced a tell-tale chill on her upper chest which announced she was wet, like she'd just stepped from a shower into a draft. She absently lifted the fingers of her right hand up to collar bone touching something warm, wet and sticky.

No, please, no.

She looked to her trembling fingers. Her breathing stilled and her head grew faint at the sight of bright crimson shining from her fingertips. A reflected glimmer of light flashed across her eyes. She felt him grab her hand and thrust it back down to the bed.

Oh, God. I'm hurt.

In that horrid instant, her confused mind couldn't comprehend why he couldn't see that she was hurt and come to her rescue.

What was wrong with him? Doesn't he care?

She tried to scream, her jaw fell agape; but no sound came forth, save a nauseous wet gurgle from beneath her chin. Her head turned to her left, a distorted image: a few inches from her ear, his right hand holding her left wrist secure. Her head painfully wrenched to her right: his left hand pushed down hard on her right wrist. Between his left hand and her wrist was a large lock-back knife. The edge of the wide gleaming blade was soiled with the same bright red crimson as was on her fingers.

Please help me....

The instinct to fight or flee had already been vanquished behind the trembling gray veil of clinical shock and utter disbelief. Hot tears distorted and obscured her vision. She could now feel the warm wetness behind her neck and beneath her shoulders.

This couldn't be happening.

It was all a fantasy, a dream, quickly fading into the shrill silence of a nightmare. Oddly, in the whirlpool of images flashing and flying through her mind, the memory of her own room in her parent's house when she was about seven magically appeared. There she was, standing in the doorway, peering inside with a tiny hand on the doorframe. She could see all the old furniture, her bed, the three drawer dresser, her toy box covered with stuffed animals, the Barbie Dream House, the tin play kitchen—

Please let me go home... just, let me.... I just want to go... home...

A gray mist floated across her eyes, slowly fading to black.

And all was quiet.

•

Oh, yes. So sweet. So sweet.

He timed his own pleasure much better this time, feeling the last mute throb subside just as the last dark red bubble oozed out of the wide ear-to-ear gash across the thing's throat. Its eyes were still open, the pupils fixed and dilated, staring eternally into space in utter disbelief. Just to satisfy his own morbid pleasure, he leaned down and kissed it once more on its slightly parted lips.

After taking a brief moment to wash up, careful to only use tissues that could be flushed away, he returned to its side and sat next to it on the edge of the bed. His calm, icy gaze found the edge of the soiled knife blade still lying next to its head in a thick pool of blood, rapidly soaking into the sheets and pillows. He lifted the blade before his face and stared at it for several moments—fascinated. A thin smile crept across his lips. With one deft stroke, he cleaned the gleaming carbide steel with his tongue. The iron bitterness sent a chill of power through him. His thighs trembled.

He glared down at the thing, what used to be something called Mandy Holden-Worth. "Ah... delicious, my love. Absolutely delicious."

He reached over and closed the eyes looking at him.

A black laugh bubbled up deep inside him, haunting, teasing. "And as you wish, m'lady... I may indeed eat you yet." His eyes returned to the gleaming edge of the knife blade. "A little at a time."

It was almost a full hour later before he had readied his latest handiwork for display to his complete satisfaction. In another half an hour he had cleaned the premises to the necessary degree, showered and dressed. With all the mirrors in Mandy Holden-Worth's bathroom, it was amazing that he never noticed the long rows of nail marks across his back from his spine to his shoulders.

PART II

SOMETIMES IT'S BETTER TO BE LUCKY THAN GOOD.

In baiting a mouse-trap with cheese, always leave room for the mouse.

Saki
"The Infernal Parliament"
The Square Egg, 1924

Plans get you into things but you got to work your way out.

Will Rogers
The Autobiography of Will Rogers, 1949

CHAPTER 13

THE CENTENNIAL TOWERS CONDOMINIUMS

Saturday
June 22, 2013

"Three roses," Ralph muttered, still in a mild state of shock, surveying the blood-soaked sheets on Mandy Holden-Worth's low, frameless Oriental-styled king-sized bed. There was so much red, everywhere, like a sloppy painter's drop cloth. A dank, spoiled, metallic stench pinched the air. He and Charlie McManus just stood there at the foot of the bed, watching the forensic team do their work.

Megan Pembrooke and her team had been there for over an hour, meticulously examining, measuring, sampling, testing, photographing and documenting. When she stood up from the bedside and faced the detectives, Ralph could see the rims of her eyes were red and moist. He imagined his were too. It was hard not to be moved by what lay on the bed. It was terrible. Megan just stared at them both for several moments without speaking, her eyes going back and forth from man to man, her jaw moving side to side. The words weren't ready to come. All the professionalism in the world couldn't veil the pain inflicted by the monstrous evil they hunted. It showed on all of their somber faces.

Even Charlie was very subdued, "Anything significant, Meg?"

Megan sniffed once and pulled off her latex gloves with an elastic snap, walking past Ralph and Charlie over to a small black lacquer Oriental writing desk in the bedroom to go over her notes, thankfully some distance away from the grisly visage lying on the bed.

It took her a few more moments to collect her thoughts and find the right words to even begin. Words seemed so impotent at that moment to convey what she had seen or how she felt. Her mouth spoke on auto-pilot of its own accord while her mind listened in the background, detached and in pain, "I'd say she's been here since late Friday night. Like the other two." She let out a long, slow breath. "And...like I feared, as you can see, his attack scenario is now accelerating exponentially."

"Obviously, Dr. Freud." Charlie shook his head in wonder.

Megan could feel her chin trembling. She held her composure, her eyes seeking out McManus', chastising and cold, "I don't think you get it, Detective. Look at her. It's a lot worse than it looks." She gestured back toward the bed, inviting the Detectives to look, "*All* of the bite marks on her arms and legs and torso were post-mortem. He opened up her throat, watched her bleed to death, and then chewed her to pieces."

"Oh, Jesus," Charlie turned away, his face going red. His gaze was reluctantly drawn back to the bed. He took a staggered breath, the nausea welling up hot in the back of his throat. Arguing with Officer Pembrooke only made the pounding in his head intensify. Even after being there for over an hour, he had yet to get used to the iron stench of slaughter hanging thick in the air—or the sight of what lay only a few feet away.

He looked again.

There on the crimson stained sheets lay what was left of Mandy Holden-Worth. Like the other two girls, she lay prone in the center of her bed, her head resting on her pillow, her upper arms lying parallel to her body, her forearms folded across her belly. Like her other two deceased sorority sisters, her lifeless hands held three long-stemmed roses between what was left of the shredded flesh that used to be her breasts. Dried blood covered most of her body in streaks and splatters, discolored and mottled by a jagged minefield of pink and purple gashes approximately four to six inches apart covering her entire body. The silver-dollar-sized lesions were more dense and grotesque around her breasts and thighs. Two large blood stains radiated out in the sheets in the area of her neck and her lower torso. He heard Megan continue speaking but very little of it registered.

Megan glanced down at her notes again. "Just like the first two, there is a similar ligature mark on the neck. However, due to the deep laceration I was able to look inside and saw that there was no apparent trauma to the back of the trachea. So, at this point I'd say, unlike the others, she didn't die from strangulation. I think she died directly from the throat wound. Blood loss. Pretty basic. She probably went pretty quick."

"I hope she did," Ralph whispered softly.

Megan nodded in agreement. "Me too." She took a deep, exaggerated breath. "And in case you want to know, in addition to the throat wound and a total of fifty-four bites, the two external pairs of..." She took another breath, lowering her voice, and quickly looking around the room, "...labia tissues of her genitals were... uh... not found."

Charlie spun around, aghast, "He cut off her lips?"

At that comment, all the other technicians in the room stopped whatever they were doing and looked at Megan, eyes wide and inquisitive, listening intently. A painful silence filled the room.

Megan closed her notebook, her face noticeably pale and grave. She gave everyone staring her way a cold accusing look which shamed them back to their tasks. She leaned toward the two detectives, whispering as discreetly as she could, "No. He didn't *cut* them off."

"Oh, shit," Ralph took out his handkerchief and covered his mouth. "What a sick fuck. I think *I'm* gonna puke."

Charlie put a hand on his shoulder, suddenly very concerned. "Ralphy, are you going to be all right?"

Ralph nodded, taking a few deep breaths of his own. "Yeah, I'm all right. But I gotta get out of here. Is that it, Meg?"

She nodded, "Pretty much. Lots more semen samples, plus I've got some good fibers and skin samples this time from under the victim's nails. The fiber appears to be wool from a suit, and a very high grade. I'll have it checked at the lab. Depending on how rare it is, it could be a break. The skin samples go in the DNA file, along with some trace blood samples. Plus now we even have some very general dental patterns based on the bite marks that could potentially be matched." She tried to lighten her tone, "Hell, we may even know his blood type this time."

Charlie sounded as exasperated as Ralph felt, "That's just fucking wonderful. We know everything but his damned address and social security number, and we still don't have a fucking clue about how to find him."

The awkward silence returned for a moment.

Ralph shrugged, trying to ease the tension, "You know, I really thought perhaps we were going to get lucky and maybe he would decide to take a weekend off."

"No such luck," Megan absently offered. "For the time being, his Friday fetish has consigned us to this ghoulish Saturday ritual. I don't see him taking a break any time soon. You know he's feeding on all of this." She dropped her eyes, "Sorry, bad choice of words."

Neither detective smiled, but the suffocating tension between them finally eased a bit.

"Well, if nothing else, he's sure got a lot of balls," Charlie stuffed his hands in his pocket, "S'all I can say. You know the bastard called this one in himself."

"What?" Megan jumped on his words. "*He* reported the murder?"

Charlie puckered his lips, "Don't get your panties wet, sweet thing. He didn't call in a convenient, digitally-recorded 911 sense. But *someone* was nice enough to call this morning to the building management and report an dangerous insect swarm problem and request an exterminator. One showed up around noon and found all of this."

"And you're sure it was him?" Megan asked.

Charlie flowed with fresh sarcasm, "Well, I don't think the lady on the bed was in any condition to make the call any time yesterday. Wouldn't you agree, Officer Pembrooke?"

Megan broke his gaze. She wasn't thinking. That was pretty basic. Why *wasn't* she thinking? The hurried pace of her heart warned her that her emotions were boiling a little too high. It was time to put them on the back burner and stoke the heat under the logic and deductive reasoning that served her so well.

Her eyes found Charlie's again. "You're right. Which means he *did* want her found today."

"It would seem," Charlie agreed. "But he couldn't count on a maid or a maintenance worker to find her over the weekend. So he had to initiate his own catalyst incident for the thrill of seeing his handiwork in the Sunday papers again."

"You really think it's just a thrill thing?" Ralph asked Charlie.

"It's what it looks like to me," Charlie retorted. "Looks like each time he kills the thrill has to be more intense to get his rocks off. I imagine in a lot of ways he's like any other crack head or a porn hound. He's addicted and needs more and more to sustain his habit."

A strange new thought occurred to Megan. "But what if it isn't that at all? What if that's just what he wants us to think?"

"What do you mean?" Ralph prompted.

Megan stood up and walked back to look at the carnage lying on the bed. "I mean, I'm getting the feeling that there's more to it than that. Look at the facts. He varied his pattern slightly, but deliberately. There had to be a reason for that. Look where we are. Somehow he knew not to go to a public hotel this week. How did he know? Why change the pattern *this* week? *Maybe* he was just being cautious. Or *maybe* he wanted more privacy to do something this gruesome. Or *maybe* he got wind of your stake-outs. Or—"

"Not a chance," Charlie tersely interrupted. "All morning we've had men questioning all the clerks on duty at fourteen different hotels in the area. They didn't turn anyone away. No good-looking guy. Nothing. He was a no show."

"*Or...*" Megan went on, "Perhaps he's thinking one step ahead of us and knew just what he had to do to keep from getting caught. He obviously wants to be chased. He likes it. But he still has no intention of being caught. He's smart. I think he *knew* you'd be looking for him at the hotels this time. That was logical. So he didn't even bother to go."

"So what do we do now?" Charlie asked no-one in particular.

"We have to get lucky," Ralph huffed.

"*Or...* think a move or two ahead of him," Megan muttered.

"How's that?" Charlie demanded.

She faced him, "I mean, you figure out what he thinks our next move will be, and then determine what he would do to counter it. Then we do something else to counter his move, but not right away, making a few moves that are expected and thereby lead to a different resolution."

"Right." Charlie threw up his hands, walking away in exasperation. "That's easy for you to say."

Ralph did chuckle that time.

"You're obviously not a chess player," Megan called after him.

Charlie didn't respond.

"What do you have in mind, Meg?" Ralph asked.

"I don't know yet," she replied. "I need to give it some thought. His patterns are becoming more defined, Ralph, even though he's presenting these new grotesque variations. But they're not *major* variations. Only minor ones, more issues of degree. You know, like a ship varying its course ever so slightly, but maintaining a general heading."

"Yeah. Or you mean like sailing a fixed distance from an uneven shoreline," he offered.

"Exactly!" she snapped her fingers, liking his analogy better. "From the ship's perspective, the course changes continually; but in reality, the overall objective stays exactly the same."

"Which is?" Charlie fired back from a few feet away.

Megan frowned, "*Which is*—the winning move, Charlie. When we figure that out, we'll know exactly how to get him."

Charlie shrugged, tossing up his palms up in mock surrender, weary of philosophizing about things he didn't give a shit about. All he was concerned with were cold hard facts. And it was high time to find some. "That's great, honey. Come on, Ralphy. Let her figure out the chess game. In the meantime, let's you and me see if we can find out where this poor girl was partying last night before she met Mr. Wonderful."

"All right." Ralph put a friendly hand on Meg's shoulder. "Call me if you get any inspirations."

Megan was willing to take a small risk. "Ralph, do me a favor. Let me know if you find out if this woman had been at either the Purple Pagoda or Jinx nightclubs last Friday night."

Ralph looked quizzical, "Why?"

"Just a hunch," she smiled.

•

Later that evening, about a quarter to seven, Megan's arms were covered with gooseflesh when Ralph called to confirm that indeed Mandy Holden-Worth had indeed been with a couple of friends earlier Friday night at the Purple Pagoda. She was also seen leaving about eleven-thirty with a handsome gentlemen matching their earlier general descriptions of the handsome strangler. Ralph wanted to know exactly how she knew where to check. She wasn't prepared to tell him just yet, maintaining it was just an intuition.

After hanging up with Ralph, sitting cross-legged on her couch, she had already marked her MAPSCO with the two new locations, numbers five and six. Consistent to the emerging pattern, the new marked locations stayed in the general line of the crescent being drawn in the lower Greenville Avenue area. She measured out an approximate equal distance beyond Mandy Holden-Worth's condo, following the general established curve, stopping almost exactly at another busy Dallas intersection with two known popular night spots: Ruby Lace and Toxins.

Would he be at one of those two clubs next Friday night?

Yes, he would. She could feel it, right down to the base of her spine. But which one? The temptation to share the information with Ralph at that very moment was overwhelming. They could be ready. They could set a trap. The department could easily stake them both out and catch the bastard.

No.

That would be a mistake. The brute realization of her opponent's skills stopped her in her tracts.

He wouldn't be caught that way. He wouldn't let it happen, for the simple reason it was too obvious. It was a trail of crumbs right into his own tiger pit. Yes. Wasn't *that* pretty basic? Then again, it wasn't very apparent to Ralph and Charlie.

The wheels of Megan Pembrooke's mind shifted into high gear. He *wanted* the police to be there waiting, so he could show them he could do it anyway, right under their noses.

Yes. Pretty basic.

His map was already drawn.

Yes. Very Basic.

It was surely drawn out in complete detail, most likely even before the death of the first girl. He was drawing the line out with the intention of being seen. Just as they thought they would catch him, all he had to do was introduce another minor variation: a disguise, a victim selected from a restaurant next door, anything really—and he'd get away with it again. It wouldn't be hard to avoid capture, if he knew they'd be looking for him.

And he did.

But why?

Because he obviously doesn't want to be caught. Which means he wants to be chased.

Yes. But why?

Malignant narcissism? Megalomania? Just to flaunt his unchallenged power and delusions of invincibility over the police? Perhaps. No, it didn't feel right. That was *too* basic, too simplistic. Certainly he was toying with them, evident from the phone call to the building management, the flowers, etc. Certainly there was an element of ego involved, but ego was incidental. No. It was something deeper. Much deeper. That's what had to be found.

Think two moves ahead.

Why be chased?

Because it was fun.

For the thrill?

Perhaps. Sacrifice a bishop to take a queen.

Yes.

The true joy of chess was to see the look in your opponent's eye as he lifts a key piece of yours from the board, then reels back in shock when he realizes doing that very thing is what closes the jaws of the trap that forces the final checkmate—THE GAMBIT. Sacrifice to win. Megan slapped her forehead in realization. It was the most fundamental strategy of the game of ancient masters.

He wants to be chased.

Why? To capture the ultimate prize.

Which is? She didn't know.

Megan felt so close, yet so far. She just needed to know that one final piece.

What was it?

Ralph's words earlier that day echoed in her mind, "...*like sailing a fixed distance from an uneven shoreline.*"

What shoreline?

She stared at the MAPSCO again. The answer was there somewhere on the page. What was it? Almost an hour later she tossed the grid-based book of Dallas metropolitan area maps down on her coffee table. Her head was pounding and her eyes were sore. She felt even more frustrated. Bruno startled slightly from his perch on her shoulder at the slap of the thick vinyl cover against the glass surface of the coffee table. His forelegs were raised, fangs defensively bared.

"Shhh," she gently stroked his fur. "It's okay, baby. Settle down."

He curled up again and went back to sleep. Yes. The answer was on that page somewhere. She could feel it.

And it was true.

•

At eight o'clock that evening, the sun had just slipped over the horizon, but the sky was still blue and bright and clear and would be for another hour. The air was still hot. The busy hum of going-home traffic could still be heard all throughout the Metroplex. A warm summer breeze pushed the leaves and grasses and weeds toward the northeast. When it abated for a moment, heat waves could still be seen shimmying up off the asphalt surfaces. The grasses were turning yellow and brown. The leaves were dull and drooping.

He took a hot breath and let it out slowly.

The streets were dry and dusty, the oily road film more pronounced and perilous. Standing outside for more than a few minutes made you feel sticky and gritty all over. Dallas could sure use some rain. The city was tired and thirsty. But he didn't care. He didn't mind feeling gritty for a short time. The objective was all that mattered.

Almost two miles from the Caribbean Club the tall, distinguished-looking man walked through the knee-high, overgrown brown and yellow weeds of a small, almost forgotten Highland Park churchyard cemetery, nestled behind an old Episcopalian church. To a passer-by he surely would have looked so out of place walking outside, dressed in a dark, double-breasted wool suit.

Almost two miles from the Rue de Royale hotel the same man stopped at an old grave with a humble granite headstone. He hadn't visited the grave in exactly one week.

Almost two miles from the Club Zanzibar the man respectfully knelt, his piercing blue eyes fixed momentarily on the brief headstone inscription. It simply read:

Touch of a Stranger

Elmyra Teasdale
1952-1991
Wife and Loving Mother

He sang softly to himself, almost under his breath, the old gospel campfire chorus, "Soon and very soon, we are going to see the King..."

Almost two miles from the Regency Park Plaza Hotel the man laid a partial bouquet of nine long-stemmed red roses on the grave, next to two other dried and withered bouquets, one with eleven shriveled buds, the other with ten.

A little bit louder, "Soon... and very soon... we are going to see the King..."

Almost two miles from the Purple Pagoda the man rose, pulled an elegant silk handkerchief from his breast pocket and cleared his nose.

Tilting his chin to the clear Texas sky, he lifted his anthem, "Soon and very soon... we are going to see the King.... Hallelujah, hallelujah, we're going to see the King."

Almost two miles from the Centennial Towers Condominiums, where Mandy Holden-Worth used to reside, the tall man closed the rusted iron gate of the old cemetery. He climbed back inside his black Porsche and drove away, chuckling softly to himself.

Robert E. Gelinas

CHAPTER 14

COUNSEL OF THE ELDERS

Thursday
June 27, 2013

Megan was drunk—very drunk, in fact. It had rapidly degenerated into a ten beer evening, and seemed to be the case for almost everyone in The Stagger Inn that night. Megan didn't go there with the intention of getting drunk, it just sort of happened sitting there on her stool solving most of the world's problems with Pete, Hal and Jesse. If there was any singular blame to be made for the general inebriation of the clientele, it would probably fall on Shannon, who had challenged her slightly tipsy comrades to Kamikaze shots. They were up to round five.

Megan knew she was S-BAR (sloshed beyond all recognition) when she let Clyde Mallory kiss her on a dare. Despite the riotous applause from everyone in the bar, it was a most distasteful event, no pun intended, for he dipped Skoal snuff and spat in an empty Styrofoam cup. However, as usual, Jesse Phillips, sitting two stools down at the end of the bar was way out ahead of them all. It was a wonder he hadn't slid off his stool yet.

With rosy cheeks and a pink nose rivaling Santa's, breathing hard, Pete Brumley listed into Megan's shoulder. She was the only thing separating him from a rapid decent to the floor. He used his hands and cigar much more, pointing a great deal, to illustrate his words when he was drunk. "I think... I think.... I said... I think...."

"What do you think?" Megan looked seriously into his glazed eyes, their noses almost touching, wavering back and forth like swordsmen in a vain attempt to align.

Pete tried again to suck-start his brain with a sharp huff, "I think we should privatize the federal government and link voting rights directly to

115

the amount of taxes you pay. You know, like buying stock in a corporation. The more tax you pay, the more clout you have on what happens."

Megan snickered, "Then the rich would just buy anything they want."

"Bullshit," Pete spat back, still using her shoulder to keep him aright. "The rich and the poor don't pay taxes. Only middle-class chumps like you and me pays 'em. *Who*...never seem to have any real say in anything, I might add. Besides, there aren't that many rich people in this country. Less than five percent of the population make over fifty grand a year. And less than one percent make over a few hundred grand. Did'ja know that?"

"I didn't know that," Megan slurred back.

"It's true," Pete nodded confidently, the massive quantities of alcohol in his system accelerating his words. "See, in my plan, corporations are still excluded from voting, but they still pay tax like nowadays. *Therefore*, the entire political power base is purely drawn from personal individual contribution. Instead of one man, one vote, it's one dollar, one vote, with votes by phone or online with a secret ID number and lots of great big fancy computers. Then you'd see the politicians run for cover like roaches when the light comes on."

Megan giggled, "I don't know. I think we depend too much on computers these days."

Pete belched and thundered on, missing her comment, "Y'see, then you wouldn't have the fucking Democrats doling out bottomless 'entitlements' to the dependent masses they've created in return for their votes. And you wouldn't have the fucking Republicans catering to high-dollar white-collar crowds and special interests for their money to fuel their political machines. Plus you'd have an incentive for the poor to stop being poor, so they'd get some say in what the fuck happens. And the rich wouldn't worry so damn much about getting out of paying taxes because it would hurt their own power base."

Megan frowned, "That's twisted, Pete. Really twisted. But you may be on to something."

"Damn straight," he pounded his chubby fist on the bar. "Give the working people—the ones toting the note on all this shit—give 'em the reins again. I say, *that's* what we need."

Hal O'Brien laughed, his head jiggling back and forth quickly like a locked doorknob checked by a giant invisible hand, "*No*—what we need, is for families to return to their basic God-given values and start raising decent kids for a change instead of turning out generations of unskilled, illiterate, hoodlums."

"*Amen*," came Jesse's moist addendum from the choir, on the heels of a heart-burning hick-up. His eyes screwed tight as he tried to swallow it back down his throat.

Megan felt like being contrary, her cheeks flushing pink beyond just the inebriation. "So what does all that right-wing rhetoric really mean, Hal? Are you really saying you want all the career women to go back to the kitchen and stay barefoot and pregnant?"

"Not all of 'em," Hal smiled. "But someone's got to rear the wee ones all proper. And the government *surely* should keep their meddling mitts off the task."

Megan smiled as sweetly as she could, "Hal, I never knew how much of a sexist asshole you really were."

Hal let out a hearty belly laugh, his slight Irish accent thickening into a deep brogue, "And proud of it, lassie. I think the Good Lord created the women-folk to do that all-important task of bringing the wee ones into the world and seein' that they get a proper start in knowing right from wrong. A sacred task it is, God-bless-us-all."

"And fathers don't have that same responsibility?" Megan countered, suddenly in the mood to spar.

"Oh, to be sure," he shot back. "But a father's *primary* task is supposed to be that of the hunter-gatherer, using that God-given strength and aggression of his to *provide* for his family, you know. Putting a good roof over their heads, clothes on their backs, shoes on their feet, and decent bread on their table."

"What if a family doesn't have a father?" Megan lashed back.

"You're *both* wasting your breath," Jesse Phillips interjected, his hazy red eyes barely open.

Hal, Megan, and Pete turned to look at him, all surprised to learn he still had the capacity to speak, let alone have something to say.

Jesse carefully set his glass down and turned toward them, his voice strangely even and eloquent. "You're just tussling over stupid logistics. All that's just on the surface, the byproducts. Men and women will spawn their young and rear them to the best of their ability, regardless of your opinion of their roles." He suppressed a deep belch with his fingers pressed tightly against his sternum, eyes tight for a second, then bulging wide as a long whiskey laden breath eased past his slightly parted lips.

Hal, Megan, and Pete could all smell it from six feet away and cringed in unison.

Jesse went on without missing a beat, "But if you want to know the real truth, I believe God didn't create women merely to bear men children." He paused dramatically, building up a moment of suspense before announcing, "I think God gave Eve to Adam..." another pause, measuring each eye of his audience, "... for the sole purpose of holding him accountable. I think it's women who have made civilization civil."

Hal, Megan and Pete all looked at one another in turn, each with his or her own skeptical wince or grimace.

Jesse's expression darkened, his voice deepening, "It's partly true, what Hal said. There *is* an aggression in man—a dark rage that burns deep down within the breast of *every* man. In many ways it's an ugly thing, a violent thing—but mind you, it's a very pure form of raw energy, like lightning. But when that most pure and devastatingly powerful form of energy is harnessed and channeled properly, it can be used to build such things as the Great Wall of China, the great Pyramids, Microwave ovens, iPads players, and yes, even great cities and great civilizations—but left unchecked, Oh," he shuddered, "it is altogether too often used to kill and slaughter by the millions. Sadly, history has shown us that far too many times, I must say."

Megan held up a finger of rebuttal and was about to say something.

Jesse cocked his head with a grin, "But take time to see the truth, my friends. It's a strong *woman* that holds her man *accountable* to provide that roof, those clothes, those shoes, and that bread. It a strong woman who holds her children *accountable* to learn their manners and do right—or face her wrath. Which we all know is a terrible thing."

Hal, Megan and Pete just stared at Jesse, all open-mouthed in complete disbelief.

As if by magic, that near catatonic, whiskey-soaked head continued its articulate discourse, "So if you want to argue about roles, you better open your eyes to the real ones. The delinquent fathers who leave single mothers behind, and all the murderers, the rapists and thieves, the depraved of all sorts, are really just so many misbehaving boys, never held accountable and taught to bridle that fire within them."

Everyone sat in dumfounded silence.

Hal broke it with a huff, "There you go, Meg. See. All of society's ills are women's fault. I knew someone would figure it out sooner or later. We've just been waiting for the right spokesman to explain it to us."

Pete spit his cigar out with a powerful wheeze, his face turning bright red, his belly bobbing with laughter.

Megan ignored them both, still looking at Jesse, "Jesse. I'm impressed."

Jesse nodded with a little toast then went back to draining the last few drop in his glass, then nodded at Hal for another.

She added, "I think that's a load of shit, but that's the most I've ever heard you say at one time in my life."

Hal and Pete both burst into renewed titters of laugher.

Jesse just winked, shrugging off the jovial rebuff, "You don't believe me? A pity." He turned to her once more, leaning closer to be heard distinctly, "Well, my dear, think about it. Just for the approval of a single woman, a man will show up on time at her door, scrubbed clean and dressed in his Sunday best, with flowers and candy in his hand. For the sake of a single woman who holds him accountable, a man will forsake all others and come home every night to her. For that same woman who faithfully holds him *accountable*, he will do just about anything—lie, cheat, steal, even fight and lay down his very life to protect her. But mark my word—without ever experiencing the shaping and molding power of that accountability in his life, a little boy almost inevitably grows up into a dangerous and most unpredictable man."

Megan had a dozen arguments to toss back into Jesse's shining, inebriated, red eyes, but at that moment all of them caught in her throat. A nervous chill fluttered within her breast. She just sat there, continuing to mutely hold his glassy gaze.

Hal tossed a hand of dismissal at him, "Oh, Jesse, you've had too much to drink. Who are you trying to fool. You're just as pussy-whipped as I am. No use crying about it here."

The conversation was getting too deep for Pete. He tapped Meg's shoulder, snapping her out of a light trance, "Okay, forget that horseshit. Now about my tax idea—"

Megan turned back facing him, insisting, "He's wrong, you know." Her eyes were deadly serious. "There's more to it than that."

Megan knew there was a *lot* more to it than that. The study of human behavior and the unending intricacies of the psyche was a lifelong field of discipline unto itself, pondered by science, medicine, and clergy for centuries. However, from the broadest vantage, Megan had been taught that human depravity basically stemmed from three primary sources: some people were ill, either psychologically, physically, or both; some people were emotionally handicapped or scarred, usually from the brutalities and neglects of childhood—and then there were the others, the ones that couldn't be easily explained, rationalized, pigeon-holed, or justified from some external stimuli, event, environs, nor circumstance. Some people were just evil. No use denying it. It was pretty basic.

Pete nodded, tossing a hand of dismissal in Jesse's direction, "Of course he's wrong." He smiled with a slight chuckle, "Then again, we both know men do a lot crazy things for a women's favor. But I think it's comes from a desire for more than just a nice pat on the head." He wiggled his eyebrows, "*If* you know what I mean."

That made Megan smile, "Well, Freud thought sexuality and aggression were very closely linked."

"Especially if she says no." Pete's eyes suddenly went wide, then he slapped his own hand, "Did I say that? Bad Pete. Bad, bad, Pete."

Megan giggled, then her smile abruptly faded back into swirling thoughts and ugly images of bruised, torn, and bitten bodies. "I wish I really *did* know exactly why some bad boys do the things they do."

Pete caught that look in her eye. "Then I gather you've not had much luck in your case?"

Her silence answered the question.

It was time for some cheering up. Despite the euphoric cloud swirling behind his eyes and toying with his equilibrium, Pete decided it was time to summon a little thrust and parry of wits. That never failed to brighten the girl's spirits. But taking into consideration how much beer and Vodka they had consumed, undoubtedly little of what he was about to say, if any, would be remembered the next day.

"You know, Meg'lin, I been meaning to tell you, based on what you been telling me, I had a couple of my own ideas to run past you." Pete looked at her, hoping her expression might liven once again.

She shrugged, "I'm open to anything at this point."

Pete switched his cigar from one corner of his mouth to the other, endeavoring to focus his mind on what those ideas were. "That's good. That's real good. Let's see, for starters, I think there's more to the roses left behind than just a signature."

"Like what?" Megan sipped her beer.

His hands were illustrating again, "Well, first of all, he's using them to number his killings. One in the first murder, two in the second, three in the third."

"Yeah. Pretty basic," Megan nodded, "So what?"

"You know roses are symbolic," Pete offered. "They're a symbol of love, affection, or extreme passion. I think they're there to make a statement that all of this about something or someone he loves, or feels deeply about."

"He *loves* to kill," she noted with terse indignance. "It's just a diseased animal thing, Pete."

"I don't think so. No, not from what you've told me." Pete shook his head, draining the last of his mug and returning it to the dark wood surface of the bar. "I think it specifically has to do with a someone. A person."

"So how does that help me?" she asked, not hiding the futility in her voice.

"Look at all the progressive symbolism in his manners." Pete leaned closer, his mind sharpening in the brewer's fog. "In the second and third killings, you said a lot of the damage he did to the bodies was after the girls were dead. Right? He hurt them when they certainly could put up no defense, nor suffer any further. While that's disgusting, it makes another statement."

"Yeah?" her eyes were opening wider, some of the mist in her brain parting by the sheer force of curiosity. "What statement?"

"A statement of pain. Don't you see? There's an anger in his statements. A vengefulness, not just a cruelty. If he just wanted to inflict harm on the girls he would have stopped at their deaths. The victims feel no more pain after they're gone. But his statement isn't about the victims themselves. They're just the canvass for the painting." Pete screwed his face up tight, "Death and Roses. No, I get the picture of an unrequited love of some kind."

"Do you get this picture from a psychic source, Petey?" Hal teased. "Crystal ball? Tarot cards?"

"Oh, shut up, Hal," Megan lashed at him, making him take a step away in surprise. Megan turned back to Pete. This was important. "Go on, Pete. Are you talking about the love of someone living or dead?"

"Unknown." Pete signaled Hal for another beer, who took his time in retrieving it. "Could be either. Could be anger over a rejected love, or possibly grief over a lost one. He hasn't given us enough clues yet to know for sure."

Megan jerked her jaw to the side in a burst of inspiration, her eyes locking on Pete's, "Maybe he has."

It was Pete's turn to look intrigued. "How so?"

"Like you said, the progression of symbolism. The progression of violence." Now Meg's hands were a flurry of illustration. "We've always assumed the pattern of degeneration was for psychopathic thrill sake, but that's what's been bothering me. It's completely inconsistent with the degree of premeditation in his acts. What he does to his victims superficially looks like deeper and deeper depths of horror, but that in and of itself could be part of the deliberate landscape of his painting."

"I'm not following," Pete said.

Megan put her hands up, "Don't you see? The first girl was strangled. Her body was barely bruised—dead, but otherwise almost pristine. The second one was cut and bruised a little, but again after the fact. The third one was chewed—*literally*. Again the bulk of the damage post-mortem."

"Yes," Pete nodded slowly, "...like a decomposing corpse."

"Exactly," she snapped her fingers. "Each one a further stage of being consumed by the worms."

"Now *that's* a revolting thought." Pete thanked Hal for his fresh beer with a wink and a nod. "But I see what you mean. So perhaps your killer has lost a loved one."

"Yes..." Megan paused, then let out a long sigh, "But knowing that doesn't bring me any closer to catching him."

Pete laughed, "You're right. Leave that for a moment. I've got another idea for you to try. Show me your MAPSCO again."

Megan reached down in her white canvass book bag leaning against the inside legs of her stool and pulled out the spiral bound directory, handing it to Pete. "Here."

Pete took it from her and opened up to the page she had marked. "You said yourself you have to stay two moves ahead in the game." He pointed the intersection she recently marked. A broad smile crept across his lips. "Look here. On site number one, there are at least a dozen fancy clubs he could have picked. He could have gone down to Deep Ellum where they're as thick as mosquitoes in an August swamp. But he didn't. He started at the Caribbean Club in lower Greenville for a reason. Why? There must have been a reason. On site number three, there are about a half-a-dozen clubs, but he picked the Zanzibar Club. Why? Again for some reason. Last Friday, on site five, he picked one of only three choices, the Purple Pagoda. See what he's doing? He's continually moving into less commercial areas, deliberately narrowing his selections."

"So what?" Megan rolled her eyes, "Look, Pete, I've been through all these scenarios. Tomorrow, he's likely to be in this area at one of only *two* places. But right now I think he *wants* me to think that, so he can turn around do something else."

"No, he'll be there all right," Pete smiled, "And, he'll certainly make sure he's undetected. But that's only the next move. Not *two* moves. Look. If you follow your pattern even further, you come to this intersection the week after." He pointed to the map once more. "There's only one club anywhere near there. *That's* where he leading you."

"What club is that?" Megan asked.

Hal leaned over and looked at the map, noting the corner. "Mmm. You're right, Pete. That's the one off McKinney Avenue, over near Inwood Parkway. I believe it's called The Inferno."

Megan dropped her forehead against the smooth wooden bar rail. "Great. He's taking us to hell."

"But he doesn't think you'll solve the puzzle of how to identify him until you're there." Pete's voice was surprisingly sober.

"And he's probably right," Megan said softly.

Hal leaned over an looked at the map, arching his brows high. He pulled a pencil out of his shirt pocket and lightly connected the dots of

Meg's numbers one through six, extending to the estimated numbers eight and nine. The entire sketch formed a very smooth arc. He grunted, "Well, look at that, will you. Your boy seems to me to like his geometry. That's a pretty exact curve."

Megan looked at the lines. He was right. It wasn't just a general deviating pattern, it was a smooth arc. "It is. Isn't it."

Hal picked up a wet glass and began to dry it, a wry smile emerging. "Now, I'm certainly no detective, and maybe it's is too obvious to be anything of note—but if it was me doing the looking, I think I'd wonder what's at the center of that little circle there he's drawing for you."

Megan and Pete's eyes froze on each other.

Could it be? No, that was too easy...

In a matter of seconds they were laying cocktail straws down on the map, trying to approximate radius angles. The measurements were extremely crude at best, involving more than one page, so they had to keep flipping back and forth. Furthermore, without a compass and a protractor and a bigger map, plus not knowing the exact locations of the last two approximations, they couldn't get an accurate measurement any closer than a five-square-block area approximately two miles from the site of the pickups and the killings.

"Damn. That's a lot of area," Pete sighed, the excitement of the previous moment fading rapidly into a cloud of disappointment. "You got several old warehouses, some residential houses, and old Episcopalian Church, a few retail strip centers, and part of a golf course."

Megan's shoulders sank as well, suddenly feeling a little stupid. "Oh, well. It was a fun idea while it lasted. Kinda like finding the 'X' on the treasure map. Thanks anyway, Hal."

Hal leveled a hard gaze at Megan, "Don't give up, Meg. You know you're close. I've seen that look in your eye before. You can feel it. The answer's down there somewhere. At least tell the detectives about what you know. Give 'em all your suspicions. It may help."

"What *do* I know?" Megan asked with a forlorn toss of her hand. "I can only give them a pocketful of half-baked theories, and our own concoction of amateur psycho-babble. If I'm wrong, then I probably won't even be on the case anymore. I can't afford to do that."

Jesse piped up again, "But Megan, that's not the issue. If you're right, another girl might not die."

That was true.

●

Ralph Weatherstrom didn't appreciate getting a phone call at nearly midnight, but he didn't mind talking to Megan. His wife Mari just slept through it. When he first heard it was Megan calling, he thought perhaps their killer had indeed decided to advance his schedule. It was only Thursday night. A wave of relief washed over him to learn otherwise. He listened to her patiently telling him of her sketchy theories concerning the city map, and referring back to his earlier question about how she knew which club was hit the past Friday.

To be sure, it was an intriguing theory, but Ralph had his own serious doubts. He wanted to believe her. However, the detectives downtown had their own map of the city, complete with large red and green pins stuck in it. Yes, the killer was systematically working a particular area, but it looked more to them like he was just moving in a general direction, not defining as precise a geographic line as Megan alleged.

Besides, he had asked her, how would they identify him at a club, even if he showed up and was standing right next to them? All they had were very general and vague descriptions. Could they arrest every good-looking man approximately six-one in height with brown hair who was trying to pick up a girl? In Dallas on a Friday night that could be hundreds of people, if not thousands. Megan vehemently begged him to assign stake-out teams at the two clubs she mentioned, but he said they had no choice but to officially stick with the hotel watch plan, looking for "a behavior" they *could* positively identify.

Megan wasn't satisfied. She hit him with a fresh idea.

Actually, as he hung up the phone, Ralph realized if it hadn't been for the impressive way she had done everything else in the investigation, he never would have agreed to her counter-proposition.

What could it hurt? Who knows? We might get lucky.

Yes. This Friday night, in less than twenty-four hours, off-duty officer Megan Pembrooke was going to keep an eye on everyone at Ruby Lace, and Detective Ralph Weatherstrom would be watching the patrons of Toxins. They both agreed with a laugh that it was probably a good idea not to mention it to Charlie until they saw what happened.

Although, just to be safe, Ralph inwardly decided he would discuss it briefly tomorrow morning in his meeting with Commissioner Bragg and see what he thought. Bragg was sharp, and wouldn't mince words. If he was flatly opposed to the idea, they could can it without any embarrassment. And if he liked it, then it never hurt to look like you were on your toes and scoring some points.

What if Megan's idea was the lucky break they were hoping for? They needed a break—desperately. Everyone involved in the investigation walked around under a debilitating gray pall of apprehension as Friday approached. Tempers were short. Patience was thin. There was little doubt the killer would strike again. And inside they all knew it was going to get a whole lot worse.

They just had no idea how much.

CHAPTER 15

A CUNNING WARRIOR

Friday
June 28, 2013

"May I buy you a drink?"

His voice had arisen out of nowhere, rich and gallant, from right be-hind her. Megan turned from the bar and looked into a pair of warm blue eyes, friendly and inviting. Her heart stilled. There he was, standing mere inches away—approximately six-foot one, medium built, with curly brown hair, wearing a finely tailored slate-gray suit.

It was just after eleven-thirty. Ruby Lace had been jammed with glamorous partying bodies all evening. Megan had been sitting at the bar by herself for almost two hours, patiently nursing a Samuel Adams lager, wearing a brand new low-cut black dress she bought that day just for the occasion. Up to that point she was getting very restless, feeling kind of foolish and conspicuous. She was still trying to stave off the same black cloud of discouragement which had loomed up on the horizon a week ago. It wasn't easy. She had scanned so many possible candidates all night, yet for one reason or another they were quickly disqualified.

But not this one.

Carol and Linda had graciously volunteered to come along again that night, but Megan steadfastly refused. They were too much of a distraction. Even Dominic wanted to tag along, but she didn't want anyone with her. No, an instinct told her that night she needed to appear alone and vulner-able, like all the other victims—that is, if she had any hope of drawing the beast out of the shadows. And she came prepared for that very thing. Her badge, gun, and micro-radio to speak with Ralph over at Toxins across the street were all readily at hand, neatly stuffed in her heavy purse.

She wasn't afraid, sitting there in public all that time, just waiting and watching. Rather, the continual trembling in her hands and knees merely stemmed from the sheer excitement of finally having a chance to get close enough to catch this wretched predator who killed so ruthlessly and easily in cold blood. At least that's what she kept repeating to herself over and over. The beer helped. She was at the end of her third one and was starting to feel it. An uncanny instinct told her (warned her?) he would be there this time. Yes, tonight she knew he would be very close—close enough to taste.

Had it worked? At that precise moment, in that one instant of time, Megan Pembrooke's greatest hope had just transformed into a most terrifying reality. Was this indeed "him" looking down into her eyes?

...just the wind...

"Uh, sure," she managed to mumble in reply, trying to keep her teeth from chattering.

He set his martini glass on the bar next to Meg's mug and signaled the bartender, who promptly fished another iced down bottle out of the cooler behind him.

"Thanks," Megan nodded.

"My pleasure." His smile was captivating. He was very sure of himself, smooth and charming.

But is it really HIM?

Megan forced her mind to focus. All the facts and figures meshed and merged as she replayed them in her mind. She had to be absolutely sure. The trembling in her knees intensified when he picked his glass up again with his left hand.

"You look a little nervous," he commented, touching her hand. "You're trembling. What's the matter?"

She tried to laugh it off, bristling at the sensation of his fingers on the back of her palm. It took everything within her not to recoil in screaming blood-curdling hysteria. She laced her fingers together down between her knees, "Oh, I'm sorry. I've just got a case of the shakes tonight for some reason. I hope I'm not coming down with something."

"Aw," he jovially put his palm over his heart, "I thought perhaps it was just me."

Megan's head began to feel light. "No. I'll be okay"

Is it really him?

How could she be sure? A confrontation? All they really needed was an identification and if this was him, he was toast. They had more than enough physical evidence to compare, the DNA samples, hairs, bite pattern, the suit fibers, the works.

Suit fibers?

The thought drew her eyes down to his jacket. Megan suddenly remembered the lab team had determined the fibers she found had come from a very expensive and rare wool. This man's elegant wool suit looked very expensive.

"I really like your suit," she smiled, doing her best to pour her bottle of beer into the fresh mug the bartender placed before her. "Where'd you get it?"

He grinned, "Thank you. I have them made for me by a tailor in San Francisco. He gets the fabric from a special mill in Scotland. It very rare, but most comfortable for my needs."

She almost dropped her mug, spilling some of her beer and splashing herself as she attempted to steady it.

"Oh, my. " He grabbed a stack of napkins and handed them to her. "Are you sure you're all right?"

Megan's face flushed with embarrassment as she dried herself off. "Yeah, I'm sorry. Just a little fumble fingered. I guess it's not my night."

He paused only a moment, "It could be."

Her eyes came up to his. She couldn't breathe.

The music slowed down to a graceful ballad.

He held out his hand, "Let's dance."

"Oh, I don't know." She wanted to run. But she couldn't. If this was him, she couldn't let him get away.

Was it him?

"I do." Without waiting for further reply he took her by the hand and led her toward the dance floor. Her feet moved of their own accord, leaving her purse on the bar – which the bartender graciously moved to the back bar. She was about five beats short of a coronary.

Megan couldn't believe she was doing this. They stopped in the center of the floor and he took her gently into his arms, slowly fading back and forth to the music. Actually, she didn't want to admit it, but it was quite nice. She hadn't slow-danced since college. Yet the thought that this man might possibly want to take her to some nearby hotel, hump her lights out, strangle her to death, and then stuff her in a meat grinder definitely put a damper on the enjoyment.

No.

A wave of revulsion bubbled up from her stomach. She suddenly felt the same way she did in college touching her first cadaver—actually coming in physical contact with death. Was the man who had strangled and cut and bit helpless women now holding her close, drawing her cheek against his chest? She began to feel nauseous. A familiar smell wafted past her nose.

Aramis. Good Lord, it WAS him!

She hesitantly looked up into his eyes, staring, her heart thundering in her chest, her bladder about to burst.

The moment came. He smiled down into her eyes. "Would you like to get out of here? Go somewhere a *lot* less crowded?"

Think, Megan, *think*, she commanded herself. You can't go with him, but you can't let him get away either.

Get help.

"All right," she whispered, doing her best to appear coy and interested. "But I need go to the ladies room first. okay?"

He nodded politely. "I'll take care of your tab and meet you by the door."

"Fine," it took hundreds of foot-pounds of force to bring her cheeks into a smile. She retrieved her purse and headed for the restrooms.

The other women in the ladies room were all wide-eyed looking at Megan screeching into her little walkie-talkie. "Dammit, Ralph! He's here! Move your fat ass!"

"Are you sure?" came the hissing response, clipped on the end with a fine hiss of static.

"You better *fucking* believe it! He's picking *me* up!" She practically mashed her lips through the small mouthpiece screen. "I've just talked with him! *I've just danced with him!*"

"How do you know it's him?" Ralph fired back.

She did her best to remain calm, "He's six-one, a hundred and eighty-plus pounds, brown hair, blue eyes, left-handed, good looking, great suit, a wad of money, and Aramis." Her legs were shaking so bad she was about to fall down.

A tall blond washing her hands gave Megan an odd look and a half laugh, "Well, honey, I been looking for something like that all night. If you got one that good and don't want him, give him to me."

"Fuck off," Megan spat, reaching into her purse and flashing her badge. "Police business."

The woman's smile faded and she hastily left the ladies room.

Ralph's voice cut in, "Meg, look. Don't worry, I'll be there in a couple of seconds. Just don't let him leave."

"Got it. Out." Megan ignored the other quizzical eyes staring at her as she left the bathroom and was immersed again in thumping music, squirming bodies, and dizzying lights. Her purse hung from her shoulder down to her waist. The zipper was open. Her hand was inside, sweating, clinging to the grip of her Beretta. Her thumb found the safety and clicked it off.

There he was standing by the door—waiting and watching.

Megan walked right up to him and stopped. The thought occurred to her she could kill him right then and there without ever having to take the gun out of her purse. It was aimed right at his belly.

No. Wait for Ralph.

She manufactured a smile, "Hi."

"Ready to go?" he asked.

Ralph rushed into the entrance of Ruby Lace, pushing people out of his way. He held his badge high. His pistol was drawn, but carried low, down by his side. His eyes found Megan. A rush of adrenaline scorched through Meg's veins.

This was it.

"I'm ready." Her sweet smile vanished as her hand whipped out her pistol and thrust in under the man's chin, beneath his look of utter astonishment, the gun sight pressing up into his soft, tender flesh. Her voice was instantly cold and authoritative, "Police! Don't even think about moving, asshole!"

He froze like a lab frog with a needle in his spine, his eyes wide, filled with terrified alarm.

Club patrons within earshot screamed and fled back, knocking a few people down and overturning and table full of drinks in the process. Glasses splashed and shattered against the floor.

Ralph rushed up, grabbed the man from behind with one hand, and slammed him headlong up against a wide concrete pillar a few feet away, the muzzle of his gun buried in the base of his skull. "You're under arrest. You have the right to remain silent..."

They'd done it! Hal was right. Sometimes it *was* better to be lucky than good. As Ralph continued to read the man his rights, Megan snapped a pair of handcuffs on their prize. It was over. They did get lucky. They got him. She felt as if a ten-ton weight had just fallen from her shoulders.

Unfortunately, the ten-ton weight would land squarely *upon* her head before the night was over.

•

"I'm *sooo* sorry, Mr. VanGoren," Megan sincerely apologized, completely red-faced. A fine rim of tears brimmed her eyes.

Dawn.

Six excruciating hours had past. Defeat had been snatched out of the jaws of victory. Megan was more embarrassed than she had ever been in her entire life. What could she say that could undo the damage? At six o'clock in the morning, her shoulders drooped beneath the burden of an entire night's fatigue. She stood mutely in the hallway of the Dallas downtown police station on Harwood Street before the poor frightened man she and Ralph had mistakenly arrested earlier that evening.

Her voice was hoarse and tired, her baggy eyes red and weary, "I hope you can understand the investigation we're conducting, trying to catch a serial-killer. I thought you...were..."

He never said a word, just shook his head sadly, turned and walked with his lawyer out the front door to make a statement to the wall of camera and microphone wielding reporters.

"Weatherstrom! Pembrooke! In my office!" bellowed Chief Moranzano from the end of the hall. "Now!"

Chief of Police Moranzano was a small, stocky, but imposing man, with a thick black bristle-brush mustache, a prominent cleft chin, and powerful arms like a wrestler. Due to the circumstances, he had been up all night as well. Ralph and Megan hadn't even taken their seats when the Chief slammed his door and bit into them, "What the fuck did you think you were doing?"

Ralph turned around and started to reply.

The Chief's next blast overrode anything Ralph was about to say, as he careened around behind his desk inadvertently scattering papers in his path. "You arrested a total stranger, an innocent man, with no evidence, no provocation, on an unauthorized operation! You've embarrassed the department! You've embarrassed me! You've embarrassed yourselves! SIT YOUR ASSES DOWN!"

They did.

The Chief remained standing, towering over them, "What in hell prompted you to arrest a businessman from San Francisco?"

Megan blurted out, "He fit the description."

"*What description?*" Moranzano roared. "There *is* no description. I've seen the files. There never has been any clear description. We don't arrest people because they fit a general description. We arrest them because we have evidence. Hard evidence. Conclusive evidence. You have none. This poor man had only been in Dallas for a day, and hasn't been here in six months! How could you have done something so stupid? If he was a suspect, you could have simply asked him for his ID, and then checked him out. That's what *we* did! We knew who he was in less than ten minutes. No arrest was necessary. That guy's probably going to sue us for false arrest. And guess what? He'll win. Are you two aware of that?"

Megan muttered, "It's all my fault, sir. I called Ralph and asked for help. He was only helping me."

Moranzano bored a hard Pontius Pilate gaze into Megan, "*And you!* You're nothing but a damned lab technician. You're *not* a detective. You exceeded and abused your authority as a police officer. You have *no business* playing detective! This *is* your fault. And as of this minute, Officer Pembrooke, you're on formal suspension, pending a full Internal Affairs investigation. You're off this case, and if I have my way you'll be off this force."

Ralph piped up, "Come on, Chief, she was just scared. The guy fit all the patterns we've found."

"Weatherstrom, I expected better out of you." The Chief sat down and buried his face in his hands, rubbing weary eyes, then glared at Ralph again. "I ought to suspend you too. But I need you to follow up on this case. You'll be getting a written reprimand. I promise. And don't you dare fuck up again. *Got it?*"

•

"I'm so sorry, Ralph," Megan whispered as they walked back down the hall together. The hot, bitter tears were already starting.

He shrugged, putting a friendly arm around her shoulders, "Hey, you tried. It's okay. Just go home. Get drunk. Take a Valium. Get some sleep. Take some time off and let it all blow over. Then just lay low for a long time and do your job. It'll all be all right. Leave it to us. We'll catch the guy." His chest heaved with a weary sigh, "Somehow."

Charlie McManus was waiting at the end of the hall shaking his head, his hands stuffed in his pockets, gloating. "So, Miss Shirley-lock Holmes. You *did* it. You went off half-cocked and fucked yourself and us. Can't wait to see the headlines this morning."

How did the cliché go, Megan wondered? Feeling like you could walk under a snake with a top hat on? No, she felt lower than that. Whale shit? No, lower. So low, she'd have to look up to see Hell? Yeah, something like that.

"Leave her alone," Ralph chastised.

"What's the matter, Ralphy?" McManus followed after them to the door, taunting, "What's wrong with you? Getting soft? You'll a little old to be thinking with that little head again."

Ralph stopped and suddenly spun around, violently lifting Charlie McManus into the nearby wall by his neck-tie. Their noses were a hair's breadth apart. Ralph's eyes burned into Charlie's with a dark ire, "I'm gonna pretend you never said that Charlie."

Detective McManus just laughed, "Oooh. Must have touched a nerve." His mocking grin dissolved into a scowl as he pushed Ralph back and straightened his tie. "Now are you gonna listen to me, instead of Miss Peaches and Scream?"

They both looked toward the door. Megan Pembrooke was gone.

•

7:05 A.M.

The sun had just lifted its gleaming face above the horizon. He hadn't slept at all that night either, just arriving back home an hour earlier. The work had been most entertaining that particular Friday night. The look on her face had been priceless. He'd remember it forever. He hit another key on the computer in front of him and the screen changed.

He was logged into the city database. He accessed the Dallas Police Department, Homicide Division case files. He hadn't read the latest updates yet. It was so much more convenient having all the city records automated these days. It saved a lot of time and energy. They were very informative as to exactly what was known, suspected, and planned. The previous night's log entries were sure to be quite entertaining.

When the latest entry came up, entered by Chief Moranzano himself at 6:35 A.M. the tall man burst out laughing. A false arrest. He read the next line. His laughter faded into a somber stare at the screen. Megan had been suspended.

Oh, no.

That was horrible. She couldn't be out of the game. That would ruin everything. But did a suspension matter? No. Not for her. She'd stay in the game until the last move. She had to. He knew she would. It's what he would do. He read further. Weatherstrom had been reprimanded. No big deal. This was becoming more and more amusing each and every day. He couldn't wait for them to find his latest piece of handiwork.

It was glorious.

CHAPTER 16

SILENT SCARS

Saturday
June 29, 2013

It was almost eight o'clock in the morning when Megan walked up to her door and shoved her key in the lock. It was already eighty-five degrees outside. Her entire body ached from her hair to her toenails. She hadn't felt so utterly exhausted and worn out since she had driven non-stop from California to Dallas two years ago in the old orange Toyota Corolla she used to have with no air conditioning. Her clothes were wringing with day-old sweat. She had been up for over twenty-four hours and wanted nothing more than to crawl into her bed and sleep for the next week or two. Perhaps when she woke up in a month or so the nightmare would somehow be over.

Yet the greatest pain was on the inside. Chief Moranzano was right. It was true. She had humiliated herself and the entire department. There would surely be lawsuits, reprimands, possible criminal liabilities. It *was* her fault—all her foolish, ambitious, arrogant, stupid fault! She didn't follow proper procedure. It *was* stupid. She didn't have any business being there at that club last night. Why did she do it? In all likelihood, short of a miracle, she'd probably just be dismissed from the force. The blackness penetrated even deeper into her soul. Even death didn't seem like such a bad option at the time.

"Hi, Meg. Are you all right?" came the familiar voice from across the hall.

Megan slowly turned around, the weariness and despair hanging from her eyes in dark bags. She just gave him a slight shrug.

Dominic wanted to walk over and throw his arms around her, but politely stood his ground. He just woke a up a little while ago and had just seen the news and heard the early reports. It was bad—real bad. Even CNN's *Headline News* was already nationally reporting the bungled Dallas arrest.

He gave her his best smile, "Can I get you anything?"

She shook her head, "I'm tired, Dominic. I just need to sleep."

"Okay," he replied softly. "But if you need anything, and I mean *anything*, I'm here."

"Thanks," she barely got the word out. Her head was starting to feel faint again. She desperately needed to sit down and lay down before she fell down.

"Hey, Meg?" he asked, desperately hoping to cheer her up, even a little bit. "In case you're interested, I heard the Ringling Brothers Circus is coming to town toward the end of July. Do you think you might like to go? I could get us some good tickets."

Anything resembling fun was anathema. Her frown stayed firmly in place, "I don't think so. But thanks anyway."

Dominic felt the lump in his throat almost double in size. "Okay. Just thought I'd ask." He started to close his door, then smiled with a fresh idea to try, "Oh, knight takes pawn. Check."

Megan pushed her door open, then glanced back over her shoulder, "Good move. I resign. You win."

•

Megan Pembrooke's door thumped shut much harder than usual, followed by a hard snap of the deadbolt. Dominic pushed his own door to without a sound, hurting inside more than he could ever remember. If only she knew how much he cared. He silently condemned himself for always saying the wrong thing. It made no sense, but in a very real way, he was certain something very important just died between them. His eyes blurred momentarily and his head was starting to feel light again. He needed to lay down. The dizziness came from time to time, usually before one of his "spells." It had been happening more so lately than usual.

Dominic suffered from a slight case of narcolepsy. At least that's what he thought it was. Occasionally, he'd start to feel dizzy and go lay down; or sometimes it would come on suddenly and he'd wake up later on the floor. Sometimes the spells lasted minutes, sometimes hours. There was no regular pattern. He knew he should see a doctor about it, but he rationalized that he never had the spare time. It wasn't that significant a problem—but he kept it a secret nonetheless.

•

Megan was no sooner inside the door when Linda and Carol rushed to her side and protectively swept her into their arms, vehemently protesting and chastising her in frantic unison. Their hands flailed in all directions for her abysmal failure to call, their own personal degree of hysterical worry, the horror of hearing the awful mess on the news, wondering what happened, and the like. They too had been up all night, worried sick. The three of them retreated in mass back into Meg's bedroom and sat on the her wide, queen-sized bed as Megan repeatedly apologized and told them everything that happened in hideous embarrassing detail. They cried together for almost an hour, pouring out much of the mutual frustration and exhaustion they all felt.

Sometime around ten o'clock that morning, they all collapsed together in utter exhaustion, all of their emotions spent, their depleted bodies huddled and twisted together like a hibernating snarl of snakes. As Megan drifted off into near-coma, covered with the comforting arms of her friends, snuggling her close, it occurred to her just how good it *did* feel just to be held.

•

When Megan's eyes stirred again it felt as though she had merely blinked. According to the bedside alarm clock, it was late in the afternoon, almost supper time. She was still dead tired and could have slept ten hours more. Her arms and legs were stiff and numb. Her right arm, pinned beneath her, was asleep and tingling with icy pins and needles. Her mouth was dry and her throat ached.

Carol and Linda were gone.

Megan ran her slender fingers through her long brown hair, pushing most of the tangles behind her ears. She yawned and stretched for almost a full minute, her back delightfully popping twice. It took three hard coughs to dislodge the choking glob of phlegm in the back of her throat. She wore only her panties and the oversized Garfield T-Shirt she liked to sleep in, but had no recollection of having removed her black party dress and put it on. She didn't really want to remember any of the pain of the previous evening, night, or morning.

Half-awake, and propelled by sheer urgent instinct to empty her screaming bladder, Megan stumbled out of bed and headed toward the apartment's only bathroom. The door was almost closed. She pushed it open and was greeted by a cloud of steam and the sounds of the shower running, a few intermittent splashes, and a mischievous volley of giggles. Carol and Linda were behind the shower curtain.

"Don't mind me," Megan croaked as she sat down on the toilet and attended to her first priority with a welcome sigh of relief and a brief shudder.

Linda's head poked around the curtain, "You're alive!"

"Sort of." Megan rose and flushed. "It's debatable."

Carol's grinning face appeared from the opposite side of the curtain. "Come on in! It'll make you feel great."

Megan tossed a hand of dismissal at her with a smirk, "I don't think so. You guys enjoy yourselves. I'll hit it when you get out. Just save me some hot water."

Carol frowned, drawing the pastel blue plastic curtain back halfway, "Oh, don't be silly. Come on. We'll wash your back. You deserve it. We don't bite."

No.

The eyes of her friends coaxed yet further, the smiles growing more mischievous. No. These were her friends. There were well-defined lines of friendship and basic trust which couldn't be crossed and have friendships remain friendships. What waited beyond the boundary of friendship? At that moment that particular specter was too frightening. Oh, yes. Megan knew all too well how crossing some lines were one-way streets which radically changed everything. The gaunt, leering face of her Uncle Bertrand in Pennsylvania loomed before her mind's eye... *coming into her bedroom... moving closer to her bed.... smiling .... telling her not to worry... professing how much he cared... untying his robe...*

Both Carol and Linda clutched each other in startled shock when they saw Megan abruptly burst into tears, run from the bathroom, and slam her bedroom door.

•

Two hours later Megan sat silently on her couch, her body completely limp, warmly cuddling Bruno under her chin. Her brilliant mind was a void, reduced to a static black-and-white test pattern. Her ears heard only a shrill monotone frequency without waver or interference. An awkward tension hung in the air around everyone. Without another word Carol and Linda had gone down to The Stagger Inn. Somewhere in the fog of her mind Megan had promised to join them later. It was a lie.

Megan didn't feel like doing anything.

A single tear dropped from her chin and landed heavy on Bruno's back, quickly soaking into his thick black fur. He awoke with a start and defensively reared his long menacing forelegs. His many eyes searched for a potential predator but found none. All was well. Wasn't it? A few moments later, the two furry appendages of the huge spider reached forth and softly stroked the trembling chin next to him, as though in some strange way he understood his matron's pain—and cared.

Megan just wanted someone to care.

CHAPTER 17

QUEEN TAKES PAWN:
NANCY CALLEDORE

Saturday
June 29, 2013

Ralph Weatherstrom crouched over the fine imported porcelain toilet in the elegant marble tiled bathroom of a palatial suite in the Ponce Du Place Hotel. His tortured lungs continued to strain air in and out of his gaping mouth. One more dry heave wrenched his bowels, and twisted his face into a red grimace of pain. He could still taste the caustic stomach acids in his nose and in the back of his throat. Ralph had never thrown up on the job in all his thirty-some-odd years. He thought he had seen it all.

He was dead wrong.

On the bed in the next room lay what was left of the most vile and ferocious act of horror he had ever beheld: Victim number four—the gruesome remains of a young woman named Nancy Calledore.

Charlie McManus stood behind him, trembling himself. He handed Ralph a wet monogrammed hand-towel, "Here you go, buddy."

Ralph took it with a frail nod of thanks. He stood and wiped his face. His eyes and nose were still watering.

Charlie couldn't look him in the eye, especially after all that had been said between them in the last twenty-four hours. "Come on, man. Let's get out of here."

"Yeah. Right now." Ralph couldn't be more pleased.

He wanted to be as far away from that place as he could get. What kind of a monster could do such a thing? Hell, even animals didn't do such things to hunt and eat. What kind of hellish creature were they up against? Back down on the street they emerged from the entrance of the building into the warm evening air. It was a sacred relief. Both men stood silent for several minutes. The shock would surely last a long time—the hideous visceral memory, forever.

Charlie broke the prolonged silence, anxious to talk about anything other than what they'd just seen up on the sixteenth floor. "How the hell did he get in there? What the hell happened to our ordinance?"

Ralph coughed into his fist. "No one even *saw* him *or* the woman this time. No check in, no clerk, no money. Completely invisible. The hotel register showed that room as vacant last night. A guest found the body late this afternoon when he checked in."

"Wow," Charlie whistled. "I would hate to be that guy."

"Yeah," Ralph nodded in agreement, then shrugged, "Although, if you think about it, it probably wasn't that hard to get a room without registering. All it takes is a master key and then knowing which rooms are empty. Any maid in the hotel could have accommodated him."

Charlie's face darkened, "Which also means we should have the duty officers up there ensure all of the house staff from last night are accounted for. Our boy doesn't seem to like witnesses. I bet we find your maid in a laundry chute or a trash dumpster."

"Good idea. You do that." Ralph's voice was drifting away in thought again.

"Did any of the...uh..." Charlie cleared his throat, "...lab techs say what they thought the exact cause of death was this time."

Ralph glared at him it utter appall, feeling a strange sense of righteous indignation welling up. "No, they didn't. And just between you and me, I don't care. I don't even *want* to know. The woman is dead. That's all that matters. After looking at what he did to that poor girl, I just want to believe she went quick and painless somewhere at the beginning. I don't want to know anything to the contrary."

"Understood." Charlie agreed wholeheartedly with his palms raised.

"I wish Meg was here," Ralph whispered.

Charlie sniffed, scuffing his shoe against the sidewalk. "Yeah, I... uh...feel kinda bad about her."

"Why?" Ralph looked over at his partner. "I thought you hated her. You gave the poor girl enough shit."

He shook his head, "I didn't hate her. I just didn't like her much. There's a difference. She's such a damned know-it-all."

"No. She was right, wasn't she?" Ralph more accused than asked, looking up the street at the marquis of Ruby Lace and Toxins in the next block. "About everything. The timing, the escalation of the violence, the locations. Everything."

Charlie ambivalently shrugged, "I don't know. She got close. That's all. But I'd say that was more luck than talent."

Ralph gave his partner a smile, "So who gives a shit? Sometimes it's better to be lucky than good. Right?"

"Right. But it's still just luck." Charlie laughed, then gave his partner a knowing wink, "You know, despite the fuck-up, she almost got the nightclub right."

"What are you talking about?" Ralph took a step closer.

Charlie confessed, "Well, 'ya see, on checking out this victim this morning, I talked with someone just up the street where you guys were—"

"You found a witness at Ruby Lace?" Ralph looked hopeful.

Charlie shook his head, "No, I talked to a bartender across the street at Toxins."

Ralph huffed, tossing his hands in the air, "Figures. That's where I was." He smacked the top of his fist against his forehead, "God! I was right near him and didn't even see him."

Charlie was quiet for another moment. "It's... uh... worse than that, Ralph."

Detective Weatherstrom felt a chill brush lightly over his face. How could anything be worse? "What do you mean?"

McManus looked like he didn't want to volunteer the information right away. "It was something I heard that VanGoren guy say to his lawyer before he left the station this morning. I think maybe our boy stopped by Ruby Lace as well."

"Why?" Ralph stepped closer still, feeling his own temperature start to rise. "What'd he say?"

Charlie appeared almost embarrassed to elaborate. "He said he thought the arrest was all part of a practical joke on Meg. That's why he ain't gonna sue."

"A joke?" Ralph was momentarily confused.

Charlie lowered his voice. "Yeah. VanGoren says that a guy came up to him in Ruby Lace and pointed Meg out sitting at the bar, saying he was a good friend of hers. He says she's supposed to be real shy, and he's helping her out—all that shit. The long and short of it is, this guy gets VanGoren to go hit on her, telling him Meg was very interested. He even went so far as to give the guy a little packet tester of Aramis cologne, telling the poor bastard it's Meg's favorite and sure to get him laid."

A sinking feeling oozed from Ralph's chest down through his tender, nauseous stomach and on down into his hips. "Let me guess, the guy was tall, dark, and handsome."

Charlie shrugged, "He didn't say. But you *know* who it was, and what it means."

Ralph nodded, "Yeah, it means he set her up. The arrogant little shit is just fucking with us, Charlie-boy. Somehow, he knows exactly what we're up to and does *just* as he pleases, *right* on his own damned schedule."

Charlie almost laughed, "I hate to admit it, but you know, lucky or not, she almost got him. He must have seen her first, sent VanGoren over as a decoy, and then headed across the street and snatched his next prey right from under *your* nose."

"Oh, thanks," Ralph blurted out. "Rub it in, why don't 'ya?" Ralph just watched the traffic drift by for a while, collecting his tangled web of thoughts. He spoke almost involuntarily, "Meg was right about something else. It *is* just a game with him, you know."

"I'd hardly call it a game," Charlie scowled, almost repulsed at the gross understatement.

"Oh, yes," Ralph insisted. "It's definitely a game. A very well thought out game. That's something else Meg tried to tell me and I didn't listen. Don't you see. He's more than just a fucking psycho. He already had *all* of this planned out. Right down to the last detail."

"But why?" Charlie wasn't expecting an answer.

Ralph didn't give him one. "Look, I gotta go."

"Where're you going?"

Ralph was already fishing his keys out of his pocket. "To talk to someone I think is a little bit better at these games than you and me."

Charlie rolled his eyes, "You really think she can help us now?"

"I think I'd like to find out," Ralph's eyes were deadly serious, "before our monster decides to take any more players out of the game."

•

"Hello, Samuel."

Samuel Ferndale, dressed in a bright silk blue and green print Japanese house-robe, was genuinely surprised to see the tall man in the dark blue double-breasted suit standing in his doorway. It was almost ten o'clock in the evening. Their usual Thursday meeting was still a long way off, he noted to himself. Had the good doctor exhausted the week's supply of frozen samples from last week with his tests so soon? Not that it mattered. After the past Friday night, there was plenty to spare. The doctor would surely be pleased.

Samuel Ferndale stepped aside with a flamboyant wave of his hand, affecting a bad German sounding accent, "Vell, hello dare, Herr Doctor."

He let the affectation drop when he saw his visitor was not even remotely amused. "Won't you *please* come in? I really didn't expect to see you so *soon* this week."

The tall man walked silently past Ferndale into the small foyer of the house, pulling off his sunglasses as Ferndale closed the front door behind him. The tall man's polished voice was even and devoid of any emotion. "Do you have my samples for this week, Samuel? I need them right away. I can't wait."

Ferndale laughed, bouncing barefoot into his living room, heading toward the recently remodeled kitchen. He led his unexpected guest along, boasting with effeminate glee, "Oh, *yes*, yes, yes. Justin was just *incredible*. I have *six* for you this time!" He disappeared into the kitchen. "And, honey, let me tell you, they were deliciously extracted over a mere four hour period. I *thought* I was going to *die*."

The tall man started to chuckle again as he stopped in the middle of the living room and reached inside his jacket. He heard a refrigerator door open and close, more mischievous giggles, then the approaching patter of bare feet on cool tiles.

Samuel Ferndale reappeared from his kitchen with the small blue thermos in hand, smiling with unabashed pride. The swift, cat-like movement of the tall man's hand, leveling the pistol at deadly point-blank range happened too quickly to react. The first bullet discharged from the cylindrical maul of the six-inch blue-steel silencer with a muted spit. It hit Ferndale squarely in the forehead, snapping his head back as the rear cranial region exploded. A thick wet splash of blood, bone, and brain tissue splattered the antique-white painted wall a yard directly behind him.

The second round struck him in the throat, just under the chin, as he was starting to fall backward. The third and fourth tore into his chest as his body collapsed back into the wall and silently slid down, leaving a bright red smear along the uneven surface of the wall. The cold thermos was still tightly clutched in his right hand, its surface beginning to bead with condensation.

Samuel Ferndale would have no more dates.

The tall man put his sunglasses back on, walked over and picked up the thermos. It was indeed a lot heavier than usual. That made him smile, his shoulders gently bobbing under his suit-coat with a slight laugh. Apparently Samuel's last evening must have been most enjoyable. Fine. He deserved it. Such a shame. This pawn had served his king well. Unfortunately, his unique services were no longer required.

One black pawn remained to be played.

CHAPTER 18

THE GAME

Sunday
June 30, 2013

The vibrantly colored computer chess model slowly rotated in a perfect three-dimensional tumble, stopping at the perspective of the black player. A match was in progress. Every shadow was perfect, every line, every detail. An ominous tune played in the background, a haunting melody based upon an old Gregorian chant. None of the pieces on the board were static images. They all breathed and restlessly moved about on their respective squares, each awaiting his imminent call to battle.

The order came.

Via the mouse, his hand maneuvered the scepter-shaped cursor on the screen over the black knight's head and clicked. In spectacular 3-D animation, the knight's horse reared high, nostrils flaring, hot breath steaming in the chilled pre-dawn air. The armored warrior drew his sword from its sheath with a ringing "SHINK" of Spanish steel. A crisp bolt of lightning crackled from the dark and threatening sky overhead, touching the tip of the two-edged sword and splintering down the blade in a shower of dazzling light, leaving it glowing white-hot at the tip and gradually fading into a glowing orange. The fierce horseman slowly rotated the sizzling blade in a small figure eight as it cooled, awaiting his next instruction.

The cursor moved over to an opposing pawn two squares up and one over from the knight's position. Another click. A strikingly realistic digitally recorded thunder-clap was heard: the prelude to a symphonic battle march. As the music swelled, the screen suddenly blazed into turbulent motion as the perspective of the viewer swooped down to the game board like a bird of prey, rushing up upon the back of the black knight and melting into his armor. The player was now inside the knight's armor, possessing his body, seeing and hearing what the knight saw and heard.

The horse pitched forward to battle, his armored hooves clapping against the marble surface below him.

The knight dismounted in the enemy square of the white pawn, who was a small battle-ax wielding foot-soldier. The pawn cried out, valiantly swinging his little ax, his eyes clearly wide with fury. The black knight's polished shield easily deflected the glancing blow, producing a brilliant flash of sparks. He countered with brutal energy and lethal precision. Through the wide visor, the black knight's blade was clearly visible swinging down hard, loudly cutting the air like a bull whip, leaving a latent arc of electric blue light in its path. The fierce blow struck the cowering enemy soldier on the shoulder of his fighting arm, severing the appendage with dull meaty-sounding chop. The amputated arm hit the white square with a bleeding bounce, the fingers still randomly twitching around the long wooden handle of the battle-ax. Blood streamed down the pawn's side. The discomfited little man reeled back, his eyes bulging in horror, crying out in fear and falling to his knees, clearly in visible pain.

The sword swung again, this time laterally, beheading the knight's screaming little foe, instantly silencing him forever. The head was seen rolling into the next square by the foot of a robed white bishop. The head and its separated carcass then burst into three-dimensional flames and magically dissolved back to a clean game board. The knight sheathed his cold, blood-stained blade and mounted his horse. Immediately the perspective of the viewer backed out of the knight's body, returning to its central, elevated, omniscient perspective in a single, fluid motion.

Dominic Callaghan was pleased.

In combat mode, holding down the right mouse button, the new routine allowed the player to use the mouse to strike at any body part on the piece being taken. He had deliberated over and over whether to retain the pawns' two blow kill factor, or go back to one. There were too many logic contradictions for the animation sequence in either scenario. Thus, he had finally decided on something immensely more intricate, involving a lookup table to determine injury relative to fatality. The algorithm added a further dimension of realism to the game, interpreting a specific blow and then judging it individually on its *potential* for fatality. Naturally, this meant that the target had to be subdivided into a much more granular anatomical grid, but that was easy to do, considering the three-dimensional sprite was already a wireframe geometric image to begin with. The cross reference to the layered color table array was the key. The resulting routine allowed the player the flexibility to finish the frightened

little opponent off quickly, or hack him to death a little piece at a time.
Perfect.

This was exciting. As soon as he compiled the new routine with a special 3-D graphics enhancer it would be ready to integrate with the Virtual Reality module. The mouse routine would be replaced with a manually stimulated tactile response system. Soon chess players all over the world would know firsthand what it looked like—and seemingly *felt* like—to cut their opponents down with the edge of a blade.

Or worse.

The higher ranking the piece, the more deadly it was, and its respective attack sequences more in depth and gruesome. A lowly pawn strove to bludgeon or cut with a small battle ax. A rook was a mad, cannibalistic castle dweller who literally devoured his opponents with his teeth. A knight cut sharply with the sword. A bishop used the purple stole from around his neck to strangle to death. And then there was Her Majesty the Queen—the most deadly piece on the board.

A queen skinned her prey alive.

When the king attacked, he was transformed into a hideous winged fire-breathing dragon. Dominic patterned the digitization and metamorphosis routine of the dragon after Disney's great flying dragon in the climax sequence of "Sleeping Beauty." However, Dominic's dragon was not a two-dimensional cartoon; rather, a 3-D computer generated Virtual Reality poly-morph—more lifelike, more threatening, more fearsome than any living creature ever beheld by human eyes. The intricate shades of chameleon greens, shark blues, scorpion yellows, cobra browns, raven black, and rich blood-red detail woven into the scales, gargoyle wings, and reptilian hide was virtually obscured by the horrifying thrashing images of fangs and talons. But fangs and talons were only to shred and devour its prey after a kill.

It killed by fire.

The flames spewing from the flying reptile's mouth literally cooked its victim's flesh, scorching and bubbling the meat, burning and consuming until all that remained was a charred pile of black and gray bones. The length and graphic detail of each sequence also escalated when the piece taken was of higher and higher rank. For a queen to take an opposing queen, the bloody result was something altogether beyond the fringe of shocking.

Dominic was certain that Megan would be so excited when she saw it. She had to be. He wasn't going to show it to her until he had it completely finished. The two player version would eventually interface with a two-station virtual reality simulator, running on a high-end graphics processor.

But Megan would enjoy it.

And soon. Very soon.

The vivid fantasy of playing the game with her was always on his mind. It would be so exciting. She'd love it. She *had* to love it. He had worked so hard. He couldn't wait. It was almost finished. There was only a little research left to do and he'd have all of the required images diagrammed, processed, digitized, and integrated.

He saved the current code listing and rose from his desk, pulling his robe around him and tying the belt in a half-knot. He hadn't dressed all day. But that was all right. A lot of important work had been accomplished. It was a good day.

Dominic shuddered as an oppressive wave of claustrophobia enveloped him, prompting a compelling desire to get out of the apartment for a while. He had dearly hoped to hear Megan come home so he could invite her out to dinner. Maybe she'd accept this time. That would be great. He'd take her to Ernie's in Addison. It was the best place he'd found in all of Dallas. It was quiet, romantic, had live music every night, melt-in-your-mouth cuisine, and service second to none. She'd love it. Unfortunately, Megan had been gone most of the weekend. He frowned. Although, those two girls were still over there. He didn't know exactly why. Something was very wrong. It wasn't good. He was still worried sick about her. She looked so bad the last time he saw her.

He laughed quietly to himself, realizing it would be just his luck to go out and then she'd show up. It never failed. But at the moment, that possibility was looking very remote. No, the decision was made. He had to get out. Now. Just for a little while. Just for a break.

But where?

It didn't matter. He'd know when he got there.

Dominic opened his closet. On the left side hung all of his custom tailored suits, most of them double-breasted. He looked better in double-breasted suits rather than single breasted. He didn't know why he bought most of them. They totally changed his appearance. He wasn't normally a suit kind of guy. But when he met with software executives, he did his best to at least look the part. Or sometimes he got dressed-up when he was just in the mood. And that wasn't often.

A top-shelf restaurant?

No, tonight he was in the mood for something casual. Perhaps just a nice drive around town, then maybe an Arby's and curly fries. He looked to the other side of the closet and selected a nice sport shirt and some khaki slacks. Yes, a drive would be great.

Standing before the mirror in the bathroom, he took off his black framed glasses and put on his tinted contacts. They made his eyes look so much more blue and bright. He didn't like wearing them all the time. They started to irritate his eyes after a few hours. He preferred just wearing his glasses. The glasses were ugly, but extremely comfortable. However, he was painfully aware of how nerdy they made him look in public. So, as usual, he left them at home.

When the elevator opened in the basement garage of his apartment building Dominic stopped, facing a small quandary.

Which one?

He owned two vehicles. One was a little red Ford pickup which he used most of the time to haul computer equipment and peripherals. It was a working-man's every-day truck, which he didn't mind if it got dirty or nicked up. He liked it a lot, like his glasses. It was a good friend. On the other hand, his other vehicle was really more of a toy—or a mistress. Unlike the druthers of most men, he didn't appreciate anyone knowing he owned it—not that he was ashamed of it. No, he was very proud of it in fact. But proud in his own unique way. For him it wasn't a status symbol. It was an adventure. He figured if people knew it was his, they'd think he just had a lot of money and get the wrong impression about him.

Couldn't let that happen.

He especially didn't want Megan to know how wealthy he was. He never wanted her to think he was showing off, or trying to impress her with his money. No, no, no. She could *never* be allowed to think of him in any other except that of an average, every-day, regular guy. That's the only way he could always be sure about her. That's how he wanted her— humbly, and with no pretentious trappings.

But wasn't the illusion of humble means a pretension?

No. It was different.

He told himself he was just striving to maintain the only lifestyle he had ever really known, save a few minor indulgences. His tremendous wealth was merely a mathematical fact, important to his bankers, lawyers, and accountants. It was only important to him in the sense that, in addition to handsomely paying the bills, it financed all his research and development work—which was *very* expensive. He constantly plowed a great deal of his royalties back into his work. And he needed a tremendous amount of money for that. Research and development was outrageously expensive.

Dominic owned and operated a dizzying array of specialized computer and image development equipment normally only found at NASA, MIT, Cal Tech, or George Lucas' Industrial Light and Magic Studios. And every day he pushed every bit of his high-tech gear to the limits of what it could do. The finished results bordered on the supernatural. He could take still photographs, computer generated animation, or live action video, and morph it into sequences so realistic it staggered the imagination—and deceived the senses. However, tonight he was bone-tired of the endless stream of bits and bytes. It was definitely time to just get out and go for a nice, exhilarating, private drive.

Dominic Callaghan walked to the opposite end of the large underground garage, his pale leather topsiders patting the smooth concrete as he made his way along. He stopped on the far side of the complex, deep in the shadows, making sure no one was around before he silently removed the canvass cover which embraced his sexy German sports car. It was a beautiful piece of automotive machinery—also custom ordered and tailored to his tastes. He had named her Elizabeth, after Elizabeth Taylor. Elizabeth was the second woman in his life. As the powerful engine roared to life, he wondered if his first woman would really ever be more than just a fantasy as well.

Time would tell.

He estimated he would know in approximately a week.

Chapter 19

Strategic Moves

Monday
July 1, 2013

"He skinned her, Meg," Ralph could barely say the words.

Megan gasped, her fingernails pressed white and trembling against the worn old bar room table top. Ralph Weatherstrom's face was as pale as her own. They discreetly sat together at a back table in The Stagger Inn, as far away from curious eyes and ears as possible. Megan noticed Pete Brumley parked in his usual seat over at the bar, who kept glancing over at them every few minutes. Pete was very suspicious of one of "the real detectives" who hadn't taken Megan very seriously. She was still embroiled in the midst of her own emotional turmoil, devastated by the official suspension, and further shocked by Ralph's story. He quickly brought her up to date on all the gruesome details of what had transpired since Friday night.

"Skinned?" Is that the word she actually heard.

Ralph's nod was more of a gentle rock of his upper body forward and back three times. He spoke with little emotion, just staring ahead into space at the unspeakable image burned into his mind he would never forget. "Every bit of her. Scalp, face, and all. He peeled every inch of skin off of her in long strips about two or three inches wide. Like an orange. Left 'em in a bloody pile next to the bed, littered like carpet scraps. Must have taken a while. When I first saw the body on the bed, all I saw was red. And the smell..." he groaned, "...just like the autopsy room over in Fort Worth at the Tarrant County Morgue." He shuddered.

Megan could tell by the tension in Ralph's voice it was very difficult for him to recall all of this.

He sniffed, "The windows were closed, but the flies had already found

150

her. I thought perhaps she was just painted in blood, another stabbing, maybe just another throat cut. When I got closer I saw all the muscles, the ligaments, the sinews." He coughed. "I ain't never seen that before. You know for a second there, it made me think of one of those 'The Visible Woman" models I'd seen back in school. Remember those? You know, the ones where you can see all the muscles under the skin?" A vain attempt at a smile peeked out for a second. "When I was kid it was kinda fascinating." The empty look instantly returned "But seeing that poor woman...." He took a deep breath, "I...uh...all I could do was run to the bathroom and puke my guts out."

Megan reached over and set her hand on Ralph's forearm, her voice reassuring. "It's okay, Ralph."

"It's not okay, Meg," His experienced eyes found hers. They were deeply disturbed. In one look they plainly told her, of all the horror he had seen committed against other human beings in three decades as a public servant, he had never seen anything like this in his life.

"Any chance it was someone else?" She didn't know why she asked that. They both knew.

He shook his head. "She was lying in the middle of the bed. Her hands were neatly folded across her middle. Four long-stemmed red roses were stuck between where her boobs used to be."

Megan just leaned back aghast. "We knew he was degenerating psychologically and escalating the violence, but that's incredible. It kind of reminds me of Albert DeSalvo up in Boston. Doesn't it? You know, with the flowers and all, like all of DeSalvo's bows and decorations?"

"Yeah, it does. With a little of Richard Speck, Ted Bundy, and Charles Manson thrown in for good measure." He gave her a half-hearted chuckle, "And if our killer was in his mid- to late-fifties, I'd be real tempted to believe all those theories about DeSalvo not really being the Boston Strangler."

Megan managed a frail smile.

"But there's another parallel I don't ever want to see. DeSalvo supposedly killed over a dozen people over a couple of years." Ralph drew close to the young woman, "I can't deal with this for years. It's gone on long enough already. Too long. We've got to do something now." The frustration came out in his voice, tired and pleading, "That's why I'm here, Meg. I want your help. I *need* your help."

Her eyes darkened, "I'm on suspension. Remember?"

He nodded, "I know. So what? You still want to be a real detective someday don't you? Well, lady, this is your chance. Are you *gonna* help me, or not?"

"What *can* I do, Ralph?" It was more a question concerning her scope of authority rather than her abilities.

Ralph's voice rose in intensity, "As far as I'm concerned, you can do whatever you want to do—on or off the force. And I think you want this guy to be found. And I think you know how to find him." He leaned back. "*Somehow.* You're getting closer. *Damn* close, in Charlie's words, believe it or not." He lifted his chin, "Come on, Meg. Anything. Just show me your map again. Please?"

She hesitated, searching his eyes.

Yes, Megan did want to be a "real" detective, more than anything else in the world, despite everything Charlie and Ralph had told her to dissuade her. They had gone on-and-on over the last few weeks about what a Herculean bitch it was to be a "real" detective: the thankless tedium; the monotonous boredom; bails of paperwork; the uncooperative and belligerent people they dealt with each and every day; the ridiculous city bureaucracy they constantly fought; and, of course, the Looney Toon morass of the judicial system. If they did manage to solve a case, the nightmare of maintaining the chain of evidence, testifying, being relentlessly assailed by defense attorneys—all of it—quite often stole away what little taste of victory they ever enjoyed. And if a case went unsolved, naturally they bore the brunt of blame.

So why bother?

For Megan Pembrooke, it wasn't a question. It was what she knew what right—what was necessary. It's what she *had* to do. It was pretty basic. Therefore, there remained no real decision, only a small superficial apprehension of getting into further trouble.

It was settled.

"All right. I'll help if I can." Megan had brought her MAPSCO with her in her book bag. When she spoke with him on the phone about the meeting, he had mentioned wanting to see it again. She opened it to the now infamous page with the six marks. "Here you go."

"You can add the two new places to your list." He gave her the exact street addresses of the club and the hotel.

Megan meticulously marked numbers seven and eight on her map. Again they both fit precisely into the penciled curve Hal had marked, without deviation. "He's right on course."

"Which means, more than likely, he'll be at this Inferno place on Friday, like you said." Ralph conceded.

Megan shook her head. "But that's so obvious." She frowned. "No, it's all wrong. It has to be."

"What do you mean?" Ralph looked puzzled.

She scrutinized the line on the page. "There are no more choices at the next spot. He would know we're going to be there waiting for him. It's...it's...."

"What?" Ralph tried to follow her, then asked hopefully, "Something he wants? You think maybe he *wants* to get caught now?"

"No," she shook her head, trying more to clear it. "He's too good a player for that. He's been very smart up to now. He still has no intention of getting caught. It's something else. I can feel it."

"What?" he implored.

The realization came. The Gambit. Megan looked deeply into Ralph's eyes, her stomach wincing, her face cringing. "It's a trap, Ralph." She paused. "For *us* this time."

He didn't want to believe her, but the pounding in his chest told him he had to. "How do you know?"

Her words were cold, like the bite of a serpent, "Because that's what I'd do if I were him."

Ralph sucked in a deep, skeptical breath. This was too much to absorb. "I don't know, Meg. Maybe you're overestimating him." He shook his head, feeling an instinctive resolve welling up, so much wanting it to be true. "But let's say you're right, and say he still isn't planning on being caught. He still doesn't think we can spot him, and he's probably right. So he *might* just be planning what he thinks is the ultimate crime. The ultimate ego rush. Think about it. To pull it off right under our noses. To do it when we *are* there waiting for him. What do you think?"

She slowly nodded, "Perhaps. It's a possibility. If he can pull it off, I'll be impressed."

Ralph's face clouded, shaking his head back and forth. "But there's still a problem. It still *has* to stop there, or he has to radically break his pattern. Look at your map. Look there." He pointed down at the page. "See? Follow your own line. It's the end of the trail. There are no more hotels or nightclubs in that direction. It's all residential. Just big old houses and few apartment buildings."

That was right. Just houses and apartment buildings.

Residential?

Megan's eyes were still on the map searching the streets: From Fitzhugh, across Avondale, to Douglass, Oaklawn, Lemmon, Cedar Springs, Carlisle, to Haskell.

Where?

•

He wound his black Porsche around the Mix-Master ramp from I-30 onto Stemmons Freeway heading north at almost ninety miles an hour, expertly dodging in and out of the flurry of cars like an arcade game. The mid-afternoon traffic was heavy. That made it all the more fun. Fenders blurred by other fenders, sometimes only a handbreadth away. It gave him a titillating rush—*adventure*. He'd be at the junction of Loop 635, the LBJ Freeway, in less than five minutes. On the radio John Mellancamp burst into the chorus of "It Hurts So Good." He reached down and turned it up.

"Come on, baby..." he sang as he hit the hands-free voice activation system and then paused his signing and commanded it to place a call to a specific number he recited from memory. The call was answered on the third ring.

"Hello," came the voice of a bubbly receptionist, probably only eighteen or nineteen years old.

"How do you do, Miss. Mr. Gibson, if you please?" He ducked into the left lane with a jerk of his powerful left hand, soaring past a slow moving group of cars.

"Gibson," came an impatient voice.

His voice was as richly cultured and smooth as usual. "Good day, sir. This is Justin Teasdale calling. I wanted to speak with you concerning a lease renewal on my Carlisle Tower apartment. If I'm not mistaken, I believe it expires at the end of July."

"*Car*-lyle Tower? Let's see, uh... that's the...uh...red brick high-rise just off McKinney Avenue. Right?" Gibson asked, not really giving his caller his full attention. He was busy murmuring terse instructions to some other administrative person in his office.

"Yes, exactly. That's the one." The Porsche picked up speed.

"Hang on," replied the voice, along with the sound of shuffling papers for several seconds and a few more muffled commands. "Yeah. Let's see here. The Carlisle Tower. Okay, okay, Teasdale. Ye-yeah. Got it. Apartment 15-C. I think I remember that one. Okay, okay. Six thousand a month. Right? Real nice. A real looker. You say you only want it another six months?"

"That's right," he replied. "I assume the rate's the same."

"Nope, sorry, bud," Mr. Gibson responded, smelling a fatter commission on total revenue. "Now it's sixty-five hundred a month. Got a waiting list for that one—cause of the view, you gotta know. Am I right? But tell you what. I can cut you some slack and give you the same rate if you sign up for a full year. Okay?"

"Then let's make it a year. Love the view." He swerved behind a silver BMW 850 back into the left-center lane, cutting off an old Chevy pick-up truck, then shooting over into the right-center lane and accelerating into an open slot. He released wheel for a second to push his mirrored sunglasses up on his nose. "I can be over at your office tomorrow to sign the new lease, if that's convenient. If you could just leave the documents with your secretary, that would be wonderful."

"Yeah, sure. Tomorrow' no problem. I'll leave 'em with Tina. Ask for her. Make sure you sign all three copies." He quickly appended, "And you know all your deposits just carry over. No refund. Understand?"

"Perfectly. Thank you for your time, sir." He ended the call. His right hand came back up to the gentle curve of the wheel, enjoying the supple feel of the calf-skin leather in his grip—like an exceptional woman.

Peasants and Pawns.

He laughed. The details of the apartment arrangement were completely irrelevant. He'd only been to the high-rise apartment twice. Once when he picked it out five months ago for the project, and once again a month later when he put some furniture in it to make it appear occupied. And in less than a week, he'd never see it again.

CHAPTER 20

TACTICAL MOVES

Tuesday
July 2, 2013

"Good night," Carol looked hesitantly into Megan's eyes. She stood in the entrance to Megan's bedroom, leaning against the doorframe. Linda was already in bed asleep.

Megan glanced in the kitchen at Mickey. He said it was almost 11:00 P.M. She was curled up on one end of her couch, her knees pulled up to her chest. They still hadn't spoken very much over the last two days. Megan's voice was soft and reserved. "Good night."

Carol walked slowly up to the back of the couch, leaned over and affectionately kissed Megan on the cheek—a close friend's kiss—whispering ever so softly, "Hey. It's okay"

Okay?

She wanted everything to be okay, but in reality she knew they were avoiding each other. Both Carol and Linda worked all day yesterday and Megan had spent most of the evening with Ralph down at The Stagger Inn. She knew she needed to talk to both of them, just to clear the air. She wanted to talk to them, she *had* to talk to them—but she really didn't know what to say to them.

Megan Pembrooke was still uncomfortably unsettled and undecided on how she felt. She knew she cared about both girls very deeply. They were her best friends. They were like family.

Hey. It's okay

Carol's words rang in her ears again. Was it okay? Maybe it was. A warm sense of ease wrapped itself around Megan's heart. Yes. In a strange way, yes, it was. That realization made her smile with a renewed warmth and a sense of relief. What a precious gift. She loved Carol and Linda all the more.

"Are *you* always gonna love me?" Megan cocked her head slightly to the left and asked Bruno, who was perched in a fuzzy ball on her shoulder.

He hunkered down a little closer, visibly pleased to feel her fingers come up and lightly stroke his back.

"Oh, shit!"

The abrupt noise above Bruno and the sudden lurch of vertigo as he plummeted down to the cushion of the couch sent him into a defensive sense of panic. He landed on his back with a plump pat, and struggled for several seconds to aright himself, angry and afraid. His mistress was nowhere to be seen. Shelter? Nine black eyes in two rows looked from side to side. A dark cavern created by a cushion leaning against the back of the sofa appeared to be the most convenient and safe haven to hide. He scampered for it as fast as his long fuzzy legs could move.

Carol and Linda both jumped up in bed as the bedroom door flew open and banged back against the door stop. Megan came rushing in.

Carol defensively held the bed sheet up to her chin, "What is it?" Megan opened the top drawer of her dresser and pulled out her Beretta, ripping it free of its thick brown leather holster, "Both of you stay here. Don't you dare come out of the apartment for any reason."

Linda was still half asleep, "What's going on?"

"Call 911," Megan ordered, checking the ammunition in the gun and snapping the magazine back in place. "Tell them to send police and an ambulance. Officer needs assistance."

Carol jumped out of bed and fled toward the door. Megan was already gone, the front door closed behind her. Carol's eyes flew to the top of the television. The red light was flashing.

"What do we do?" Linda helplessly called from the bed.

Carol spun back and screamed, "Make the call! Hurry!"

•

So tonight was the night. So be it.

Megan switched off the safety of her pistol, holding the deadly weapon steady with both hands near her face, the barrel pointed skyward. Carol and Linda's apartment was in another wing, but on the same floor. The door was closed. Megan pulled the slide and chambered a .40 caliber hollow point round. A whirlwind of thoughts and emotions cascaded from her heels to her tightly knit eyebrows. Could she really do this? She wasn't a street cop. She'd never had to use deadly force in any situation, and in her job, would potentially never have to. She was a forensic technician! Her training had barely touched on face to face confrontations involving lethal weapons.

Who cares.

In that instant, a cold-blooded instinct bubbled up within her, telling her there was still no other choice. She had to do what she had to do. All alternatives were unacceptable. It would continue until it was stopped. The animal had entered the trap. It was time for it all to stop. Her heart was racing. Breaths seethed through her teeth at a staggered interval.

It was time.

Holding the pistol aloft in her right hand she opened the door with her left, pushing it wide slowly and quietly. The lock on the door was broken, the wood of the jam looked like it had been splintered with a crowbar. Her hand found the light switch and turned on the overhead light, quickly recoiling, leveling the gun, prepared to fire at the first sight of any threatening human form.

Nothing.

The living room had already been ransacked. Her breathing arrested when she heard the crackling noises of violent destruction emanating from the bedroom: the sounds of wood and glass being bludgeoned with something heavy. The bedroom door was closed, but the light was on inside, evidenced by a thin line of light peeking out along its bottom edge. Megan kept telling herself over and over, if she had to, she could do it.

Go on.

She reclosed the front door, then walked over and took a seat on the couch. No sense precipitating a confrontation. She could wait. There was no other way out of the apartment, unless he wanted to jump from a fourth floor balcony. Her mind told her not to make a noise. A noise would cause alarm. In a state of alarm he would surely come bolting out of the room, running headlong for the door. Moving targets were harder to hit. Besides, she knew he wouldn't take very long. For him, time was precious commodity in short supply.

As usual, Megan Pembrooke was right.

In less than two minutes Troy Bigham emerged from the bedroom carrying a long black crowbar. His first sense of surprise came with the discovery of the living room light turned on. He stopped cold in the bedroom doorway, but failed to notice Megan Pembrooke sitting patiently on the couch with her elbows propped up on the arm, steadying her trembling petite hands which held fourteen rounds of death pointed directly at him.

"Freeze, shit head. You're under arrest." A formality for conscience sake.

Their gazes locked in the next instant: his filled with a blood boiling rage and then a strange mixture of alarm, instantly recognizing the petite woman who had so completely humiliated and debased him in their last encounter; her gaze was cold and steady.

Megan had often played out in her mind how this scenario would transpire when this day came. The decision to live or die would always be his; but she knew long ago what he would choose—and what a terrible decision she would then be forced to make. Many times in her fantasy, she confronted the man, holding him at gun point and further exacting a prolonged verbal retribution before the final "High Noon" styled show down. But the chess player in her continually reminded her that such dialogues were reserved for the movies. In real life, any time she allowed him to move was time she herself was in danger. The two white dots on rear sight of her weapon converged with the single dot of the front sight.

"Fuck you, bitch," he spat with baleful venom, lifting the crowbar and beginning to take a single step forward.

One deafening shot ripped through the night.

Troy Bigham's adrenaline charged heart was torn in two with one powerful penetration, which also managed to brake his spine before knocking him off his feet, landing him in a sprawl, six feet back atop the clutter he had just created in the bedroom. He was dead before he hit the carpet.

Megan dropped the pistol to the floor, her entire body quaking. Tears filled her eyes as she ran out the front door to the fourth story rail, leaning wide, and threw up on the decorative shrubbery far below.

Sirens screamed in the distance.

•

Almost an hour later, just before midnight, still standing at the cold iron rail holding onto her stomach, Megan was finishing making her oral report to the two Plano duty officers. The ambulance crew had already taken the body away. Oddly, the two uniformed patrolmen seemed to be most pleased by what had happened, but Megan was still sick to her stomach and badly shaken.

Even while she spoke to the officers in an uncanny sense of detachment, a strange thought pricked her soul. Now she too, knew what it felt like to kill—and as far as she was concerned, it was something she prayed she'd never to have to do again as long as she lived. Every time she closed her eyes, the grizzly image replayed of Troy Bigham's chest exploding, just past the end of her gun muzzle.

"Hey, little girl," came the warm, paternal voice of Ralph Weatherstrom from down the walk. It was a welcome voice, comfortably familiar.

She looked up without speaking, her chin quivering like a hummingbird's wing and rushed to him. He folded her into his arms and held her close. She clung to him like a frightened kitten, the tears hot and fresh.

His fingers petted the back of her head, "Shh, shh, shh. Hey, I heard what happened on the squawk-box and came right over. When I heard you plugged one, my first thought was that our Mr. Friday Night heard what a good job you were doing, found out where you lived, and decided to pay you a neighborly visit." He gave her a half-laugh, "To tell you the truth, I was actually a little disappointed to find out it was just some street scum."

Megan kept her eyes tightly clenched. Her chin started to quake again, her stomach knotting and writhing in revulsion.

Ralph leaned back and his expression clouded when he looked down saw the pained look on her face. "Hey, honey, you gonna be all right?"

She cuddled tighter against his chest. "I...I killed a man tonight, Ralph."

"I know," he tried to sound comforting, like a father, but fortunately came across more like a friend. "That's why I'm here." His fingers stroked down through her long brown hair once more. After a thoughtful pause he added, "I've had to put down four men in my career. I can still remember every one of their faces. I won't say you ever get used to it. It's horrible every time. Yep, you can remember each and every one. Even when you don't want to. But it *is* part of the job, you know?"

She huddled closer still, her eyes tearing up yet again. "You don't understand, Ralph. This was different. I knew he was coming. He wasn't just a prowler. He's been stalking two friends of mine. I knew this was going to happen." Her voice hardened, "I *knew this* was going to happen. I knew he'd come and I'd have to do this."

"So?" His eyes weren't concerned.

"So..." she didn't know what else to say.

"So, Officer Clements here, one of Plano's finest, tells me the stupid motherfucker had a crowbar in his hands. Zat right?" He took her by the shoulders, pushing her back to arm's length, and facing her squarely. He paused for a second when she didn't reply. "And no matter what, sure as shit, he would'a caved your pretty head in if you didn't do what you had to do. Ain't dat right?"

She nodded faintly. There was so much he didn't know.

"And now your two pretty friends can sleep at night. Idn'at right?" He did know.

"Right," she whispered.

He crouched down so his eyes were at her level. "Hey. It's okay."

Hey. It's okay

For the second time that night she heard those words. And for the second time they conveyed a desperately needed sense of release. She clung to them and repeated them silently over and over in her mind.

"Are you sure?" she asked.

Ralph stood tall and laughed, "Hell, you'll probably get a fuckin' commendation." He laughed, "Who knows? It may at least get you off of suspension."

She failed to see any humor at all; but she was very glad Ralph had made the trip over this late at night to see her. It meant a lot.

Wow.

Someone cared.

•

When Megan came through her own front door at just after twelve-thirty in the wee hours of the morning, she was once again greeted with the anxious arms and worried faces of Carol and Linda.

Carol implored, her words spilling out in a flood, "Meg, are you all right? We heard the shot and saw the sirens and people running and the lights and everything and we just stayed inside like you said after we called and..."

Carol's voice trailed off and an awkward silence filled the room.

Linda hesitantly asked, "Did you get him."

Megan sniffed hard, looking down at her toes. "It's over. You can both go home now." It was a command, not a fact.

Carol and Linda both just stood there dumbfounded.

"I'd like some time by myself. I'll talk to you guys later." With that, before Carol and Linda could pour out their heartfelt thanks, Megan went quietly into her bedroom, closed the door and locked it, then fell flat on her bed and began to sob until she fell asleep from exhaustion.

CHAPTER 21

CALCULATIONS AND REVELATIONS

Wednesday
July 3, 2013

Megan didn't get up the next day until almost noon. A horrible empty feeling swirled around inside her head and refused to go away. Her extensive education and training taught her it was merely the routine symptoms of an emotional wound which would literally just take time to heal. That knowledge did little to minimize the pain. Common sense told her the best thing to do was to get her mind off of what happened and busy on something else—as quickly as possible. It turned out to be a good plan; plus it kept her from bursting into tears every few minutes.

She took almost an hour to help Carol and Linda get their things back over to their own apartment, but she refused to go in. The girls graciously understood, but made her promise to meet them at The Stagger Inn later that evening to all get sloppy drunk and sink into a deep pool of forgetfulness. Megan considered this a sound medicinal recommendation as well.

However, the thing which focused her mind the greatest was throwing herself headlong back into her work. The more she allowed herself to concentrate on assimilating the facts and figures which had emerged about Mr. Friday Night—*thankfully*—the more detached she began to feel about everything else. It was perhaps this almost clinical sense of detachment, this complete absorption in rational deduction and logic, which finally led her to the critical break they had all been praying for.

Although, at the time, Megan didn't realize what it was she had found.

It happened shortly after Dominic had come over, just after lunch. He timidly kept his distance, but offered to be of service. Megan had promptly dispatched him over to the Albertson's grocery store to buy her the largest city map of Dallas he could find, a compass, a straight-edged ruler, and a protractor. Spread out all over her small brass and glass coffee table, the picture slowly became clear.

Dominic sat on the sofa watching her transcribe the exact locations from her MAPSCO to the four-by-six foot city map. "So you really think there's a connection between all the locations?"

"Yep," she didn't even look at him, intent on making her measurements as precise as possible.

"Why?" he shrugged. "Wouldn't that be stretching things a bit? That would mean the locations are more important to him than the victims, unless there's something supernatural at work here."

"Exactly," she replied, making a final dot for the Ponce Du Place Hotel where Nancy Calledore was found. "In the area of town he's been striking, there are more than enough locations to choose. He could've gone up to Addison, over to the West End, or down to Deep Ellum. But he didn't. These places *have* to have been selected for a purpose. They are his priority."

Dominic just rolled his eyes. "Okay. So how do you match them up?"

She peeled the thin cardboard backing off the package holding the compass. "With a little geometric engineering, my friend."

Dominic peered at the map, watching her run her finger along the dots, intrigued by what she was doing. "How do you know how big to make the arc if you don't know the center."

"Ah!" she brightened, "The center is what we're looking for. That's the goal, not the beginning. And that's what the arc itself will tell us."

"But you need the center to draw the arc," he sounded contrary.

"No I don't," she contradicted. "I just postulate that it is a continuous arc around one point and then let it tell me where that point is."

Now he was *very* intrigued. "Show me."

"Okay. Watch."

Megan took a pencil and the straight-edged ruler and connected dot number one and dot number four, then drew another line from dot number four to dot number eight. She put the point of the compass down on dot number one, opened the arm a little wider than half the length of the segment she constructed, then drew a light semi-circle, perpendicular to the segment. Without changing the compass's angle, she put the point on dot number four and made another semi-circle in the opposite direction, overlapping the first semi-circle inscribed from point number one. The two semi-circles overlapped at two equidistant points, one on either side of the segment.

"What does that do?" Dominic asked.

"It bisects the segment," she replied, "and points the way to the center."

With that, she picked up her straight edge and drew a long line, first connecting the two points where the semi-circles over lapped, then extending further creating an elongated potential radius of the curve.

"Wow," Dominic ran a hand through his hair. "That's neat."

Megan put the compass point down on dot number eight. "Now, we repeat the procedure and we have a triangulation pointing directly at the true center."

Dominic was dumfounded to see the second radius line cross the first. He registered his skepticism, until she did it twice more, with a small segment from point three to point six, and then a large segment from point one to point eight. All of the radii crisscrossed at the exact same spot.

"Now check this out," Megan challenged. "We'll confirm."

She took the compass and put the point on the intersection of the four radius lines she had created and opened the arm of the compass to point number one. As she swung it slowly toward point eight, the arc of the pencil in the compass neatly touched points two through eight without deviation.

"I'm impressed," Dominic said.

"Told you," Megan smiled.

Dominic wasn't smiling. He swallowed once. "And now you know the center."

Her smile faded as her heart began to pound. "That's right." Her eyes flew down to the map, locking on the defined center point. Theory had momentarily distracted from purpose. "It looks like the northeast corner of Douglass and Potomac. What's there?"

Dominic swallowed, "I don't know."

"Well, let's go find out." Megan was already grabbing her keys car off the breakfast bar next to Bruno's aquarium. In her excitement she failed to notice the aquarium was empty.

•

Megan's car came to an abrupt stop in the dusty parking lot of St. Andrews Episcopalian Church. The tall stone structure stood silent and dark. Long shadows fell from its three-story buttresses. A few of the towering stained glass windows had been broken out. A starling flew out of one window and winged off in the cloudless sky. Weeds grew from the gnarled cracks in the stone steps leading to the entrance. It looked as though it had been abandoned for some time. Megan's heart sank. Was this "his" idea of a joke? To lead her to an old run-down church?

"It's a church," Dominic commented devoid of emotion from the passenger's seat, peeking over the top of his sunglasses.

"Yeah, I can see that." Megan made no attempt to hide her disappointment.

"What do you want to do?" he asked.

She sighed, "We're here. Let's take a look around anyway. All right?"

"Sure," Dominic was already getting out of the car.

It was almost a hundred degrees outside and the humidity was unusually high with very little wind. A city bus spewed the stench of diesel into the air as it roared up Douglass Avenue. Megan's clothes were already sticking to her skin. Dominic's face and armpits were perspiring. Lazy heat waves rose up from the hole-pocked and weed-mottled asphalt parking lot as they walked together up to the tall wooden double-doors of the old Gothic sanctuary, further surprised to find it chained and padlocked shut. A yellowed, weather scarred "For Sale" sign was tacked up at eye level with a telephone number to call if interested in the property.

Megan wiped a layer of dust off the oversized brass door handle with a sweaty finger and huffed in disgust, "No one's been here in years."

"Oh, well," Dominic shrugged. "You want to go...or look around and see what we can find?"

"Come on. We might as well see what's here," Megan lamented. "Like I said, we're already here."

They wandered around the somber atrophied building, staring up at the relic's decaying artisanship and architecture. Megan estimated it must have been quite an impressive structure in its day. When they rounded the corner at the rear of the sanctuary, both of their feet involuntarily picked up speed at the sight of the rusty gate to the churchyard cemetery a few yards away. Megan's heart started to pound again.

There.

The answer was in there. She knew it.

The grave took only a few minutes to locate. There was no mistake. It was the one.

Both Megan and Dominic stood in awe at the foot of the humble granite headstone. Four withered bouquets of long stemmed roses lay at its base, each at a different state of decomposition. Megan could see one had eleven stems, another ten, another nine, the least decayed group with only eight.

"Elmyra Teasdale," she read.

"I wonder who she was," Dominic mused, more to the air than to Megan.

Megan's temples were pounding. Was this it? Had she indeed solved the puzzle and found the missing link to Mr. Friday Night.

She could hardly speak, trembling with excitement, "I'm going to find out."

"How?" Dominic asked.

She shrugged, "I'll go to the court house, look up records. There's got to be a death record for this woman sometime back in 1991."

Dominic smiled. "There's a much easier way."

"How?" she asked.

"Google," he replied.

•

DeWayne T. Bragg threw the day's edition of *The Dallas Morning News* on his desk, making Ralph Weatherstrom jump. He scowled, "Have you seen this shit?"

"Yes, sir," Ralph replied, holding out his hands. "You know we're doing everything we can."

Bragg sat down, "Come on, Ralph. Don't you start sounding like Moranzano on me."

Ralph smiled, "Sorry, sir. But we did get pretty damn close to him last week."

The commissioner huffed, "I heard about that. Your forensic puke got suspended as I recall. Fucked up big time. Busted some dipshit bystander stupid enough to hit on her."

"… uh…something like that," Ralph wasn't very loud.

"Don't get your drawers twisted up in your crack, Ralph. I know what she was doing." Bragg shrugged, "Look. If it'll make you feel better, I was already planning to call the Chief and have him put her back in action. The way I see it, fuck-up or not, she's come a hell of a lot closer than you and that jug-head McManus."

Ralph's cheeks reddened. "I'm sure she'll be pleased to hear that." Charlie, not so much.

Bragg slapped the paper again, "But Weatherstrom, this bullshit press has to stop. And I mean *now*. They're calling for my fucking resignation if we don't turn anything up soon."

Ralph cleared his throat, "We think it's highly likely he may only strike one more time."

"Why?" Bragg demanded.

"A couple of reasons." Ralph opened his notebook and flipped up a page. "First, Dr. Jamison, our beloved shrink, says our boy's been demonstrating a degenerating psychological pattern, which is...how did he say it...here it is... 'which is likely to take a parallel toll on the assailant, lending to suicidal or martyrdom obsessions.' That's it."

"So Jamison thinks he's about to self-destruct?" Bragg was openly incredulous. "That we should be so lucky."

"Well, actually, sir," Ralph closed his notebook and took a deep breath, "I put more faith in Officer Pembrooke's theory which indicates he's running out of places to hunt. I'm willing to support her theory that he's likely to show up at another meat-market dance club called The Inferno this Friday. Only, she believes it may be a set up. Either way, it still looks like it's all about to come to a head."

"How many men do you need?" Bragg picked up his pen to write.

"Five," Ralph answered directly, pleased he didn't have to lobby for them. "I don't want an army or we'll scare him off. I just need all the exits covered. Charlie and I will be inside waiting for him."

"How will you recognize him?" the Commissioner asked.

Ralph raised his brows high, "That's the trick. And that's why Meg needs to be there too."

"It's done," Bragg nodded.

•

A few hours later Police Commissioner DeWayne T. Bragg sat alone at the bar at Dave & Busters, watching all the dapper young suits and painted dollies suck down beers and frou-frou drinks, play shuffleboard or shoot pool. The music was upbeat and festive. It was nice to be around people having fun. He needed it, especially now. The bartender pointed to his empty glass and Bragg nodded, letting him refill his club soda and toss in another fresh wedge of lime.

Despite the lack of progress and the screw-ups in the case, he had complete confidence in Weatherstrom and McManus. They were both hard-working veterans with solid records. Even this new face, this girl Megan Pembrooke, despite taking some unnecessary knocks, seemed to be helping as well. They'd come through.

Eventually?

How could they know why this case was so important to him? The city elections weren't that far away. New budgets were being allocated. His enemies on the city council—which was most of them—wouldn't even bother to piss on him if he was on fire. He was in deep trouble. He needed a win, a big win, not more embarrassment.

Yet, as each week rolled by, as another gruesome Friday night slaying was discovered, the media came out of the woodwork to exact their own pound of flesh—and his ulcer acted up all the more. The public relations spokesmen said all the right things to the legions of reporters, but he knew in his gut the investigators were still no further along than they were on day one. Whoever was doing this was making them look like total incompetents—and doing a *helluva* good job at it. The pressure was taking a savage toll on him physically as well as emotionally. It was the most stressful case of his career. He had even started taking his heart medication again. He inwardly prayed Ralph was right and it was almost over. They really needed a lucky break.

"Hey, old man," a friendly hand touched his shoulder.

"Hey there, fireball," Bragg turned with a forced smile to see his son walk up and slide onto the stool next to him. He could tell by the concerned look in his son's eyes the fatigue in his face showed more than he wanted it to. The last thing he wanted to do was burden his son with worry. Nonetheless, spending time with the young man was a pleasant distraction and a good tonic to relieve much of the stress which constantly plagued him. It was such a welcome change from the distressing years past.

So much had changed over time. Bragg and his son had had their differences years ago—*big* differences, with many hateful words and a ledger full of regrets. But Bragg knew even back then much of the stress gnawing at his soul was job related. He worked so many hours in the early years, night and day, trying to build a career and develop his own fortune. Now it was to maintain all he had built. Richard had been such a headstrong and stubborn boy growing up, just like his mother. Neither of them liked his constant civic activity. It only multiplied the frustrations. Oh, sure he had a hero wall full of accolades to show for it; but at such a costly price. He had loved Richard's mother so much. The image of Sara, his first wife, came to mind. So fair and beautiful with those heart-breaking eyes of hers. She passed away of Leukemia seventeen years ago. She was only thirty-five.

Sara's passing was so hard on both of them for those three years they lived alone. Dealing with the grief, plus trying to be a single parent, was almost more than he could cope with. It wasn't until he met Daphne that his life started to come together again. She was half his age, but she was such a balm. Admittedly, there were still a few points of tension at home. But after Richard graduated from SMU and went off to Harvard Law School things seemed to improve dramatically. In fact, all of their lives seemed to change for the better. That was good. DeWayne desperately needed the peace and quiet.

Daphne was now involved in a great deal of social work, and played the perfect hostess in an unbelievable litany of society functions. Richard was now a successful practicing attorney, and over the last three years the two men had actually developed what could legitimately be called a healthy friendship. The esteemed Commissioner openly sought his son's expert advice, and Richard gave it freely. He was a bright young man. And right now, DeWayne Bragg needed bright minds around him. There was a comforting sense of security in feeling like they were at least doing everything they knew to do to apprehend this mysterious monster stalking the streets of Dallas, plundering an unwitting fair maiden every Friday night.

Richard ordered a Kettle One on the rocks and looked at his father with taut-browed concern, "Dad, are you all right? You look tired."

"I am, son," Bragg lamented, taking another sip of his club soda. "I guess the damn pressure's getting to me again. It's all right. I just gotta take it easy."

"Why don't you take some time off. Hell, dad, you deserve it. Your guys'll get their man," Richard tried to make his dad laugh. "They gotta catch him soon. From everything you've told me, they sure know a hell of a lot about him—shoe size, underwear brand, favorite gum...."

Bragg huffed with a half-laugh, "Yeah. Everything but his fucking address and phone number..." He added, "Oh, and...who he is."

•

"If we get lucky, we might even come up with his name and address," Dominic pecked on the keys of his computer.

"How?" Megan's eyes watched the screen on Dominic's desk as he closed several browser tabs, then brought up the Google home screen.

He grinned, "The Internet has virtually every magazine, newspaper, and regular periodical ever published."

"Great," Megan scooted her chair a little closer to the wide screen.

Dominic typed in the name Teasdale. He looked at Megan once. They exchanged a hopeful look of anticipation as he hit the Return key. A page full of results popped up. One of them was listed as the obituary of Elmyra Teasdale.

"There," Megan pointed. "Pull that up."

"Okay." Dominic clicked on that entry.

A second later the graphic image of a newspaper Obituary flashed up on the screen. Two pairs of hungry eyes devoured it.

Dallas Morning News. July 5, 1991. C-5D
Teasdale, Elmyra Denise — loving and devoted
wife of Herbert Allen Teasdale, was laid to rest
today at St. Andrews Episcopal Church. Mrs.
Teasdale past away yesterday at Methodist Hospital from complications resulting from a tragic fall
down a flight of stairs at her home. Elmyra was a
member of the St. Andrews choir and participated
in many local civic and charity events. She is sur-
vived by her husband Herbert, her son Justin, her
sister Gladys who lives in Euless, a brother in
Texarkana, and many nieces and nephews. Services will be held tomorrow at St. Andrews,
burial to immediately follow. Donations for the
family may be made at the church office…

"Justin Teasdale," Megan whispered, with a trace of reverence. She
could see Dominic's fingers were trembling. "Okay. Find me some more.
Do a search on that name."

The excitement waned a degree when the new search came back with
no further matches other than those already listed.

"Shit," Megan spat, grabbing Dominic's iPhone on the desk. "We're
going to do it my way now." Her index finger stabbed in the digits,
thankful to get a ring instead of a busy signal.

"Who are you calling?" Dominic asked.

She answered his question by directing her call request to the operator
who answered, "Records division, please." She paused giving Dominic a
hopeful smile while the call was transferred. "Hi, who's this? Sergeant Or-
tega, this is Officer Pembrooke. Could you please do a records search on
one Justin Teasdale. I'll take anything. Criminal record. Parking tickets.
Warrants and Priors. Donations to the Policeman's Ball. Hell, I'll take a
driver's license number. Great. I'll wait." She pulled the phone down
while she was put on hold again.

Dominic was pressing more keys. A few seconds later another screen
popped up. Dominic's eyes dove into the results.

A minute later Meg's expression faded, "Really? Well, thanks anyway." She hung up. "Dammit. They've never heard of him."

Dominic pointed at the screen, "Well, take a look at this."

Megan looked at the screen, "What is it?"

"One of the other matches. It was the only entry after the obituary, listed as Teasdale Investigation."

Her eyes were scanning and scanning, then widened with surprise on a passage near the end which read:

> ...officials suspect Mrs. Teasdale's accident wasn't an accident at all. Her husband Herbert, who was out of town on business at the time of the incident, told authorities of the often times violent conflicts between his wife Elmyra and son Justin. These alleged incidents were corroborated by two neighbors. Ten-year-old Justin was brought in by Dallas country authorities for psychiatric evaluation. However, three days ago at Parkland Medical Center he bit an orderly and disappeared from the hospital. To date, officials have not located him, but report...

A follow-up cross-reference indicated that the boy was found two weeks later and spent two years in a juvenile detention center down in Austin under psychiatric care, but no formal charges were ever filed in connection with the accident concerning his mother. At the time of the article he was being placed in foster care. Megan imagined it probably wasn't his last stop. The slurred words of Jesse Phillips rang in Meg's memory about bad little boys never being held accountable by their mothers.

"What do you think?" Dominic asked tentatively.

Megan swallowed hard, "Well, obviously, it would appear we need to find young Master Teasdale before he gets into any more mischief."

CHAPTER 22

TO CASTLE:
A ROOK TAKES THE PLACE
OF A KING

Thursday
July 4, 2013

"Mr. Justin Teasdale?"

"Who are you?" Justin Teasdale asked, waking from a slight slumber and squinting up at a dark silhouette of a tall man standing in the path of the sun. He didn't appreciate anyone disturbing his privacy.

"May I?" without waiting for a reply, the tall gentleman dressed in a dark formal suit tossed his jingling key ring with the gold Porsche emblem into his left front pants pocket as he sat down on the iron deck lounger next to Justin Teasdale.

The two men were completely alone at poolside in the upscale North Dallas apartment complex 11:15 in the morning. He knew they would be. He knew Justin Teasdale liked to sun-bathe between eleven and one almost every day the sun was shining. Samuel said sun-worshipping was only one of Justin's many passions. And to be certain, the tall man had been to the apartments twice before to ensure the meeting could be held in complete privacy.

Actually, the tall man knew a great deal about Justin Teasdale—an incredible amount of information—like the fact that Teasdale made his living as a high-dollar bisexual prostitute. Funnily enough, it was one of the primary qualifications for the project. It ensured a certain propensity to the tasks required, and a sure measure of secrecy. Both were essential to success. Teasdale also lived with two roommates, a pilot and a pharmacist. His apartment was leased in the pilot's name, so Justin had no recorded address. This was necessary to prevent any premature interruption from the authorities. He carried no credit cards and bore no traceable debts. Justin Teasdale was an all but invisible man. That, plus his physical attributes merited his final selection for the project.

He was perfect.

Justin Teasdale lived in the shadows, and certainly wouldn't be missed after he was gone. But such was the case of most who lived their lives on the dark fringe of legality. Now, in all truth, amid the precision execution of the web of painstakingly planned logistics, the tall man was genuinely pleased to finally have the chance to meet the one and only Mr. Justin Teasdale face-to-face.

It seemed only fitting at the end.

"What do you want?" Justin sat up, stretching his tanned, athletic arms in a lethargic yawn. He lifted the top half of the lounger up into a sitting position, clicking the support to its highest setting, and summarily adjusting the long neon-green beach towel back in place after it slipped down behind his back. He wore only a low-rise fire-engine red bikini brief and a pair of Ray-Bans.

The tall man nodded a silent approval. It was uncanny. Teasdale was in fine shape, his skin uniformly darkened. The variance of hue to his own was of no consequence. The only people to ever see him undressed never had the opportunity to mention it to anyone.

The tall man pushed his sunglasses up on his nose with his left forefinger while holding out his right hand for a formal introduction, "You can call me Larry. Larry...Taylor." He suppressed the urge to laugh. It was as good a name as any.

Justin took his hand, "Do I know you, Mr. ... *Taylor?*"

"We have a mutual friend," the faux Mr. Larry Taylor replied. "Samuel Ferndale?"

Justin grinned, "Ah, old Sammy. Hey, you know, that little bitch was supposed to call me this week so we could get together." He looked Mr. Taylor over from head to toe with a sudden renewed interest in his handsome visitor. "You're a *friend* of Sammy's?"

The tall man smiled politely, "We've had some *business* dealings. As a matter of fact, he's out of town this week on business on my behalf. I assume you received his message about my proposition? He did mention that I was coming today, yes?"

Justin gave him a blank stare.

"Oh, I'm so sorry," the tall man feigned embarrassment well. "Then this much seem most awkward for you. Please accept my sincere apologies." The tall man checked his watch. "Well, now that I'm here, if I could trouble you for a few moments? This will only take a moment." He paused slightly, giving polite opportunity for objection.

None was offered.

He continued, "You see, Mr. Teasdale, Samuel *highly* recommended you for a very special project I'm doing. Something I believe you'd be very interested in."

"What kind of project?" Justin asked with a trace of apprehension, a little dismayed at the thought of not seeing Ferndale that Friday. He paid extra well. Three hundred a night minimum. Sometimes more.

The man unbuttoned his double-breasted jacket and loosened his tie. Even before noon the temperature was already above ninety. "You see, I'm a film maker, Mr. Teasdale. And I need someone who exactly fits your description, with your *professional* qualifications, for a very particular role. It's very important to me."

"Porno flick," Justin said matter-of-fact.

"Adult entertainment, you might say," the fictitious Mr. Taylor smiled with enthusiasm. "But of a very unique variety, to say the least."

"What do you mean?" Justin leaned over on one elbow. "I've done a few fuck flicks. Nothing too hard core. Just stupid stuff." He wasn't that interested. "Are we talking girls or guys or what?"

Larry Taylor lowered his voice slightly. "Let's just say it's a *spontaneous* erotic film, more in keeping with a hidden camera type theme."

"What?" Justin Teasdale started to laugh. "What do you want me to do?"

The tall man chuckled, "Quite simply, I want you to seduce a total stranger and bring her to a specially arranged apartment for the shoot. There will be hidden cameras all over the place, then—"

"So it *is* babes?" Justin interrupted, wanting to make sure he understood that point clearly.

"Oh, yes," Taylor affirmed, holding his condescension in check. "*Babes*, as you say. Or *babe*, singular, in this instance. I only require one woman. And when you've secured an appropriate participant, I want you to bring her to the master bedroom where, as I say, there will be a vast array of very discreetly positioned cameras at various angles and cinematic perspectives. There I want you to completely and totally seduce her. I'll be filming it all."

Teasdale looked side to side, ensuring they were alone. "This is just a private film. Isn't it?"

"What do you care?" the tall man asked.

"Cause I don't want to get in any trouble," Justin insisted.

"You won't," Taylor assured him. "But your insights serve you well, Mr. Teasdale. You're right, it is a *private* film." He smiled, "Just between you and me, I like to watch. And I have some rather...*unique* tastes..." The smile faded, "...and I can assure you, no one will ever see it but me."

"I don't know. Sounds pretty weird, dude. How much we talkin' about here? This sounds like I could get nailed if the wrong parties saw it—*if*, you know what I mean." Justin nodded like he knew what he was talking about. He might consider doing it for a thousand.

"Well, your compensation depends entirely on how successful you are," the tall man replied. "First of all, the young lady absolutely *must* be a complete and total stranger. I'll check on the young lady's credentials afterward, and if it's a set-up you forfeit all bonuses."

"Bonuses?" Justin raised a skeptical brow above the edge of his sunglasses.

"Oh, yes," the man nodded without emotion, reaching into his breast pocket, removing a thick legal-sized envelope, and holding it up. "I pay you ten thousand dollars today, in cash of course, for acceptance of my offer."

Justin Teasdale pulled his glassed off. His eyes went wide and his heart began to pound.

Did he say ten-thousand? Dollars?

The man in the suit continued, "If you are successful in picking up a young lady at the particular establishment I specify, and successfully bring her to the prearranged apartment, I pay you an additional five thousand. If you can get her in the master bedroom and undressed, you get another five thousand. If you can...*handcuff* her to the brass bed, another *ten*-thousand. There will be four pairs of cuffs available. I want both hands and feet secured. And then for every unique sex act you can think of, and successfully perform thereafter, I'll pay you an additional ten thousand dollars. No limit. Orgasms by either party are optional, but carry an additional one thousand dollars bonus each. We'll have the entire interlude on tape to assure accurate accounting."

Justin Teasdale's mouth was hanging open in complete shock. He never graduated from high school, but he could certainly add. His palms came out in front of him, fingers wide. "Let me get this straight. If I pick up some chick, *any* willing chick, and take to your place, shackle her down, and pump her lights out, you're going to give me forty grand or more?"

"Your math skills serve you well, Mr. Teasdale," his rich cultured voice intoned. "As I said, no financial limits whatsoever. You shall be restricted only by the limits of your charm and your talents. I think with a little creative imagination, you could easily garner yourself perhaps as much as a hundred thousand dollars for just a few hour's work. So what do you say?"

"I don't have to snuff her, do I?" Justin teased, half-laughing.

The man returned his chuckle. "Don't be silly." He wouldn't dare let anyone else have the privilege.

"Okay!" Teasdale eagerly held out his hand, still in disbelief over his good fortune. "I'm in. When?"

"Soon," the tall man shook Justin's hand politely. "Tomorrow night, in fact."

"Wow. Right away. Well, all right. I'm in," Justin grinned. "Where do we meet?"

The tall man leaned forward. "All in due time, my friend. All in due time. But we have a great deal of work and preparation to do before the actual event. We have security card issues and procedures to discuss. Time tables to go over. Plus, you absolutely must be properly costumed for my film. Please go and get dressed and we'll attend to that detail right away. As an added extra bonus, I'm going to have you fitted for a new suit. It will be yours to keep, naturally. We have an appointment for a fitting this very afternoon. So please be prompt. I'll be waiting for you out front in the black Porsche."

CHAPTER 23

MIRROR IMAGES

Friday
July 5, 2013

Friday night. It was almost 11:00 P.M. Dallas, Texas was dressed to kill. The energetic lights of the city blossomed to celebrate the end of another week's profitable toil. The young, nouveau-riche stepped under the kaleidoscope shower of lights to dance, to laugh, and to indulge their infinite passions: a well-fed herd gathered at the watering holes.

The predators waited in the shadows.

Megan Pembrooke stood nervous in front of the bathroom mirror in the ladies room at The Inferno Club touching up her make-up. They had been there since nine o'clock. She could barely hold her hand still to draw a straight line with her eye-liner. Her brilliant mind was a voracious tornado of disjointed thoughts and misplaced anxieties. Was she ready to face this? Were any of them? Were the theories sound? Had they considered everything? Would he really show up? How would they know him? And where the hell was Bruno?

Bruno was missing. It wasn't that big a crisis. It had happened before. He'd scamper off and turn up in a couple of days when he got really hungry and couldn't find any crickets, roaches, or moths. Regardless, Megan was worried sick, and it only added to the queasiness bubbling within her. She moved over to a vacant stall and peed for the fourth time in two hours.

This particular Friday night had descended upon them all far too soon. Even the date sounded a loud chord in her mind. July fifth: the very same day Elmyra Teasdale was buried in St. Andrews churchyard. The macabre tragedy drew ever nearer to its sordid finale. Nothing could stop it now. It was here.

On the way out of the restroom Megan Pembrooke stopped and looked at herself in the mirror one more time, catching the hard, determined gaze staring back. Her nerves were still humming like a downed power line after a storm. But there was no turning back. Not now. She knew she could do it. She had done what she had to do to help her friends, and she'd do what she had to do now.

...just...the wind...

Taking in one more deep breath, she walked back out in the midst of the pressing throng. The loud dance music, the lights, a thousand voices, and the smoke and perfumed air swallowed her the minute the door swung open. Ralph Weatherstrom was waiting for her at the small round table where she left him. He seemed more ill at ease than she was.

"You know, we might get lucky just by carding everyone who comes in," Ralph stated flatly above the thundering music at The Inferno as Megan sat back down.

He could hardly sit still, his eyes darting to and fro every second. As far as he was concerned, The Inferno looked just like every other neon plastic nightclub he'd ever been into. It was quite a bit larger than most of them, but decked out like all the rest. Four bars lined each wall on the lower level. Two more were upstairs. The upstairs was really more of a horseshoe shaped balcony which hemmed the enormous dance-floor. An amazing collection of used and antique musical instruments lined the edge of the balcony. They were mostly old electric guitars: Fender Stratocasters, Gibson Les Pauls, a Gretch, two Beatles vintage Rickenbackers, a beat up old yellow Kramer striped with dirty adhesive tape and signed by Eddie Van Halen, two new Ibanez models, and even an old Gibson Chet Atkins special autographed by Roy Clark. In between the guitars were a shiny array of saxophones, from soprano to tenor; trumpets and fluegel-horns, clarinets and flutes, violins and a nasty-looking finger-stained pair of bongos. Apparently celebrity patrons donated them when in town performing.

Ralph remembered coming in this place back in the seventies when it was a disco and the dance floor had lights beneath it. Now it was polished hardwood, and the dizzying display of lights were nested above it. The lights were the same confusing array of spinning wheels, bright green lasers, and colored LED pots that every other club deemed standard equipment these days. However, to complement the Hades/Perdition theme of the club, most of the lights were red; and far too often for Ralph's taste, thick clouds of gray smoke would billow out from four smoke machines at each corner of the dance floor. A DJ station was located behind an angled glass window at the back of the dance floor, elevated about six feet above the fray. The DJ on duty tonight was gracious enough not to ratchet-jaw between *every* song, but kept the music continuous to the delight of the jubilant patrons.

Megan took a sip of her ginger-ale. She desperately wanted an ice cold beer—*but no*—she was on duty. She leaned forward and raised her voice to be heard, "You really think we're just going to card him? Like he would use his own ID? Come on, Ralph. You know as well as I do, he's led us here by the nose. I don't see him screwing up over something that trivial."

Ralph just shrugged. They had already issued a citywide APB for one: Justin Teasdale. They both knew that it was another waste of time. Megan wanted to make a television announcement on all the local stations to enlist the public's help in locating him. Someone knew who Justin Teasdale was. But legally they couldn't. They couldn't risk another false arrest. Justin Teasdale's guilt was still just another theory—and a pretty farfetched one at that.

After a thorough DMV cross-check, they did manage to discover Teasdale had a three-year-old driver's license, the only document their computers listed with that name. Unfortunately, the address was a small apartment over in Fort Worth. A SWAT Team had raided the place earlier that morning, only to find he had moved away two years ago. He left no forwarding address, naturally. Thus, they had no choice but to stake out The Inferno according to Megan's plan.

If he showed, they were ready. Two detectives were stationed at each of the two entrances, wearing Inferno T-shirts, masquerading as bouncers. Charlie McManus was in a back room control booth with the club's own security team watching the crowd on a wall of closed-circuit monitors. They were all in communication via state-of-the-art FM radio micro-miniature ear pieces and lapel-pin mikes obtained that morning from the local Secret Service division down at the Treasury Department in the Federal Building. Commissioner Bragg had called in a favor to make that happen.

Fortunately, the management of the club was being extra cooperative, even if it meant the possibility of closing early and losing a little Friday night revenue. Ralph and Charlie were most gracious to the manager and the owner, pretending to believe the management's help was due to their civic-mindedness, rather than from direct orders from their attorney concerning law suits should anyone get hurt on the premises. It didn't matter. The job would get done one way or another.

"What do you *really* think is going to happen, Meg?" Ralph sincerely wanted to know. "I feel so stupid and out of place just sitting here."

Megan thought long and hard before answering. "I think he's going to surprise us. Or at least, he desperately wants to. I can feel it. But somehow, we're going to get our shot at him tonight. We just have to be ready."

"I know," Ralph nervously looked down at his well-chewed fingernails for the tenth time in as many minutes. "That's what bothers me." He laughed, shaking off a flutter of nerves, "Only this time, let's make sure it's the right guy."

Megan nodded, "Definitely."

If she was honest with herself, Megan had no business being there that night. Inside she was still an emotional wreck. Her suspension from the force had been lifted that morning by direct order of Commissioner Bragg, but not without the loud protestations of Chief Moranzano, who made it very clear to her he had a long and indelible memory—especially when it came to Mavericks and flagrant violation of proper police procedure.

Actually, the brief meeting with the Police Commissioner had been most pleasant. She knew of his bad reputation, but after her own firsthand experience, Megan didn't feel it was warranted. Yes, he was a little coarse around the edges, but he was most courteous and complimentary. He told her straight out that he recognized her considerable efforts in the case; and even when the department missed a step, like in the incident with poor Mr. VanGoren from San Francisco, he understood it was in the line of duty trying to get the job done. He said he liked that kind of initiative; and consequently, she liked him.

And just like Ralph, she had been very impressed with his wall of accomplishments. Megan didn't even feel like she was brown-nosing when she complimented him on the handsome picture of his family. He was a lucky man, even though she could tell that inwardly he was a very troubled man. But outwardly, Bragg was gracious and expressed his thanks openly. Nonetheless, the sinking feeling in Meg's stomach told her it was going to take a long time before Chief Moranzano did anything but scowl and curse when he saw her coming.

Poor Dominic, bless his heart, was trying his best to be so cheery and helpful, but he had degenerated into a complete pest. He even wanted to come on the operation that night. Megan forbid it. Although, knowing him, she figured he was probably outside somewhere in his little red Toyota pick-up, watching the entrance, worrying, and panting like a puppy.

In a way she realized it was kind of sweet. She hated herself for being so abrupt with him earlier that very evening. He insisted that he had a surprise for her that he wanted to show her—something so important it couldn't wait, something for both of them he had been working on for a long time. She had to be positively rude about saying no, promising him

180

she'd see it later, perhaps tomorrow. But by the look in his eye, she knew tomorrow morning she'd be apologizing for hurting his feelings.

Megan glanced at her watch. It was exactly 11:15. If he wasn't here already, somewhere in the dense crowd, he'd be here soon. For now, all they could do was silently watch and wait.

•

The tall man answered the door at the Carlisle Tower apartment, two blocks over from The Inferno nightclub on McKinney Avenue. He looked at his Rolex. It was 11:20. Right on time.

"Good evening," he smiled at Justin Teasdale, who was eagerly standing in the hall.

"Hi. Am I late?" Teasdale was wearing the navy blue custom tailored double-breasted suit the tall man had purchased for him yesterday. Even the fragrance of Aramis announced his presence, as instructed. He looked perfect.

"No, not at all," he replied, opening the door wide and inviting his special guest into the lavish accommodation. "This way, please."

He directed Teasdale into the living room. It was a cavernous, but comfortable chamber with beautifully vaulted ceilings. The far wall was a series of French-styled glass arches, with fan-shaped panes, overlooking an ornate wrought-iron-railed balcony. The fifteenth floor view of the downtown Dallas skyline was unequaled anywhere in the city. A wide stone fireplace hugged the left wall, flanked by floor to ceiling built-in mahogany bookshelves, lined with an attractive collection of leather bound volumes, brass knick-knacks, and various colorful trinkets. A wide, inset marble wet-bar adorned the wall to the right. Also on the right-hand wall was a hand-hewn stone archway which led to a small Spanish tile hallway and the rear bedrooms. The tall man strode over to the wet bar and lifted a bottle of Vodka, expertly mixing two martinis.

He handed Justin one of them, "Let me hear you repeat it all once more."

Teasdale nodded, "Okay, with my new Louis Vuitton shades on, I go downstairs in the elevator and wave and the guard at the desk again and use the security card to get out. I walk down to McKinney and use the ID card you gave me, just in case I'm carded, and then hit The Inferno. At the club I order myself a James Bond special: Vodka martini on the rocks, shaken not stirred. Then I score myself a babe, who can't be a friend or a whore, and then be back here no later than twelve thirty. I got the key and security card you gave me to get back in."

"Excellent," the tall man replied as he walked toward the archway. "Follow me, please, Justin."

The tall man led Justin to the master bedroom suite. It was even more spacious than the living room, its own ceiling fifteen feet tall and artistically molded in with a turn-of-the-century Parisian motif. A king sized brass bed was the most eye-catching furnishing in the room, with tall brass corner posts and a bone white gossamer canopy crowning its top. A six-foot by four-foot beveled glass mirror hung on the wall opposite the bed in broad portrait-styled gilded frame. Beneath it stood a wide, waist-high dresser which matched the nightstands on either side of the bed. On top of the dresser stood a crystal vase displaying a dozen fresh long-stemmed red roses.

The man pointed at the mirror, "It's two way. The camera is set up behind there in the spare bedroom. Please do be considerate of the angles. The handcuffs are in the top drawer of the nightstand." He walked over and opened the upper drawer of the two drawer white Queen Anne piece and pulled out one of the pairs of cuffs, demonstrating the twelve-inch length of the connecting chain. "Don't worry, the keys are also in here for later." He pointed back to the bed. "Be sure your fair young maiden is centered on the bed for the best cinematographic perspective. Yes? You can attach the cuffs to any of the spindles of the headboard and foot board. They should all reach quite nicely."

"Got it," Teasdale nodded.

The man walked up to Justin, their eyes were at the exact same level, "Well then, my dear Mr. Teasdale, are you ready?"

Justin smiled, "Can't wait."

"Then you'd best be on your way," the tall man instructed.

Justin nodded with confidence, "I won't let you down."

"I know you won't," the man replied with a broad smile as Justin shook his hand and left.

After Justin Teasdale had gone, the tall man walked over to the bedroom closet and opened it. He brought a hat box down from the closet shelf and carefully set it on the bed. From inside he removed a Gen 4 Glock 19, 9mm semiautomatic pistol. He hit the magazine ejector, and checked the ammunition, ensuring that all thirteen rounds were loaded. Satisfied, he shoved the magazine back in place. He lifted another object wrapped with a white cloth. He grabbed one corner of the cloth and the weight of the object caused it to roll free and fall in his lap. It was a six-inch cylindrical silencer. He carefully screwed it into the muzzle of the Glock. Also in the box was a much smaller box, about the size of a paperback book, wrapped with bright silver foil and a green ribbon. A present.

She'd love it. The sight of it made him laugh. He couldn't resist. This was all such grand fun.

He stood and slipped the gun behind his back, securing it in the waistband of his trousers. It was time to go. He buttoned his jacket, then picked up the little present. With a confident stride and a smile on his lips he left the apartment, and headed toward the elevators. He too would be at The Inferno for Act I of tonight's little drama.

The curtain was just going up.

CHAPTER 24

FIVE MOVES TO MATE

Friday
July 5, 2013

Lynn Evans was a reasonably attractive blond, and a bookkeeper by day. Her mother told her she drank too much, and she often told her mother to go to hell with no reservation. Lynn sat alone at the bar in The Inferno nightclub, hoping something really exciting would happen that night. It had to. She needed something special—*something wicked*—after everything that had happened. She had just broken up with her boyfriend Kevin two and a half weeks ago, and couldn't bear sitting home alone for another weekend.

Broken up? Is that what she told herself?

No, she got dumped, like Arlo Guthrie's VW microbus full of Alice's Restaurant garbage. He just showed up and said it was all over. Simple as that. Just took his shit and left. After *two* years. It was all just...*over*. But even that wasn't true. She knew the two-faced lying-assed bastard was seeing that dried up slut Tanya Blakley.

Whore. Tramp. Bitch.

Lynn bristled with rage even at the thought of Tanya's name. The revolting image of Kevin and Tanya commingling together made her positively nauseous. She'd show him. If she had her way she'd land the finest looking, richest, smartest, most charming guy in town—that very night, if possible. And when she did, she'd show that guy the best time of his life—better than Kevin Culvert ever *dreamed* about.

"Vodka martini, please. On the rocks."

Lynn turned and saw the handsome gentleman standing next to her, ordering his drink.

Wow... This one would do in a heartbeat.

She leaned forward slightly to catch his eye.

He gave her a sideways glance and tossed her a devilishly disarming smile, "Hello there."

"Hi," she raised her eyebrows and folded her shoulders forward with obvious interest. He was certainly handsome enough. And that suit said he was rich enough. Time to go to work.

Lynn was decked out in a brand new black and white party dress she found at Neiman's at Valley View that afternoon. It was outrageously expensive, but she felt like after what she had just been through, she deserved it. It was cut low, slit up the side, built for speed—styled explicitly to attract a lot of attention—that is, the right *caliber* of attention. At that moment she felt like she was definitely getting her money's worth.

"May I get you something?" he asked.

"Sure," she revealed an even row of white teeth, framed by warm, wet ruby red lips.

He signaled the bartender, who promptly refilled her wine glass with a house White Zinfandel. Justin Teasdale continued to engage his target in small talk, confident he would be collecting his money even before midnight. This was too easy.

•

From the balcony above, the tall man watched the interaction between Justin Teasdale and his attractive new acquaintance, most pleased his task was proceeding so promptly. He had chosen well. She would do nicely. He had no doubt everything would go superbly. Justin was a most capable fellow, handsome and outgoing. He was chosen on that basis.

Well, hello there...

The tall man was further amused when he noticed Officer Megan Pembrooke and Detective Ralph Weatherstrom seated at a small table near the dance floor. They stuck out like such sore thumbs. Ralph was old enough to be her father. They both appeared to be so visibly uncomfortable. Although, she looked exceptionally attractive this evening. Yes, dear sweet Megan. The red lights bubbled and boiled in a fresh puff of fog. Ralph was coughing. He laughed.

Amazing.

What did they possibly hope to observe? Until he chose to make himself known he was quite invisible. Then again, as he stood there watching, they weren't really looking at *anything* at the moment. They appeared to be in fervent discussion among themselves. The temptation to go down and ask her to dance was almost overwhelming. No. Couldn't do that. However, what he had planned would be just as effective—and infinitely more entertaining.

•

"Meg, this is stupid," Ralph scowled. "I believed everything you said. *Everything!* But we don't even know who we're looking for!"

"I know," she admitted. "I just feel like I have to be here. Somehow he'll show himself. He has to. He's led us here for a reason. It's pretty basic, Ralph. His ego won't let him leave before his purpose here is successfully carried out."

"So the ball's in his court?" Ralph challenged.

"Yeah," she nodded.

"And so we just sit here on our asses, getting a headache and suffocating?" He desperately wanted to go outside and get some air.

"Yes," she raised her voice above a sudden swell in the music. "Until he makes his move, all we can do is wait. You know the drill. When he shows, we alert the team. There's only two doors on this place. If he shows at all, we've got him. All we have to do is close the bar, then go through every inch of it till we filter him out. Petty basic stuff, you know?"

Ralph nodded, "Yeah. Pretty basic. But this waiting is killing me. I can't just sit here. I gotta get some air."

"You and me both," she shot back. Her eyes scanned the bars again. Everywhere she looked, attractive men in suits were talking to young ladies. Were any of these pairs Mr. Friday Night and victim number five?

•

"So you're an attorney?" Lynn Evans cooed.

"Yes," Justin lied. "I graduated from Princeton in eighty-six. Been practicing here in Dallas for almost three years now. Love it here. I just got myself a beautiful place right here in the area, over at the Carlisle Tower. Do you know it?"

Did she? It was only one of the most prestigious and beautiful high rises in the city. "Yes, I think I've heard the name before. Do you like it there?"

"It's great," he babbled on. "Got a great view of town. It's up on the fifteenth floor. Wet-bar. Jacuzzi." He hoped it had a Jacuzzi. "The works. You should drop by sometime. I'd love to show it to you. I think you'd really like it."

"I'd love to," her smile broadened.

He lowered his voice and leaned down close to her ear, "You know, you really should see it at night. The city lights are positively mesmerizing. It's very romantic."

Lynn swallowed hard. "Sounds great."

He looked at his watch. It was 11:53 P.M. For time and bonus sake he needed to know if this one was a go or no go. "You know, I'm really getting kind of tired of this noise. My place is only a short walk from here. Could I interest you in a quiet nightcap? Perhaps some champagne?"

A rush of felon's guilt surged up Lynn's spine, but it quickly faded as the grinning face of Kevin Culvert holding Tanya in his arms flashed across her mind.

"What are we waiting for?"

•

The tall man in the balcony checked his watch when he saw the attractive blond take Justin's arm and head for the door. It was 11:55 P.M. Perfect. Ahead of schedule in fact. Excellent. Step one complete.

Time for step two.

After he was certain Teasdale and his pretty young date were safely gone, he summoned a long-legged cocktail waitress carrying a round tray overloaded with drinks. Still standing at the balcony rail, he pointed down to Megan and Ralph's table. He handed the young lady a hundred-dollar bill, "Do you see that young woman down there with the older gentleman? The woman there in the green dress?"

"Yes, sir." She had his complete attention, despite the urgent calls from other tables.

"First of all, my dear, before you anything else, would you be so kind as to bring me a glass of your absolute finest champagne," his voice was so rich and smooth.

"Certainly sir," she replied. This one was sure to get a napkin with her phone number on it.

He handed her the silver wrapped present with the green bow, "After you've fetched me my drink, then I'd dearly like you to go down and deliver this little token of my affection to the young lady down there. Would that be too much trouble?" He tossed another hundred on her tray.

"My pleasure, sir." She took the package. "Who shall I say it's from?"

He grinned, "She'll know. But please be so kind as to point up this way." He grabbed her arm as she started to leave, his eyes sternly commanding, "But not until after she's opened it. Understand?"

"Yes, sir," she returned his broad smile, enjoying being part of romantic gestures. "I'll be right back with your champagne."

He looked over the rail. Megan's eyes were still scanning the crowds along the bar rails and in the shadows, where the routine mating games were played. Such a two dimensional thinker, he mused.

•

"What time is it?" Megan asked, noticing Ralph looking at his watch for the hundredth time.

"Twelve-oh-five," he looked up and gave her a disheartened look. "Your boy may be a no show."

Her face twisted up, "No! I can't believe it. We have to keep waiting. Just a little longer."

Ralph leaned down toward his lapel mike. "All units report in."

All three teams chimed in his ear piece with a noticeable trace of boredom in their voices.

"Fuck you, Ralph," Charlie's voice cut in from the control room. "This ain't working. Let's call it a night and get out of here. Pembrooke's going to make us all look like assholes again."

"All units just stand by," Ralph harshly fired back, thankful Megan wasn't wearing a receiver.

"Miss?" a female voice interrupted.

Megan turned to see the young waitress from upstairs standing behind her. "Yes?"

The waitress handed the silver package with the green bow to Meg, "This is for you."

"What?" Megan looked around the bar once more, her face flushing red. "Why? What is this? Who's it from?"

"From your secret admirer, I guess," the waitress replied with a grin. "Go on. You're supposed to open it."

Ralph leaned over the table to see what was going on. He spoke into his lapel, "All units, alert." He had a bad feeling.

Megan hastily pulled the ribbon off and lifted the lid of the box, not considering the fact that it might be ticking. Fortunately, beneath the lid lay a plain three-by-five index card atop a thick layer of jeweler's cotton. On the card was a brief note. She quickly read the neatly typed card, doing her best to remain calm.

It simply read:

My Dearest Megan,

I won't be in need of this tonight. It's entirely inadequate to the task. But I trust you will add it, and a few other enclosed tokens of my affection, to your collection of memorabilia about me. I'm sorry to say farewell. But I'm afraid I must bid you adieu. I'm going home now, and regrettably, won't be seeing you ever again.

Yours Always,
J.T.

Megan's fingers anxiously snatched up the cotton. Beneath it was the closed lock-back knife laying on a bottom layer of cotton. The cotton batting was stained with the dark brown hue of dried blood. Four long, thin, shriveled pieces of dried tissue about two inches long, resembling pieces of beef jerky, were neatly tucked in the corners of the box.

Oh, Good God Almighty…

Her thoughts instantly knew what they were—his hideous souvenirs ripped from the body of Mandy Holden-Worth. Meg's hand flew over her mouth. The wrenching aversion of her gaze was the only thing which prevented her from violently retching.

Ralph jumped to his feet.

The petite police officer was on her feet in the next second, her hand gasping the front of the surprised waitress' blouse in a powerful claw, yanking the startled girl's face close. The waitress' tray spilled to in a crash of glass and beverages. A few drunk bystanders applauded.

Megan bellowed in the girl's face, "Where is he!"

The frightened and confused young girl tried to pull back, pointing above. "There. The tall guy up there."

Ralph spun around, looking high.

Megan's heart skipped a beat when her eyes scorched up to the balcony. Twenty feet above and fifty feet across the dance floor, above the ring of classic guitars and other instruments, amid the haze of smoke, fog, and the ominous red lights—

There he was.

All she could really see was a tall male figure standing at the rail, holding out a long-stemmed champagne flute. He lifted it in a silent toast to her and took a long sip. With flamboyant panache he held the glass over the rail for a teasing instant, and then let it fall. To Megan it seemed to descend in slow motion, falling almost completely vertical. The delicate goblet exploded on the hardwood of the dance floor in a shower of glass and white foam. Startled dancers jumped back in fright and anger. Megan's eyes flew back up to the balcony.

He was gone.

"Get him," Megan shouted at Ralph.

"Lock it down," Ralph bellowed into his mike. "We got him."

Megan still had the poor waitress in her grip, "Come on. You're coming with me, honey. You're going to point him out for me, up close and personal."

In less than ten seconds the front door was closed and bolted tight. The rear team in the kitchen had already bolted the back door. It was only opened when a card-carrying employee had a need to use it. However, Charlie McManus in the control booth reported no sign of the man in the balcony. It didn't matter. Ralph knew there was no other way out. And their boy didn't have time to get out otherwise. They'd done it. The trap had finally snapped shut on Mr. Friday Night.

But it was no time to celebrate. The danger was far from over. There were too many potential hostages and victims. The house lights came on and the music was abruptly stopped. The crowded throng of patrons became still in an tense air of alarm. Ralph suddenly became nervous. The last thing in the world they needed was panic. People would die.

He raised his voice, holding out his badge and walking to the middle of the dance floor, "Ladies and gentleman." He yelled louder, "Ladies and gentlemen may I have your attention please!"

The buzz of voices sweeping across the crowd slowly diminished with each of Ralph's urgent appeals. A few drunken catcalls were thrown out amid shouts of irritation and inconvenience. Ralph thought about firing a round into the ceiling, but decided against it. In all likelihood, considering the part of town they were in, someone in the crowd would return fire. "Ladies and gentlemen, *please*, we need your complete and total cooperation. We need you to please remain calm. I'm sorry, but the club is now closed. Please leave in an orderly fashion."

Megan dragged the frightened waitress to the front entrance where a long line of angry and frustrated faces were already waiting restlessly to be allowed to leave. She instructed the two detectives to let patrons out one at a time, only after the waitress had ensured it wasn't the man who had given her the present. The detectives, Megan, and the waitress formed a small gauntlet and began the slow process. Ralph joined her, and all four police officers stood there, weapons in hand, carefully scrutinizing each face and body as it past.

Instinctively, Megan knew in all probability, after everyone was gone, they'd have to find him hiding somewhere inside. That was all right. Ei-

190

ther way it was just a matter of time.

What she didn't know was that he'd already left the building.

•

From the moment the champagne glass hit the dance floor, signaling the completion of Step Two, the tall man was already initiating Step Three. He quickly made his way into the upstairs men's room and entered the last stall. With all the commotion outside, the bathroom quickly emptied. He stepped up on the toilet seat and lifted the smoke-stained acoustical tile in the ceiling and removed the canvass gym bag he had placed there the day before. It contained a complete change of clothes: a pair of black slacks, black Nike running shoes, and one of the red souvenir T-shirts worn by the bouncers at the nightclub. He wadded up his suit, shirt, tie, along with his shoes and stuffed them into the canvass gym bag.

Slipping discreetly out of the bathroom, he made his way down a rear set of stairs and walked down to the kitchen. It too was a bee-hive of confusion. The regular bouncers didn't know him, and assumed him to be one of the Dallas detectives. The detectives guarding the back door didn't recognize him and assumed him to be one of the regular bouncers. Without drawing any undue attention to himself, he dropped the canvass bag into the trash chute, which would be compacted and buried in a landfill within a week.

The tall man then proceeded into the storage room and quietly closed the door. Climbing the rear set of wooden shelves, he pushed up another acoustical tile and crawled up into the false ceiling. The tile was replaced without any evidence of disturbance.

It was thus a simple matter of crawling across the half-wall over the Chinese restaurant next door and dropping down into their kitchen. The restaurant closed at 10:00 P.M., and everyone was always gone no later than 11:30. There was no alarm system. He'd checked carefully. However, his Glock was waiting in the ceiling above the restaurant, just in case someone decided to work late. There were always contingencies to be planned for. More likely than not, some poor employee would probably get chastised or fired the next day when they discovered the back door unlocked.

The black Porsche was parked only a few feet beyond the Chinese restaurant's rear door. Even as he climbed into his car, he knew the police would be cordoning off the streets to search cars for a five block radius. That was fine. He only had to drive two blocks.

Step Three complete. Time for Step Four: the fun part.

There was still plenty of time. The Inferno would be thoroughly searched for at least two hours. By 2:00 A.M. they would initiate the house-to-house hard-target search, following the mapped curve. Miss Pembrooke surely knew the curve, otherwise they wouldn't have been there at all that night. Yes. Hostile invaders could be expected to storm the Carlisle Tower any time after 3:00 A.M. The old fossil of a security guard would positively verify the Teasdale residence, but wouldn't allow access, not even to the police. Search warrants would take another hour or two to obtain, waking up amiable judges in the middle of the night and such.

They'd find the bodies just before dawn.

But alas, too late again. Despite the amount of work involved, it would all be over before 3:00 A.M. It was time to get to it.

He couldn't wait.

CHAPTER 25

THE STORM

Friday
July 5, 2013

The storm approached—cruel cumulonimbus battalions, robed in black, advancing to the battlefield from the south, heralded by the crisp howl of the wind through the streets. The traffic lights and street signs swayed. Awnings flapped. Flags stood straight, quivering along the fringe. Pedestrians moved faster to find their cars or reach their destinations. The distant drums of thunder echoed over the horizon.

Inside The Inferno, one by one, the disgruntled patrons marched past Megan and the trembling waitress. Half of them were already gone. Ralph and Charlie had already started searching the club from top to bottom, suspecting he might be inside hiding somewhere. The crowd was painfully aware they were hunting for someone. Fortunately, the sight of the police moving about with weapons drawn had a welcome sobering effect. The people obediently pressed toward the exits and patiently waited their turn to leave and find their cars with a sense of relief.

Standing in the doorway Megan was getting more and more frustrated with each passing moment. The wind pushed her long brown hair over her shoulder. It sent a shudder through her. She didn't like the wind. Her mind was whirling again, the gears meshing and picking up speed. The machine tabulated with a fluttering twinge behind her eyes.

Something was wrong.

What was it? Would he have suspected a trap? Would he have known this vulnerability? Of course he would. Would he merely hide? Hell no, he'd surely be found. And he'd know that too.

Think, Pembrooke. Think.

Her thoughts focused, the incredible organic mechanism between her ears picking up RPMs. *What would you do if you were him?* Only two doors. And an eye witness. He's trapped. *Therefore*—he'd have planned another way out. Yes. In every gambit, there's always an escape. Just like Dominic finding the bishop move. If studied carefully enough, a way could possibly be found—but if planned for—*always* found.

He's gone—and we're wasting time.

But where would he go? Megan violently spun around, looking outside into the night. The wind caressed her face now, scented with the approaching swell of rain. She remembered his flamboyant three-by-five note: *Home.* Ralph's words from days ago flashed across her mind:

It's the end of the trail. There are no more hotels or nightclubs in that direction. It's all residential. Just big old houses and few apartment buildings.

Residential.

Almost involuntarily she was walking out into the middle of McKinney Avenue, adjusting her canvass shoulder bag up a little higher and more secure on her shoulder as the wind licked at her skirt and furled her hair around her shoulders. A dark, brooding sensation embraced her like a heavy knitted shawl on a chilly winter's eve. The temperature was dropping rapidly. It was still in the nineties, but she felt a chill ripple up her spine.

Where?

Her eyes looked across the rooftops toward downtown Dallas to get her bearings. She could just barely make out the old Southland Building, The Bryan Tower, The Mobil Building, The green light trimmed Jolly Green Giant, the light ball of Reunion Tower—yes. The webbed image of her well-studied map came to mind. Other familiar landmarks popped up, orienting her in the proper direction. She spun around again on her low heels, this time facing the direction of the arc on her map.

That way!

A deep resonant rumble tumbled out of the black overcast sky above. A momentary pale of light flashed across the face of a towering cloud bank, illuminating the dauntless approaching army of purple thunderheads. The stratospheric attack was about to commence. A dark shudder dug its way through Megan. She vehemently hated storms. As a small child she used to imagine angels up in the clouds taking pictures with huge antique flashbulb cameras. According to her wicked aunt (stepmother?), the thunder was supposed to be a heavenly bowling tournament, or some such other innocuous activity which quieted the fears of children beneath a tender veil of compassionate deception.

It was a lie.

Megan knew full well about storms. She never believed her aunt. Aunt Gwendolyn was the one who said Uncle Bertrand would always love her and never hurt her.

She lied. Even the fleeting memory of his face still hurt.

No, this night, as the dark ominous storm approached, Megan's innermost fears rose to the surface, exposed and raw. Yes, she knew all too well the dangerous and destructive power of storms—but even more so— the ferocity of the beast they now hunted: an animal that offered love but only gave pain; a betrayer of trust; a liar. Yes. She knew this animal all too well. A few cool drops lightly touched her cheeks. One hit her shoulder, then her forearm. The rain began its quiet hissing overture. The wind continued its assault from the south, pregnant with the musky scent of the imminent deluge.

Ralph's voice called to her from the curb, "Meg, what is it?"

"You won't find him in there," she called back.

He jogged to her side, his heavy girth bouncing along as he came. "Why not? There's still a lot of people in there. It could take a couple of hours to go through them all. He has to turn up."

"And he knew that," she threw back. "So while we're here, he's doing as he pleases...at his home."

"What?" Ralph looked offended. "He couldn't have got past us. There's no fucking way!"

With a hissing rush, the rain came down heavier, accented with a stinging clap of thunder from the inverness sky overhead. The wall of thunderheads in the distance flashed again, brighter, the pales of light reflecting up the ionized chimney within, percolating with mounting energy, a destructive energy waiting to be unleashed—only seconds away now.

Her gaze cut through him, "We both know he's gone. For God sake, Ralph, think about it. If he wanted to surrender he would have done so. He still wants to make us look like incompetent fools. And just between you and me, he's doing a pretty damn good job."

The downpour increased dramatically, as though a giant sprinkler spigot was opened in the heavens. The rush of droplets grew louder, pushed down at an acute angle by the driving power of the wind. The temperature dropped further. The sky growled again.

Completely soaked, Ralph had to raise his voice above the rain pelting their bodies and bouncing up off the street, "Then where the hell is he?"

The assault of hard droplets flattened Megan's hair and sheathed her thin green dress to her skin, revealing every contour and hue of her slender frame. Neither officer took any notice. Such things were now irrelevant, like the storm. She pointed southeast with a trembling finger, "That way. He's at home."

"What?" Ralph put his hands on his hips. "Are you sure?"

Megan looked firmly into his eyes. "Leave McManus in charge of the search detail. Have them keep looking and checking the people as they leave. But *you* have to come with me." She reached forward and grabbed his dripping lapels, pulling her dripping face nose to nose with his, "I'm right about this, Ralph. Come on!"

"Where the hell are we going to go?" he demanded, wanting to believe her.

"That way," she pointed again, stabbing harder into the downpour. "We'll find an apartment building or a rented house. *Something!* And he'll be there."

•

"Oh, you're right!" Lynn exclaimed, "The view is absolutely stellar."

It truly was. Beneath the dark canopy of clouds overhead, the lights of the Dallas skyline twinkled up from a dense carpet of light fifteen stories below. Her eyes followed Justin as he casually drifted over to the wet-bar, opened the small refrigerator and pulled out a bottle of champagne. An eager chill of excitement washed over her. She giggled at the sound of the thick mushroom-shaped cork popping out of the bottle. A glistening tower of white foam ejaculated from the spout, dripping down to the white carpet below. He smartly filled two tall crystal flutes and offered her one. She didn't need much more alcohol, but she accepted it anyway. Her head was light enough already.

Light enough for what? she asked herself.

It didn't matter. She was primed for anything.

Her handsome stranger needed neither invitation nor coaxing to escalate the intoxication of the evening to the seductive realm of intimate desires. She wanted him (or someone just like him) to take her that night—she was ready to give it all. She wanted it all. This gorgeous guy was a dream come true, an apparition right out of a fairy tale: handsome, rich, charming, polite, clean, and well-mannered. She could barely contain herself. A long, luxurious night of romance and passion would show that stupid Kevin Culvert and Tanya-the-Whore a thing or two. Tonight would be the most memorable night of her life.

This was true...in a manner of speaking.

Ten minutes after arriving at the lavish high-rise apartment, what began as fantasy had now been transformed into tangible titillating reality.

Her mysterious lover was exquisite. His lips feasted and devoured her own; his slow, firm hands caressed her; his strong arms held her—all of it, so tender and gentle, with such consideration and sensitivity for her pleasure. When he lifted her into his powerful arms and carried her into the bedroom she was so aroused wanted to eat him alive. Her first glimpse of the brass bed with the gossamer canopy made her mouth water. She couldn't get out of her dress and pantyhose fast enough.

Justin shot a furtive glance at the wide framed mirror on the wall as he undressed. He assumed it would be acceptable to do it at least once the old fashioned way before going right to the handcuffs. Before he got his fire-engine-red bikini briefs all the way to the ground, there was no choice to be made.

The most eager Miss Lynn Evans grabbed him and pushed him down on the bed, kissing and sucking and kissing and licking and kissing and nibbling and kissing. She was almost *too* eager to please. However, in Justin's professional opinion, her oral talents rivaled even those of Samuel Ferndale; so, for the moment he withheld any objection.

A distant rumble of thunder signaled an approaching storm.

•

The first warm drops of the summer rain hit the windshield of the Porsche as it pulled up to the heavy steel garage gate at the rear entrance of the Carlisle Tower. He reached out the window and punched in the six digit access code, then hastily closed the window as the drops grew heavier. Idling low and throaty, like a big jungle cat, the exquisite automobile rolled into the underground garage and proceeded down to the second level.

He parked in a visitor's slot and killed the engine. The 9mm Glock was in the passenger's seat beside him. His eyes strayed around the garage, taking inventory of all that moved and all that did not. It was deserted, as expected.

Good.

He checked the ammunition in the gun once more, then climbed out of the car, slipping the weapon to its familiar place behind his back in the waistband of his trousers.

The excruciatingly slow garage elevator would take him to the lobby, where he would move quickly to the opposite side to summon one of the two residence elevators. The dithering old security guard would be half-asleep and take little notice, if any. Besides, the guard had already seen a Mr. Teasdale and his lovely guest retire for the evening through the front door less than thirty minutes ago. Once up in the apartment, assuming Mr. Teasdale was successfully doing his prescribed part, they'd not hear him come in, nor change his clothes in the spare bedroom.

Perfect.

While waiting for the other elevator in the lobby he noticed how hard it was now raining. The lobby windows were being assaulted in undulating sheets of water, blasted in almost horizontally by a powerful wind, completely blurring the images beyond. It was a comforting sight. Bad weather only slowed down urban activity. That meant a greater margin of error. The silver elevator doors slid open and he stepped inside, hitting the button marked "15." He glanced at his watch again. It was 12:37 A.M. Perfect. Still ahead of schedule. His smile came out again. Everything was proceeding exactly according to plan.

"Soon and very soon..." he softly sang.

•

"Keep going," Megan shouted, drenched to the skin and shivering so hard her teeth chattered. Her soaked canvass shoulder bag felt like it weighed a hundred pounds. She was carrying her shoes, running barefoot in the inch of water running across the streets.

"Meg, this is insane," Ralph cried, winded and weary. Silhouetted by the amber street lights above. Rain water spewed from his lips with every wheezing puff. He knew he couldn't press on much further without collapsing dead in the street. Not until that moment had he ever regretted chomping down a single doughnut. He was in pain. They had beat on the doors of every house in the last block which even remotely appeared occupied. So far all they found were angry sleepers, irritated TV watchers, or embarrassed lovers. Ralph was getting tired of apologizing.

"I know the approximate distance," Megan insisted. "It has to be within a block or two. Let's at least hit these big condos up ahead."

They were on Carlisle street. The next block contained four high-rise apartment buildings: The Westmont, The Grenadier, The Carlisle Tower, and The Royal Jamaican Renaissance.

"All right," he agreed, holding a hand to his chest feeling the harsh pounding against his fingers. A quick glance at his watch told him it was 12:39 A.M. "One of 'em might be the place. I think he has a thing for places with a view."

•

Lynn Evans had already had two devastating climaxes in the first fifteen minutes on the bed, seemingly choreographed by nature in concert with the raging intensity of the storm raging outside the bedroom window. While bright white talons of lightning clawed at the earth, amid each deep detonation of thunder, waves of pleasure penetrated her, consumed her, destroyed her strength like a burning tree reduced to ashes. However, Justin Teasdale was beginning to get exceedingly concerned about his compensation. He had to get to the cuffs on soon or he was going to be out a lot of money.

Don't wait. Just do it...

When he abruptly stopped and withdrew from her body, she looked at him with longing, puppy-dog eyes. "What's the matter, lover?"

He slid over to the edge of the bed, reaching for the nightstand drawer. "I want to drive you wild. Are you game?"

She cuddled up against his shoulder. "Oh, baby, you're already doing that. But I'm game for anything you want, sugar."

He lifted up one pair of the cuffs. "Anything?"

She frowned, "Oh, no. Not that, baby. I don't like that."

Always the consummate capitalist, Justin implored her, "Come on, sweet thing. Do it for me. It won't hurt. I promise. I just want you to hold still, while I make you come at least a dozen more times. It's really a lot better when you feel a little helpless and..." he grinned, "...*vulnerable.* You know? Can't you imagine it?"

She frowned. "I don't need those to make me hold still. B'sides, I like to move."

Justin Teasdale was clever. He switched tactics, drawing his face into a look of disappointment. "All right. But I don't know then. Maybe we should just knock it off for tonight." He sighed with forlorn longing, "You know, I really thought you were special. Unafraid to try new and exciting things. That's the kind of girl I'm looking for. That's the kind of girl I would want to take care of and buy nice things for, cover her in diamonds, show her the world, and perhaps have stay with me in a great place like this."

He actually thought he saw her drool.

She grinned, her natural common sense circuits quickly shorting out. "Well...okay, lover. But just for a little bit. All right?"

He buzzed open the first cuff with a grin. "You're after my own heart, darlin'. I hope you know that."

She just giggled with delight.

A few moments later, Lynn Evans lay prone in the center of the brass bed. Both of her hands were shackled above her head, and both ankles spread wide and secured to the foot rails. Justin Teasdale, now almost fifty-thousand dollars richer, suddenly realized just how much fun this was. He'd have to get some handcuffs for himself. She *did* look so helpless and vulnerable. A bolt of desire shot through him.

Oh, yes…

He genuinely wanted her again, without delay. Justin climbed between her legs and heard her gasp with ecstasy as her eyes clenched shut. Her body felt exquisite. But it wasn't just the sex—the mere sight of this defenseless woman chained beneath him was getting him off like never before.

Lynn Evans squealed with wanton glee, approaching delirium. She writhed in delight. Her tongue came out and encircled her lips in delight, her mouth going dry with shallow breaths.

Oh, yes!

This was *soooo* nasty. It was *soooo* dirty. This was absolutely, positively *wicked*—and she loved every minute of it. At that moment Lynn desperately wished somehow she had a picture of it all to show Kevin. He'd just die. Yes, she knew beyond the shadow of a doubt if Kevin even suspected, he'd absolutely swell up *and die*. He'd never gotten more than old fashioned hump between the sheets or a blow job in the front of his pick-up truck. Nothing, repeat *nothing*, like this.

At that moment neither Justin nor Lynn was aware they were no longer alone.

•

"Teasdale?" the septuagenarian guard asked, lifting his spectacles up above his long, wiry eyebrows and wiping his dim eyes. He replaced his glasses and looked oddly askew at the soaking wet small woman and the huffing and puffing older man standing in front of his desk. The water draining from their clothes loudly dripped onto the carpet.

Megan put a wet arm on the marble counter top with moist squish and leaned forward. Her rain soaked shoes were still in her hand. She spoke louder in case the old fart was hard of hearing, "Yes. Justin Teasdale. Does he live here?"

The old man sniffed once, then asked, "I'm afraid that's privileged information ma'am. Who's asking?"

This was it!

Ralph's eyes flew to Megan's. They were as wide and charged as his own. If he didn't live there, security always said so and sent you on your way. The brutal fatigue he carried in the door with him was dripping of into the carpet with the rain water with every breath he took. Fresh waves of energy warmed his face.

Ralph started to pull out his badge, but Megan caught his hand, unseen on the other side of the counter by the old man. Her mind was whirling with a strategy that might save them some time—and maybe a life. There was no time to play it by the book. Evidently, that's what Mr. Friday Night kept expecting them to do.

How else did he stay to precisely ahead of them?

She did her best to sound pleasant. A phenomenally accurate south Dallas accent arose out of nowhere, "See, I'm Meg. And this here's Ralph. I'm Justin's baby-sister? Ralph here's our uncle on our mama's side. Y'know?" She knit her brow together with mock concern, "Why, didn't he tell you we was coming?"

Ralph clamped his lips between his teeth. Damn, she was good. The accent was flawless.

The geezer shook his head, running four stubby fingers over his thin pate of gray wisps of hair vainly covering a mottled field of age spots. He peered over at a clipboard. "Nope. He didn't." He looked back at Megan. "So let me see some ID, young lady."

"Surely." Megan fished through her purse and presented her driver's license, her heart suddenly pounding, struggling to sound convincing. "He *is* home id'n he?"

"Yep, B'lieve so." The old man tottered to his feet, pushing his thick pair of bifocals up on his nose. "But already got some company as I recall. Perdy young thing too. Probably doesn't want to be disturbed."

Megan squeezed Ralph's hand with her free one.

The guard leaned close to Megan's little plastic card, peering through the bottom lens at her name. He looked back and forth through the top lens from the picture to Meg's face several times before declaring, "Says Pembrooke, missy. Not Teasdale."

"Pembrooke's my married name," she said sweetly, with a touch of forlorn helplessness thrown in for good measure.

The guard sat back down and looked at his computer monitor. "Is Mr. Teasdale expecting you at this late hour?"

Megan nodded, "Why, yes he is. Well... sort'a. Y'see, we's horribly late. We was supposed to be here hours ago to spend the long Fourth of July weekend with him. But we broke down in Waco yesterday. And with that bad storm out'tare moving in, you'd a know'd it slowed us down terribly. Hell, mister, we got stuck in all the way up I-35. See, there was this eighteen wheeler overturned at the Hillsboro turn-off? Good Lord, what a mess."

Ralph looked up at the ceiling, about to burst out laughing. The realization of why there were there faded his grin and sobered his vision. It did nothing for the thundering pace of his heavy heart.

"Well, missy," the old man grunted, "I'll have to call up to see if he'll authorize you to go up. It's the rules."

"Oh, do you have to?" Megan looked mortified. "Truth is, sir. We'd hoped to surprise him." That was no lie. "He ain't seen us in years. Not since mama died. It would be so great when he opens up his door and sees us standin' there. He'll be so tickled."

"I still have to call," the surly guard threw back firmly. He was missing a good portion of Sports Center online on account of these trailer trash. He huffed, "He'll be just as tickled to learn your down here than at his door. And if he don't want to see you, you'll have a shorter walk back outside to go back to wherever you come from." He started to dial.

Megan's eyes flew to Ralph's, the accent noticeably dropping, "No. He'll run."

Ralph's lurched across the desk and pushed down the switch-hook on the telephone key system. "Don't do that."

"What the hell's wrong with you, young fella?" the old man was positively chagrined, leaning back in his chair. "I told you it's the rules. Now get your hand off that thing."

Ralph's fingers stayed planted. He turned his face to Megan, "No good. Use your cell phone. Call in the cavalry. We have to seal the building first."

The guard stood up, putting his hand on the .38 special in his holster. "Who are you?"

Ralph pulled out his badge, "Easy, pops. Dallas Police. Sit down, don't move. And do as you're told."

As she dialed, Megan noticed the time readout on her iPhone. It was 12:52 A.M.

•

"Splendid," the rich voice cut through the room.

Lynn was submerged beneath the waves of euphoric ecstasy, consumed by all the erotic sensations, sounds, tastes, and smells. It took several moments for the foreign sound of intrusion to capture her attention. She looked up to her lover's smiling face and saw him looking toward the doorway. Her head likewise turned toward the door. She gasped, shocked to see another man standing there. All four pairs of handcuffs jingled simultaneously.

"Hi," Justin greeted the stranger with familiar decorum. "Did I screw something up?"

"Oh, no," the tall man assured him, waving a dismissing hand in the air. He was wearing bright orange workman's coveralls. "Everything's fine. Excellent work thus far."

About to die from embarrassment, Lynn seethed up to Justin, "What's going on? Who's that?" The cuffs jingled again.

Justin smiled down at her, "Sorry, love. My boss." He started to laugh, "Smile, you're on Candid Camera."

"You're shittin' me," her red face grew stone cold.

"Not at all," the tall man assured her, coming to the edge of the bed and sitting down next to Lynn, like a good-natured physician at bedside. "But don't worry, love. It's all just a bit of innocent fun. You'll treasure seeing it later. Everyone gets a copy of the tape. I just want to request a few special shots."

The red-faced pallor of Lynn's face was starting to dissipate, aided by the fact she was still very drunk. What the hell, she thought. She'd show her copy to Kevin. Who knows? Maybe she'd even make him one so he could always know what he was missing. Then again, she mused, this new guy was even better looking than the first one. He had a sultry air about him, a certain poise, a confidence, an unspoken charm that made her think of more wicked things, nastier things. Who knows? Perhaps the night would get even better as it went along. Two might be twice as fun as one.

"What do you want to see?" Justin asked.

The tall man pulled a plain white handkerchief out his back pocket and waded it into a little ball, "Well, my friend, first of all, I need a strict measure of silence from your lovely companion." With that he reached over and roughly stuffed the wad of silk into Lynn's mouth. "We don't want to disturb any of the neighbors."

Justin just sat there and grinned. It was at that moment he noticed Mr. Larry Taylor was wearing thin, almost completely transparent, latex surgical gloves. What did he have in mind? It didn't matter. He liked his new friend's kinky imagination.

Lynn's eyes instantly went wide with fear from the moment the cloth parted her lips. It caught her completely by surprise. She gagged and sputtered, frantically trying to spit the hankie out. However, the tall man swiftly opened the bottom drawer on the nightstand and pulled out a thick roll of duct tape. He peeled off an eight inch strip and fastened it over the woman's cheeks, firmly securing the cloth in her mouth.

"There we go," he said, satisfied with his handiwork. "That should suffice nicely. Time to get back to work. What do you say, my friend?"

Humming, moaning, whinnying, and snorting through her nose, Lynn struggled vainly against the handcuffs, causing the headboard and footboard to bow in and out. Steel against brass clanked and chinked and scraped and rattled.

"I'm ready. What do you want *me* to do?" Justin eagerly wanted to know. This was getting *really* fun.

The man scratched his chin thoughtfully, "Well, before the next scene, I want you to go down and kneel on the floor at the foot of the bed, like you're worshipping your mistress in bondage here."

"Cool," Justin hopped off the bed, moved to the foot, and did exactly as he was instructed. "That'll be great. You can get a shot over my head right up her box canyon."

"Exactly," the tall man nodded thoughtfully, moving over next to Justin and squatting down. "Then, you'll crawl up..." his voice trailed off discreetly as he leaned toward Justin's ear.

Lynn strained to hear. All she could make out was Justin giggling again. She felt the burning sensation of panic rapidly growing in her bowels. Something was very, very, *very* wrong. She could feel it. This was no movie. Due to the height of the bed, she couldn't see much down the length of her body, down through the valley between her breasts, over the little stubble of pubic hair, and between her parted knees. All she could effectively discern was the back of her lover's head, his brown curly hair barely visible above the horizontal brass rail at her feet. The stranger continued to kneel beside him, on her lover's right, whispering further covert instructions in his ear.

A taut moment of still silence past.

She heard the stranger in the orange coveralls say, "Now close your eyes," just before she heard a small click, like a latch or a lock opening. The next sound was a startling, dull, metallic cough. Something wet and solid splashed the wall to her right with blinding force. Her eyes flew in that direction, straining to comprehend what she was seeing. Red dots spattered all along the once white wall, some of the drops thick enough to start dripping down vertically. Her mind froze in confusion and panic. She had no idea what was going on. The next sight made her lose all control of her bodily functions, soiling the bed in one wrenching burst.

Oh, God, NO!

There between her feet, she saw the stranger in the orange overalls lifting her lover's limp body aright with his powerful left hand clutched around the back of his neck. The limp head flopped back and forth once. In that one instant of motion she saw his right temple was burned black, all around a hole the size of quarter. The left side of his head was gone—

just gone. A shredded gaping hole of red, black and white remained. Blood was thickly oozing down his neck to his shoulder. But the horror of that grisly visage was eclipsed by the sight of the huge black maul of a pistol with a long distended barrel held aloft in her lover's lifeless right hand, enveloped by the stranger's own hand.

The muzzle was aimed directly at her face.

With all her might she labored to scream for help. Hot mucus flew from her nose. Salt laden tears burned down her cheeks, blurring her vision. The cuffs cut into her wrist and ankles. The bed frame bowed back and forth, back and forth. The gossamer canopy flapped up and down. She pulled harder. The pain of her extremities was of no consequence. In that moment she would gladly rip off her hands and feet to be free. A single pop and a flash of light went off before her eyes. Feathers exploded with a rush of hot air inches from her face. The hot stinking breath of burned gun powder and machine oil filled her nose. The searing acid sting of bile roared up in her throat and flooded out her nose. Her lungs went into involuntary spasms. She was drowning.

Another flash and a pop.

A momentary burning sensation touched the bridge of her nose. A lightning sensation of vertigo detonated behind her eyes.

And there was no more.

•

It was done.

The tall man let Teasdale's body flop over to its left. It landed in a limp heap, the smoking gun still clutched in his dead fist. Assisted by gravity, a large red stain was quickly forming on the carpet beneath the four inch exit wound on the left side of his head, radiating out in an expanding concentric circle.

He looked the body over from head to toe. He glanced back to the bed. Most of the woman's head was gone. Well, that wasn't entirely true. It wasn't actually *gone*. It wasn't where it was originally. The messy red and pink and white and gray fragments were sprayed all over the brass spindles of the headboard and thickly splattered along the wall behind it, dripping to the baseboard.

Amazing.

He rose again to his feet, backing up a few paces, carefully surveying the entire scene. It was glorious. All was how he had envisioned it. It would be completely convincing.

He walked to the waist-high dresser beneath the mirror, pulled a legal-sized envelope from the top drawer. It was neatly addressed to Megan Pembrooke. He laid it on the polished surface next to the flower vase, then lifted five of the long-stemmed red roses out of the crystal vase and returned to the bed. He laid the fresh flowers down by her feet.

No, not yet, he silently chastised himself. They were for later. Mustn't get ahead of ourselves. There was much work left to do. He checked his watch again.

It was 1:18. He estimated his remaining labors would take just about an hour to go from head to toe.

Step Four was now complete.

Time for Step Five: the finishing touches, the completion of the set. The game was nearly finished.

He reached into the bottom drawer of the nightstand again and removed several other necessary items for his work: a double-filtered respirator, a pair of carpenter's plastic goggles, a welder's striker, and a small propane torch. He put the respirator on, opened the valve on the tank, and lit the torch. The small blue tongue of fire rushed out of the flanged end of the angled brass tube with a fine hiss. He adjusted the small black knob at the top of the thermos-sized blue tank to increase the flow to a fine white and orange spike.

He wasn't fooling himself. The respirator was the best he could find, commercially available, that is. But it was inherently designed for painters, to filter out dust and paint particulates, not to stop a smell. With that much flesh, this was still going to stink. Thankfully, the quilt on the bed wasn't flammable.

He mumbled beneath the rubber mask, "Ashes to ashes, my dear, and dust to dust."

It was at that moment the telephone on the opposite nightstand rang. The screams of sirens could be heard in the distance.

"Oh, my," he whispered.

PART III

IT'S ALWAYS
THE LITTLE THINGS

There are some frauds so well conducted
that it would be stupidity not to be
deceived by them.

Charles Caleb Colton
Lacon, 1825

What renders us so bitter against those
who trick us is that they believe themselves
to be more clever than we are.

La Rouchefoucauld
Maxims, 1665

Necessity can turn any weapon to
advantage.

Publius Syrus
Moral Sayings, 1st Century B.C.

CHAPTER 26

KING TAKES PAWN: LYNN EVANS

Friday
July 5, 2013

"Hello?"

Ralph was stunned when someone actually answered the phone. They couldn't risk losing Teasdale now in legal screw-ups. Thus, they couldn't technically trespass on the property or enter his apartment to apprehend him without a proper search warrant and a warrant for his arrest. All the proper documents were already signed by Judge Alton Stone five minutes ago and were on their way over. Four back-up squad cars and the SWAT van had already arrived to secure the building, a dozen more were en-route. Yet, even with the building secure, it didn't mean Teasdale couldn't surrender of his own accord if asked. Granted, it was a stupid idea, but nonetheless, proper form and by the book. It didn't matter, the stairwells and elevators were already covered. He wouldn't slip away this time, even if they had to go door-to-door.

"Hello?" an even voice repeated, patient, with no trace of alarm.

"Mr. Justin Teasdale?" Ralph asked.

Megan's eyes grew wide, standing in front of Ralph, still dripping wet. It was still raining, but the harsh downpour had slacked off dramatically in the last few minutes.

"That's right," the voice replied.

Ralph raised his eyebrows and shrugged. "Mr. Teasdale, this is Detective Ralph Weatherstrom. Dallas Police. Would you please report immediately down to the lobby?"

There was a long, dead silence on the line.

Then the voice calmly requested, "Let me speak with Miss Megan Pembrooke, Detective Weatherstrom, if you'd be so kind."

Ralph pulled Megan's iPhone away from his ear, hugging it to his chest. "He wants to talk to you."

"Me?" Megan felt a shiver run through her. "He asked for me? Why the hell does he want to talk to me?"

Ralph held out the phone to her, the tension inside of him bubbling forth, "How the fuck should I know? Why does he do anything? Maybe he wants to know how you liked your present."

She took it, hesitantly holding it up to her ear. "This is Officer Pembrooke."

The smooth distinguished voice simply stated, "Ah, Megan. I'm so proud of you. It looks as if—for the time being—you've won. Well done, well done. I humbly resign." The line went dead.

Ralph just looked at Megan. "Well?"

"He said he resigns. Then he hung up." She felt as confused as Ralph looked.

"Do you think he's coming down?" Ralph didn't sound too hopeful.

A Dallas blue and white came roaring up to the front of the Carlisle Tower. More cars and vans had been arriving every second. Ten officers from the SWAT team, decked out in black with Kevlar tactical vests and carrying military issue M-16's, saw the car and assembled in formation by the elevator.

Megan smiled at Ralph, "Doesn't matter. Cavalry's here."

The driver of the car jumped out and ran in carrying a legal folder. He called out, "Got 'em. Let's do it."

The lobby burst into motion.

The man presented the documents to the old guard, "This is a court order by Judge Alton Stone to grant entry for any and all police officials on this premises, and to gain access to the apartment of one Justin Teasdale, to wit, to search..."

As the deputy assistant district attorney droned on, half of the Swat Team was already pouring up the stairs, weapons at the ready, safeties off; while the other half piled into one of the two elevators. Megan, Ralph, and three other uniformed policemen entered the second elevator. One of them carried a battering ram.

In less than three minutes the hall on the fifteenth floor was flooded with armed warriors, closing in on their prey. A barrel-chested SWAT team member beat on apartment 15-C's door with the heel of his fist. He ordered any occupant to surrender.

No reply.

A door, two doors down, opened up. Twenty gun barrels swiveled toward the sound. An elderly woman in a pink house robe and curlers in her hair poked her head out. She held a Jesse James Colt forty-five six-shooter in her quaking old hand. Her eyes went wide when she saw the crowd of officers.

The nearest officer, standing just on the other side of her door, deftly snatched the gun out of her hand, admonishing, "Thank you, ma'am, but we have all the help we need. Just go back inside." He politely pushed her back inside her apartment and pulled the door closed. He kept her gun.

The SWAT tactical commander nodded to the officer with the battering ram. He stepped up to the door. As he pulled the heavy device back, all the bolts and actions of twenty weapons clicked back like popcorn going off. They were all leveled and prepared to fire when the ram struck the deadbolt lock, splintering the doorframe and sending the door flying inward, banging against the wall.

The team rushed in.

•

For the next five minutes apartment 15-C was filled with a dense black swarm of motion and confusion. Megan and Ralph waited in the hall until the SWAT commander came back out, looking shaken and bewildered. He nodded to them. The gray pall on his face instantly announced something was terribly wrong.

"Was he there?" Ralph demanded, expecting to be told to the negative, fearing they had been outwitted yet again.

The commander grabbed Ralph's arm. "He popped himself, Ralph."

Ralph and Megan exchanged an incredulous look.

"But not before taking another one with him," the commander added, shaking his head back and forth. "Sick piece of shit."

"Let's have a look," Megan tugged at Ralph's arm.

Dead?

"Yeah," he nodded, still dazed by what he heard. Could it really be over?

They passed through the stone archway, walked down the Spanish tile hallway and entered the bedroom. There they were instantly greeted by a mixed cloud of bitter stench: sex, blood, burned powder—and burned human flesh. Megan started to gag. Ralph pulled out his handkerchief and covered his mouth and nose. Megan lifted her wet sleeve to her face. Two other SWAT officers just walked out, both of them breathing hard and looking a little pale. Megan carefully approached the figure lying on the bed. Ralph walked slowly to the foot of the bed and looked down at the nude body of a young man lying in a twisted pile. The blood on the carpet was still wet and glistening. *If anyone ever deserved it*...he mused with bitter disdain.

Ralph looked on top of the bed and saw the body of a woman handcuffed spread-eagle to the headboard and footboard. She had been almost completely decapitated. Five roses adorned what was left of her, like all the rest of his prey. What was left of the lower portion of the woman's face, her neck, and the tops of her shoulders was scared and charred red and black, hideously bubbled up and burned. He noticed the small propane torch sitting on the nightstand. Ralph had to look away. It took everything inside him not to kick the corpse lying at his feet and spit on the miserable carcass. He was starting to feel nauseous again.

Meanwhile, Megan was scurrying around like a royal attendant bee, her hands and eyes, searching, probing and taking in everything she saw. Ralph watched her meticulously examining everything: the woman, the man, the woman again, the bed, the man again, the woman again. She was becoming more visibly agitated as she went along. He was becoming light headed.

Ralph walked over and leaned up against the dresser by the mirror. "Megan. What the hell are you doing? It's over. He's dead. We got him."

"I know," Megan mumbled absently. "But let me do my job. I just have to be sure."

"Of what?" he challenged.

She was examining how loose the headboard was to the frame, shaking it slightly. "That it's really over."

Ralph looked down at the body of Justin Teasdale again. "Well, honey, I don't think he looks like he's going to be hurting anyone else any time real soon."

She ignored the comment, walking down to the foot of the elegant brass bed and knelt down next to Teasdale's body. She rolled him over on his back, staring into his wide, frozen eyes.

"Is it him?" Ralph asked, almost terrified to hear the answer, wanting to savor the few moments of relief which teased him just moments ago. He took a quick visual inventory: brown curly hair, blue eyes, handsome features, and appeared to be the right height and weight.

Megan leaned down near his neck and sniffed.

"Aramis?" Ralph asked.

She nodded. "Aramis."

His hand brushed something on the dresser top. It was a man's personal effects: keys, wallet, Rolex watch, a black ebony Mont Blanc pen and pencil set, and some loose change. He picked up the wallet.

"Here," he handed Megan Justin Teasdale's driver's license. "This the same guy?"

Megan took the card and compared it to the face. It matched. But something was wrong. She still didn't feel right. "Yeah, it looks like him. But we don't have any prior prints to run. There's only one way to be *completely* sure."

"How?" Ralph asked.

"The DNA tests," she replied. "We compare all the semen samples we've found at each of the previous crime scenes to what's smeared all over the girl and see if they match."

"Okay," Ralph nodded. A pang of apprehension grabbing his heart as he asked, "And if they don't match?"

"Then we've just got another one of his VanGorens here," she noted, feeling that familiar twinge of doubt in her gut. "But if it matches, then it's settled. You've got your boy. Case closed."

"All right," Ralph looked a little happier, inwardly praying the samples matched. "How soon can the test be done?"

She stood up, her eyes still on the body. "I'll order them right away. We could get technicians out of bed and started tonight with the right authorization. We have the equipment at Baylor Medical. If so, we might have something back by tomorrow afternoon if we're lucky."

"No problem," Ralph was starting to feel energized again. "I'll call Commissioner Bragg directly right now. He can guarantee we get whatever we need."

"That's great," she almost whispered, still looking down at the lifeless body, curled up in an almost fetal position.

Ralph turned to leave, but stopped short. A few inches away from all the loose change was an envelope. The name scrawled on the front caught his eye.

"Meg," he whispered softly.

She was still looking down at the slain body of Justin Teasdale, shaking her head. Something still didn't feel right.

"What's the matter?" she asked.

"Take a look?" he said.

She glanced over and saw the thin envelope. Her heart picked up its pace.

He handed it to her. It was scented with Aramis. Her eyes detected a small crimson spot on the underside. It didn't seem significant at the time. Its contents were all she was interested in. Her fingers quickly tore the fragile brief open, pulling out the folded piece of stationary, desperate to know what it said. Its neatly typed text read:

My dearest Megan,

The game was played down to the last player.
You've found me at long last, as I always knew you would. But look at how dear a price has been paid along the way. Isn't it a pity that law enforcement in this day and age is so impotent? It only prevails after all the damage is done.
Too bad brilliant minds such as your own don't proliferate the profession. Then perhaps the white hats might have a fighting change. Perhaps they should think of re-staffing, perchance even some new leadership. You know what they say, a fish stinks from the head down.
But alas, we are at the end of this game. Even I must now leave the board. But for you, Miss Pembrooke, there will be many other games, perhaps some even more thrilling and challenging than the one you've just played.

Best of Luck,
J.T.

She handed the letter to Ralph and let him read it.

His eyes flew back and forth as he quickly absorbed the message. When he reached the end he grunted, "Oh, Bragg's just gonna love this." He folded it back up and put it in his pocket, leaving the discarded envelope lying on the dresser.

Megan brought her hands together under her chin, "Wait a minute. This wasn't written after you called. And it's typed. There wasn't time." She huffed, thinking for a moment. "It looks like you were right. It *was* the end of the line. He was planning to end it all here tonight no matter what."

"Arrogant little shit. Right to the end." Ralph looked down at Teasdale's body once more, his anger welling up in his throat, "But look who's dead, and look who's still around to play the game." He did spit toward the body that time. Without another word, he spun on his heel and marched out of the room.

The crime scene technicians and coroner's team had just arrived and were opening their satchels.

The end of the game?

Megan just stood back out of everyone's way, leaning against the dresser, her arms protectively folded across her damp chest. Something still felt wrong. Her eyes roamed around the room, watching her colleagues do their work. The tiny spot of red on the envelope lying on the dresser caught her eye again. She picked it up and looked at it more closely.

Blood?

Yes. It *was* blood, and freshly dried. The small mark was a wide spot, and a smear, like the edge of a finger. From its position, holding the envelope straight, and reading the addressee, it would have to have come from a left forefinger. She looked at it closer. From the shape she could tell it was surely a finger impression, but there were no print marks. That couldn't be. The blood would have left a beautiful print, or at least a partial. Why not? Gloves? Her eyes went back to Teasdale's hands. They were both clean.

His hands.

The 9mm Glock was clutched in Teasdale's right hand. Entry wound was on the right side of this head, exit wound on the left. That couldn't be. Or *shouldn't* be. Or could it? She moved quickly to the corpse, knelt down again and lifted his upper lip, examining his teeth very carefully. What she saw surprised her. She sat back with a huff. That made no sense. This man wasn't left-handed.

•

Amid all the commotion of police officers running in and out of the building, none of them noticed a tall uniformed police officer walk right out the front door of the Carlisle Tower. Had Megan been down in the lobby, she might have noticed he was the only officer leaving the building whose uniform was dry.

After he had hung up the phone with Ralph Weatherstrom prior to the raid, he knew he had at least five more minutes, even if they had warrants in hand. The elevators were excruciatingly slow. It wasn't very difficult to take a minute to at least produce a token of his finishing work with the torch, put everything in order, then take the stairs to the roof to change into the official city police uniform. It was then merely a matter of waiting and watching, timing the buzz of confusion just right. Safely outside, he'd catch a cab home to his own apartment, then return tomorrow for his car.

Perfect.

Well, almost perfect. The authorities were inconveniently early. There was no time to artistically complete his crowning masterpiece, save a smoldering sample. However, there were always contingency plans available to adjust to any miscalculations in timing. Although, it was certainly kind of the police to call ahead and at least give him a few minutes to respond. Had they waited a few moments longer and entered completely unannounced and found him engrossed in his work, they might have actually won the game. Evidently, that was not to be.

It was his destiny to win.

Oh yes, they were allowed to think they had won for the moment. It was a required part of the strategy of the game. That would make the overall effect that much more powerful when the game began again, when Justin Teasdale miraculously returned from the dead—like a pawn who reaches the eighth row and becomes the most deadly of all players, a queen.

He could hardly wait.

CHAPTER 27

ATTENTION TO DETAIL

Saturday
July 6, 2013

At just after eight o'clock in the evening, The Stagger Inn was completely abuzz with celebration in honor of the woman of the hour, Officer Megan Pembrooke. Megan was continually congratulated by everyone who came and went, a good deal of them strangers. Hal told Megan her money was no good that night, even if she wanted to drink herself sick. Pete Brumley kept clapping her on the back, laughing, and lauding her brilliance in finding Teasdale's apartment. Her face had been on TV all day. All over the Metroplex she was the heroine of the hour.

Shannon Bolinski had made a huge crock of homemade chili and was serving bowls to everyone. Jesse Phillips sat red-eyed on his usual stool, quietly nursing a bourbon and coke and philosophizing about abortion, gays in the military, and congressional term limits with Hal. Stanley and Clyde were in a heated life or death dart tournament for the championship of the world. Even Carol and Linda were there. They kept a little distance from Megan, but both received a warm hug from her. All her friends were gathered there to honor her.

So why did she still feel so bad?

Megan Pembrooke was an instant celebrity. The press was going wild. Her phone wouldn't stop ringing. She was the super sleuth who had outwitted the master butcher of Dallas. Professionally, she was sure to be promoted to Detective years ahead of her peers—perhaps even sooner than she dreamed. She felt all the attention was unnecessary. Finding the body of Justin Teasdale and his last victim seemed too anti-climactic. Her gut was reluctant to accept the fact that her opponent had so blithely opted out of the game without a more dramatic finish. Was it disappointment she was feeling?

She was scheduled to meet with the Chief of Police and Commissioner Bragg at City Hall on Monday. Bragg wanted to commend her personally. Ralph and Charlie were also to be there. She knew they'd at least give her an eight dollar plaque or a laser printed certificate, shake her hand, and then take a few pictures for the *Dallas Morning News*. After weeks and weeks of negative press, embarrassment, calls for high-level resignations, the endless tasteless jokes—all the shit—the whole department had been miraculously vindicated, literally overnight. The danger was past.

But was it?

There remained small, irritating, inconsistencies which relentlessly tugged at her heart-strings, playing dissonant melodies and out-of-tune chords. She wasn't a perfectionist. She knew that things were often a little ragged around the edges in any investigation. Not all the square pegs had square holes. It wasn't an absolute requirement. Nevertheless, the nagging feeling wouldn't go away. She wanted it to. She wanted it to all be over. Then they could sleep again.

"Hey, Detective," came a familiar voice.

She turned around and saw Ralph Weatherstrom standing behind her. "Hi, Ralph." She raised her eyebrows, "Did you call me a detective?"

"Well, you're almost one," he smiled, then noticed the downcast look on her face. "Hey, what's wrong?"

Pete Brumley piped up, seated next to her on his stool, "Oh, she'll be all right. She's probably just a little shell shocked."

"Oh, give her a kiss, Petey," Jesse cackled from down at his end of the bar. "Come on, it'll cheer her up."

Pete rolled his eyes, his plump cheeks growing pinker.

Megan slid off her stool and grabbed Ralph by his tie, "No. *You*. You come give me a kiss. I want you." She needed to talk.

Ralph chuckled, his wide girth bobbing up and down. Everyone standing around laughed and applauded as she dragged him back to a dark table in the back of the bar.

Jesse called down to Pete, "I told 'ya, Pete. She wanted an older type. You should'a gone for it. Snooze 'ya lose."

"Fuck you," Pete shot back with an indignant glare.

Hal and Shannon burst into sputtering laughter.

Seated in the shadows, Ralph's own sense of relief and euphoria was evaporating in Megan's sober mood. He didn't understand. "I don't get it, Meg. What's wrong. It's over. You were a hundred percent right. We got the results back a couple of hours ago. The DNA samples matched perfectly. The semen that came from all the other crime scenes *all* came from Justin Teasdale. Unless he's got an identical twin with the same DNA, it was him. And he's dead. Verified, documented, and nicely on ice down at the Parkland morgue."

She shook her head and looked him in the eye, "I'm not so sure."

He was starting to get irritated, "Sure of what?"

"I'm not so sure it's him," she said with deadly calm. "...and I just want to be."

A nervous flutter washed over Ralph, "How can you say that?"

"Two reasons," she fired back. "One, the man who killed Sandy Depaglia, victim number two, was left-handed. I'd swear to it. Justin Teasdale was right-handed."

"How to you know that?" Ralph challenged.

"The gun was in his right hand. And based upon dental wear the man lying dead on that floor brushed his teeth with his right hand." She looked smug.

"So what?" Ralph threw back. "So he shoots and brushes with his right hand and uses a knife with his left. Maybe he's ambidextrous. Some people are. I don't buy it. Come on, Meg. Give it up. We got the damned DNA! It doesn't get any more conclusive than that. We won. It's over. Let it go. *Please.*"

"Two, the envelope." She was shivering with excitement, nervous excitement.

"What envelope?" Ralph didn't like this a bit. It was over, and he wanted it to stay over.

She kept her eyes on his. "The envelope with his final note to me."

"What about it?" he asked, wary of the answer.

"It had a small drop of blood on it," she replied. "Made by a finger, but didn't leave a fingerprint or partial."

"So?"

"So, Teasdale's hands were clean." She took a deep breath, collecting her thoughts. "And there were no gloves found anywhere in the room, or anywhere in the apartment for that matter. I searched it. I had three people from the lab team search. If he had used gloves he would have no reason to hide them, nor an opportunity to get rid of them before we got there. He supposedly didn't leave, remember?"

"So what are you saying?" he wanted her to get to the point.

Megan spoke matter-of-factly, the weight of her statement making Ralph's face flush. "The person who put that letter on the dresser, got blood on it. Justin Teasdale didn't have blood on him, except on the area of his own self-inflicted wound—assuming is *was* self-inflicted."

Ralph waved his hands like he was shooing away a cloud of mosquitoes, "Hold the phone. You think there was a third person in the room? Someone who killed Teasdale *and/or* the girl? I don't buy it. Teasdale definitely killed the girl. He had powder traces on his palm. *He* pulled the trigger. And even if there was an accomplice of some kind, where did he go? When I talked to Teasdale the building was surrounded with cops. No one came or left that building."

She didn't answer. "I don't know what I think. I just have this unnerving feeling that it's not all quite finished yet. And it's bugging the shit out of me. I have to know the answer."

Ralph counted his own logic on his fingers, "Meg, we checked the guy out. Justin Teasdale was a small time hustler, a drifter. No one has ever seen him lately on a Friday night. He apparently had something important to do *every* Friday. Now we know what it was. We checked the cemetery like you said. We saw the dried bouquets with the missing flowers, matching the crimes perfectly. It was *his* mother who died when he was only eleven."

Megan started to say something in rebuttal.

Ralph droned on, "All of the semen samples positively put him at the scene of the crime in all the other killings. Every one! Plus, only three rounds were fired from the gun. Your team found one in the wall next to the girl's head. A clean miss. Both that round, and round number two that killed the girl, were fired from the exact angle and height Teasdale's body was found in. The third round dusted Teasdale himself from point blank contact range. He shot the girl, then shot himself. Simple. Even the DA could convict on as much as we have. No questions asked. Open and shut."

"But don't you see. That's what bothers me. There was a hell of a lot more going on between those two bullets." Her voice raised in intensity. "Let's say you're right. He's kneeling at the foot of the bed and shoots the girl. But then, for some reason, he gets up and burns her with the torch. He puts the flowers on her. For some other unknown reason he walks over and maybe touches her with the envelope and gets a little blood on it, somehow without getting any on himself. Then he returns it to the dresser. Then you call. After he talks to me, he hangs up, and then he kneels back down at the end of the bed and pops himself. Does that make any sense? That's stupid. Why even return to the same spot?"

"So you have another explanation?" he challenged.

"Not exactly," she replied, her own candor making herself feel very disturbed. She was trembling again too.

"So what do you want to do?" he asked flatly.

"I just want to be sure," she pleaded, placing her palms flat on the table. "That's all. Look. I think it would be good to have the lab team go over everything we have. Just one more time. Especially, I want to see all the skin samples I've collected tested. I want to order DNA matching tests to compare all the skin with the semen samples."

Ralph laughed, "For what? You know they'll match. You think a different guy killed all those girls, but somehow he managed to figure out a way to fuck them with Teasdale's dick?" His face darkened. He pushed himself back from the table with a terse huff. "Give me a fuckin' break, Meg. I'm not bitin'. The case's closed."

"Semen can be obtained in other ways," she offered weakly.

"A gallon of it? All from the same guy?" Ralph slapped his forehead. "What do you think your phantom butcher was doing, puttin' a milk bucket under Teasdale and jerkin' him off in his sleep? I don't think so."

The absurdity of the image Ralph painted shamed her. Megan's face drooped, her cheeks turning red. "You're right. It's stupid. I'm sorry. I don't know why I'm doing this. It's like a fever."

Ralph felt a little better. He didn't want to admit it, but she started to worry him there for a minute. He put a fatherly hand on top of hers. "Hey, it's okay I tell you what." He caught her eye and smiled, "I'll let Commissioner Bragg know that we're doing all the proper follow up for our files and for the Serial-Killer specialists and forensic teams. We'll get all those other tests run you want. Even if it's a waste of time and taxpayer money. That way, no matter what, we'll all sleep good at night knowing we got our man. Fair enough?"

She smiled, "Thanks, Ralph." When she leaned over and kissed his cheek, the gang at the bar started clapping and hooting and making a general nuisance of themselves.

Megan blushed again.

•

Ralph felt good about his talk with Megan for almost two hours. That is, until her pesky concerns started to nag at him again. Dammit. What if there *was* a third party, an accomplice who had slipped away in all the commotion? Was that even possible? Did it even matter anymore? Who was this shit-bag Justin Teasdale anyway? His own words came back to haunt him: Justin Teasdale was a small time hustler, a drifter. What the hell was a drifter doing leasing a high dollar place in the Carlisle Towers? Where'd he get the money for the clothes? The furnishings?

Drugs? Organized crime connections? No. It didn't feel right.

As usual, he knew Megan was right. There were still some things that just plain didn't feel right. Since it was Saturday, he called Commissioner Bragg at home, using a pay phone at the Seven-Eleven across the parking lot from The Stagger Inn. He glanced at his watch. It was almost eleven. That was all right. It wasn't too late to call. Over the past few weeks he began to feel more and more comfortable with the crusty old city bureaucrat. They came from the same generation and shared a lot of the same bottom-line values and concerns. During the course of the investigation DeWayne T. Bragg had asked Ralph to call any time he needed to, day or night, home or office.

This was one of those times he needed to call.

Truthfully, at that moment Ralph just needed to talk to Commissioner Bragg about Megan's concerns, get the old man's thoughts, and let him know about the follow up to be sure everything was but to bed. He just needed some reassurance. The phone rang seven times before it was answered.

Unfortunately, the Commissioner and his wife weren't home. According to their son, who was visiting, they were out celebrating the victory themselves, and weren't expected to return until late. Ralph just left a message asking for Bragg to call tomorrow morning, and dictated a brief note about initiating the follow-up on Monday. Ralph knew if Bragg had a problem with it he'd be on the phone later that night or at first light— in plenty of time to nix the deal before Monday. But deep down inside Ralph knew he wouldn't. The Commissioner would instinctively share the same concerns he and Megan did. All three of them would eagerly await the outcome of the additional forensic tests.

•

Tonight was the night.

He had to do it. It could no longer wait. The tall man walked over to the desk and sat down in front of the computer terminal. His fingers flew over the keyboard with familiar aplomb. All contingencies had to be accounted for. There could be no mistakes. There could be no interruptions, not from nosy neighbors nor inopportune friends.

He logged onto the City of Dallas public database, his fingers pecking and stroking even faster as the excitement built. He had all the necessary passwords. For enough money you can have most anything. Soon he was into the telephone records, typing in new information and amending old. There wasn't that much to change. A simple "Sort & Replace" command altered information in huge blocks. It wouldn't be noticed right away. Not that it mattered. It wasn't intended to be a permanent change. However, it would assure adequate quantities of valuable time before backup records could be accessed for verification and correction. And like he always said, timing was the key to everything.

Perfect.

The required transactions took less than ten minutes to complete. Central Office telephone switches weren't that difficult to reprogram. He chuckled softly to himself as he switched his computer off. He then went to his closet and selected his finest navy-blue, double-breasted suit, and dressed for the evening. He pictured the face of Megan Pembrooke and smiled. She'd be *so* surprised.

She was.

CHAPTER 28

CHECK

Saturday
July 6, 2013

He woke up from another brief nap with start, still sitting up in his chair. Had he dozed off again? It was late. He had been working so hard lately, he seemed to need more and more sleep. Tonight was *definitely* the night.

It was finished.

Megan would surely love it. All the hoopla of the murder case was now behind them. She was now a hero. He knew she would be. He wanted her to be a hero and get her wish of becoming a real detective almost as bad as she did. There wasn't anything he wouldn't do to help her. When he heard her coming up the steps outside, he rushed to the door.

It was 11:30 P.M.

"Hi, Meg," Dominic Callaghan called out across the hallway, just sticking his head out the door.

She looked tired, her eyes glassy. "Hi, Dominic. How are you?"

"I'm good," he tried to sound cheerful, but noticed the listlessness in her eyes. "Are you okay?"

She listed against the doorframe of her apartment, her keys still jingling in her hand. "Yeah, just had a few too many Sam Adams down at the Inn. Beddy-bye-time for me."

His smile returned, "I have something to show you, Meg. I really want you to see it."

Not this again. Megan looked into the warm, innocent puppy dog eyes. What? A new stamp collection? A gift from his aunt Flossy in Maine? Not tonight. She really wasn't up to it, but she hated putting him off one more time. She gave him a forlorn sigh, "I'm really tired, Dominic. How about first thing in the morning. Okay?" It was then she noticed he wasn't wearing his heavy black-frame glasses. His face was quite striking. How odd she hadn't noticed it before.

He persisted, "No, Meg. Come on over. Please? I've got a present for you. Something I've been working on for a long time. Just for you. You'll love it. I promise."

"Do I *have* to?" she resisted.

"Yes," he constrained. "Please? For me?"

She looked back at her door, then back to Dominic. Her sleigh bed was sweetly calling. She could hear it distinctly. Those pitiful eyes across the hall were begging.

"Will it take long?"

He did his best to keep smiling, opening his door and stepping out in full view to welcome her, "It doesn't have to. But you can take as long as you like."

Megan's jaw dropped. Dominic was wearing a beautiful tailored suit, dark blue and double-breasted. He was gorgeous. Megan rubbed her eyes. Maybe it was an illusion. She looked again. No, it was Dominic, standing there more handsome than she'd ever seen him before. He held his hand out and warmly beckoned her to come inside.

"Wow," she half-laughed, "You look great. What's the occasion?"

"Come and see," he said, his voice uncharacteristically smooth and even.

She put her keys back in her canvass shoulder bag and walked across the hallway. "Okay, so what's this big surprise?"

"A new adventure," he said, taking her hand and leading her over to the couch and gesturing for her to sit. He pushed the front door to, but it didn't latch, drifting back open about two inches. It was unimportant. He was far too excited about the moment.

Megan was fascinated with the complex array of electronic devices arranged on the coffee table. In the middle of the table was a large plastic box, about the size of an older DVD player. Connected to the box by long spiraled wires were two sets of wrap-around goggles, each fitted with ear-phones. Two pairs of heavy gloves, not quite as big as hockey gloves, but larger than work gloves, were also tethered to the central box by numerous wires.

"What is this?" She was starting to feel an excited tingle of childlike curiosity.

"Quite simply, it's the ultimate game," Dominic replied, handing her a headset and a pair of gloves. "Here. Put these on."

She looked at them apprehensively, "What do they do?"

"They take you on a whole new adventure." His eyes grew wide as he slipped his hands in his own pair of gloves and started adjusting the chin strap on his headset.

"Okay," the euphoric light-headedness she brought home with her from The Stagger Inn gave her a bold sense of confidence. What the hell. Dominic had crafted some pretty neat games in the past. What could he have come up with this time?

"Is this a new game?" It was a stupid question, suggested by Samuel Adams.

Dominic stopped, "Oh, it's more than just a game, Meg. It's the greatest thing I've ever done." He looked into her eyes, "And I did it for you. You inspired it."

She looked back into his bright blue eyes, her cheeks turning pink. She was genuinely touched. "You did it for me?"

He nodded.

"And am I the first one to see it?" she asked.

He shrugged, "Well, you're the first one, besides me, to ever play it. Other than my accountant and business manager in New York who puts together the marketing packages, my lawyer here in town who does the patent and copyright work, and two Virtual Reality engineers at Cal Tech, you're now the only other person in the world who even knows it exists. But not for long. It's almost ready to publish."

"Did you say Virtual Reality?" Megan caught her breath. She had read several articles about it, and was fascinated by the audio-visual technology which could seemingly make you a part of the game instead of merely a spectator. "Let me see!"

Dominic was glowing with pride. "Okay. Put your headset on. I'll start the program and just run the demo first. If you like it, I'll run the tutorial for you. You need to see that before you can actually play the main module. But it's completely self-teaching. So you don't have to feel like you're missing anything while you're getting the hang of it."

She was excited, slipping her hands into the gloves and pulling the headset firmly into place. "Okay. Cool. Let her rip!"

Dominic reached over and activated the play mechanism. Massive optical terabyte disc drives spun into action as the system booted. Hundreds of megabytes of digitized information poured into Random Access Memory registers like water filling acres of microscopic ice trays. The graphics processors initialized. The images interfaced with the audio/visual/tactile response system.

The game had begun.

"Oh, wow!" Megan moaned, her hands reaching out in front of her as if groping for balance.

Inside the simulation, she had emerged from darkness, flying at high speed like a bird through the clouds banking and diving, moving over the open sea toward a distant crooked crag of a shoreline. An orchestra played a chilling, dissonant overture as she approached a dark and menacing castle perched on a sheer cliff. She circled the enormous gargoyle encrusted structure once, landing on the massive wooden drawbridge on the land side. The animation was breathtaking, perfectly lifelike, three dimensional, more realistic than a movie. At the castle gates she was stopped and challenged by a uniform gatekeeper, armed with a crossbow.

"What's thy bidding?" he inquired with a heavy brogue. "To watch the games, to enter the academy, or to try thyne own skills?"

"What do I do?" Megan asked.

She heard Dominic's voice muffled in her right ear. "There's a microphone in your headset, attached to a speech recognition processor. Tell him you just want to see the games."

"How?" she asked.

"Anyway you want. It's pretty smart. It can even detect gender."

She looked at the gatekeeper, "I want to see the games, sir." This was fun.

"Aye. Take the stairs to the left. But watch thy step, fair lady."

It actually felt like she was walking forward, entering the huge carved stone gates of the castle. The archway just inside was lined with niches, each containing a marble statue of a Roman warrior. Her character saw a long staircase and headed for it. Other live action characters ran up and down in full period costume. One, a motley bard, bumped into her, and she actually though she felt a shove. Megan thought the sensory effect was even better than 3D IMAX shows.

At the top of the staircase she walked out on a wide parapet. To her left, over the top of the wall, was the rolling sea, crashing against the cliffs below. Gulls shrieked across the sky. Straight before her lay a large open air gallery. It was crowded with medieval characters, some cheering some hissing and throwing bits of food. A young boy, a page, politely showed her to a seat beneath a covered tent, near a nobleman's box. The sight beyond the waist-high stone wall, looking down in to the castle's enormous courtyard made her gasp with glee. The yard was marked off into a giant black and white marble chessboard. Black and White forces opposed each other in their traditional starting positions.

Megan squealed, "A chess game! Ah, Dominic, you wizard! And you made all of this for me?"

The nobleman next to her, turned to her and replied, "Quiet, lass, or I'll have you flogged. The games are about to begin."

She held her tongue.

From her "fifty-yard-line" vantage, Megan sat in dumfounded wonder. She was actually there, magically transported over time and space to an enormous fortress somewhere in the middle ages watching the most ancient of ritual battles about to commence. How did he do this? Who cares? At that moment she just wanted to watch. In the back of her mind she remembered that he said that you could actually play the game and not just watch. That would be fun. Maybe she would stay and both enroll in the academy *and* try her skills before she went home.

The nobleman next to her raised a large white handkerchief, blown lightly by a gentle wind coming in off the sea. Trumpeters on the wall heralded the commencement. The blue sky began to darken as a series of black clouds rolled in as if summoned by witchcraft. The handkerchief drifted down to the playing field in a lazy serpentine. As soon as it touched the soft earth below, a foot soldier on the front lines of the white army marched out two squares in front of his queen and stopped.

Megan giggled again. It was at that time that she noticed the generals of the armies. Behind each army, high up in what could only be described as a Feudal press-box, sat an ominous looking uniformed and robed general on a small throne, flanked by two armed attendants. Each general held a jewel encrusted scepter in his hand. These were obviously the actual players. Megan's eyes went to the Black general

He pointed his black scepter down to the game board. A beam of light flew from the end of the wand in his hand to the head of his king's knight. Megan expected to see the knight move, but what preceded it chilled her. The Black general seemed to become more spirit than man, dissolving into a misty apparition, swooping out of his elevated box like a black specter and soared down into the knight, becoming one with the knight, possessing his body. The knight's horse reared and rode forward two squares and to his right one square. The spirit returned to the general's box and materialized back into flesh and bone.

Amazing.

Megan was totally engrossed in the action. Dominic sat next to her on the sofa, just watching her body language, knowing exactly where she was in the demo module by the way she'd cheer for one piece or another. The first capture was coming up soon. He hoped she liked it and didn't take any offense.

Thinking ahead, Megan's expectation was for pieces to engage in simple combat. She wasn't prepared for what lay ahead. The first piece to fall in battle was a pawn, taken by a bishop. The holy man removed the purple stole from his neck and strangled the foot soldier to death. It wasn't quick and efficient like in a typical video chess game. It took several moments. The soldier, more of a gnarled Hobbit in relation to the size of the bishop, struggled and fought for his miserable little life. Megan could actually see the poor pawn's face turning red, his melon-ball eyes bulging out, and his leather-mail clad arms and legs twitching in his death throws. The clergyman's arms tensed and trembled, his haggard old face angry, his crooked teeth bared and clenched, squeezing tighter and tighter until the dwarf moved no more. When the small body fell to the playing board, it burst into flame and was quickly consumed, then instantly vanished.

Megan's heart was pounding. The only person she had ever seen firsthand actually lose his life was Troy Bigham. She had just seen another life extinguished. She wanted to take the headset off and run away, but she couldn't. She was completely entranced. Her mind was locked into the game. She knew what moves were to be made. Which one would the general choose?

The next capture was a white knight taking a black knight. They fought with broadswords, sparks flying every time a blade made contact with shield or armor. The white knight prevailed with an expert slice across the black knight's throat, catching him under the edge of his helmet. Blood spilled on the battleground. The black knight fell to his knees, his gauntlet covered hands clutching at his throat as his heart pumped fountains of blood from his body. When he hit the board, face first, he too burst into flames and disappeared. Megan could feel herself trembling. It was the most grisly thing she had ever seen—until the black rook attached a white bishop.

The small stone castle opened and a hairy beast emerged, part man, part animal—all lethal. The bishop knelt and prayed for his life, his cries for mercy echoing in Megan's ears. The animal didn't care. Long tines of drool dripped from its bared fangs. It's nostrils flared with a blood lust at fever pitch. The bishop prayed for God's grace. The blood-thirsty rook martyred him regardless, tearing the cleric's flesh from his bones with his teeth while the victim was still alive. The minister's screams were almost more than Megan could endure. She had to look away.

The nobleman looked down at her, "What's wrong with you, m'lady?"

She looked back up at him, completely oblivious to the fact that she was sitting on a couch in an apartment, not in a private box watching the gruesome carnage. "I can't bear to see anymore."

"Nay, thou art able," the nobleman contradicted. "Open thyne eyes. Her majesty the queen sets upon the vile rook just now. Justice will thus be served."

Megan's eyes returned to the board. She didn't want to look, but she had to. The white queen spread her arms and approached the castle. The beast screamed in terror and ran back inside its gray stone lair. The queen pointed her own scepter at the tiny structure. Lightning flashed from its tip. The rook's abode exploded in a shower of stone fragments, disintegrating into rubble around the cowering beast's feet. The monster bellowed its futile protest. The queen's wand pointed again. A cruel wooden whipping post rose from beneath the rook's square, towering up almost twenty feet in the air. Another wave of the wand and the beast was spun around by invisible hands and shackled to the post. The royal warrior spoke her indiscernible command and the whipping post rose another two feet, lifting the beast's flailing feet off the ground. He continued to groan and bellow in terror.

The queen grasped the ends of her wand and pulled it apart. The air was filled with a brief shriek of steel. Inside the wand was a thin gleaming blade, like a Samurai warrior's hare-kare sword. Megan could actually feel the nausea in her stomach start to bubble up to her throat as she watched the bejeweled woman approach the screaming animal.

The queen cut it near the shoulder with the tip of the blade, carving out a small flap of its hide. Dark rivulets of blood were already running down its back, matting into its thick fur. It groaned in mortal pain. But the superficial wound was inconsequential to what lay ahead. Her Majesty the Queen grabbed the dangling flap with her free hand and ripped down hard, tearing the beast's skin from its howling body to the applause and cheers of the gallery. The mortal cries of the wounded creature echoed throughout the arena, penetrating into Megan. The blade came up and the torture was repeated. The strips of hide were dropped in a pile like carpet scraps. Megan couldn't breathe. She was watching the animal being skinned alive.

Skinned alive?

A strangulation.

A severed throat.

Bites.

Skinned.

It all rang too familiar—specific details she had spent the last few weeks of her life wrestling with, things never made fully public, terrible things she never told him, things only the police and the killer knew. The blood was draining out of Megan's face. Her eyes closed. Her entire body was trembling.

Don't panic.

229

She pulled off the tactile-response gloves and slowly reached up and took off the Virtual Reality headset, doing everything within her power to remain absolutely calm. As the visor came free, she instantly returned to her own space and time. There sitting next to her was Dominic, just grinning, his eyes brimming with expectation—a Dominic she had never seen before, dressed so handsome, so charming. What lonely girl wouldn't succumb to the wiles of a guy who looked like that? It must have been so easy for him.

His eyes continued to search hers, waiting for a response. He was obviously most concerned about her reaction. Did she like it? Was it too graphic? Was she grossed out? His heart was pounding almost as hard as hers.

She had to ask, remembering the propane torch on the nightstand in Apartment 15-C at the Carlisle tower. Her voice was strangely detached and hollow, "And when the king attacks, does he burn his victims?"

Dominic looked surprised, "How'd you know that?" He grinned, his excitement growing, "It's really cool. Do you want me to skip ahead to that? He turns into this great big dragon... and... then ..." his voice trailed off into confused silence at the sight of tears in Megan's eyes.

"Why, Dominic?" she asked. "Why did you do it?"

He was puzzled, his expression so childlike and pure, "I told you, Meg. I did it all for you." He blushed, "I really care about you."

He couldn't look her in the eye anymore. The weight of realization crashed down on him. She was offended. He'd made her cry. He'd screwed up again. How could that be? He really didn't think she'd be that sensitive about it. After all, it was only a game. He wished everything would just go away. He wished he could just make it all go away. His head started to feel dizzy again.

Megan watched Dominic's eyes flutter for a second.

He opened them again, strangely calm and serene. His voice was smooth and even. "I'm sorry, Meg. I really thought you'd like it. Silly. Yes? I'm so sorry you didn't."

She opened her mouth wide and sucked in a staggered breath. Her purse was next to her. Her gun was in it. She looked him right in the eye, "Dominic, I'm sorry too." She glanced toward his kitchen as an idea formed, "Could I please have some water?"

"Oh, certainly," he rose quietly from the couch, his eyes fluttering again as though he were momentarily disoriented. The smoothness in his voice vanished as abruptly as it came. "... j-j-just a second."

A second was all she needed.

He disappeared into the kitchen. Her hand dove inside her bag, finding the grip of her pistol. She heard a cabinet open and close and the tap ran for a second—then the sound of footsteps.

Megan was ready.

Over her gun sight Megan watched Dominic drop the full water glass on the tile below when he came back into the living room and heard her scream at the top of her lungs, *"DON'T YOU FUCKING MOVE!"*

"Meg, what are you doing?" he shouted back at her, his feet came up and down like he was standing barefoot on hot pavement, splashing in the spilled puddle of water.

She kept the muzzle of her Beretta pointed directly at his face, speaking slow, her words measured and deliberate, "I... said... don't... move."

Dead silence.

He stood stone-still, his head was still spinning in confusion. His stomach hurt, twisting and knotting. Was she kidding? He started to relax with chuckle of realization, shaking his finger at her, "Oh, that's a good one. I get it."

She didn't move a muscle, her jaws tensing.

He threw his hands up, apologizing, "Meg, I'm sorry if the game scared you." He let out a heavy sigh of relief, "Okay, we're even. You scared the piss out of me." He started to bend down and retrieve the fallen glass, "I'll get you another glass of water and some paper towels."

The thunder of the pistol was deafening.

The front of Dominic's microwave oven in the kitchen behind him exploded in a shower of glass and electrical sparks. Megan could see a wet stain spreading in his pants as his own urine tickled down his pant leg into his shoe. The pungent odor filled the air. His chin was trembling in fear; his eyes were two pools of sheer terror and disbelief.

"Maybe you didn't hear me. I said, *don't* fucking move." The hard glare in her eyes said she wouldn't repeat it again without drawing blood and/or severing an appendage with the next round.

Dominic was frozen where he stood with fear. This certainly wasn't the reaction he expected. His words came out amid a stammering sob, "Oh, God, I'm sorry, Meg. I really am. *Please!* Come on. Would you *please* put the gun down. Please?"

She kept her weapon trained on his face as she moved over to an end table and lifted the phone handset out of its charging cradle. She dialed 911, heard a click and a voice answer. She screamed into the receiver, "Officer needs assistance." She rattled off the street address. "Code three. Notify Detective Ralph Weatherstrom, Dallas homicide. *Now!* Get here *NOW!*" She hung up the phone, never taking her eyes off of Dominic.

He stood there stunned and trembling, about to fall down.

She spoke, slowly, evenly, struggling to stay in control of her faculties. "Now we wait."

"Are... uh... the *police* coming?" Dominic timidly asked.

"You better believe it, sonny," she scowled, her knees knocking violently. In another moment she'd empty her own bladder in her jeans. "Scores of 'em. And you're not getting away this time."

He gave her another puzzled look. "Meg, what are you talking about? Get away from what?"

She wanted to pistol whip him for his insolence. "Just shut up and stand there. You so much as twitch and you'll be dead before your worthless carcass hits the floor—which is more consideration that you showed any of your victims."

Dominic's eyes narrowed, his eyes starting to flutter once more. He had that strange sensation that one of his spells was coming on. He didn't want to faint in front of her. His voice was smooth again, unusually calm, almost detached, "Meg, it was just a game. An illusion. You're going off the deep end here. Calm down. I know you've been under a lot of pressure lately, but you need to relax. Okay? I'm not going to do anything, but stand here like you said. Okay? Look, if you really hate the game that much, I swear to God I'll erase it. It's not that important to me. But you are. I mean that."

The dizziness was returning.

There was an innocence in his eyes which throttled Megan's raw adrenaline down a notch. Something felt wrong again—desperately wrong. That face before her didn't look capable of committing such acts of abomination. But looks were so often deceiving. She'd just seen the brutality and the horror in his game, a product of his own self-admitted imagination. It was a horror she had seen firsthand five times in as many weeks. The odds of one technique being similar could have been coincidence. But all five? Astronomical.

No. Impossible.

Her mind raced to understand. He was ill. Hell, who knows? Perhaps it was one of those split personality things. Jekyll and Hyde. Sibyl. The Seven Faces of Eve. Hell, it happens. God, she wished the cavalry would get there soon. Her forearms trembled. Her elbows were screaming. The weight of the gun in her hands was getting painfully heavy. The gun's sight quivered as she steadfastly struggled to keep it held aloft, leveled at his face.

"If you'd please be so kind as to lower your weapon *ever* so slowly, Megan dear," a rich, cultured voice interrupted from the doorway.

CHAPTER 29

ADVANCE OF THE KNIGHTS: RALPH AND CHARLIE

Sunday
July 7, 2013

It was after midnight. Charlie McManus was as restless as Megan Pembrooke that night. He couldn't sleep. His face was aglow with the soft light of his computer monitor on the third floor of the Harwood Street Police station. He was logged into the Department of Motor Vehicles, fastidiously pecking in license plate numbers.

Ever since he walked into the Carlisle Tower late Friday night and saw the dead man on the floor and the dead woman in the bed, something didn't sit right with him either. He heard some of Megan's remarks, mumbling to herself as she painstakingly looked over the bodies. He noticed a few of the things to which she was paying special attention. He even helped in the search for the missing gloves. They found nothing.

And yet...

Normally, he would have just let it go and not given it a second thought. The case was neatly wrapped up. They couldn't have asked for a more tidy conclusion to Justin Teasdale's obvious reign of terror. On Monday, Chief Moranzano and Commissioner Bragg would pat them all on the back for a job well done.

But how well done was it?

Shit. The twitch in his stomach was all Pembrooke's fault. Why did she make it all feel so incomplete? He had to be sure himself. Pembrooke poked around like there might have been more than two people in that room that night. As implausible as it might seem, it was something he had to put to rest in his own gut. And he was bound and determined to do it *his* way, the old fashioned way, with hard work, raking through the tedious dung heap of insignificant details.

Was there an accomplice?

If so, he had to get to the scene of the crime somehow. Perhaps he drove. Charlie laughed softly to himself, thinking sometimes it paid to be both good *and* lucky. A few things he knew for sure. The log at the lobby desk of the Carlisle Towers that last Friday night only showed one guest, a lady escorted by tenant Justin Teasdale. No one else in the building had visitors that night. That would mean that every car in the secure underground parking garage that night supposedly belonged to a tenant. No cars came or went from the building from the second it was secured. He had spent over an hour Friday night walking the two levels writing down license plate numbers. Even now he was feeding them into the computer, one-by-one, then checking residents names off a master roster as he went. So far every car belonged to a tenant.

When a vehicle came up registered to Justin Teasdale, he felt that familiar detective's flutter in his stomach—the gray and purple butterfly that mysteriously whispers to pay careful attention to something you may not presently understand. It was an old 1996 Chevy Malibu.

What the hell?

He couldn't picture someone who lived in high-dollar digs like the Carlisle Tower, wearing thousand dollar suits, driving a fucking late-model piece-of-shit Chevy. He knew from some of the follow-up reports earlier that day that Teasdale was a male-whore, but just assumed he was good at it. Surely one of the many Lexus, Mercedes, Infinities, BMWs, or Porsches he saw down there was his. Maybe it was a second car, or a loaner. Maybe he had a nicer one in the shop. Who knows. Charlie's head started to hurt. He kept typing in numbers.

The minutes became an hour.

Charlie stuck his pencil in his mouth as he lazily pecked in the next license plate number from a black Porsche convertible. He remembered it. It was a nice looking car. The computer chugged for a few seconds, then a file popped up with the current registration of the vehicle. Charlie read the name.

Charlie stopped breathing.

He blinked twice and read it again. His face flushed red. The pencil between Charlie McManus' teeth fell out and tinkled onto the floor. His hands suddenly flew to the keyboard. His fingers quickly selected the record for a driver's license cross reference. The name, address, and description came up on the screen.

There it was—Height: 6'1". Weight: 185 lb. Eyes: Blue. Hair: Brown. "Oh, dear God," he whispered as his hand lunged for his phone.

•

Ralph Weatherstrom had been sitting on the edge of his bed in his pajamas, staring at the phone on the nightstand for almost half an hour, thinking it might ring. His wife Mari was snuggled down in their bed, rolled over on her side with her back to him, soundly asleep. He checked his watch. It was just after 1:00 A.M. The red day-and-date on the face of his watch indicated it was already Sunday.

He made up his mind.

Bragg wouldn't mind. He'd understand, even if he was already planning on calling in the morning. He dialed Bragg's number again.

A weary male voice answered on the fifth ring, "Hello?"

"Commissioner?" Ralph asked, embarrassed that he bothered the old man so late at night. This could have waited until morning.

"Yes?" the voice replied. "Who is this?"

Ralph flirted with the fleeting temptation to just hang up, but heard himself say, "This is Detective Weatherstrom, sir. Uh...did you get my message?"

Ralph could hear Bragg, coughing and fumbling around for a second, then tersely asking, "What message? Dammit, man, have you any idea what *time* it is?"

Ralph swallowed hard, "Yes, sir. I spoke with your son earlier and asked him to have you call me. Didn't you get the message?"

"No," Bragg fired back. "I came home and went to bed, like I always do. What's so damn important?"

Over the next ten minutes, Ralph did his level best to explain all of his concerns and doubts about the conclusion of the case.

The Commissioner threw up as many objections as Ralph did to Megan, before conceding in sheer fatigue, "All right, Ralph. Fuck it. I'm tired. Do what you want. I don't care anymore. It's over. Order the damn tests, so we can put all of this to bed. Which is *exactly* where I want my tired ass right now."

"Thank you, sir. I'll follow-up with you on Monday." He hung up the phone.

A funny thought struck him. Why hadn't the commissioner's received the message? There was no way his son could have failed to grasp the urgency of the situation. It didn't make any sense. The more he thought about it the more it bothered him. Was it just indifference? Was he too

busy? Was the fancy Harvard lawyer too good to dirty his hands with police business? Hell, it was his father he was asking for. What was the
fucking problem?

He looked at the phone again.

There was only one person who might be able to make some sense of
it. It didn't matter how late it was. He picked up the receiver again and
started to dial Megan's number, then stopped. He felt stupid again. She'd
think he was being as paranoid as she had been.

He sighed. No, he'd wait. It could wait till tomorrow. He cuddled up
next to Mari. His eyes wouldn't close.

CHAPTER 30

A MOST WORTHY ADVERSARY

Sunday
July 7, 2013

Megan Pembrooke looked to her left.

Dominic Callaghan looked to his right.

There in the open doorway of Dominic's apartment stood a tall, hand-some man: about six-one, a hundred an eighty-seven pounds, with brown curly hair and the most piercing blue eyes Megan had ever seen. He was wearing a dashing silk navy-blue double-breasted suit—one very similar to Dominic's—and a blood-red silk tie. The man just stood there smiling and relaxed, leaning against the door frame with his left foot crossed over the right. He could have been Justin Teasdale's fraternal twin brother. Unfortunately, just like the late Justin Teasdale, this man also held a men-acing black 9mm Glock in his hand—his left hand—complete with long, slender silencer. Only, this one was aimed directly at Megan.

"Please?" the tall man requested with such polite gentility.

Megan didn't move for a second. She blinked twice in stunned disbe-lief. Her mind was struggling comprehend what she was actually seeing, seriously questioning her own sanity.

He added, "My dear, in the event you may be tempted to do some-thing rash, I can surely pull this trigger much faster than you could hope to spin, level, and fire. I assure you. Please don't feel the slightest inclina-tion to put the theory to the test."

"Rick, what the hell's going on?" Dominic asked the man standing in the doorway. "Thank God you're here. What the hell did I do? Am I being arrested for something?"

Megan's eyes went back to Dominic, then back to the smiling man standing casually in the doorway, who was gesturing toward the floor with the muzzle of his gun. She obediently dropped her Beretta to the floor with a thick clatter, her eyes abruptly returning to Dominic's perplexed face. "You *know* this guy?"

Dominic nodded vigorously, "Of course. He's my attorney."

"*Was* your attorney," the man in the door amended. The muzzle of the gun swung quickly to the man's left, toward Dominic. It spit once.

In that fleeting instant, as she felt her bowels clench tight, Megan saw a bright spot of red open up in Dominic's upper chest. Glistening crimson spots splattered the doorframe and wall beyond him. He never said a word, nor cried out, nor made any noise of protest or anguish at all, save a stifled gasp. His body left the floor, tumbling backward and crashing hard into his breakfast bar, then tumbled heavy to the floor, lying on his back, still and lifeless. His eyes were closed. Four distinct streaks of fresh blood drew thin lines down the front of the breakfast bar to the baseboard.

"*No!*" Megan screamed. Fresh burning tears instantly boiled out of her eyes and rushed down her cheeks. She started to move toward him. Another metallic spit discharged. A thick piece of the carped directly in front of her was torn up by an invisible claw. The stench of burned fibers filled her nose.

"Ah, ah, ah," the man in the door chastised. "This way, my love."

She looked back to the tall man. A light of recognition came on. His face wasn't altogether unfamiliar. It was a strikingly handsome face. She knew that face. She instinctively knew she'd seen it only once, but quite recently.

Where?

Rick? That's what Dominic called him. Those eyes. That smile. That finely chiseled nose. The angle of his jaw. The way he carried himself, even standing in the doorway, so regal, like a prince. Yet the fleeting image she had of him buried back in a dark recess of her mind wasn't in a tailored suit. The image slowly came forward in her mind's eye, blurred and foggy at first, then sharpening clear and distinct. No. That striking face she had seen had not been attired in a lawyer's raiment. It was set atop a body arrayed in a burgundy cap and gown. The gold leaf outline and the Latin motto of the Harvard crest—Ve Ri Tas, came to mind.

Then she remembered. She knew exactly who he was.

"I know you," she whispered, almost to herself in shocked realization. But it couldn't be. Yet it was. "The old man's son."

"Why, yes! *Very* impressive, Megan dear." He gave her a genteel nod of genuine admiration. "You know, from your reputation I feel like I know *you* so well. But regrettably, I'm afraid we've never been properly introduced. So how, may I ask, did you arrive at that remarkable deduction?"

"Your picture," she mumbled, still in dumfounded shock.

"Ah," he smiled, proudly commending, "Simply amazing. There aren't that many of them. You've obviously been to my father's office or his home on at least one occasion. Very good. *Very* good indeed. I knew you were the best one all along, Megan. You have *such* an eye for detail. It's patently uncanny. Not that it matters at this point." He sighed with exaggerated melancholy, "It's such a pity to have to quench such a noble flame."

She swallowed hard. "What are you going to do?"

"I told you," he gestured with the gun, "This way. And do be *ever* so quiet. Yes?"

Her eyes glanced around. Her gun was out of reach. If she screamed she'd be dead before she hit the carpet, just like Dominic. Nothing came instantly came to mind.

Patience.

The little voice inside spoke plainly and distinct. She reverently heeded it's counsel. Yes. It was time to wait and watch—and pray.

Trembling down to her toes she hesitantly walked toward him, realizing that if he just wanted to shoot her, he would have already done so. A moment later that wasn't such a comforting thought.

What else might he have in mind?

He discreetly marched across the concrete hallway her over to her own apartment. The door was unlocked. He'd left it that way. Inside, he bade her take a seat on her couch while he closed her front door. "You know, I've been sitting over here waiting for you for almost an hour. I was beginning to think you'd *never* get home. You have nothing good to read in this pitiful little apartment of yours. Most disappointing." He glanced at the huge TV, "Really, dear, you should read a bit more. A woman of your incredible caliber should well know television only rots the brain and lowers the IQ."

Megan said nothing as she timidly sat down of the left side of her sofa, defensively bringing her knees up close and hugging her legs in an almost fetal position. The shaking wouldn't stop. The old images started to come back, the taunting demons, the black winged ones with the sharp talons. She closed her eyes and willed them away.

Just the wind... the wind... the wind...

He walked over beside the coffee table, standing before her, casually glancing around the apartment, taking another visual inventory. He wasn't impressed with anything he saw this time either. "I was *soooo* bored. And you know what a miserable pain boredom can be for intellectuals like you and I. Yes?"

She wasn't the least bit amused by his glib banter.

He half-laughed, gesturing back toward the front door with the gun muzzle, "But *then*... I heard the shot come from across the way. What could it be, I asked myself." His smile blossomed. "Naturally, I raced over to see for myself. For a moment there I thought perchance you'd saved me a step on tonight's sordid errands. When I saw you holding the poor lad at gun point, I could only surmise with a deduction of my own that poor Dominic *must* have shown you that wonderful game of his. It impressed the hell out of me, I must say." His fingers came up and absently scratched his right temple. "Didn't really think he'd show it to you so soon, to tell you the truth. Must have been quite a shock. A little *déjà vous*? Yes?"

Megan felt like she was about to faint. Her heart was about to pound its way out of her chest. She held her legs tighter, her chin resting between her knees. How did it happen? She'd come so close and miscalculated again, almost killing an innocent man with her own hands. And now it looked as though she was indirectly responsible for his death anyway. She didn't want any more death. Her tears flowed freely.

"Oh, don't cry," he reached into his pocket, pulled out a fine linen monogrammed handkerchief and offered it. When she refused, he stuffed it back in his pocket, gliding over with his lithe, cat-like moves, taking a seat on the other end of the couch, to her right.

She cringed toward the arm rest.

He smiled warmly, almost affectionately, "Oh, it's not so a great loss, Megan dear. Just another pawn. Yes? No one would ever miss the miserable little computer geek. I'll grant you, he was a well-spring of good ideas." He furrowed his brow, "Then again, the lad did have quite a brutal imagination." He shrugged, "On the other hand, *you'll* be sorely missed. And Detective Weatherstrom will be *certainly* be missed."

She stifled a cry at the mention of Ralph's name. Her eyes jerked to his.

... the wind...

He nodded into her wide-eyed expression of horror, "Oh, yes, 'tis true, love. Unfortunately, poor overworked Ralph is scheduled to have a massive heart attack in but a few days hence, via a special little cocktail I'll serve at a celebratory party at my father's house. Daddy Dearest and the good Detective Weatherstrom are getting ever so close, you see." He clucked his cheek once, "Ah, yes. Poor, poor Weatherstrom. Everyone knew it was coming. He should have taken better care of himself. I guess the excitement will be a little too much for him. There won't even be an autopsy." An evil leer slithered across his lips. "I guarantee it."

Megan wiped her wet cheeks with the heels of her hands, sniffing hard, "And what about me?"

"Ah, yes, *you* my dear." He scratched the top of his head with the sharp gun sight. "Well... just thinking out loud, mind you... as far as everyone else is concerned, officially, I think perhaps you'll take a much needed leave of absence, after hearing about the tragic robbery and unfortunate slaying of your good friend across the hall. Add to that all the weight of the stressful investigation you've just ended, it's only natural that you take a little time off to get away. You know, to rest and relax, and 'get your head together' as they say. Unfortunately, you won't see fit to return to duty—*ever*. The department will get your short and sweet letter of resignation in a few weeks. And they'll understand. Some people just aren't cut out to carry a badge."

She openly sobbed, "How can you do this?"

He leaned forward, his impish smile fading into a vicious grin, almost a carnivore's snarl, "With pleasure, love. *With pleasure.*"

Her legs went back down to the floor and she half-turned to face him, an anger of frustration welling up inside her. This was completely illogical. Her lips vehemently protested before her brain had a chance to stop them, "But it was over," she shook her head in wonder. "You won. You fooled us all. Why are you doing this? All you had to do was walk away. Why Dominic? Why Ralph? Why me?"

He held the gun up between them, "Oh, Dominic was incidental. A bothersome pawn. Nothing more. But you, Megan dear. You're being far too modest, my love. You wouldn't *let* me just walk away. Dear old Ralph called me just tonight and explained about all your pesky little concerns. Like the gun in the wrong hand." He sighed, "It's true. I screwed that one up." He gave her a half-hearted shrug, "No one's perfect. And I was in a hurry. But that was of no great concern. It could easily be explained away a hundred different ways."

"Right," Megan nodded. "So why are you here?"

His eyes went wide with mock appall, "Ah! But dear Ralph also made specific mention of the additional DNA matching tests you wanted run on some...skin samples? I believe. Oh, no, no, no. I couldn't have that." He sighed with a mock crestfallen countenance, "Bad Megan. Bad meddling, clever little Megan. That's why I had to rush right over tonight and pay you this brief visit." He scolded, "Dearest, you just couldn't leave well-enough alone. Could you?"

Megan just shook her head in open-mouthed wonder.

He leaned back, looking rather pleased, "But all's forgiven. Not to worry. All things considered, I rather like it ending this way instead. As I listened to my asinine father's accounts of your puny progress I was most impressed with your efforts in particular. I sincerely hoped we'd get the opportunity to have this little chat. You were a most worthy adversary. Most worthy indeed. Yes, it was only fitting we meet face to face at least once." He grinned, "It was...only sporting."

"It's *him*, isn't it?" she whispered, her winsome voice now drained and empty. "Your father. You hate him."

"The good Commissioner, the Alderman, the Man of the Year?" His eyes went wide with sparkling glee. "How utterly Freudian of you to say so." He inched closer on the couch, keeping the gun muzzle pointed at her head, his finger carefully clutching the delicate trigger. His lips pursed thoughtfully, "Well...to be perfectly honest, perhaps you could say he's possibly a wee part of it." His smile reappeared, "But don't you think it'll be grand, in the city's moment of triumph, for Justin Teasdale to suddenly rise from the dead? Or be reincarnated in the life of some other miserable little pawn? And then bodies start showing up all over again?" His evil laughter filled the air.

Megan nodded, with a rush of twisted understanding, "Yeah. He'd lose everything. He'd be even more embarrassed. The whole department would. You'd make it look like after everything we did, after all the celebrating and gloating, we got the wrong guy again." She could smell his Aramis clearly, so teasingly sweet and sultry.

He winked at her, sliding even closer, just inches away, knowing by the look in her eye she could palpably feel his presence. "I really like you, Megan dear. I really do. You're so clever. So *very, very* clever. But you see, that's your trouble. You're so damned focused on the minutia, you don't think *ahead* far enough."

The gun muzzle touched her throat. She was confused for a second, then a pang of apprehension seized her heart: he was going to kill the Commissioner.

He confirmed her fear with his next statement. "It's even better than you could imagine. Think of it. Without his precious dignity, drummed off of his high horse for gross incompetence and driven out of town by a fearful public, it will only make perfect sense when he puts a gun to his own head, just like poor Justin did... and...*boom*." He gleefully added, "Naturally, after putting a bullet hole or two...or ten...in his pretty little trophy wife as well." His eyes fell to his lap, "No loss there. She was nothing but a gold-digger like all my pretty roses." His eyes found hers again as he sighed, "Yes, it's absolutely horrible what these unstable executive management types will do in a fit of desperate rage."

"But I still don't understand. Surely you value economy of effort. Why go to all this trouble just for revenge or hatred or whatever your problem is with him?" she asked, puzzled anew, "Why not just kill him outright? You're obviously clever enough to make it look like anything you want. Why all these games?"

He laughed, his bobbing hand driving the muzzle of the gun into her throat, the sharp edges of the silencer scratching the skin. "Oh, now where's the fun in *that*?" He paused, studying her eyes, "But to tell you the God's honest truth, my love, having dear old dad bear the brunt of the project was merely a fortuitous byproduct. Perhaps merely a convenient rationalization on my part. I didn't really give tangent motivations that much thought."

Megan was all the more confused.

He continued, "But I do want you to understand. An intellect such as yours deserves that much," His eyes went toward the ceiling, musing philosophically, "I guess it's like a mountain climber's summit, you might say. The climber says it's the goal, but the climb itself is his true love. Yes? It's true I don't care much for him, nor his beloved...*Daphne*. But in all candor, my dear, I hope you can now understand, my actions and motivations are really not so different from those whom I've...how shall I say?...*entertained*? The lovely flowers I've picked?"

She gave him a quizzical stare.

"Don't you see, Megan my dear? Each of my young ladies were all victims of their own unbridled fantasy. Each and every one, just wanted to see what an indulgent adventure felt like," he whispered, bringing his lips up next to her right ear. "Yes. Each and...*every* one. They were all willing to make themselves completely and utterly...*vulnerable*...to a complete and total stranger...to make a sordid dream come true...to relish in a lust-filled night of temporal pleasures and wanton desires, with promised of fantasies yet to be explored. And this they handsomely received...in exchange for their mortal souls."

His haunting laugh curdled Megan's blood. She felt his body press close against her right arm. Her stomach wrenched tight. She could feel his breath touching her skin, hot and moist. The nausea boiled hot within. Her eyes were clamped shut again. She shakes were intensifying.

"You see, Megan, I know these fair maidens merely wanted to *feel* good. So they acted upon their desires, their passions...their *hungers*." He shrugged with no remorse, "I merely did as well."

She dared a glance and saw his face pressed so hideously close. She had never seen eyes so malevolent, so cold, so unholy.

"Like they say, 'If it feels good, do it?' Yes?" He wiggled his eyebrows, his voice dropping low and menacing, "And it felt *soooo gooooood*. So *exceptionally* good. I admit, I rather like the game—*all* of it. The planning. The execution, pardon the pun. Baffling the keystone cops, from A to Z. It's a delightful hobby that I think I'll enjoy for a good long while." He frowned, "Though I admit, having full computer access to all the police files is surely bad form, and not terribly sporting. I may amend that practice in the future." He tipped his free hand back and forth, "Just to level the playing field a bit. Yes?"

Megan felt a hot wretch well up in her throat again as his lips made teasing contact with the side of her neck, just below her ear. His heat of his breath caressed her neck, but there was no pleasure. It was the breath of the beast. She started to pull away, tensing her legs, but the blunt contact of the silencer's end jammed against her windpipe arrested her movement. Her lungs froze.

He kissed her neck—the serpent tasting its prey.

Her body went rigid in toe-curling revulsion.

She felt his lips drifted down her neck with featherlike touches down to her collar, then followed the long, thin, strained tendon back up again with the tip of his tongue, like a serpent inspecting the lifeless body of a small rodent it just killed.

His seductively whispered, "Mmm. You taste ever so sweet, my dear. I can't begin to tell you how arousing your trembling is."

Megan didn't reply, biting down hard on the inside of her bottom lip to prevent totally hysteria. The pain helped her focus. She had to focus. The trembling uncontrollably shivered up and down her body. She started to cry again, hot and salty. She stammered, "So what do you want from me?"

She gagged when she felt his fingertips touch her side. She felt his free right hand coursed up her stomach, over the loose T-Shirt she wore, and cupped the small swell of her right breast, his lips pressing briefly against her temple. In another moment she knew she was going to scream. He leaned back a hand's breadth, and the gap flooded with relief.

His voice grew very matter-of-fact, professional, "Well, first, we have a little house cleaning to do. I want you to get all of your files and books pertaining to the case and give them to me. Everything. Computer files, whatever you have."

She glanced at his eyes again—still devoid of life, cold and hard. She could scarcely get the words out, "All I have is in my bag. Back over at Dominic's."

He frowned, "How can I believe that?"

"Have I ever lied to you?" she said weakly.

He laughed out loud, rocking his head back, leaning back further yet, "Good. Very good, Miss Pembrooke. Keep your humor to the very last. It's most noble and becoming of you." He shook his head, answering her question. "But then again, this could be the *first* time you've lied. Many a nobleman and infidel alike have lied to save their skins in a moment of desperation. I really can't afford to take that chance. Don't want any post-humous loose ends."

She was thankful when he pulled away from her. The air seemed to lighten.

The room grew silent.

What was he thinking?

His face brightened when his eyes found the little fireplace, "Yes! Of course! A fire! Oh, yes. How silly of me not to have thought of it sooner. Fires have the wonderful propensity to purge a great many sins. Wouldn't you agree?"

... the wind...

Megan's stomach churned anew. How many would die in an apartment fire this late at night? The units were crowded with families and lots of small children.

He was quite pleased with his inspiration, "Oh, yes. It's perfect. Yes, yes, yes. I think, our silly young friend Dominic next door perhaps had.. an electrical problem? *...yes...* with all that high-tech equipment of his. It's only natural a roaring blaze would take quite a few units with it, yours included, of course. Oh, yes indeed. That ought to tend to things quite nicely."

"I thought you said I just disappear, not die in a fire," her tears were flowing again, hot and stinging, with no sense of release of relief. It had been at least five minutes since she called 911. Why didn't she hear the sound of sirens yet? Didn't any of the neighbors hear the gun shot and call themselves? A frail, thin voice within her told her if she could just stall long enough, she might live.

It's just the wind...

However, at that very moment Megan Pembrooke had no idea that the click and the voice of 911 she heard when she called from Dominic's apartment was nothing but an electronic telephone switch recording, dispassionately advising her to stay on the line until the next operator became available. Nor was she aware her frantic instructions were given over the sound of classical music playing while she was on hold. She hung up before the line was transferred to an emergency attendant.

No one was coming.

"Oh, no dear. The fire's not for you. Not for my dear sweet Megan." He leaned back into her once more, kissing her earlobe, suckling it for a second. "Oh, no. I have something very special in mind for you."

Her diaphragm jolted with one violent spasm. It took everything within her to remain still.

He retreated again, reaching into his trouser pocket and pulling out his jingling key ring. "You'll be far away from here, my love. As I said, after all you've done, you deserve at least that much—to depart this world in privacy, with dignity. I'll be back to tend to the apartments later. They can wait a few hours."

Just a little longer, she vainly prayed. "So where are we going?"

His voice grew hard, dropping to a cold-blooded whisper, "Well, my pet, first I'm going to take you out for a long, quiet, romantic drive in the country. We'll stop under the stars, somewhere discreet and secluded. We'll make desperate love, with you tied Fay Wray awaiting King Kong style between two trees. I promise you'll like it. They all do. I'll undress you ever so slowly—with the edge of a blade. It'll drive you wild. I'll arouse you beyond your wildest dreams. You'll reach climaxes poets have not yet dared to imagine. Then, in the wake of your ecstasy, I'll show you the most wonderful set of antique surgical instruments I recently purchased—at a garage sale of all places. I've cleaned the rust off of most of them." He seethed, "With those precious instruments in hand, I'll treat your body to a whole new dimension of intimate pleasure derived from pain—then throw what's little there is left of you in the Trinity River for the fish to eat."

She noticed his jingling key ring with the large gold Porsche crest as he rose to his feet and stood directly in front of her. Her knees defensively came back up to her chest. The jingle was a signal to go.

Stall.

She looked up into his eyes, "Well, as tempting an offer as that is, I think I'd prefer for you to just shoot me, if it's all the same to you." It didn't occur to her until she had said the words that he might accommodate her.

He laughed again, heartily this time, his eyes brimming with tears of mirth. "Megan, I shall certainly miss you. On any other day, I'd have half a notion to let you go, just to prolong the chase. It's so deliciously amusing. You are *more* than a worthy adversary."

"Sounds good to me," she nodded.

He only laughed harder, cradling his stomach and wiping his eyes. He pulled in a deep breath and sobered in an instant. "On your feet, my love. It's time to go. Your personal adventure awaits."

CHAPTER 31

TIMING IS EVERYTHING

Sunday
July 4, 2013

"What's the matter with you?" Mari Weatherstrom leaned on her elbow, staring at her husband. Her low-pitched, raspy voice was thick with a classic Texas inflection. It sounded that much more like a hound's growl when she was half asleep. But at that moment she was genuinely concerned. Ralph had been tossing and turning for the longest time, and keeping her awake. "Are you sick at your stomach? I can get you a Zantac..."

He was sitting on the bedside with his back to her. "No, punkin. Just can't sleep."

"How come?" she sat up and rubbed a loving hand on his shoulder blade.

It felt good. "Cause I got something buggin' me."

She waited for him to continue, rubbing his shoulders with both hands the way he liked. She'd known those shoulders, and the rest of his tired old carcass for over forty years, and knew exactly where to rub to make the tension go away.

"Something weird is going on, babe," his voice betrayed a twinge of concern—no more than that—a deep sense of foreboding. "I need to talk to Pembrooke."

"So call her," Mari said mater-of-fact.

He winced when her fingers found a tender spot, "Don't know if I should. She might think it's stupid."

Mari huffed, "I think if it's keeping you up, then it's stupid not to call. She can always tell you to go to hell and call tomorrow. Then you can at least get to sleep."

Ralph smiled, then leaned back and kissed his wife. "I ever tell you I love you?"

"Not enough," she grinned.

Ralph reached for the phone.

•

"I said, it's time to go," he repeated.

Megan just sat still, frozen to her spot on the couch, in her little fetal ball, hugging her legs close to her trembling body. Her eyes looked away, "I can't. I can't move."

THWACK!

Without warning, her next sensation was the blunt impact of the pistol crashing cold and hard into her jaw. It dazed her equilibrium. Burning pain radiated across her jaw. She tasted the bitter iron bite of fresh blood in her mouth.

"I think you can," he advised.

Stifling her frightened sobs, willing her body to comply, she struggled to her feet.

They both startled when the landline telephone on the breakfast bar rang.

Her eyes flew to his.

"Just let it ring," he ordered. "They'll think you're still out."

The tumblers of her mind clicked over and unlocked. An idea formed. She did her best to sound sincere, "The only people who would be calling me this late were all at the bar this evening and know I'm home. If I don't answer, they'll worry and then come check on me."

The phone rang a second time.

He stood still, keeping the gun muzzle in her ribs, "So let them worry. You'll be gone before anyone gets here."

"Not if it's Carol or Linda," she shot back. "They only live about a hundred yards from here, and saw me go in. They'll see us leave."

The third ring chimed.

"You're in the shower," he sparred.

"They still come," she parried.

The fourth ring.

He chewed the corner of his mouth. "Very well. But make it very short and very sweet. You drank too much. You're tired. You'll call them tomorrow. Nothing more. *Anything* more, and you'll get your wish. You die here and now. Quickly and cleanly, right through the head."

Rushing to the breakfast bar Megan lifted the receiver in the middle of the fifth ring. The answering machine would have switched on with the sixth and her chance would have been gone. She tried to sound cheerful and awake, "Hello?"

"Meg, I need to talk," Ralph started.

She interrupted, "Carol, hi!" Her eyes went back toward the couch with shrug.

He stood tall, with both hands projected straight out in front of him, one hand supporting the other, his right eye closed, sighting the gun directly at her face. Her legs were trembling. This was her only chance. Her mind threw out words of its own instinctive accord.

"Carol?" Ralph grunted. "No, Meg, I said this is Ralph."

She cut him off again, "I'm sorry, Carol, but I can't really talk right now. Too many Heineken's tonight. Did me in. I'm beat. Can I call you in the morning?"

Heinekens?

Is that was he heard? Nothing but a Samuel Adams would ever touch Pembrooke's lips. A bolt of fear ripped through Ralph. "Meg, if you're in trouble, just say good-bye and hang up."

"Good-bye." She hung up.

"Very good," the tall man lowered the weapon slightly. "Smart girl. Now let's go."

The emergency team had to be there any second. What the hell was taking them so long? Standing further away she felt a little more brave, and desperately wanted to stall, "It's already too late, Mr. Bragg. I called 911 from Dominic's apartment. The cavalry's on its way."

"I don't believe you." He shook his head, still smiling, almost gloating. "But it doesn't really matter, even if you did. I never enter a vulnerable situation unprepared." He chuckled, "It's amazing what you can do these days with computers." He fanned the gun at the door. "Now go."

•

In less than sixty seconds Ralph Weatherstrom had already thrown on a jogging suit, kissed Mari good-bye, and was already out the door, in his car, and on his portable radio summoning every unit in the vicinity of Meg's apartment, screaming into the mouthpiece, "Get every available unit over to Officer Megan Pembrooke's apartment. Now!"

The dispatch operator replied, "Do you know the exact street address Detective Weatherstrom?"

"No," he screamed back. "Dammit, she's a Dallas cop. Pembrooke. Megan Pembrooke. Call it up on the damned computer! It's in Plano. Just off 15th Street!"

"Spell the last name, please," came the official voice.

"You gotta be fucking kidding me!" he screamed, "P-E-M-...brook something. Hell, honey, you can damn well figure it out."

"Affirmative, sir," came the reply. "Pembrooke. Megan Olivia. Address on file. Transmitting broadcast. All units, respond. All units, respond. Code three."

"*Olivia?*" Ralph grimaced like he'd just tasted something nasty. It was worthy of a healthy laugh, but none came. If she was still alive, he'd laugh later.

As Ralph's car sped down LBJ Freeway toward the Central Expressway interchange, the data transmission from central dispatch went out to all active patrol units on their mobile data terminals. Within seconds, all over Plano, parts of Richardson, and even from sections of North Dallas, sirens came on and lights started flashing. Unfortunately, the nearest patrol unit to Megan's apartment complex was over seven minutes away. Megan Pembrooke didn't have seven minutes to wait. She was out of time.

What's more, police response time was completely irrelevant. Following the information in the city's locator database files, the battalions of shrieking emergency units weren't headed to the Stratford Arms Apartments just off 15th Street.

It's amazing what you can do these days with computers.

CHAPTER 32

A LITTLE LUCK

Sunday
July 7, 2013

Oooooooh....

He groaned softly, his eyes fluttering ever so gently, focusing on nothing. The pain was more intense than he could have ever imagined. Wasn't it supposed to numb after a while, he thought? Dominic Callaghan felt like there was a hot lance piercing through him just under his left collar bone. Every tiny breath he squeezed in and out created a ghastly gurgling noise. He didn't know it then but he was only staying alive on one lung. The left one was collapsed, filled with blood.

It took everything within him to roll over on his stomach. Tears of pain and anguish bubbled out of his eyes again when he saw the thick ooze of blood pour from his mouth.

He had to get to the phone.

He moved. Groans of agony accented each and every tiny motion. Bolts of excruciating torture radiated through him. Yet, he managed to snake across the carpet on his belly the twelve feet from the bloody pool at the base of the breakfast bar to the end table. He was barely able to reach the wooden leg with his right hand. His left arm was virtually useless. It took almost ten tries before he was able to topple the small piece of furniture toward him. The small telephone handset clattered down on the side of his head, the sharp corner of the little table barely missing his cheek by less than an inch.

He pressed the greed call button and the sound of dial tone made it all worth it. He stabbed out 911 and pulled it to his ear.

He heard the click and the recording, *"Thank you for calling 911. All lines are busy right now. Please remain on the line and your call will be answered in the order that it was received."* He heard the sound of a violin orchestra.

Almost three minutes past before a voice mutely asked, "Emergency service, how can we help you?"

He started to speak. All that came out of his mouth was another cup of dark blood. He started to gag. Hot tears flowed from his eyes and nose. His face was drenched with sweat. The pain in his chest ceased to matter. He had to tell them.

The voice called, "Hello? Please respond if you are able."

He tried to speak again, only producing more slimy strings and heavy drops of blood amid his wet rasps.

NO! This couldn't be happening.

He was going to kill her. That couldn't happen. Dominic's hand was still on the key pad. He couldn't think of anything else. He put his forefinger on the star button and started pushing. He'd been a Boy Scout. Maybe someone there was too, or a maritime sailor.

Please, God...

He pressed three times, quickly: *Deet-deet-deet.*

Then three times slowly: *Deeeeet, deeeeet, deeeeet.*

Then three times quickly again: *Deet-deet-deet.*

He repeated the sequence over and over.

"Billy, come take a look at this." A 911 operator, turned to her supervisor, an unusually skinny man with long arms and legs and a fuzzy crewcut. He stepped over and looked down at the amber monochrome display screen in front of the operator. The computer monitor read-out employed the Caller ID service, which accessed residential databases. It specified the caller's phone number, name and street address.

The operator pointed at the screen, "I think I'm getting what sounds like an SOS from a Mr. Sherman Burns residence over in the Starlight Terrace Apartments in Plano. I thought it might just be kids, but didn't you have a code three at the Starlight Terrace, over on Parker Road, just few minutes ago?"

The skinny man with a headset on bobbed his head once, "Yeah, we've got all units en route to that location. Officer in trouble. Could be a shooting. All ambulances are standing by for that. Why?"

She pointed to the screen. "I've got this call, but no one talking. Just beeping."

The supervisor plugged his headset into the operator's station, "Mr. Burns. Hello? Whoever you are? Sir? Ma'am? This is 911 Emergency service. Can you hear me?"

The SOS stopped

Billy, the supervisor, spoke louder into the clear boom mike wrapped around his jaw in front of his teeth. "If you can hear us. Units are on their way. Stay calm. Help is on the way. Please stay on the line if you can. Signal if you acknowledge."

Dominic caught the last bit of what the voice said about someone being on the way. He pressed the star button once more and sighed with relief. It had worked.

The little distant voice repeated, "Help will be there in just a few minutes. So just hang in there."

Dominic looked toward his front door. How many precious minutes did Megan have?

•

Megan looked helplessly into his eyes, "Please don't do this. It doesn't have to end this way. Just go. You'll get away."

He shrugged, "Sorry, can't do that, love. Besides, you'd be so disappointed in me if I did. Now, come on."

She walked hesitantly toward the front door and nervously started to open it. He stepped up next to her, then abruptly caught the door when it was open only three inches, cautiously peering out, peeking over her shoulder before he let her walk out.

He saw a movement, a body. He yanked her back inside, keeping her to his left, pushing the door back to its jam, leaving a fine crack to spy out. The gun stayed trained on her face.

He whispered, "Not a sound, or whoever it is dies three seconds after you do."

Three doors down, an old woman in a ragged pale-blue nightgown and fuzzy red slippers, with a half-smoked cigarette in her hand, was letting in a fat orange tabby cat. He leaned up against the door frame, pressing his right eye to the crack, watching the woman cuddle and chat with her plump furry pet. He was careful to keep Megan safely in the peripheral vision of his left eye.

He was mumbling to himself, "Go on back to bed, old bat."

His shoulder was at the exact height of the cheap bookshelf screwed to the wall on slightly rusted angled brackets. The long one-by-eight board of the bottom shelf just came in contact with the top sleeve stitching on his jacket. Two more painted one-by-eight board shelves rose above it on more brackets. They were there when Megan had moved in and held only a few knick-knacks and old books she never read. Due to the fact Megan could barely reach them, they were a prime collection spot for dust, cobwebs, and dead moths. The thick, sculptured shoulder pad of his finely tailored double-breasted coat prevented him from noticing the small presence moving toward him with stealth and hungry determination.

Megan had gingerly stepped back a pace from the door, waiting for the inevitable, knowing she dare not try to physically attack him. He'd overpower her in an instant and rip her limb from limb. A faint movement near his right shoulder caught her hawk-like eyes.

Oh, shit!

She almost cried out in surprise.

There, in all his plump and hairy glory, stepping lightly onto the tall man's right shoulder, was Bruno, drifting silently toward the tall man's neck with every languid step of his many legs. Funnily enough, her next thought was to forget her own plight and chastise the spider, having been missing since last Tuesday. In all the commotion and chaos, she had forgot to find him. He had to be starving. She caught her breath with a glimmer of inspiration. Yes. Right now, her fat, furry little friend just might be a hero.

Whirrrrrrrrrrrrrrr!

He spun his face toward Megan when he heard a long high-pitched squeaking chortle coming from her tongue pressed behind her front teeth. It sounded oddly like the song a field cricket.

"Shhhh," he commanded, putting the barrel of the gun to his lips. "What the hell's wrong with you?"

When he turned back to the door, something brushed the side of his neck, just behind his right ear. His head reflexively spun to the right in alarm, his chin coming in contact with something large—and moving.

Whirrrrrrrrrrrrrrr!

Megan gave the cricket call again, as long and loud as she could.

In that one instant, all he saw was what appeared to be the disembodied hand of an alien, with elongated hairy black fingers, lunging for his face. Two searing darts of pain stabbed into his lower lip like he'd been skewered with a barbecue fork.

He shrieked in alarm and stunning pain. The pistol clattered to the floor with a heavy thump. Both of his hands flew up to the writhing source of the piercing agony. He wrenched the hellish thing free and instinctively flung it far from him.

Bruno flew through the air, end over end, holding all eight legs out rigid against the nauseating sensation of vertigo. He clattered through the long fronds of an overgrown fern next to the television. The leaves slowed his flight. He tumbled to the carpet with a heavy plop.

He was pissed.

His forelegs aggressively climbed high in midair, his long black fangs clicking together, looking for another soft target, instantly ready to attack anything that dared to move in his path. Miraculously, none of his legs were broken, and his guts were still intact. He scampered over to the couch and disappeared beneath it. There was nothing under there but a collection of dust bunnies, two forgotten magazines, and a blue plastic comb. He bit the comb four times just out of spite, then curled up in a ball and stayed mad for over an hour.

Meanwhile, the instant the wounded man had flung the gigantic spider from his face, he dropped to his knees gasping for air. The pain in his face was excruciating. His fingers touched his chin and lower lip. It was bleeding—badly. His heart was still pounding fiercely. He was at a loss to fully understand exactly what had just happened. His mind raced to refocus. The Glock lay the carpet between his knees. He looked up. The front door stood wide.

Megan Pembrooke was gone.

He could still hear the sound of frantic footsteps running away.

No!

With molars grinding he staggered back to his feet, picking up the pistol and pulling the slide back again into firing position. His entire face stung. His chin started to throb. His eyes were watering, his nose running. He lunged headlong out of Megan's front door.

There.

Seventy-five feet away, at the end of the concrete hallway he saw Megan's petite body turning into the stairwell. He fired once, the silencer spewing muted death, tight and crisp. A chunk of stucco exploded in a fine white cloud inches from the doorframe an instant after her head ducked within. He swore under his breath, and started to take chase.

Something caught his left foot.

He tumbled headlong against the concrete hallway, his wounded face making contact first, sliding a few inches over the hard surface. He screamed in pain and rage, rolling over on his back. Images before his eyes swam in a pool of near delirium. His gut went into an involuntary spasm, but he stifled a retch. A few feet away he heard a raspy wet chuckle.

He clambered to his feet and saw Dominic Callaghan laying in a wide puddle of his own blood, just outside his front door. He walked over and towered over the wounded man laying prone on the cold concrete. From the pool of red, a dark bloody trail went back inside the apartment. Dominic's right hand was still outstretched where he had caught the tall man's foot. There was fresh blood all over his beautiful hand-made Italian shoe.

Their eyes met.

"Foolish young man," he seethed. *"Adieu."*

His mouth stung again when he spoke, sharp and icy, like a vicious slap. He winced more out of anger than pain as he put a hasty bullet in Dominic's back, then turned and ran, wiping his torn face with the sleeve of his jacket.

The hot lance had skewered Dominic once again. His eyes screwed down tight. He couldn't breathe, save a few wet, crimson wheezes. His bloody, smiling face landed against the flat stone surface with a gentle wet slap. The coolness of the concrete felt good against his cheek.

It didn't matter anymore.

He'd helped her get away. He'd given her a few extra seconds of time—time to live. That's all that really mattered now. Sideways, he watched Richard Bragg race down the hallway and quickly disappear in the same stairwell door Megan did moments earlier. She'd get away. He knew it. She had to. The princess was always rescued at the end of the game. That thought brought a gentle calm to his heart. The pain began to fade into the cold numbness he had heard about.

And then all was still.

It grew deathly quiet around him.

Dominic could feel his tender little heart tapping lightly in his temples every once in a great while. He didn't know how long he just laid there, staring at a sideways world. Time didn't mean anything. Nothing meant much anymore. All his money was insignificant. His beautiful silver toy, Elizabeth, the Mercedes SL65 AMG roadster down in the garage, was just an empty machine, a thing—now a completely insignificant thing. Even his work was nothing more than a mere pastime. And now it seemed his time was past. Game Over. An eerie peace washed over him.

So this is what it's like, he mused.

Amazing.

His eyes were still open when the darkness came. Yet faintly, in the darkness he could have sworn he heard the sound of sirens; but for some strange reason, they quickly faded away.

CHAPTER 33

THE THRILL OF THE CHASE

Sunday
July 7, 2013

Ralph's Ford Taurus roared up North Central Expressway at over a hundred miles an hour. Fortunately, between 1:00 and 2:00 A.M., with most folks out of town on a long holiday weekend, Central Expressway was almost deserted—a rarity at any hour of the day or night. His magnetic emergency red strobe-light was affixed to the roof just over his window, tethered to the cigarette lighter by its tangled wire.

Ralph assumed the flashing red emergency light was on. However, he hadn't shoved the electrical plug deeply enough in the 12 volt socket. The light was dark. As he blazed past Beltline Road, a Richardson motorcycle cop picked him up on radar and took off in pursuit. Ralph collected another Richardson cop sitting under the Collins overpass in a late-model Chevy Caprice. Ralph saw the two policemen in his rearview mirror and naturally assumed they were lending assistance. As his car approached Renner Road, it was doing a hundred and fifteen.

Inside the ugly Caprice sat Officer Harold "Buddy" Weaver, who had been eating a Burrito Supreme from Taco Bell and reading the personals in *The Dallas Observer*, laughing at the perverts. The car reeked of refried beans, stale coffee, and an open pouch of Red Man chewing tobacco. When Ralph's Ford flew by with a Richardson bike on its tail Buddy almost choked at the radar reading: 113 mph. He abruptly tossed the Burrito in the passenger seat next to him, hit his lights and sirens, and joined the bike in the chase. The Ford showed no signs of slowing nor acknowledging the supreme authority of the law. Mistake.

Probably some shit-bag crack head.

Doing almost a hundred himself, Buddy Weaver played it by the book and radioed ahead to the Plano Police Department, but was quickly told by the dispatcher that no units were available to assist with a reckless speeder. All active Plano units were busy responding to an officer shooting at an apartment complex.

Mighty fine.

Buddy decided to handle it on his own. He'd catch this piece-of-shit his'sef, even if he had to chase him all the way up to fuckin' McKinney. He switched his radio over to P.A. and shouted to the Ford from the loud-speaker in the radiator grill, "You in the Ford. Pull over. Now. That's an order."

At a hundred miles an hour, sound doesn't travel forward very well, let alone drown out a powerful Detroit engine pushing a ton of steel at over a hundred miles an hour. Ralph didn't hear the verbal commands, but appreciated the escort nonetheless.

"Pull over—or prepare to be stopped." Buddy waited another ten seconds before reaching to his right and unlocked the brace holding his shotgun.

Fine, shit-head. We can do it your way.

Buddy Weaver had practiced this move many times, especially when sitting bored on traffic detail, anticipating the day he'd get to do it for real. His heart was pumping with adrenalized excitement. The day had finally come. With pistol-grip of the Mossman shotgun pressed against the floor board, the portly cop chambered a twelve gauge shell with one hand, snapping the pump action down hard under the short barrel. He accelerated the Caprice, passing the bike and rapidly closing the gap on the Ford. The bike officer nodded as he passed.

Ralph appreciated the urgency of his Richardson colleagues. His thoughts were still on Megan, praying he'd get there in time.

Buddy laid the shotgun down on the seat beside him. He reached down and hit the power window button. The passenger's side window buzzed down on its motorized lift. A howling roar of air blew in the car as the glass came down. He picked up the microphone and called again, "This is your final warning. Stop the car. Now!"

Ralph obliviously barreled on.

Just a little bit closer.

•

"He's still not in yet," a weary DeWayne Bragg rubbed his eyes and opened the door for Charlie McManus. "Come on in."

"Thank you, sir." Charlie walked in the Commissioner's front door and stood in the foyer. The Braggs lived in the Bent Tree Area, just west of the Dallas North Tollway, off the Trinity Mills exit. Charlie looked at Bragg, still wearing a full-length royal blue bathrobe over his night clothes. Charlie thought he'd be dressed. But no, he just stood there, looking unusually tired and harried—older. The old man's hands were trembling slightly.

"Have you told anyone about this?" Bragg's eyes twitched slightly, his thin lips quaking at the corners into the briefest semblance of a smile— but he wasn't smiling. He was afraid.

Charlie shook his head, "No, sir. I figured you'd want to know about this first."

Bragg returned a humble nod of thanks, and closed the front door behind McManus. "Good man. Come in and sit. Let's talk. He should be home any time."

Charlie never felt more awkward in all his life. In his urgency for immediate action he had just blurted out what he found to the Commissioner on the phone without thinking about how it might affect him. How does a man react when he finds out the son he's so proud of is quite possibly a diabolical serial killer? He was taking it well. Bragg showed Charlie into the family room and offered him some coffee. Charlie declined.

The Commissioner sat in a tall leather wingback chair, his elbows on the arms, his hands covering his mouth and chin, staring off at nothing. He mumbled into his palms, "Could there be any legitimate reason why Richard might have been at that building that evening?"

Charlie swallowed hard and recited matter-of-fact, "Six-one. A hundred an eighty-seven pounds. Brown hair. Blue eyes. Well-heeled."

Bragg lowered his hands and glared at Charlie, his eyes screaming their refusal to believe, "But the semen tests were all conclusively Teasdale!"

Charlie nodded. "Oh, Teasdale was definitely involved somehow, sir. We don't know how yet. My guess is that Richard wanted us to believe it was Teasdale all along. The perfect alibi. It's brilliant, really."

"Well, I'm still inclined to believe it *was* Teasdale all along. We'll just see what Richard has to say when he returns. I'm sure there's a perfectly reasonable explanation." The old man buried his tired face in his huge hands, muttering with despair, "It just can't be. Not my Richard. Not my boy."

Charlie could feel the thick lump in his throat and the hot moisture around his own eyes. The room grew painfully quiet. Only the crisp interval of tick-tocks from the grandfather clock in the hall pierced the air. As each second past, the ticks became much louder. Both men startled slightly when the clock struck one-thirty, signaled by a single brass chime. Neither man said a word.

They both jumped when the phone rang.

Bragg rose from his chair, walked to an antique railroad master's roll-top desk and answered the call. "Bragg." His face went ashen. There was an eternal pause, then he said quietly, "I understand. Thank you. Keep...keep me informed."

Charlie's heart was pounding. He stood, his fingers lacing and unlacing. His eyes looked for contact with Bragg's.

The Commissioner looked completely disoriented. He appeared to be going into shock.

Charlie went to him, tentatively touching the old man's shoulder, and bowing his head slightly, "Sir, are you all right?"

Bragg waved the detective back, taking a deep breath and summoning all the dignity he possessed. "Certainly, McManus. I'm fine." He tried to sound casual, but professional, gesturing at the telephone instrument, "That was... Headquarters." His looked back to Charlie. "Apparently...Detective Weatherstrom has reported Officer Pembrooke involved in a shooting at her residence. Units are responding as we speak."

"Oh, no! Meg's been hit?" Charlie turned to bolt. "I'm outta here. I'll call you."

Bragg caught his arm, his eyes pleading, he couldn't bring himself to say the words, "Please....*don't*...."

Charlie felt the lump again, "They'll do what they have to, sir. You know that. Do you want to come with me?"

The first tear in over twenty years made its way down the hard lines on the Commissioner's face. He shook his head with a tense shiver, eyes crushed closed, unable to say anything more. He turned his back and lifted a single hand of dismissal.

Charlie didn't see it. He was already out the door.

•

Megan screamed when the stucco exploded less than a foot behind her head. A shower of stony fragments pelted the back of her neck and lodged in her hair. She crashed through the steel fire door, rushing into the narrow concrete stairwell. She was greeted with a thick stifling cloud of stagnant, humid summer air.

Run, Pembrooke. Run!

Her feet took the steps two at a time, terrified all the while she might fall, twist an ankle or break a leg, and be laying there helpless when the fiery bullets came to shred her to pieces. But there was no alternative but to go as fast as she could. Blind instinct instantly taught her The Gazelle School for Defenseless but Mobile Prey, Rule #1: Distance from the predator is in direct proportion to the measure of safety and the potential for longevity.

Pat, pat, pat, pat, pat, lunge, lunge.

She cleared the first half-flight of stairs, her mind analyzing what lay before her with mathematical precision. Each of the four floors of the complex had two half-flights of stairs with a small concrete landing in between each set of stairs. There were ten steps per half-flight. Every other landing had a teal colored steel fire door painted with the floor number. Two lunging strides, per landing. Her own apartment was on the fourth floor. Therefore, there were six flights to the ground floor, eight to the basement garage. At ground level, the stairs emptied into the open courtyard. From any floor she'd be an open target from above.

No choice: the garage.

Pat, pat, pat, pat, pat, lunge, lunge.

Door number three loomed past. Megan's heart pinched in her chest when she heard the door above bang back against the inside wall. He was in pursuit, one floor above. She thought about rushing out on one of the other floors. But where would she go? All the hallways looked like hers: stucco walls lined with front doors; each a dead end; all overlooking the central courtyards and swimming pools. No, she'd be trapped. The underground garage was dark and vast, as big as the entire six hundred unit complex, filled with cars and potential places to hide. She moved faster.

Pat, pat, pat, pat, pat, lunge, lunge.

CLANG!

Megan froze, her body reflexively recoiling hard against the stone wall to her left. Her right hand instantly went numb, throbbing up to her elbow. She pulled her forearm to her chest. It *hurt*. There were drops of blood on the side of her index finger and thumb. Metal fragments and paint chips were all over her hand. The rail right next to where she had grasped to steady her flight was dented and mangled as though someone just hit it with a sledge hammer. Her eyes picked up traces of lead and copper on the rail.

"Oh, God," she whispered.

The sound of leather shoes on stairs echoed from above. Her feet instantly set to flight again in the next instant.

Pat, pat, pat, pat, pat, lunge, lunge.

She soared past door number two, fearfully wary of getting anywhere near the center hand rail again, staying as close to the outer wall as she could. However, the smooth concrete wall wasn't as helpful as the rail to maintain speed, and moving further out only increased the distance necessary to be traveled. The net result was a slower decent. The Gazelles were right. The sound of leather shoes was getting closer. She was crying again, wiping the tears away with both fists.

Paat, paat, paat, paat, paat, step, step, step.

A patter of footsteps echoed from above—leather against concrete, moving in precise rhythm, like a dancer, *tap, tap, tap, tap, tap, tap, tap, tap, tap, tap, scuff.*

She could see door number one below.

Paat, paat, paat, paat, paat, step, step, step.

The leather feet louder, closer: *tap, tap, tap, tap, tap, tap, tap, tap, tap, tap, scuff.*

Two more flights to go to the safety of the darkness.

Megan screamed when the concrete behind her right heel exploded, hungry fragments of stone bit her calves through her jeans.

Jump!

She leaped like frog crashing down on the landing below. The shock of impact jammed up her spine as her knees bent tight, the backs of her thighs mashing down hard against her calves.

God, that hurt.

She took one long stride across the landing and leaped again, crashing down on the garage floor landing. Her ankles and knees were on fire. Darts of heat shot up her back. It didn't matter. She sprang up and hit the fire door full force, barreling out into the garage—aghast to see they had recently repaired most of the lights.

Not far behind: *tap, tap, tap, tap, tap, tap, tap, tap, tap, tap, scuff.*

•

Ralph was in the far right lane, preparing to exit off of Central Expressway. He had no idea why the Richardson police cruiser had just pulled into the right center lane to his left and started to pass him. Didn't this guy know where they were going? The 15th Street exit was coming up next, hell, they were almost on top of it. They had to take 15th to the Stratford Arms Apartments. It was the most direct route. The Stratford Arms was at the corner of 15th and Stratford. If you missed the 15th Street exit you had to go all the way down to Park Blvd., and then double back. That was way the hell out of the way. The Richardson cruiser pulled up alongside as they went under the train bridge at Plano Parkway.

Where the hell was he going?

Ralph glanced to his left and saw the open passenger-side window and the gaping black muzzle pointed at him.

Oh, fuck!

His hands reacted an instant before the orange and red flash and the blue and gray smoke roared at him. It was an instinctive move, like slapping at a mosquito. He jerked the wheel to the left, sideswiping the Caprice. The clash of steel rang out amid a shower of orange sparks. His driver's side window exploded in the same instant. A hurricane of wind thundered into the car, sending papers in the back seat into a slapping flurry.

A moment earlier Buddy Weaver had recalled reading in *Soldier of Fortune Magazine*—or was it on an HBO special?—anyway, of how a short-barrel twelve gauge could take a man's head clean off at close range. This fucking dope-eater wouldn't be endangering the lives of any good citizens any more. Buddy had felt the blunt metallic impact of the cars just as he pulled the trigger. His right hand rocked up. The blast tore the top of Buddy's door frame off, shattered the Taurus' window, and disintegrated Ralph's emergency light. The bulk of the blast was expended on the defenseless light. Its wire flopped down along the door, scraping it at high speed.

So, the prick wants to play.

Buddy set the shotgun butt to the floor and violently jerked another shell in the chamber.

"What the fuck is wrong with you!" Ralph screamed out his broken window as more glass chips toppled down inside the door and out on the roadway, bouncing high. The left side of Ralph's face was cut from small pieces of flying glass, but fortunately none of the nine deadly projectiles inside of the twelve-gauge shell found him. He was burning with outrage. His eyes blurred with anger. His right hand groped for his 357 magnum, preparing to return fire. He literally screamed with rage when he saw that he missed the 15th street exit.

Buddy leveled his shotgun again.

Ralph instantly stood up on his brake pedal with both feet. A blue-gray plume of smoke cooked off his tires as his car skidded onto the right shoulder and came to a smoldering stop. Buddy saw the Taurus disappear behind him in a squeal of rubber. He dropped the shotgun in the seat, grabbed the wheel with both hands and braked hard, swerving into the right lane and coming to a sideways stop fifty yards further down the highway.

Ralph saw a fat unformed cop jump out of his car, shotgun in hand and throw himself down across the trunk of the Caprice, leveling the weapon at him again. The sound of a powerful motorcycle engine roared up behind his car. He looked in the rearview mirror and saw the cop on the bike dismount and draw his side arm, taking refuge behind Ralph's trunk.

And angry voice from behind his car bellowed, "All right, you! Out of the car! Now!"

Fuming, Ralph picked up his portable radio from the seat beside him and hit the talk button, "Dispatch, this is Detective Ralph Weatherstrom. Dallas Homicide. Third Division. Get me whatever asshole is in charge in Richardson tonight. And I mean fucking *now*."

"I said, out of the car!" the voice of authority screamed again.

Ralph slowly opened his door, keeping his hands raised in plain sight. More glass chips crumbled out on the roadway. The two officers closed in rapidly. Buddy Weaver ambled up with an ear-to-ear leer, huffing and puffing with wide-eyed excitement.

Ralph turned and faced the motorcycle cop. He felt the blunt shotgun muzzle poke him in the back of the head. It was still warm. His rear molars squeezed tight, but he stayed in control. The motorcycle cop's weapon was leveled directly at his face.

A voice crackled from the radio in Ralph's hand, "This is Lieutenant Jacobs, Richardson Police. What can I do for you tonight, Detective Weatherstrom?"

Ralph held the radio out to the motorcycle cop, "It's for you."

Chapter 34

Face to Face

Sunday
July 7, 2013

The stagnant garage air mixed with the stifling summer heat was unmerciful. Megan crouched down in the long shadows between a freshly washed Ford Explorer and a badly needed-to-be-washed Mercury, doing her best not to make a sound. Her knees were tucked under her chin, her arms cuddling them close.

...the wind...

The smallest vibration or resonance was magnified a thousand times in the concrete cavern. Megan scarcely dared to breathe. It was excruciating. Exhaling was fairly smooth and easy, but taking in a breath snagged and staggered amid half-sobs. It took all of her will power to force her lungs and heart to calm slightly. Her right hand still ached all the way up to her elbow, a ticklish pain, like she had jammed her funny-bone. There were drops of blood on the back of her pant leg as well as her hand. She knew he'd be there any second.

Just the wind...

The darkness, the solitude, the deadly danger—it brought back the old memories, the images, the demons—things longs forgotten and buried beneath the scars of a young and tender heart. The old ugly images returned in a montage of painful recollection, so clear and vivid. She couldn't will them away this time.

Oddly, it was one of the only memories she had left of her real mother. It all happened just a month before her sixth birthday. They had crouched together in the damp storm cellar of their small rural Kansas home. It was so dark and hot. The humidity was unbearable in the late spring: tornado season. It was hard to breathe. She had huddled tight against her mother's bosom, clinging to the old worn gingham dress, waiting in terror for the deadly twister to pass. She could still remember the smell of her mother's dress, warm and soft, the home-spun cloth scented like fresh cut hay.

It's just the wind baby. It won't hurt us. It'll pass. We just to need to stay out of its way. We'll be safe down here. Don't worry honey. It's just the wind...

Her daddy had gone to let the animals out of the barn and bring the water jugs. The wind was so loud, like a monstrous freight train coming closer and closer. It drew nearer and nearer, closer and closer, thundering louder ever louder as it came. When the raging, swirling terror roared the loudest, they had both heard a different sound. Even the memory of the sound frightfully twisted Megan's bowels. It was a high-pitched dissonance which cut through the tornado's roar like a single silver orchestra bell piercing over an entire symphony orchestra. Megan had never heard that sound before.

The shriek.

It was a human voice—screaming for its mortal life. To this day, she had never heard any human being consumed in that much pain and fear. It was her daddy's voice. Her mother had yelled at her above the roar to stay put while she ran to help.

And Megan was left alone.

Just like she was at that very moment, little five-year-old Megan Pembrooke sat curled up in a little fetal ball, all by herself in the dark for over fourteen hours, until a Kansas State Trooper heard her crying. The farm was completely destroyed. The bodies of her parents were never found.

Just the wind...

•

SWANG!

Megan choked in a half-breath of panic when she heard the fire door from the stairwell fly out of its jam and bang hard against the concrete wall behind it. The terror had arrived. The memory vanished. The menace was real. And it had come for her.

Why weren't the police there yet? Where were her state troopers?

Silence.

Thirty agonizing seconds crawled by.

Screeeeee—BANG.

A loud metallic creak, rang out shrill and sharp, echoing throughout the three-acre concrete cavern. Megan dropped down to the cool surface of the garage floor, peering intently under the cars. She was about thirty yards from the stairwell.

There he was.

All she could see was his feet over by the trash dumpster, right next to the stairwell. He had apparently thrown back the heavy steel lid to search inside. Breathlessly, she saw him go up on his tip toes and heard a rummaging sound of paper and plastic. His heels came back down and turned in a slow calculated circle. She could hear the sound of the leather on the bottom of his shoes gently scuff the concrete as he pivoted. She still dared not breathe.

He was listening too.

When she saw his knees start to part, her stomach sank. He was crouching down to look under the vehicles as well. She pushed herself into a sitting position and pressed her back up against the left-rear tire of the Explorer, again holding her arms and legs as close together as possible, just like she did when she was five. For the first time in her life she was truly thankful God had made her so petite.

Leather footsteps patted the concrete—slowly, cautiously.

All was silent again.

This time almost a full minute of the unnerving quiet pressed by. Megan dared only to suck in mere thimblefuls of air, desperate not to betray her location. Her mind told her as long as she could hear him, she could crawl away in the darkness and stay in the safety of the shadows. She couldn't hear anything.

Another empty minute past.

What was he waiting for?

Megan ventured a peek around the edge of the tire. Her eyes puddled with fresh tears of terror. She bit down on her lip to keep from screaming. The handsome pair of hand-stitched Italian leather shoes were right where they were two minutes ago. No one was in them.

•

The mangled Ford Taurus pulled into the parking lot of the Stratford Arms Apartments. There were no legions of patrol cars surrounding it, no flashing lights, no wailing sirens—*nobody*. Ralph got halfway out of the car, his right foot still trailing in the glass covered floorboard, his left elbow draped over the open car door. Was he at the right place? Yes. The huge gold sign at the leasing office plainly read: Stratford Arms Apartments. That's where Megan lived. He'd picked her up once for breakfast two weeks ago. This was definitely the place.

"Where the hell *is* everybody?" he said out loud to no one. He grabbed his radio and started lumbering toward Megan's apartment as fast as he could go. "Dispatch, this is Detective Weatherstrom again. What the fuck's wrong with you people? Where are units you *supposedly* dispatched to Stratford Arms Apartments for Officer Pembrooke?"

The radio crackled as Ralph ran into the entrance gate, a slightly irritated official voice declared, "Negative, sir, on the address. Not the Stratford Arms. Our database reports Officer Pembrooke's current address in on Parker Road in Plano. The *Starlight Terrace* Apartments."

"*What?*" he screamed at the handset as he stabbed the elevator button in Megan's wing five times in quick succession with his blunt middle finger. "No, that's bullshit. It's the Stratford Arms, on the corner of Stratford and 15th. I'm here right now. Dammit, I know where she lives."

"Not according to our file," the voice tersely rebutted.

"Fuck the file," he screamed. "Get everyone over here right now!"

The radio hissed. "I will relay information, sir, and try to reconfirm the data. Please stand by."

"Micro-Idiots," he clicked the radio off and shoved it in his jacket pocket. More heads would roll first thing in the morning in addition to two gung-ho Richardson hot-rod ticket clerks. His hands flew up in exasperation. "Why does this *always* fucking have to happen?"

•

Megan felt sure if she could just slip inside a car or a truck without being seen, he'd never find her. Someone would eventually come along and then he'd have to flee. She was now squatting behind a brand-new red Jeep Grand Cherokee, huddled in the dark, peering intently underneath the high carriage of the vehicle, looking for bare feet. She shivered uncontrollably, though her body wrung with sweat.

A dark, sinking feeling crept up her sides again. It was obvious to her now. No one was coming to rescue her. No cavalry. No white knights. No state troopers. They'd have been there long before now. Somehow he'd done it again. Somehow he'd made sure that even calls for help were somehow transformed into more of his deceptions and illusions. Somehow he'd deceived them all one more time.

Her eyes closed in frustration. She inhaled long and slow through her nose. The air hung still in the garage, thick and pungent with the humid odors of lingering exhaust, road film, oil, grease, mixed with faint traces of days-old cigarette smoke and discarded trash from the dumpsters. The scents seemed to cling to her arms, legs, and face like the ninety-two degree heat, right down to her pores. A heavy drop of sweat fell from her chin and landed on her knee, quickly soaking in to the faded denim. It was soon joined by another.

"Megan, my love!"

Megan bumped her head against the hard wall behind her with a fitful start. The voice came from *very* nearby, perhaps only ten yards away. She leaned down and looked under the Jeep again. The smell of a slightly leaking oil pan was much stronger with her nose under the front bumper.

Nothing. Where was he?

Think two moves ahead, Pembrooke.

The tumblers in her mind clicked again. Play the game. Play to win. Where was he? What was he doing? What were his available moves? What were his options? What would *she* do if she were the hunter? Yes. That's it. What does he know? Her mind quickly calculated and enumerated:

1. His prey is trapped and can't get to an exit without being seen.
2. His prey is unarmed and no physical threat.
3. His prey is afraid and emotionally on edge—vulnerable.
4. He doesn't need to find her if he can flush her out with fear.

Her mind catalogued and analyzed the facts, then quickly plotted a counter-strategy. One, she needed a diversion or distraction to escape. Two, she needed a weapon of some kind. Three, she needed to remain calm and quiet—especially quiet. And four, above all, she must not be afraid.

Oh, yeah. Right.

Another tear fell from her quivering chin and joined the drops of sweat on her knees.

His voice rang out again, reflecting off the grim garage walls, closer still, "Megan, dearest. Don't hide, my love. We both know it's only a matter of time before I find you. There's no way out of here, and no one coming to help. You know I'll eventually find you. And when I do...then we'll do the terrible things. *Gloriously* terrible things."

Where was he?

Megan slowly slid up the wall, her back gently scrapping along the smooth surface. Her eyes scanned furtively back and forth, peering through the windows of the Jeep. And there he was—sitting barefoot on the hood of a big old Chrysler. The pistol was still leveled in both hands, ready to fire in an instant. From his vantage point he could easily see the stairwell as well as the two entrances on either end of the garage. His eyes narrowed, scanning, his head cocked slightly at an angle—listening. Listening for the faintest of sounds, a gasp, a breath. An audible sob of fear?

No.

That he couldn't have. Megan made up her mind. He could shoot her dead, but he wouldn't do it in the back. It would happen head-on, face-to-face, player against player. A burning ire twisted its way up from her somewhere deep down in her hips, up through her guts, wresting a firm grip on her heart. The racing thump within her chest began to subside. The little voice inside declared—if it's a battle of minds he wants, then screw him: Let the Games Begin.

Step one, a distraction or a diversion.

Megan's eyes scanned the cars to her left and to her right and back again, finally locking on Dr. Eubanks' new BMW 750. It was also along the wall to her left, down about seven cars. It would do nicely. She silently unbuckled the leather strap of her wrist watch and held it dangling by the square metal buckle. Her eyes went back to Richard. He was still nesting on his perch, his eyes slowly panning back and forth, like a closed circuit security camera. She waited until his face was at its farthest point away.

He called out to the regiments of shadows, "Megan!"

Now.

Megan hurled the watch at the BMW like a knife, throwing as hard as she could, spinning it end over end, and quickly ducked back down in the safety of the shadows. The watch struck the rear window of the car and its alarm launched into a deafening, wailing screech, echoing throughout the entire garage. Megan watched Richard Bragg leap from the Chrysler and race down toward the BMW. As he moved quickly to her left, she moved to her right, heading back toward the stairwell—her nearest avenue of escape.

As she crept along in the darkness, covered by the incessant screams of the auto alarm, Megan grabbed the chrome antenna of a very old little white Nissan near its base and snapped it off, collapsing its telescopic sections down to the ten inch base section. Step two complete—a weapon: an instant ghetto blade. The torn end of the antenna was quite sharp and formidable at close range. Inwardly, she realized she had no intention of getting within close range. So far so good. However, she was still trapped.

The Glock vomited death again. The BMW's front windshield exploded in a crumbling shower of glass. It fired again and again and the radiator started spewing liquid on the concrete in front of it, mortally wounded. A few more shots and the alarm grew quiet.

Megan's bowels clenched again.

Good God, he killed the car!

At that moment she was only two cars away from the stairwell entrance. She didn't have anything left to throw and didn't want to risk taking another peek above. She dropped to the pavement again.

Megan screamed.

Barely a hundred feet away, in a well-lit area, Richard Bragg was lying on his stomach, arms wide, elbows up and back, like he was at the bottom of a push-up. He was staring directly at her.

"Hello, my dear." The Glock swung around to greet her.

CHAPTER 35

KING TAKES KNIGHT: STALEMATE

Sunday
July 7, 2013

Ralph bolted out of the elevator and ran toward Megan's apartment. He could see the body of a man lying at the end of the concrete hallway. When he made his way to it, he recognized it as her neighbor-friend, Dominic, the computer guy. He reached down and pressed his fingers against the young man's neck. He didn't feel anything. Both Megan's door and the neighbor's door were open. He checked Megan's apartment first, bursting through doors with his 357 drawn, but finding no one. The same was true of the apartment across the hall.

"God, what would Megan do?" he asked himself out loud.

Details.

Pretty basic, Ralph, her voice seemed to whisper in the back of his mind. It's the little things.

Yes.

He looked back down at the poor young man lying face down in a dark pool of blood. His right arm was outstretched, back in the direction from which Ralph had come. The hand had fresh blood on it. A few inches beyond the hand, there was what appeared to be the edge of a shoe, drawn also in blood. A foot print, heading back toward the elevators. A large footprint. A man. Whoever it was, was running now.

Running after Megan?

Yes, Ralph. Follow the details. Follow the little things.

Ralph ran back to the elevator. Would Megan have taken the elevator?

Not if she was running and had a choice. Was she running? Yes.

Details.

The bullet hole in the stucco wall next to the stairwell entrance answered his question. She was running and under fire. But there was no blood. He missed her.

Ralph crashed through the fire door on the fourth floor and started descending the stairs, going as fast as his heaving lungs and pounding heart could stand.

The little things, Ralph. The little things.

He saw the gun blast in the hand rail. No blood. He missed again. She was still free and headed to basement to get away. Yes. That's what she'd do. A car alarm squealed below, confirming his logic. Yes, she was down there somewhere. He tried to move faster, taking the steps two at a time. Just a little further. The alarm abruptly stopped. Ralph didn't. He moved faster, his heart pounding like a bass drum. He heard a woman scream. It sounded like Megan.

Move, Weatherstrom!

Ralph crashed through the basement door, gun leveled. He turned to his right, his eyes scanning back and forth, looking intently for the next bread crumb of her trail. A sudden movement in his peripheral vision, just to his left, spun him in that direction. A hundred feet away a man was lying prone on the concrete floor and rolling toward him. He was holding something small and black in his hands.

Gun?

By reflex, Ralph's revolver started to take aim.

A familiar voice, a female voice, very close, screamed something unintelligible. Whatever it was the man lying on the garage floor was holding belched a puff of smoke at him.

Nooooo!

It was over in less than a single second in time; but it all felt like it was mired down in a surreal slow-motion, like one of those dreams where you see the danger, you feel it, you know it, and you even know what you have to do—yet all of your limbs move through a semi-paralyzed limbo, impotent and ineffective. It's the most torturous of all frustrations. Megan barely had time to scream a warning before she saw Ralph leave his feet, just like Dominic a few minutes earlier.

An invisible line-backer buried his head and shoulder in Ralph's stomach and decked him to the pavement, slamming his body down hard in one meaty thud, like dropping a side of beef. The invisible opponent then stood up on his gut and proceeded to maliciously grind in his steel cleats down into his bowels without end. Ralph could only see the oil-stained concrete ceiling above him. He was wheezing. His right hand still clung to his revolver. His free hand absently reached to his stomach to see if he could dislodge the invisible foot standing on him and ease the burning. All he found was wetness—thick, sticky wetness. Despite the Dallas heat, Ralph Weatherstrom suddenly felt cold.

Megan snapped out of her stunned trance at the patter of an approaching sound: Bare feet running on concrete, getting louder, closer: *Pat, pat, pat, pat....*

It would be her turn next. Her body instinctively moved of its own accord, spinning and scraping around the end of another car, snaking down the wall and hiding behind another tire.

Richard Bragg spun around the front of the car Megan had been hiding behind a second earlier, gun muzzle first, genuinely surprised to see her gone. His eyes scanned to and fro.

Nothing.

He dropped to the ground again, looking under the cars.

Nothing.

He stood back up, his rich voice resonating loud off the smooth walls, "That makes two who have died in your place tonight, Officer Pembrooke. The blood of two souls are on your hands. How many more will you see die before you come to me? It's only you I want now, my dearest...only you." His dark laughter bounced off the walls. And then he began to sing: *"...only you... can make.. all this world seem bright....."*

Megan cringed when she heard him start to sing the fifties classic, "Only You." It struck her that the Platters' "The Great Pretender" would have been more appropriate.

He stopped on the second line, interrupted by anther familiar sound: the frantic scream of approaching sirens. More contingencies and interruptions. He sighed. There should have been more time. The databases shouldn't have been reconciled until the morning. It had to have been done manually. He glanced back at Ralph, wheezing and bleeding like a freshly-hit dog on the side of the road. Yes. Somehow, the old fart had muddled things. But not to worry. It was fitting. And it saved him another trip. But as far as lovely Megan was concerned, his most worthy adversary had managed to squeak out a stalemate in this frantic encounter. That was luck. The next time she couldn't depend on luck. She'd have to be good.

"Damn," he swore under his breath, genuinely disappointed. He raised his voice again. "Ah, my dear," he let out an accentuated heavy sigh, "alas, you've missed your chance for our dance tonight." He bellowed even louder, "But rest assured, I'll come calling for you again... very soon. I can't tell you when. Sometime, *day or night*. You'll never know *exactly* when, or *how*. You'll never see it coming—and you'll certainly never be able to prevent it from arriving. But it will come. And I'll enjoy it. *Adieu*."

Megan peered around the wide, radial tire and slowly raised herself up over the dusty trunk lid, smearing some of the wheel-well grime into her sweat-soaked T-Shirt, just in time to see Richard disappear into the stairwell. She moved closer, hesitantly, with tentative little Gazelle steps, expecting him to reappear any second. Her ankles trembled. Her knees quaked. Any movement whatsoever would send her diving between the nearest two vehicles. She had the broken antenna in her throbbing, sweaty fist, poised to strike. The fading sound of bare feet running up the stairs elicited a sigh of relief. Another fire door slammed somewhere above. Perhaps he was gone.

God, I hope so.

Ralph. She ran and dropped to her knees by his side.

The sight of him lying there in his own blood brought her heart up into her throat. A thin trickle of blood dribbled out of both corners of his mouth and his left nostril. His body was trembling and jerking in minor spasms. He tried to smile when he saw her.

"Hey," he gurgled, "I been lookin' for you."

Fresh tears welled in her eyes, her chin bobbing anew. She looked down at his wound, just above his navel. It was bad. It looked like he'd been gored by a bull.

Her eyes found his, "Oh, Ralph. Look what he's done to you." She felt something hard and heavy touch her hand. She looked down and saw him sliding his revolver toward her.

He coughed once, his face constricting in a twisted grimace of pain. When it subsided, he wheezed, "Go get him, Detective. Don't let him get away. Not...not this time. Just remember to tell the good guys where to find me."

The sounds of sirens grew even louder. Megan could see flashing red lights winking in at both garage entrances on either end of the building. Her eyes looked back to Ralph once more.

"Go on...*Olivia*," he ordered with a glimmer of a smile. "Finish it."

Megan's tears dripped over her frail smile. She nodded once, then leaned down and kissed him softly on his wet cheek. Her eyes puddled again with thanks as she accepted his warm look of encouragement and confidence. She jumped up and was on her feet running toward the flashing lights, screaming for help, yelling "Officer down!" and bellowing orders for an ambulance.

CHAPTER 36

A CLASSIC DEFENSE: MASS PANIC

Sunday
July 7, 2013

As his own car negotiated the ramp from LBJ Freeway onto Central Expressway North and sped toward Plano, Charlie McManus lifted his portable radio to his lips, "What's status at The Stratford Arms?" He glanced at his watch.

It was 1:55 A.M.

The dispatcher's voice came back, "Ambulances are en route, sir, transporting two gunshot victims to HCA emergency. One DOA. One critical."

"Who are they?" Charlie was afraid to ask.

"Unable to confirm at this time, sir," the voice came back. "Consult the watch commander on site."

"Shit," he threw the radio down in the seat beside him and accelerated.

Charlie noticed a large gathering of Richardson police vehicles on the side of the expressway, headlights all pointed inward like a drug bust. Two uniformed officers, a thin one in rider gear and a fat one, seemed to be surrounded by four others. A short man in a black suit was screaming into the fat one's face.

"Wonder what the fuck he did?"

His car flew on.

•

Richard Bragg emerged from the stairwell on the first floor and entered the landscaped courtyard. Police vehicles were screaming up from all directions. Lights and sirens were waking up the whole neighborhood. Heads and concerned faces started popping out of doors.

Perfect.

That's what he needed.

Still dressed in his suit and stocking feet, he walked down a concrete hallway and pounded on the closed door of a unit he estimated to be a one-bedroom flat. "Police. Open up."

A few seconds later, the peep hole went dark, then light. The door opened a crack, "Yes, officer?"

Those were the nervous little man inside's last words. Bragg put the silencer's muzzle squarely between the man's eyes and sent the back of his skull, and everything in between, spraying all over the dead man's living room. Richard was through the door before the corpse flopped to the carpet. He closed the door behind him and proceeded directly to the bedroom. The man lived alone. That was good: less work and conservation of ammunition. In less than a minute he tore the soiled double-breasted suit off. He found a pair of jogging shorts in a drawer, plus an extra-large souvenir T-Shirt in a closet which he was able to get over his large frame.

He was halfway home.

To proffer an unimpeded departure, he decided it was time for a bigger confusion factor, enhanced by the wonderful hazards of crowd management. Richard tucked the gun in the waistband of the shorts and pulled the T-Shirt down over the grip. He walked back through the dead stranger's living room and into the kitchen. He found some cleaning spirits under the sink. As expected, a box of wooden kitchen matches was stored in the cupboard above the stove with the spare light bulbs, like in everyone's home. As he walked back into the living room and opened the sliding glass patio door, he laughed at the childlike ease of his task. Air flow was important. The bottom hem of the hideous orange drapes were saturated with the spirits and then set ablaze.

Perfect.

He watched the bright orange flames lick up the dry cloth until he was satisfied it would produce the desired effect. For good measure he pushed the late occupant's sofa against the flames to increase the fuel supply. It caught quickly as well. Barefoot, with his car keys and wallet in hand, he turned and left the apartment, walking casually to the end of the hallway. He looked out across the courtyard and saw a legion of armed police officers storming Megan's wing. Smoke was starting to curl around the end of the building. He chuckled softly to himself.

It was all so easy.

He reached up with his free hand and yanked the fire alarm. Obnoxious buzzers blared into the night, like huge constipated geese, honking and honking, amplified by air-horns to over a hundred decibels. Four blocks away, firemen were jumping into their rubber boots and pants and dashing to their trucks. At the Stratford Arms, men, women and children began to anxiously filter out of their units into the concrete hallways, heading for the stairwells, each with the barest of belongings in his or her arms, some carrying children or pets, musical instruments or stereo gear.

Naturally, they all believed it was a real fire. It was—or at least it would be in a few minutes. It was certainly a real emergency for the time being, and that's all that was important. They could see all the lights and hear the sirens surrounding the complex. None of the good citizens would question the fact that the good guys had actually arrived before the fire was even reported. Modern efficiency was to be commended and applauded don't-cha-know. Richard chuckled again and joined the throng of lemmings in their march to safety.

•

Megan's face went pale when she heard the honking wail of the fire alarm. She was standing next to the watch commander, Lieutenant Franklin Mulrooney of the Plano Police department. Ralph's 357 magnum was still in her right hand, the broken radio antenna in her left.

She gasped, "Oh, no. He'll get away!"

"Oh, that's all we need." The commander quickly shouted into his radio, "Detain all residents. That's an order. All units. Do you hear me? Acknowledge. Detain all residents. It's a false alarm."

"Negative, sir," came a field officer's voice in urgent reply. "It's real. We've got a fire."

"Oh, wonderful," Mulrooney moaned, then held the radio to his lips again, "Well, assist in evacuation, but keep looking for the suspect—tall, blue suit, no shoes."

"Affirmative," crackled the reply.

A gray wisp of smoke ascended above the rooftop of the wing adjacent to Megan's. It swelled thicker and blacker as each moment passed.

A crowd of spectators from nearby homes and apartments had already begun to gather around the spectacle as well. A good fire was as entertaining as the circus. Local news crews listening to the emergency channels on their mobile scanners were pulling up and leaping out with arm-loads of camera and sound equipment. A helicopter swooped overhead, shining a search light down on the area of the smoke. In minutes there would be hundreds of bodies and faces milling around, like fire ants in a kicked-over mound. Megan was seething with anger. He was clever. Very clever.

How the hell am I supposed to find him now?

More sirens, punctuated by the honking bleats of air horns and powerful diesel engines, signaled the approach of the fire companies. Megan's shoulders fell. Hell, in five minutes, the Dallas Cowboys could walk in and out of that building without being seen.

Not happy.

She sniffed once, slipping the antenna into the back pocket of her jeans. She tucked the heavy revolver in the front of her pants. It was time for both talent and luck. She couldn't let him get away. She *wouldn't* let him get away. In every gambit there was always a way in and a way out. You just had to find it. What would he do next? Just walk away? Her eyes strayed over to the commanders gold badge pinned to his shirt. It triggered a memory, an image of something she'd just seen that night. She instantly knew what she had to do.

"Hey where are you going?" called Lt. Mulrooney.

Megan was already out of earshot, running as fast as her tired, aching legs would carry her. There wasn't much time.

•

It was destiny, he mused, feeling a surge of power an invincibility. No one even looked at him twice. He marched right past several police officers, who were running and shouting urgent phrases and codes into their little toy radios at one another. It was comical, but he kept his face sober and concerned like the rest of the frightened refugees fleeing the disaster. He even endeavored to make eye contact with them, but they completely ignored him. He was even so brash as to ask one what all the commotion was about, only to be dismissed and told to move along.

Amazing.

He had walked all the way out of the complex, across the street and down the sidewalk without a single challenge. He laughed as he drifted from the crowd, walked past a throng of spectators pressing in, and casually made his way to his car parked a block down the street beneath a thick overhang of trees, in the darkest shadows of Stratford Lane.

The alarm system in the sleek, black Porsche was turned off. It had to be. He didn't need his own car going into frantic spasms like that BMW from some kid leaning on it and attracting any undue attention. He climbed into the driver's seat and set his Glock in the passenger's seat, still within easy reach should an unwitting passerby take more than a cursory interest in him. He had suffered enough nuisances for one evening. He sucked in a long deep cleansing breath, held it for several seconds, and then let it out slowly.

Victory.

The night was alive with motion and noise. He sat quietly for several moments, watching other tragedy voyeurs dashing back toward the apartment complex to satisfy their morbid curiosities, followed by another wave of bleating emergency vehicles. The sounds of fear and trauma overlapped with the shrill whines of the machines of mercy to produce the dull roar of pandemonium. The longer he sat there the louder it grew, resembling the cacophony of a parade or a riotous stadium event.

As it should be.

The tinted windows were rolled down half-way, for the night was hot, but it wasn't enough. It was time to feel the wind. He started the powerful German engine, recessed all the windows, and then hit the button on the console which retracted the convertible top. It folded back into its nest between the trunk and the little back seat. A gentle breeze of the night air, scented with the husky fragrances of the trees and manicured grasses of suburbia, whispered across his face.

Perfect.

A perfect ending to a perfect escapade. Well, it was *almost* perfect. Now he would have to modify the operation to facilitate a new identity, a new base of operation, a new target criteria. It wasn't difficult, just inconvenient—and now mandatory. Lovely little Miss Pembrooke knew who Richard Bragg was. He clucked his cheek once.

Unfortunate.

Yes, it would have been so much easier if he had dispatched her in the apartment. But then where would the fun be in that? No, all things considered, this was best. It would be altogether so much more grand when next they met. He'd cook up a very special dish for her, a very special one indeed. Oh, yes. No shame in that. A strategic retreat at present to fight another day, and all that rot. Yes? He laughed again, loud and full, his shoulders bobbing with glee.

Simply amazing.

His bare left foot pushed the clutch to the floor as his right palm pushed the leather-clad stick forward and found first gear. With a smooth rush of German engineered RPM's, the black Porsche glided out of the inky shadows, into the amber streetlights, up Stratford Avenue. He turned east on Park Boulevard heading back toward Central Expressway, and disappeared into the night.

CHAPTER 37

THE FINAL MOVE

Sunday
July 7, 2013

Charlie McManus couldn't believe the spectacle unfolding at the Stratford Arms Apartments. He had to show his badge to get past the erected barricades. His jaw hung agape in complete awe as he slowly drove past the dizzying array of rescue equipment. An entire wing of the complex was ablaze. A billowing tower of gray smoke snaked high into the sky, illuminated by the orange and red flames beneath. It looked like the Hindenburg had crashed there. Three full engine companies had the conflagration surrounded with stiff, swollen water hoses. Long arcs of high-pressure water blasted into scorched windows and rained down on the rooftops. Scores of police officers and fire fighters were still busy assisting residents in their evacuation. Charlie stopped his car at a safe distance and got out. An officer on site pointed out Lt. Mulrooney.

"Did you get him?" was all Charlie asked the watch commander, after holding up his badge and identifying himself.

Mulrooney's silence answered the question.

"Fuck," Charlie completely spun completely around in anger.

"We're still looking," Mulrooney declared. "He may still be here somewhere. A man wearing a blue suit and no shoes shouldn't be too hard to spot."

"Unless he's no longer wearing a fuckin' blue suit," Charlie shot back as thought the Lieutenant were the most perverse of idiots on the face of the earth. "That thought ever cross your mind?"

Mulrooney started to say something in rebuttal, but was interrupted by an urgent voice on his radio. He shouted more instructions into the electronic black brick, suddenly oblivious to Charlie.

Charlie raised his voice, "Where's Officer Pembrooke?"

Mulrooney waved an irritated hand in return, still in fervent radio conversation.

Charlie stepped over and pushed the device away from the Lieutenant's face, "I asked you where Megan is?"

The hard-faced police commander stepped back, grossly offended, "She's fine. She was here just a minute ago."

"*Where...*is she now?" Charlie demanded.

Mulrooney shrugged, "Hell if I know." He indignantly hocked a thick wad of phlegm out of his throat and spit on the pavement to his right, "She just turned and run off like she left something burning on the stove."

"Great," Charlie turned and walked back to his car, staring up at the stars, as if some semblance of his sanity could somehow be found up there.

•

The black Porsche cleared the traffic light at Alma and Park Boulevard, carefully winding around the gentle curve to the left. No time to stop, he thought. The obvious next step would be to return home and eliminate the good Commissioner and his whore—tonight, right away, amid all the confusion and commotion.

Yes. Splendid idea.

It would be sort of a parting epilogue, a final bow for Richard Francis Bragg, before he officially became either Rudolph Perkins, Michael Grafton, Serge DiPescalini, or Bartholomew Genviere. He had masterfully forged passports in his possession printed in all of those names—each from separate countries, of course. Furthermore, he had tucked away just over two million dollars cash in his Geneva bank under an another name, as well as almost three million in bearer bonds in an off-shore Cayman Bank safety deposit box. Contingencies and necessities, always planned for, always ready.

More than enough.

Besides, after finishing the work of the night, a little vacation was certainly called for. Yes. A lovely night drive to San Antonio, then a short Southwest Airlines flight in the morning to Vegas for a little relaxation. Perhaps a stopover in Palm Desert for a little golf before heading down to Costa Rica was also called for. Yes. So many possibilities. So easy.

The Porsche turned right onto the Central Expressway access road and conservatively accelerated to fifty-five. Nothing as trivial as a speeding ticket would impede him now. The warm, sultry night air felt so good rushing through his brown, curly hair, whistling past his ears. He flexed his fingers and rewound them tightly around the hand-stitched leather steering wheel cover, his palms comfortably perched at a perfect ten and two.

Something hard and cold jabbed him just behind his right ear. He froze with a gasping start, the car swerving for a second, then coming back under his control in the center lane. He apparently wasn't alone.

A harsh female voice: "Keep both hands on the wheel, sweetie-pie, and pull it off the road gently and easily."

Dearest Megan. How wonderful.

Richard's pounding heart slowed from the instantaneous sense of alarm. His abdomen suddenly percolated with a rolling laugh as he considered the situation. He was most impressed at the cold pair of eyes staring at him in the rear view mirror.

Megan's hands were still quaking. She knew what she was doing was insane, but there was no other way. From the moment she saw the gold shield on Mulrooney's shirt, it reminded her of the Porsche crest on Bragg's key-ring. His move to start the fire was brilliant, but she knew what his next move would be: to find his car. It couldn't have been parked very far from the complex. There weren't that many streets to check. All in all she got lucky. When she saw the beautiful black Porsche sitting on the curb with the windows half down, her gut told her it was his. When she shook a fender and an alarm didn't go off, she was almost certain. When even the interior lights remained dark upon opening the driver's side door, she was absolutely certain.

The most frightening part was curling up into an almost fetal ball in the black shadows behind the passenger's seat and waiting for him to come. There was always the possibility it was the wrong car. And she knew she had to wait until he was driving and no longer had the gun in his hand to take him—when he was most vulnerable. She hadn't intended to wait so long to confront him; drawing upon the thin reserves of life and death courage one more time didn't come so easily. A wall of paralyzing apprehension had to be scaled. That same, simple childlike fear, like standing on the side of the deep aquamarine swimming pool on an early Spring afternoon, toes curled over the edge, looking down on the chilling cold waters just inches away, apprehensive of its shocking total embrace. Once committed to jump, there was no turning back. It kept her frozen to the spot until sheer determination, and realization of no other course of action, compelled her to act.

That time had come.

"Very good, my dear," he nodded with genuine appreciation. "Once again, I am *most* impressed."

"Well, your brains are going to be *com*pressed if you don't pull this piece of shit off the road right now," she commanded. "And, mister, I mean now!"

"I don't think so."

The car accelerated. At 2:12 in the morning, for the most part, the highway was still deserted.

She pushed the gun muzzle of Ralph's 357 harder into the back of his head. "It's over, Bragg. I said stop."

The car went faster, the wind around them rushing harder, louder.

"And I said, I don't think so."

Holding the heavy weapon with both hands, she pulled the hammer back, which rotated the fat cylinder, positioning the next .357 caliber brass hollow point cartridge behind the firing pin.

He laughed, "Darling, we doing just over ninety miles per hour right now. If you pull that trigger, my brains will be on the windshield about four seconds before yours will be all over the roadway, that is, when this vehicle flips and rolls about fourteen to seventeen times."

Megan pulled the pistol back a fraction of an inch. Her mind quickly calculating. No? Yes? Maybe? Would he really kill himself and take her with him? No. Impossible.

"You don't want to die," she challenged, her lips almost touching the rear gun sights, yelling above the hurricane force wind in her face. "You've worked too hard to stay alive and free."

"Do you really think so?" he giggled like a child at the circus.

The needle on the speedometer reached a hundred. They blazed by the group of Richardson policemen still chastising their errant brethren. The sight of the Porsche sent them scrambling to their vehicles and radios. Dallas police were notified. Units were on duty at the Park Central Plaza, five miles south, near the intersection of LBJ Freeway and Central Expressway. They would try to intercept.

Megan's legs tensed when he started veering the car back and forth, rocking it hard with the steering wheel, making it slalom between the two center lanes of the freeway. The high-performance radial tires screamed in protest. Still gripping the revolver in her left hand, she hugged the head rest of the passenger seat with her right arm to keep from spilling side to side. Amid the careening thrashes, she saw his right hand slowly sliding down on the wheel toward his lap. She could see his pistol in the seat beside him.

"No," she screamed. "Hands on the wheel."

"Soon and very soon," he sang, *"we are going to see the King."* His hand

kept inching down. Only twelve short inches now from the Glock and closing. She'd be dead in a matter of seconds, and the matter concluded. *"Soon and very soon—"*

The explosion was deafening.

The pistol almost flew out of her hand with a thundering recoil. Megan had pointed the barrel at the windshield directly in front of his face and pulled the trigger. The disintegrating sheet of glass shattered inward, clawing at his face as it stormed by, pressed by the one hundred mile an hour winds. The car swerved back and forth even more severely, careening and squealing. Megan clung to the back of the passenger seat with both forearms. Both of his hands gripped the wheel to steady it, but his bare right foot never relaxed a hair's breadth from the accelerator. Straining against the fierce breath of wind, she had the gun pressed into his neck before he could release the wheel again.

That should get the bastard's attention and let him know she wasn't kidding, she thought. Yet inwardly, she wondered if she could really pull the trigger again on another human being. The ghostly image of Troy Bigham flying away from her in slow motion brought back the fluttering nausea in her stomach. Part of her brain pleaded for her to stop analyzing and just do what she knew she had to do. The other part really didn't know if she could apply that four pounds of pressure to that little tongue of steel beneath the ball of her left forefinger.

Why couldn't he just stop?

Again, she screamed in his right ear to stop, unaware he couldn't hear anything with it anymore, save an icepick sharp whine.

Richard grit his teeth and strained to see. He could feel the stinging lacerations of his beautiful face. His lower lip was still numb and throbbing. He spit a crumb of glass out of his mouth. His eyes squinting shut at the sound of the blast was probably the only thing that saved his vision. The pain in the right side of his head was maddening. He struggled to maintain control, but refused to slow down. The sassy little bitch couldn't win. No matter what. No, she'd cling to her life to the bitter end.

Yes.

His mind focused—and that would be her undoing.

"Throw the gun out of the car," he demanded, accelerating to a hundred and twenty. "Or we both die together. Here and now."

Megan's hands were violently shaking, that beautiful mind weighing and considering. If she dropped the gun, he'd kill her. If she didn't drop it, he'd kill her. A brilliant move. A knight's fork: threatening from two different directions simultaneously by the same piece. She'd lose either way—and this time, there was no resigning from the game.

"Throw it out," he screamed as they hit a hundred and thirty, his face dripping with fresh rivulets of blood, fanned out across his face by the whistling jet stream. *"Now!* I'm not going to jail, Megan my love. I'll die here with you, or you'll let me walk away. Those are the only choices."

"And you'd let *me* walk away?" she screamed back at him.

It was almost demonic the way his bloody face rotated on his neck around to almost face her. His shoulders barely moved. The car hurtled ahead at almost a hundred and forty miles an hour.

He snarled a hellish grin, "Trust me."

Megan's eyes clenched tight. The final move of the game. Her move. The last choice. Resignation was death. Persistence in the game was death. Killing him would bring death.

Did there remain a winning move?

The Classic defense: Separate attacking elements. Divide and conquer.

Her mind spun as fast as the tortured racing tires on the Porsche humming beneath her. The intersection of Central and LBJ freeway was looming up, less than a mile away.

His gambit: Sacrificing his life for a draw, gambling for a win on her instinct for survival.

They both knew it.

Two choices with the same end: her death. She swallowed hard as she forced her mind to focus. A two pronged attack. Death by gun or death by car. She couldn't reach the gun from where she was without becoming vulnerable. And even if she could, with a spin of the wheel he could still execute death by car. Her eyes sharpened. The tornado tearing across her face seemed but a gentle blur of reality.

"Decision time, Megan my love," he roared, the streams of hot blood dripping from his chin increased, lapping at his throat. "Lose the weapon, or we say hello to the rather immovable bridge supports just ahead. I've not tried death. It might be glorious just to see what it feels like—together, you and I. Into the pit together? Yes?"

And there it was: the answer.

There it was, hiding right there in plain sight beneath the golden Porsche crest in the center of the steering wheel.

Do it!

BOOOOM!

Ralph Weatherstrom's 357 fired point-blank at the golden Porsche's proud crest in the middle of the wheel. The Porsche's airbag instantly detonated, crushing its driver back in the seat. As designed by the German engineers, the steering mechanism locked, keeping the car headed perfectly straight.

BOOOOM! BOOOOM!

The gun fired again, and again, this time destroying the entire instrument cluster and ignition assembly, shattering the complex electronic circuitry behind it and completely severing the electrical connections which kept the engine running. When the engine died, with the precision transmission still in gear, the car stuttered forward like it had been hit in the rear by another vehicle. It coughed and choked until the rear wheels locked, tires screaming. The discomfited and shocked driver swam in a billowing white cloud of inflated vinyl.

The sudden forward jolt of the skidding car threw Megan's body hard against the back of the passenger's seat, painfully bending her right arm at an impossible angle. She screamed in pain. The 357 flew out of her left hand and clattered down behind the driver's seat. The G-force inertia of going from 137 mph to zero at a full drag, kept her pinned behind the seat as though an elephant were leaning into her. The tires wore down to the steel belts, cut through, and slid on the bare alloy rims, leaving parallel orange fountains of sparks in their wake. The car came to a complete stop almost a quarter of a mile down the highway from the entrance ramp to the LBJ Freeway.

The crippled Porsche rocked back and forth with frantic human motion inside. A totally dumfounded Richard Bragg was still wrestling with the deflating white balloon in his arms. Unfortunately, his reflexes were much more acute than Megan had anticipated. With most of the air within it expended, he whipped the folds of vinyl sharply to his left. The murderous outrage in his eyes glowed red and hot. His right hand flew down to the seat beside him and felt the cool surface of the Glock. He had it in his grip, a round chambered, and his arm flying between the seats in less than two seconds.

One more shot was fired in the Porsche that night.

CHAPTER 38

CHECKMATE

Sunday
July 7, 2013

Mulrooney had advised Charlie McManus about Ralph and Dominic being shot. Charlie wasn't aware of either one's condition. He was on his way over to HCA Hospital in Plano to check when he heard the frenzied chatter on his car radio. A black Porsche was picked up flying down Central Expressway. Richardson and North Dallas units were responding. He spun his car around on 15th Street and headed back toward Central with his own siren and light turned on. It was Bragg. But that made no sense. Why was he running? He got away. Why would he risk it? Why didn't he just casually cruise away? Was someone chasing him?

Megan.

Bless her heart. He grabbed the portable radio in the seat next to him and called the dispatcher, "Is there any other civilian vehicle in pursuit of the Porsche?"

"Negative, Detective," the voice came back. "Only one vehicle moving at high speed. Two Richardson units are giving chase. Three Dallas Metro units and a State Trooper are going to set up a road block at the LBJ intersection."

Then what the hell is he doing?

Charlie went faster.

•

When Richard Bragg spun around in the seat to fire the Glock he was seething in livid, temple-pounding, red-faced rage. Miss Megan Pembrooke was irritatingly clever, far too clever for her own good. But not clever enough. Game Over. Here's where it ended. It was time for Miss Pembrooke to die.

Goodbye, Megan.

The Glock coughed once through the narrow divide in the bucket seats. Chunks of leather and cotton batting puffed into the air. The tiny back seat of the Porsche was filled with nothing but dark shadows and silence.

What the hell?

Dumbfounded, Richard leaned forward through the seats and peered into the empty darkness, looking at the torn empty seat. He felt a polite tap on his left shoulder.

No!

He violently lurched around to his left, catching the small feminine figure in his peripheral vision. Her right arm was swinging violently at his face, sweeping laterally from her left to right.

Stupid bitch. Now you're mine.

The Glock came whipping around to—

SPLUTCH.

Richard Bragg screamed in mortal agony. His icy shrill cries pierced the night. His head rocked back against the leather head rest, straining the seat back, stretching the leather taut. He writhed back and forth, bellowing and shrieking. His legs locked and kicked and thrashed and banged under the dash.

For an instant, Megan froze at the hideous sound: the demons were back, flying and clawing, teasing and taunting.

No. Do it.

There had been no time to spare. She knew what he would do, and she knew what she had to do. No choice. Megan had not wasted an instant when the car came to a screeching halt: popping out of the back seat, rolling down the trunk, and crawling along the driver's side of the car on the hot Dallas pavement. She couldn't waste a precious moment. She leaned forward to finish it, her trembling hand reaching out through the taunts of the demons, past the leathern wings and the sharp claws, beyond the shrieks and wails.

Now.

Blood was running down the left side of his nose, spraying forward in gruesome spurts, atomized by each deafening howl. The Glock clattered down against the folds of the withered airbag and down into his lap as both of his hands desperately flew up to his face. His fingers curled around the long thin piece of metal jabbed deeply into his left eye. His body lurched forward in one giant spasm. The pain digging all the way down to the core of his spine was so intense, Richard Bragg was barely aware of the fingers—small but strong fingers—gathering up a fistful of curly brown hair from the back of his head. His entire upper body was hauled back against the seat again with one massive jerk, then violently thrust forward.

Finish it.

Standing in the roadway, next to the driver's-side door, with her left hand braced on the windshield frame, her right hand gripping a white-knuckled fist full of hair down to the scalp, Megan wrenched the bellowing head forward and down with all the adrenaline-charged power and might her small frame could muster. The end of the thin stainless steel antenna, sticking out of her nemesis' left eye socket made blunt contact with the flat plate which used support the airbag in the steering column, providing immovable resistance. It stopped. The shrieking and bellowing skull in her hand continued forward with the power of her one-armed thrust another three inches.

With a sudden hot squirt of blood and a flood of clear liquid, the squealing high-pitched shrieking abruptly ceased. The arms and legs kept twitching for several seconds, as though he were being electrocuted at spastic intervals, until, at long last, they too ebbed into the bloody darkness.

And all was silent.

For the second time in her life, Megan Pembrooke had heard the wind and the screams.

The demons grew silent—for a season.

Megan spun around and vomited hot bile in the roadway as police cars closed in from both directions. She was still dry heaving, hugging herself in a tight little ball, her body wrenching with wracking sobs for several agonizing minutes, until strong arms lifted her to her feet and pulled her away from the car and held her close. The arms belonged to Charlie McManus. The quaking and the tears didn't subside for almost an hour, and he didn't let go of her until they did.

EPILOGUE

HORIZONS AND SUNSETS

Friday
July 9, 2013

Five terrible days had past. Megan sat at the bar in The Stagger Inn mutely staring at the etched mirror behind the bar. It was just past noon. She hadn't slept more than a few minutes at a time all week, and even then it was short dozes, jumping up with a start at every little sound. The face of Richard Bragg had joined the winged demons that returned in her dreams to taunt her. The little voice told her they wouldn't stay gone long.

Megan knew she looked like shit. She felt like shit.

Sitting next to her on Pete Brumley's usual stool was Detective Charlie McManus. Pete wouldn't get off work till five and didn't usually show till six or seven, so he wouldn't mind. Both Megan and Charlie were drinking coffee, and for Megan even that was hard to keep down.

It had been the hardest week of her life.

"I still think you're making a mistake," Charlie said softly. "It's too soon to be making any big career decisions. Hell, Meg, it hasn't even been a whole week. Give it some time."

She shrugged, "It doesn't make any difference, Charlie. I can't go back now. It's a no win situation for me. And the way I play the game, when there's no way you can win, you have to resign."

Charlie put a friendly hand on her shoulder, "But, dammit, Meg, you won. You got him. It's done. It's over."

She looked him coldly in the eye, "That's right. I got him. But look at what price."

He nodded somberly.

She sighed, "Hell, Charlie, you know I can't go back to the department. I killed the damn Police Commissioner's son. I'm the foolhardy maverick the Chief of Police can't wait to see drummed off the force. I overstepped the bounds." She lifted a hand of futility, "And I know I always will. That's just how I am. I'll never do it any other way. I just can't." She shook her head, "Look, Charlie, I don't mind friction or a good challenge, it's not that. But come on. I can't live my life, or do a job where it's all uphill. I gotta have someone on *my* side. You know? It's pretty basic."

He was quiet for a second, cleared his throat and then asked, "So what are you going to do?"

"I don't know exactly." She took another sip of her coffee. It was just as she liked it, steaming hot, a little bitter and black. "Strike out on my own, maybe? Who knows."

The telephone rang at the end of the bar. Hal was leaning next to it and picked up the receiver.

Charlie squeezed her shoulder, finding her eyes, "Well, no matter what. You'll always have at least one guy on your side. I mean that. You can call me anytime. No matter what."

Her left hand came up and patted the back of his hand, holding it in place, "Thanks. Coming from you that means a lot." She brightened, "Which reminds me. I need to go visit another friend."

"Hey, Megan?" Hal called.

She turned to him, "Hmm?"

"It's Carol." He covered the receiver with his hand, "Are you here?"

"No, I'm just leaving." She slid off her stool. "Tell her I'm going over to the hospital and expect to be there for a while, but you can tell her I'll be back here later tonight."

Hal nodded and spoke into the receiver again.

Megan turned back to Charlie, their eyes holding each other's pained gaze for a while. She leaned forward and hugged him close. "I'll see 'ya. Promise."

Charlie nodded with understanding and watched her leave. She was right. He really needed to make a visit too.

•

Megan pushed open the door of the semi-private hospital room. It still smelled of bitter antiseptics and dried blood. She brought a small bunch of carnations in her hand and a wore a warm smile on her lips. She had been there to see him every day that week, and stayed till the nurses ran her off after visiting hours. She had to.

He watched her come in and it made him smile. And even the simple act of smiling was hard. His whole body still ached, even after five days in the hospital. The heavy narcotics in his system took the edge off the pain, but only the edge. His eyes were still glassy and the lids hung at half-staff.

He hadn't regained full consciousness until Tuesday and had been tethered to a tangle of tubes in his arms, nose, and mouth; as well as taped up to a vast array of beeping monitoring equipment in ICU until yesterday. Thankfully, the doctors said his chances were very good, but they still had a few more deep fragments to remove from near his spine. More surgery was scheduled in two weeks. He'd been told by the specialists that he'd be in bed for at least a month and then into the whole rehabilitation ordeal for several more months before he was fully back on his feet.

"How are you doing today?" she asked softly.

He managed a brief smile, "I've been better."

Megan forced a laugh. She swore she wouldn't cry again, but it was hard—very hard after everything they'd been through. "Well, you know I just had to come by and check in on you again. Make sure you weren't pinching all the nurses and running up and down the halls bothering all the other patients."

He shook his head slowly, "No. Not today. But I tell 'ya, that late night nurse, Hilda? She gives great bed pan."

Megan giggled, actually somewhat thankful that the tension in her throat was able to ease in the light of his good spirits. She set the flowers down on his serving tray and looked deeply into his eyes. No words would ever be able to tell him just how sorry she was, or to ever make everything right again. But she wanted to do whatever she could. She reached into her purse. "Hey, I brought a surprise for you."

He raised his eyebrows with interest. "God, I sure hope it's a big fat Snickers Bar?"

"No, silly," she pulled out a blue and yellow envelope with a radio station logo on the side. She opened it up and pulled out two printed tickets and held them up, "I got permission from Dr. Hennessey to take you on a little field trip the week after next, before your operation."

He looked puzzled till he read the title of the event: The Ringling Brothers Barnum and Bailey Circus. It was Dominic's turn for his eyes to puddle.

•

Charlie McManus laid the small bouquet of flowers he picked up at the grocery store next to the tall marble headstone of his best friend. He hadn't been back to the cemetery since the funeral on Tuesday. He had stood tall beside Mari Weatherstrom and held her close while she cried and cried. He cried with her too, and with her three grown children. He couldn't stop the hot tears from trickling down his cheeks when the entire Dallas Police department, and numerous members of several other neighboring forces all stood in attendance. Ralph Weatherstrom got a hero's twenty-one gun salute as his Medal of Valor and the folded American flag was presented to Mari.

He deserved it.

A police widow's pension was far from a fortune, but Ralph and Charlie had a private pact between them, that if anything ever happened to one of them, the other's family would be taken care of. Charlie was already honoring his end of that bargain. He was picking up chicken and fixings at the Colonel's that evening and taking it over to Mari at her sister's house in Grand Prairie.

"We did it, buddy," he spoke to the fresh sod. "We got him. It's finished."

Charlie chatted to the marble headstone for almost an hour before running out of thoughts to share. He'd be back next week to update his friend on all the latest gossip.

It was time to go.

Charlie came to attention, delivered a crisp military salute, turned about-face, and trudged silently back to his car.

•

That evening Megan Pembrooke quietly stood on her small apartment balcony for well over an hour, just silently staring off to the west at the vast expanse of the Texas sky, until the plump orange globe of the sun oozed beyond the rim of the planet, dissolving the radiant blue heaven above into a gradually fading band of crimson to violet. Perched securely on her shoulder, cuddled tightly against her neck, was an eight legged ball of fur who loved her more than a fat, slow-moving cricket. She tilted her head and gently rubbed Bruno's back with her chin. A grateful flurry of his two long forelegs against her cheek confirmed that he had forgiven her for all the recent trauma.

In a few minutes she knew she'd head down to The Stagger Inn and join her large and colorful surrogate family. But for now the brief solitude felt good; the serenity was relaxing and refreshingly peaceful. Down at the Inn she was never alone. And that was good too. There she was never lonely. Like always, they'd all sit around and tell bad jokes, laugh anyway, swill beer, throw darts, and swap stories of adventure and family embarrassment. And all would be well. All would be as it should be. All would be as it ever was.

Or would it?

Things had changed.

So much had happened. The future wasn't nearly as certain and smoothly structured as it appeared to be just a few short months ago. Was Scarlett O'Hara right? Was tomorrow *just* another day? No. It wasn't. Tomorrow was now a mystery—but for Megan Pembrooke, the thought of solving a good mystery excited and warmed her heart more than anything.